PRAISE FOR *THE SWAP*

"full of page-by-page surprises"

–Kirkus Reviews

"**Mary Higgins Clark meets London**… The pace of Boyarsky's story and the thrill of surprising new developments lead to a nail-biting adventure whose thralls are difficult to escape. Nicole's evolution… places her amongst the most intriguing leads in the genre. *The Swap* contributes to the women-driven mystery field with panache."

–Foreword Reviews

"Well written, non-stop, can't-put-it-down suspense."

–Charles Rosenberg, bestselling author of *"Death on a High Floor"*

"I loved this Hitchcockian thriller... Taut, suspenseful, and fast-paced, *The Swap* is a terrific read. I recommend it highly."

–Laura Levine, author of the *Jaine Austen Mystery* series

"Delightful. Set amidst the quaint neighborhoods of London and the wild lochs of Western Scotland, this tale of a house swap gone criminally wrong will appeal to mainstream mystery fans. Skulking strangers, assumed identities, and the protagonist's increasingly distant husband amp up the paranoia and suspense."

–Denise Hamilton, bestselling author and editor of the Edgar Award-winning short story anthology *Los Angeles Noir*

THE SWAP

a Nicole Graves mystery

NANCY BOYARSKY

The Swap
Nancy Boyarsky
www.nancyboyarsky.com
nboyarsky@lightmessages.com

Published 2017, by Light Messages
www.lightmessages.com
Durham, NC 27713 USA
SAN: 920-9298

Paperback ISBN: 978-1-61153-188-6
Ebook ISBN: 978-1-61153-187-9
Library of Congress Control Number: 2016952720

This book is dedicated to
Bill, Jennifer, John, Anabelle and Lila
and in loving memory of Robin

One

Afterward, Nicole blamed herself for not sensing something wrong that very first day, when she stepped across the Lowrys' threshold into their shabby front hall.

But what, really, was there to notice, beyond the fact that the house was less than she'd expected? She was too exhausted from the long flight. If she was worried about anything, it was Brad's silence, the impenetrable gloom that had enveloped him since they'd left L.A.

After a day or two, when she began to suspect she was in danger, it was impossible to get anyone to believe her. By the time the car blew up with that poor man inside, she understood this was no random act of terrorism. They were in serious trouble. Yet try as she might, it was impossible to convince Brad that the car bomb had anything to do with them, or the house swap, or the Lowrys, for that matter.

But that was later. After landing at Heathrow on that first morning, Nicole followed Brad through the airport, struggling to keep up. With Brad, activities as routine as finding their luggage and getting through customs were competitive sports.

Nicole had been unable to sleep during the long plane ride. She'd spent the time hatching schemes to fix their marriage and, at alternate moments, trying to figure out what had gone wrong. Now, in the airport's fluorescent glare, the rift between them was like a buzzing in her head—an insistent noise that blocked out everything else.

They were just leaving baggage claim when Nicole said, "Wait." Brad kept walking, so she grabbed his arm. "My other bag," she said. "Where is it?"

"Your other bag," he repeated, setting the suitcases down and staring at them as if he'd never seen them before. He was tall and lanky with a broad face and dark brown hair that insisted on separating into curls despite stern measures taken with a blow dryer. The curls and his wide-set eyes usually gave him the look of an impish little boy. But this morning he was wearing a scowl and, after sleeping fitfully on the plane, seemed unusually cranky and distracted.

Looking back, she saw that the luggage carousel was empty and had stopped revolving. Nearby sat the only remaining pieces of unclaimed baggage, a carton tied with rope and a large aluminum trunk that looked as if it might contain a piece of movie equipment. The bag in question—black with tan leather trim, a slightly-larger version of the one slung over her shoulder—was nowhere in sight.

She opened her mouth, then closed it again. She could have sworn she'd pulled both of her suitcases from the moving belt. Now she wasn't sure.

Locating the claims office and filing a lost baggage form consumed the better part of two hours. Before that, they'd spent forty-five minutes waiting in the long line in immigration. As they headed through customs toward the exit marked NOTHING TO DECLARE, Brad trailed along behind. His silence seemed to blame her for the lost suitcase and the delay. If she hadn't come, she imagined him thinking, he'd already have checked into a hotel and be on his way to the office.

They took the express train from Heathrow to Paddington Station and, following Mrs. Lowry's instructions, "queued up" for a cab. About twenty people were ahead of them. Brad stood at the edge of the sidewalk, as silent and remote as one of the lampposts that lined the street.

At any other time, Nicole would have been watching the other travelers, trying to pick up clues to the lives they led, their secrets and pretensions. She was insatiably curious about people, and the occasional chance to do some detective work was the one thing about her job she still found interesting. When the law firm wasn't in chaos, she abandoned her role as office manager to help the resident private investigator. She had a gift for prying things out of people, figuring out connections, unearthing information no one else could find.

This morning, however, all of her curiosity had evaporated. Instead of staring at the people around her, she watched the red double-decker buses come and go, breathing in the reek of their exhaust. Jet lag, along with Brad's abstraction, made her feel like a ghost in the final stages of dematerialization. Not for the first time, she was having doubts about the trip.

At last they climbed into a cab, and it carried them to Chiswick, about thirty-five minutes away.

The Lowrys' next-door neighbor was pacing up and down in front of the house, waiting to let them in. He was enormously relieved to see them, a tall hunched man in his sixties who introduced himself as Mr. McGiever. Despite the brisk wind, he appeared to be sweating. "Brought the fine weather with you," he said, mopping his brow with a crumpled handkerchief.

Nicole gave a puzzled smile and glanced at the sky. Between the gray clouds, thin scraps of blue peeked out. If this was a fine day, what could they expect of a normal summer day?

When they shook hands, McGiever's was moist and sticky. It made Nicole's skin creep, but she tried to be polite, waiting while he recited a welcoming speech that sounded as if he'd rehearsed it. Something about feeling free to call on him if they needed anything. "It's no trouble," he said. "No trouble at all."

Nicole wasn't paying much attention to the man; she was too distracted by the surroundings. Like its neighbors, the Lowrys' house was a stunted-looking two-story brick with moldings of dingy white stucco outlining the windows and the eaves of the peaked roof. In front, a wrought-iron fence enclosed a yard just big enough to accommodate eight sick-looking rose bushes, four on either side of a cement path. Instead of lawn, the ground was covered with a layer of yellowing gray gravel.

The drapes were drawn, and the house looked deserted. Nicole prayed this meant the tenant was away. It wasn't until her third email that Mrs. Lowry had even mentioned a tenant. "She's quiet and respectable, a qualified nurse specializing in home care. She only uses the room between cases."

Nicole, who had been ready to sign the agreement, balked at the idea of sharing the house with a stranger. She called Brad at the office to complain. For, while Brad had adamantly opposed the house swap, it was he who'd actually found the Lowrys' house through a contact at work.

"Oh, yeah," Brad said, when she asked him about the boarder. "That's something they do over there. Only she's not a boarder; she's a tenant. You don't have to cook meals for her. Wait, hang on," he said. There was a click, then silence, while he put her on hold. Then he was back. "I've got to go. Look, if you don't like this arrangement, find something else."

"For God's sake," she said. "We're leaving in three weeks..."

"Maybe you should consider staying home."

"Brad..."

"Do what you want, okay? Gotta go. Love ya!"

After some soul searching, Nicole signed the agreement. But the tenant remained on her list of worries. What was the etiquette in dealing with such a person? Did the tenant share the kitchen with them, and how would that work? What if this "quiet young woman" had wild parties? Nicole pictured herself encountering strange men in the hallway at night.

"Now if you'll allow me," Mr. McGiever was saying, "I'll show you how to unlock the front door. Mr. Lowry is a great believer in household security, and there's a bit of a trick to it." He produced a set of keys and eagerly escorted them to the door. The locks were rather complicated, requiring one key to release the doorknob, a second for the deadbolt, and yet a third for a lock near the bottom of the door.

There was a bad moment when Brad caught sight of the front hall—the peeling paint, the cracked tile floor, the worn tweed carpeting on the steps to the upper floor. It was all there on his face, his objection to her coming with him, to her being here at all. Never mind that he'd found this particular house. She was the one who'd insisted on this whole arrangement. It was on her.

There it was again—the rift between them, the hopelessness of ever fixing it. But she would, she told herself. That was why she'd come. She squared her shoulders and took a long gulp of air. Then, while Brad was getting rid of Mr. McGiever, she hurried through the first doorway on her left.

She found herself in a small dining room with dark wood paneling and a stone fireplace. It was crowded with furniture: a round oak table and chairs and two substantial china hutches. A narrow buffet table, shoved against one wall, held an array of condiments. She moved closer to read the labels: ketchup and Worcestershire sauce, some squat jars of mustard in several shades of nasty brown, chutney, jam, jelly, marmalade, lemon curd, honey, and small cruets of vinegar and oil. Despite the clutter, the room had a cozy charm.

The kitchen, through another doorway and a step down, was bright and airy. Looking around, she recognized it from Mrs. Lowry's description, the new stove top, the stacked washer and dryer. Nicole was amazed at how small the appliances were, especially the oven, which looked like it dated back to the 1930s. A toaster, electric kettle, can opener, and coffee mill were lined up on the beige Formica counter. Each had a note—written in large, flowing script with a bright blue marker—taped in front explaining how it worked.

At the sight of the kitchen, Nicole's spirits lifted. This was going to be okay. "Brad, come here!" she shouted.

After a moment or so, he appeared in the doorway, smiling. "They've got a 65-inch LED TV," he said, "and killer speakers." He seemed about to say something else, then hesitated, eyes dancing with amusement.

"What?" she said.

"You've got to see the painting in the dining room."

She followed him back across the entry hall and through a nicely-furnished living room. It was a little bland for her taste, all beiges and browns. Beyond it, a good distance from the kitchen, was a formal dining room with a long mahogany table and twelve chairs. Hanging over an elaborately-carved sideboard was a mural populated by four repellent looking creatures, all nude. They were wrestling, or maybe embracing. She couldn't tell. Nor could she determine what sex they were. Each had breasts, as well as a penis, five-o'clock shadow and long-painted fingernails. The artist possessed a certain amount of skill; the painting was interesting and provocative. But there was something weird about it that went beyond the androgynous nature of the figures.

She spent the next half-hour poking through the house. The sight of that painting had stirred her curiosity about the Lowrys. But the house offered no other clues to their proclivities. In fact, the place appeared disappointingly normal and—except for the front hall—decently maintained. There were quite a few antiques.

A piece that especially caught her eye was the large armoire that loomed at the top of the stairs. Up close, she noticed the carvings were of malevolent-looking creatures that might have been gargoyles, trolls, or dwarfs. Whatever they were, she didn't like the expressions on their faces, the way they seemed to stare right at her. The armoire was finely crafted and odd in that there were no visible knobs or pulls for opening any interior compartments it might contain. She ran her hands over the carvings and tapped the heavy wood. Unable to figure out the trick, she gave up and moved on.

At the rear of the upstairs hall was a room she decided must belong to the tenant. She tapped on the door, waited a bit, then tapped again. No response. She waited a moment longer, then tried the knob, but the door was locked. With a sense of relief, she continued down the rear stairs, which led to a back door. From here, she walked down a short hallway and back into the kitchen.

It seemed strange there weren't more clues about the Lowrys, about what kind of people they were. She'd gotten the impression Mr. Lowry had a job in banking or some sort of financial institution and that Muriel was a full-time housewife. Yet, other than the small appliances on the counter, the kitchen lacked cookbooks and equipment beyond the most basic pots and pans. From this, Nicole concluded that Muriel invested little time or effort in cooking. Nowhere had she seen clues to any other interests or hobbies.

There weren't any books, not even magazines or newspapers lying about. The CD collection, a set of thirty-six recordings titled, "Great Masterpieces of World Music," had been purchased as a set, complete with its own fitted rack. Only one of the disks had been removed from its cellophane wrap.

When she ran out of rooms to investigate, she found Brad upstairs in the master bedroom, unpacking his things. Then she spotted something she hadn't noticed before. In one of the room's two closets (the other left empty for Nicole and Brad) was a huge, old-fashioned metal safe, painted light green. The Lowrys' clothes were jammed into the remaining space. She wondered how they'd gotten the safe through the bedroom door and into the closet. She reached out and gave the knob a tug. It was locked.

When she looked around, Brad was standing behind her.

"Well, what do you think?" she said.

"That is one big safe."

"No, silly," she said. "The house!"

"Not too bad," he said. "Not too bad."

"It's great," she said, beaming at him. "We'd never have found anything this good through an agency."

He smiled, accepting this as praise. Then he stared at her a moment, tossed his suitcase onto the chaise lounge, and pulled her onto the bed.

Making love in this strange house, on a bed that actually squeaked, deepened her sense of unreality. At one point, she noticed that the bedroom door was open and remembered the tenant. She had an uneasy sense of someone else in the house, someone about to walk in on them. Then she was caught up in the warmth of him, the feel of his lips, the slow movement of hips and thighs. The strangeness of the house, England, the problems they'd been having—everything disappeared except the two of them.

Afterward, Brad dropped off to sleep while she drowsily took in the unfamiliar bedroom. Except for a few spots of dull turquoise, this room was done up in the same beiges and tans as the downstairs. Looking around, she wondered if the Lowrys' marriage could possibly be as dull as their bedroom.

As she snuggled against Brad's back, wrapping her arms around him, he pulled away and burrowed deeper into his pillow. She rolled onto her back, trying not to feel rejected. It was enough that he'd felt like making love again. A little at a time, she told herself. The chill was beginning to lift. She'd been right to insist on coming.

The leave of absence from her job—that seemed to be what infuriated him the most. The money, and the fact that she'd left without any guarantee her position would be there when she got back. He'd get over it. If they weren't extravagant, they could manage on his salary for a while. She could always find another job.

She did feel bad about leaving Stephanie to cope with their father. Their mother had been dead over a year, and he still hadn't recovered. Not that the marriage had been happy. On the contrary, his grief reminded Nicole of the old saying about it being easier to survive the loss of your best friend than the death of your worst enemy.

Despite her feelings of guilt, she'd felt compelled to accompany Brad to London. He would be gone the whole summer, his fourth trip in a year. Each time, he came back more distant. She worried that, after all this time apart, their problems might be irreversible.

After seven reasonably happy years of marriage, the chill between them puzzled her. Granted, they were two very different people. Nicole down to earth and practical, her energies focused on her small circle of friends and family. Aside from being an accomplished techy, Brad was something of a futuristic visionary with enough charisma to attract followers, people who believed in him. She'd always thought their differences were the reason they made such a great team. What had gone wrong?

She shivered, pushing the thought away, then kissed Brad on the side of the head and got up. She found a clean T-shirt among his things and pulled it on. The sleeves came almost to her elbows, the hem to mid thigh. She rolled up the sleeves, using her fingers to rearrange her hair. Only last Saturday, she'd had it trimmed and streaked with gold highlights to brighten up her natural color, a drab sparrow brown.

She moved closer to the mirror to study her face. At thirty-two, she still had no lines, no sign of crow's feet. Today, in this unfamiliar setting, she looked different—faded somehow, like an overexposed photograph. Perhaps it was the light.

She rubbed her cheeks to bring back some color then turned from the mirror to trot downstairs and see what there was to eat. As agreed, the Lowrys had left enough food for the first day. Nicole had done the same at home. She pulled a loaf of bread and salad makings from the refrigerator, then she located a can of tuna in the cupboard. When lunch was ready, she covered it with paper towels. (No telling what sort of creatures might be running around in an old house like this.) Then she went back up to see if Brad was awake.

Finding him already up and dressed for the office, she felt a pang of disappointment. He was installed at a desk in a corner of the bedroom, talking on the phone while typing furiously on his laptop. This was something he prided himself on—the ability to do two, even three things at the same time. "He'd better get one thing straight," he was saying. He paused a moment, absorbed in what he'd just written. Then, fingers flying over the keyboard again, he went on,"Britcomp isn't in charge anymore. We are."

She came up behind him and put her arms around his neck, her cheek against his. At her touch, he recoiled. This wasn't a conscious gesture; he simply twitched and pulled away. It was enough to let her know he was talking to Brenda, his assistant. She'd arrived in London a week early to set things up.

The thought of Brenda made Nicole's stomach knot. As she released Brad, she could almost hear Brenda's little-girl voice at the other end of the line. Brenda was another reason Nicole had been so determined to come along.

She began to root through her remaining suitcase, trying to assess which of her carefully packed possessions had disappeared with the missing bag. Meanwhile, Brad said goodbye and hung up. He busied himself shutting down his laptop and putting it back in its case. This done, he reached into the closet for his blue sports coat.

"But I made lunch," she protested. "You don't have to leave this minute, do you?"

Instead of answering, he kissed her absentmindedly on the top of the head. Then he was clumping down the steps, two at a time. "I'll be home early, around seven. Don't bother about dinner," he shouted up to her. "We'll take Brenda to that Indian place Dennis told us about." There was a brief silence before he added, "Take a nap or something."

The front door slammed and she was alone.

Two

Despite her exhaustion, Nicole was too keyed up for a nap. Instead, she put on shorts and a T-shirt and set off for a jog around the park she'd noticed on the ride in. The people she encountered were mainly elderly, sitting idly on benches or doddering along the paths with rickety metal shopping carts and string shopping bags.

As she began jogging, her mind drifted back over the last few months and the enormous effort this trip had required. It wasn't just a matter of preparing the condo for the occupation of strangers and figuring out what to pack. The hardest part had been the battle over whether she should come at all.

"Look. It's not going to be much fun for you in London," he'd said, in one of his more conciliatory moments. "Why not wait until next summer? Then we can both take off: go to Asia, backpack our way across India, see Tibet, the Himalayas."

She replied that she couldn't wait a year. Besides, he'd been talking about that same trip since college, and he was never going to get around to it. Sensing her resolve, he accused her of being headstrong and impulsive. It was a familiar charge, one he seemed to drag out every time they had a fight.

And it was true that Nicole, growing up, had a reputation for being impulsive. In family lore, several favorite stories illustrated this tendency, the most famous being the time she'd stopped on the shoulder of the Santa Monica Freeway to rescue a dog. She was sixteen at the time, newly licensed to drive.

Nicole's parents were furious at the way she'd imperiled herself "for a stupid mutt." They'd suspended her driving privileges for the entire summer, an eternity in her young life. Even so, the family kept the dog, a short-legged, red-haired creature who looked like a cross between an Irish Setter and a dachshund. For many years, Franny was their much beloved pet, a fact that gave Nicole great satisfaction. She'd never seen the decision to rescue the dog as rash—quite the contrary. She'd been certain, when she pulled onto the shoulder of the freeway, opened the car door, and called, "Here, doggy," that the story would have a happy ending.

As her feet pounded along the path, she wondered once again why Brad so opposed her coming. "I have enough on my plate," he'd said, "without having to worry about you." This argument didn't make sense when, on several previous assignments, he'd seemed genuinely disappointed that she couldn't get time off work to come along. Now she wondered if his earlier protestations had been entirely sincere.

As she started around the park for the third time, sweat began dripping in her eyes, and she slowed to a walk. Pulling off the red kerchief she was wearing as a headband, she wiped her face. Only then did she notice she was the park's only jogger, the only woman in shorts and (as far as she could see) the sole person under sixty. People were staring in a way that implied joggers weren't an everyday sight on Turnham Green. Suddenly self-conscious, she strolled out of the park, still heading away from the house.

After another few minutes, she came to a large brick supermarket called Sainsbury's. Inside, the smell of food was intoxicating: bread baking, chickens roasting. Cruising the fresh produce, she noticed tomatoes, melons, strawberries, peaches, and cellophane packs of lettuce bearing labels from countries like Spain, Portugal, Israel.

She had a sudden inspiration. They could go to that Indian restaurant any time. Tonight she'd make a nice dinner.

She'd brought along her credit card. The prices here seemed reasonable—that is, until she got to the checkstand and realized she was spending pounds, not dollars. But what difference did it make? Eating at home was bound to be less expensive than going to a restaurant.

As hostess, she reasoned, she'd be in charge. She could refuse to let Brad and Brenda dominate the evening with shop talk. They were always doing that, shutting her out of the conversation.

When she turned the corner and the Lowrys' house came into view, she spotted a stranger emerge from the backyard. He headed purposefully up the front steps and appeared to be trying to look in the windows.

The man and his behavior alarmed her. Was this even the right street? She made a hasty detour into Mr. McGiever's flowerbed, pretending to examine a scruffy outcropping of plants while she took another look. Yes, she decided, that was the Lowrys' house. If this man was a door-to-door salesman, he was certainly aggressive about it. She considered the wisdom of waiting behind the hedge until he left.

Just then, a curtain parted in the window nearby, and Mr. McGiever peered out. She felt exposed, caught in the act of trampling his garden. But she wasn't about to walk up to his door and ask for help. That would be more trouble than it was worth. She could handle this herself. After readjusting her load of groceries, she walked on.

As she reached the Lowrys' gate, the man hurried forward to open it, and she noticed he looked a little like Brad. The two had the same general coloring, only this man was taller, more muscular. And, while Brad had a tendency to slouch, there was something about the way this man stood, the set of his shoulders. He was, in fact, much better looking than Brad, with almond-shaped eyes that reminded her of the actor who starred in the old movie, American Gigolo, a particular favorite of hers.

His gaze was admiring and, at the same time, unsettling. It made her aware of the wind whipping her T-shirt around and of her bare legs, the inappropriateness of her skimpy white shorts in this sedate London neighborhood. On her outing, the only other female she'd seen with legs on display had been a girl in a leather miniskirt. She'd been no more than eighteen, skinny as a stick.

He was holding the gate open. After a moment's hesitation, she stepped into the yard. Then, as the gate clanged behind her, she remembered the way he'd been snooping around. She noticed that the street looked empty, the windows of the houses dark and unyielding. Next door, where Mr. McGiever had been peeking out only a minute ago, the place appeared deserted.

She thought of the self defense class she'd taken and its cardinal rule: "When approached by a stranger, no matter how respectable he looks, prepare to defend yourself." The stance came back to her—hands ready to push against an assailant's chest, knee poised for a quick jab to the groin.

But that was ridiculous. She never doubted her ability to take care of herself, even in a place like L.A. And this was London, the most civilized city in the world. No one would attempt robbery, rape, or mayhem on a quiet, residential street, certainly not in broad daylight. Besides, this man appeared to be as solid as the Bank of England. Her memory flickered. Was there really a Bank of England; if so, was it still in business?

Meeting his glance, she felt her cheeks flush. Get a grip, she told herself. Then, aloud, "Can I help you?"

"I'm looking for Frederick Lowry," the man said in clear, BBC English. "I need to get in touch with him rather urgently."

"I'm afraid he's away. Out of the country." The words were out before she had time to consider whether this was something she should be telling a stranger.

"Do you know when he'll be back?"

Again, she hesitated. But what harm would it do to tell him? "After Labor Day," she said. Then, remembering this was England, she added, "The third or fourth of September."

"That's a bit inconvenient," he said. "Isn't there any way to get in touch with him? A telephone number?"

"I'm sorry," she said. "I really don't know where he is right now." This was a lie. On their way to L.A., Muriel had said they were stopping off in Dallas for two days to visit family. In the interim, Nicole's sister was watching the condo, watering the plants, and feeding the dog.

As his smile dimmed, it occurred to her that he might be a policeman. But no, she decided, his jacket was too expensive, and that gold watch he was wearing was a Rolex. Brad had a fondness for designer knock-offs, and she knew such things could be faked. This one looked real enough.

"Mr. Lowry and I have a small business venture together," he said. "I can assure you he'll be most anxious to hear what I have to tell him."

If that's so, she thought, why didn't he tell you he was leaving the country? Then, aloud, "All right. If he happens to call, I'll tell him you want to speak to him."

"I wonder if I could persuade you to contact him."

She felt weary and out of patience. "Listen," she said, "I already told you…" She stopped and made an effort to be polite. "I haven't any idea where he is. His wife said they wouldn't be using a mobile on this trip, so I can't reach them by phone. Why don't you give me your number? If they happen to call, I'll pass it on."

He studied her a moment, his expression doubtful. "Just tell him Reinhardt said to get in touch," he said. "He has the number." For the first time, he seemed to notice the load of groceries in her arms. "I say, that shopping looks heavy, and I've kept you standing there. Please allow me…" He moved forward, as if to take them.

At that moment, an alarm went off in her head. She thought of the appalling incident in the condo down the hall from theirs, the brutal rape of a young woman. The assailant had been wearing a business suit, a respectable-looking stranger who'd offered to help carry the woman's groceries. The crime had inspired the residents association to offer the self-defense class. Until then, Nicole had felt invulnerable, removed from the city's violent nature, immune to the car jackings, ATM robberies, muggings and parking-structure stabbings, the drive-by shootings and freeway snipers. For the first time, a self-defense class had seemed like a good idea.

"No thanks," she said, gripping the bags tighter and taking a step back to let him pass. "I'm sorry I couldn't be of help."

For a moment, he didn't move; as he stared at her, she could see he wasn't used to being dismissed. His expression darkened, and she noticed a feral cast to his eyes, the look of a predator. "I'm sorry to have troubled you," he said stiffly. He started for the gate, then turned back to add, "Good day."

She watched him walk across the street toward a small black sports car and waited for him to get in. Then she set her bags down and unlocked the front door.

She was in the kitchen, unloading her groceries when she suddenly remembered seeing him come out of the backyard. She went to the back door and inspected it. Her knees went weak when she saw that it wasn't locked. She told herself that she must have forgotten to relock it earlier, when she was exploring the garden.

After securing the lock, she walked back to the front door and peered through the small, eye-level window. He was still out there, sitting in his car. She couldn't tell what he was doing, but he didn't seem to be looking at the house.

She wondered, suddenly, why this man was so desperate to find Lowry when he'd only just left the country. This troubled her, raising questions about the family she'd trusted with their condo. When Brad first told her about Lowry, he said he'd run into him in his company's London office.

Pressed for details, he said, "I don't think he actually works there. He's a consultant or something. Tell you what. I'll call over there and ask about him."

"Never mind," she said. At the time, a good two months before their departure, it hadn't mattered that much. Now, after her little talk with Reinhardt, she began to wonder. Was Lowry a deadbeat a step ahead of his creditors?

For a moment, she was tempted to call Brad. Yet she knew this was a bad idea. He'd say he had enough on his mind without having to worry about his wife at loose ends in Chiswick, having hysterics.

And really, what was there to be so rattled about? The man had been nothing less than polite. When she wanted him to leave, he'd left, without making trouble. So what if he was out there, sitting in his parked car? It wasn't against the law.

Still, she couldn't shake the thought of him, the way he'd looked at her. She stepped over to the hall mirror to inspect herself, running her fingers through the mess the wind had made of her hair. She grimaced a smile and two dimples appeared. Those dimples were the problem, she thought—the reason people were always assuming she was a sweet little thing when she had no intention of being sweet at all.

Perhaps that was what had happened out there. The sinister look on his face had been nothing more than astonishment at being dismissed by this "sweet little thing."

Perhaps he really was Lowry's business partner and the two had a falling out. Or, more likely, Lowry owed him money.

Reinhardt might even be a process server or a repo man—even if he didn't look the part.

As she began to put away the groceries, she remembered that she did have a way to reach the Lowrys. In her last message, Mrs. Lowry had mentioned they wouldn't be using their mobile phone because it wouldn't work in the States. Instead, she'd given Nicole the number of the relatives in Dallas. Nicole had printed out the message and put it in a folder with their trip information. On her way upstairs, she peeked out again. The black car was gone.

The folder was in a zippered side compartment of her one remaining suitcase. After locating the number and figuring out the codes for an international call, she heard it ring at the other end of the line.

A woman's voice, heavy with a Texas drawl, came on. "Hello. This is Jeannie Bennett. We aren't around right now. Please leave a message, and we'll give you a ring when we get home. You all have a good day, now." At the end of each sentence, her voice went up, as if she were asking a question.

Nicole explained that someone named Reinhardt had dropped by and wanted Mr. Lowry to call him. She said he seemed to think it was important. (Somehow she hesitated to use the word urgent. After all, these people were on vacation.) As soon as she hung up, it struck her that the woman had said her name was Bennett, not Lowry. She began to wonder if she'd reached the right number.

Her shoulders and legs had started to ache. She decided that this, like her anxiety, was a symptom of jet lag. Even so, she was determined to start dinner.

She trudged back downstairs and seasoned the free-range chicken with garlic and fresh herbs. Then she cut up vegetables—onions, potatoes, carrots, and some miniature ears of corn she'd found at Sainsbury's. They were the sort that only came canned and packed in brine at home. But these were fresh, imported from Thailand.

She put the chicken and vegetables in a bright-orange enameled casserole and slid it into the oven then studied the temperature control. Whatever numbers had once surrounded the dial were now too faded to read. After a moment's consternation, she twisted it to the left and waited for the burner to ignite. Then she turned the temperature down about a third of the way, to a point she guessed should be about 350 degrees. She set the table and made a salad. When she was done straightening the kitchen, she decided to do the sensible thing and take a nap.

Her travel alarm went off with a rasping buzz, and she sat up with a start. For a long, panicky moment she couldn't remember where she was. Outside it was daylight, and her travel alarm—gold, with BABY BEN painted on its face in curly letters—said 6:00. Then she remembered. She was in London. She'd set the alarm to go off in an hour so she could check on dinner and get dressed.

She took another look at the clock. Brad would probably arrive around 7:00 with Brenda in tow. She perched at the edge of the bed, stretching, trying to shake the thick fog that filled her head. It felt like 3:00 in the morning. She did a quick calculation. Since L.A. was eight hours earlier, that meant it was 10:00 a.m. Except for her hour-long nap, she'd been up all night. No wonder she felt so groggy.

Forcing herself up, she pulled a green knit dress from the suitcase and put it on a hanger. In the bathroom, she hung her dress on the shower curtain rod and turned on the hot water to steam out the wrinkles.

She ran downstairs for a peek at the chicken. It hadn't begun to brown. The oven was barely warm. She turned the dial to what appeared to be the highest temperature.

When she got back to the bathroom, she discovered that a shower was out of the question. The "shower bath" Mrs. Lowry had mentioned consisted of a hand-held rubber hose with a nozzle. Even turned up full blast, it leaked rather than sprayed.

She settled for a bath, which turned out to be exactly what she needed. As she relaxed into it, she let go of her anxieties and considered the three months ahead, the opportunity to live in London. One of the things that had drawn her to the swap had been the chance to see how people lived in a foreign country. She imagined herself rethinking all her old assumptions from the ground up. The visit to Sainsbury's had confirmed this—the array of unfamiliar household products, bins of bulk candy in dazzling variety, exotic fruits and vegetables, some prepackaged like cuts of meat.

The nitty gritty of daily life was just one aspect of the discoveries to be made. Above all, London was famous for its cultural life—theaters, museums, bookstores. As she considered all of this, she found herself wondering if three months would be enough.

She must have dozed off for a moment, for she was startled awake by the creaking of floorboards, the sound of someone creeping up the stairs.

"Brad?" she called. "Is that you?" The creaking stopped but there was no response. Then she remembered the tenant and called out, "Is someone there?' As the words left her mouth, she recalled Mrs. Lowry mentioning that the tenant always used the back stairs, which led directly to the rented room. The sounds she'd just heard had come from the front of the house.

As she raised herself out of the bath water and reached for the towel, she heard several clicks, as if someone was trying to open the bathroom door. She froze, heart pounding wildly and cursed herself for not locking the door. Only then did she notice that there was no key in the lock.

The noise stopped. She waited, holding her breath, listening intently, but the house remained still. After what seemed like a long time, several minutes perhaps, she got out of the tub, wrapped herself in the towel, and slowly crept to the door. As quietly as she could, she turned the knob. It was locked.

Then she heard sounds down the hall. Someone was walking around in the bedroom. She tiptoed to the window and looked down at the yard. It was too far to jump.

She thought of Reinhardt, the man on the porch, and felt chilled. But if he was going to rape and murder her, why would he lock her in the bathroom while he rummaged through the house? One by one, possibilities occurred to her, none of them reassuring.

Looking around for something to protect herself, she spotted a metal towel bar next to the sink. She tugged and pulled, struggling to wrench it from its brackets, but it was solidly attached. Finally, she reached under the sink and pulled out an ancient blow dryer that felt pathetically light in her hand.

She flattened herself against the wall by the door so she'd be behind it when it opened. After an interminable wait, the footsteps started toward the bathroom again. She stood, gripping the hair dryer, not daring to breathe. As the sounds got louder, it was hard to separate them from the pounding of her heart.

Then the noise grew fainter. The intruder had passed the bathroom and was now running lightly down the stairs. In the distance, she heard a door close, then silence.

She tried the door again, then rattled the knob and yanked it hard. She'd just begun to beat on it when she could hear the distinctive chime of her cell phone. She knew immediately who it was. Brad was calling to say he'd be late. Damn it, he was out there somewhere with Brenda. She counted while the phone chimed a dozen times, then stopped.

That was when she smelled it—smoke. Her heart began to thump in her throat. Stepping back from the door, she could see a wispy veil of smoke leaking under the door.

She hurried to the window and tried to open it, but it was stuck. As she struggled with it, she saw that it was painted shut. Looking around for something to pry the window open, she noticed something else. The smoke smelled a lot less like a house on fire than barbecued chicken. Only then did she realize it wasn't the house that was burning. It was the casserole she'd left in the oven, the chicken and the tiny ears of corn.

As the phone started up again, Nicole put every ounce of her strength into beating on the door. Once in a while, she made a run at it, slamming into it with her shoulder. But the only damage she managed to inflict was to herself.

She pounded on the door until her fists ached and tears of frustration ran down her face. But it was useless. There was no one to hear.

Three

The smoke grew thicker, stinging her eyes and making her throat and nasal passages burn. She renewed her battle with the window, bracing her feet against the floor and pushing with all her might. Still, it wouldn't budge.

She struggled to calm herself. She had to stay focused on one simple goal—opening the window. First, she picked up the hairdryer and gave the window frame three or four sharp whacks. Jerkily, in stops and starts, the window allowed itself to be raised. But as soon as she took her hand away, it slammed shut, and she had to start over.

She held it open until she figured out the problem. The sash—the pulley of rope that held the window up—was frayed through. Looking around for something to prop it open, she grabbed the hair dryer from its resting place on the sink and jammed it into the gap. As the weight of the window settled on it, a big chunk of the dryer's plastic case broke off and clattered to the floor.

With a grunt of disgust, she kicked it into the corner. Her eyes were running and sweat was trickling down her face. She leaned out the window to take a deep breath of fresh air. One look reaffirmed her earlier judgment; jumping was out of the question. Directly below—about fifteen feet beneath the bathroom window—a concrete slab was set up for use as a patio in warm weather. White wrought-iron furniture, covered with clear plastic, was stacked against the house.

Her cell phone had just stopped chiming when the Lowrys' house phone started in. It wasn't exactly a ring but a muted double rasping sound that reminded her of a hiccup. As it rang, she wondered how long she'd have to wait before Brad got home. She knew from experience that if he was calling, it meant he wouldn't be leaving the office for a while, perhaps not for hours.

She leaned a little further out and called a tentative, "Help!" To her ears, her voice sounded thin and shrill, verging on hysteria. She waited perhaps a full minute and tried again, this time louder. "Help me! Help!"

The silence persisted, and the knot in her stomach grew. "Help!" she screamed. "Fire!"

She shouted until her throat was raw, her voice frayed and reedy. The only response was the distant cawing of a bird.

The house directly behind the Lowrys'—another grim-looking brick crackerbox—appeared deserted. Trees obscured the houses on either side. She wondered if it was possible for all the neighbors to be out at the same time. She thought about Mr. McGiever and his eagerness to be of help. Where was he?

As she extracted her head from the window, she noticed that the smoke seemed to be growing denser. She took off the towel she was using as a sarong and plugged the crack at the bottom of the door. This seemed to staunch the leak, at least for the moment.

She pulled her dress on, then looked around for something to use in the keyhole. She had no idea how to pick a lock. But if those delinquents who regularly broke into the condo complex could do it, how hard could it be?

There was nothing useful on the countertop or the back of the toilet. She began working her way through the medicine cabinet and the drawers next to the sink.

Here, when she was in no mood to appreciate it, was a treasure trove of information about the Lowrys: four different brands of laxatives, a bottle of diet pills, and several types of over-the-counter uppers—so-called "energy boosters" with mega-doses of caffeine. A jar of petroleum jelly was almost empty, as was a container of thick pink lotion labeled "Itch-No-More." She also found some peroxide, strawberry-blond hair coloring, and an assortment of nail polish in shades of crimson. An image of Muriel Lowry flashed through her mind: a nervous blonde, given to constipation and a habit of scratching herself with her long scarlet fingernails.

The phone, which had been quiet for a while, started in again. She tried to ignore it, focusing her attention on the cupboard under the sink. At the far back, pushed to one side of the pipes was a shoebox. She lifted it out and took off the lid. It was filled with pill bottles. She stared at them for a moment, puzzled by the fact that none of them bore labels or any sort of identification. Then she put the cover on, shoved them under the sink again, and stood up.

The smoke, temporarily stemmed by the towel at the bottom of the door, was now leaking in at the sides. She went back to the window and leaned out, hoping to spot a trellis or drainpipe that might support her weight. It was a straight drop, without even an awning or overhang to break a fall. As she pulled her head in, something gouged the palm of her hand. She drew her hand away, and there was the answer to her prayers—a jumbo bobby pin.

She separated the prongs and unbent the pin into a straight piece of wire. Then she went to work on the lock. After a half dozen failed attempts, she dropped to her knees and peered into the keyhole. It was completely dark, as if something were blocking the view. She sat back on her heels and, after a moment's thought, realized it must be the key. He must have left the key in the lock. She could use the bobby pin to dislodge it. Then, when it dropped to the floor, all she had to do was pull it under the door.

She shook out the towel and tried to feed it through the gap at the bottom of the door so it would catch the key when it fell. But the towel, limp and damp, kept bunching up no matter how carefully she guided it. Finally, she gave up.

Knocking the key out of the lock was a little easier. She poked this way and that, and at last, the key gave way and tumbled to the floor. She reached her fingers into the crack under the door—smoke was too thick to risk a look—but there was no key within reach. She repositioned the towel over the crack at the bottom of the door and went back to the window. Since her first cries for help, several birds had appeared in the Lowrys' tree and seemed to be watching with great interest.

Wearily, she renewed her cries. "Fire!" she croaked. "The house is burning down!"

"Who's doing all that shouting?" someone called back. "And what's this about a house burning down?" The voice was female, the accent Irish. At that moment, a woman with bright red hair appeared in the yard below.

Nicole was so happy to see her she almost cried. "The house isn't on fire." Her voice was gravelly, unrecognizable from the strain of shouting. "My dinner's burning, and I'm locked in the bathroom. I'm Nicole Graves. Are you the Lowrys' tenant?"

"Aye," the woman said. "McConnehy's the name—Alice. Hang on up there, Nicole. I'll switch the oven off and be right along to let you out." She disappeared into the back of the house.

It seemed a long time before Nicole heard heels clicking up the stairs. "Jesus, what a reek," the woman called out. "Like the whole house is going up." When she reached the door, she turned the doorknob, then shook it, rattling the door. "It is locked," she said, "Now Nicole, tell me how it happened."

Nicole quickly explained about the intruder, how he'd locked her in the bathroom.

"Are you serious?" Alice said. "He didn't hurt you, did he?"

"I'm fine," Nicole said. "I didn't even get a look at him." Then she explained about the key and told Alice to look around on the floor for it.

There was a silence, punctuated by the creaking of floorboards. Then the key sounded in the lock, the door swung open, and there she was, a woman with red hair pulled into a careless topknot. She was small, not much taller than Nicole, and rather pretty, with wide-spaced blue eyes.

"That's a powerful bad thing to happen your first day here, Nicole," she said. "But you say you didn't actually see the man?"

Nicole explained the earlier encounter with Reinhardt and her hunch that he was the intruder.

Alice was quiet, considering this. Then she said, "But you don't know it was him, now do you?"

"I didn't actually see him in the house," Nicole said, after pausing to reflect. "But there was something odd about the way he peered in the windows when he thought no one was looking, and he'd been snooping around in back."

Just then the phone started ringing again. Alice moved aside as Nicole bolted into the bedroom to get it. Only as she reached the desk did she decide that she wasn't going to answer. Any other husband would have been worried enough by now to leave the office and rush home. If he called again, she'd let it ring. She'd let it ring all night.

Alice appeared in the doorway just as the phone stopped ringing. "I'll open some windows," she said. "You'd better check your valuables."

Nicole looked in her purse. Her credit cards were still there. She went over to the desk and opened the drawer where Brad had put the passports, credit cards, and some £20 notes. It was all there.

"How weird," Nicole said. "He didn't take anything." She looked around at Alice. "Don't you want to check your room?"

The woman shook her head. "My door was locked, and no one would bother with my things." She paused and seemed to consider this. "I'm not in the habit of keeping valuables in my room. I like to keep my life as simple as what I can fit in a suitcase."

"You know, now that I think about it, I didn't hear him go into the back of the house at all," Nicole said. "I don't get it. He wasn't interested in our passports or credit cards or even the cash we left in here. It's like he was looking for something else in this room, something he expected to find here."

"The police should be able to sort it out for you." Alice shrugged. "We'll have to give them a ring, you know."

"First I want to look downstairs," Nicole said.

In the kitchen, where Alice had already turned off the oven and opened a window, the smoke was thinning. Nicole located some potholders and opened the oven door. Smoke billowed out, and she shut it. The two of them opened the rest of the windows and the door leading to the yard. Then Nicole went back to the oven and, braving the smoke, pulled out the blackened casserole. The heat seeped through the pads as she darted into the yard. She set the casserole down in one of the rear flowerbeds. Using the potholder, she lifted the lid.

The chicken was a crusty black mass and now seemed to be a permanent part of the pot. The little ears of corn had completely disappeared.

She left the casserole sitting in the dirt and went back into the kitchen. Alice was standing at the sink, filling the electric kettle. She turned around and gave Nicole a distracted smile. For the first time, Nicole had a chance to study her. Aside from her pretty eyes, she had a slightly turned-up nose, and lots of freckles. She didn't appear to be wearing any make-up, but her cheeks and lips were rosy with natural color. Although she wasn't as slender as current fashion dictated, she was well proportioned and looked fit. She was wearing white nylon slacks, a pink T-shirt and sensible, white lace-up shoes with crepe soles.

The most striking thing about her was her relaxed, friendly manner and sensible, down-to-earth way of expressing herself. Nicole had the feeling that given time, the two of them would become good friends.

"I'm just thinking of what's happened to you, Nicole. And I don't want to speak out of turn, but…"

Nicole nodded, mystified.

Alice studied her a bit longer. Then she said, "It wasn't your husband who locked you in, was it?"

"Brad?" Nicole gave an incredulous laugh. "He'd never do a thing like that. Besides, I'm certain someone broke in."

"Broke in," Alice repeated, almost to herself. "Here," she handed Nicole a box of tea and pointed at the kettle. "I wonder if you'd mind starting the tea while I take a look round."

Alice went out the back door to inspect the lock from the outside. Then she walked through the house, and Nicole heard her open and shut the front door. When she reappeared, she said, "It doesn't look like anyone has tampered with the locks. You know, Freddy keeps this place secured like a fortress. You're sure you locked up?"

Nicole remembered coming back from the store and finding the back door unlocked but decided not to mention it. "I double-checked the doors before I went upstairs," she said. "That guy had me spooked."

"Then someone else has the keys. You're absolutely certain it wasn't your husband?"

"I told you," Nicole said, beginning to lose patience. "He's at the office."

"He could have popped back for something he needed."

"He never does that. I don't even think he took the key. Once he gets involved at work…"

Alice appeared deep in thought, leaning against the refrigerator and staring into the distance. "You know," she said. "There are three possibilities: It could have been your husband, but you're certain it wasn't. It could have been a burglar, perhaps that chap who came 'round asking for Freddy. But I'm thinking—maybe it was Freddy himself."

"Freddy?" Nicole repeated.

Alice nodded. "Frederick H. Lowry." The way she said this made it clear she didn't think much of him. "What if he forgot something important and came back for it?"

The conversation was beginning to make Nicole dizzy. "But they've left the country," she said.

"Oh, they told me about their trip to the States," Alice said.

Nicole stared at her. "But you think he's still here?"

"No, I suppose not," Alice said slowly. "It's only..." Another pause. "You can't ever tell with Freddy." Then to Nicole's puzzled look, she added, "What he's up to, if you get my meaning."

Before she could ask Alice to explain, Nicole found herself being ushered to the kitchen phone.

"While the tea is brewing," Alice was saying, "we might as well put in a call to the police."

Alice dialed the number. Nicole described the incident to a man at the other end of the line. He promised to send a constable as soon as possible.

By the time they sat down and Alice poured the tea, it was as black as coffee. This seemed to suit her. "Gorgeous," she said, as she took the first sip. There was also a dish of chocolate-coated wheat-meal biscuits, which Alice had put on the table at the last moment.

Even after Nicole added milk and sugar, the tea was so strong that she could only take small sips. As they sat in companionable silence, drinking tea and munching chocolate biscuits, she studied Alice and was struck, once again, by how much she liked her. There was something profoundly comforting about the woman. Just being in the room with her made Nicole feel calm and safe.

Soon they were rehashing the break-in. When Nicole described Reinhardt, Alice was sure she'd never seen anyone like him visit the Lowrys. "They have very few visitors," Alice said, "and no social life to speak of." When she heard about the arsenal of pills Nicole had found, Alice said, "Really?" without a bit of interest.

"You don't understand," Nicole said. "There were at least several dozen bottles filled with pills: red ones, blue ones, rainbow assortments—none of them labeled."

She waited for a response, but there was none.

"I mean," Nicole continued, "that's a lot of pills, and if she got them from a pharmacy—you know, a chemist—they'd be labeled, wouldn't they?" Just thinking about it made her feel anxious. She had a sudden vision of the Lowrys shuttling her new Volvo between the pawnshops in Santa Monica and the seamier part of Venice, swapping components of her home entertainment center for the latest in pharmaceutical highs.

"Now that I think about it," Alice finally said, "Muriel does have allergy problems. She's always dosing herself with one thing or another. But I never saw her acting strange, if that's what you're getting at." She was quiet again and seemed to be considering this. Then she added, "On the other hand, I've never spent much time with her. Or Freddy. To tell you the truth, I prefer not to know much about them."

Nicole gave her a puzzled look. There was nothing she didn't want to know about the people she met, including Alice.

"Let me put it this way," Alice went on. "Some folk you prefer not to get pally with—especially when you share living quarters." Her tone was dismissive. "Besides, I'm away a great deal for my work. It isn't as if I have the opportunity."

"Mrs. Lowry said you're a nurse."

"Home nurse," Alice said. "Terminal cases. I take over in the last phase. See the family through, lay the body out and all."

Nicole stared at her, trying to take this in. It was hard to imagine someone as wholesome as Alice laying out a corpse. She swallowed hard and groped for something to say. "I'll bet that's a very good field," she murmured.

Alice nodded in agreement. "That it is. Given a choice, most folks would choose to die at home, close to their own people, the things they love. So I'm doing them a good turn, the way I see it. The money's grand, and I'm never starved for work." She yawned and stood up. "Sorry. Finished up a case last night. Didn't get much sleep. If you're all right then, Nicole, I'll just pop back upstairs for a wee lie-down."

On her way out of the room, Alice stopped and glanced back. "Oh, by the way—I may have a few days before my next case. You said your husband would be tied up with his work. Maybe you'll let me show you 'round."

Four

After Alice went upstairs, Nicole remained seated at the table. She thought of that moment at Heathrow when she'd first noticed her suitcase was gone. In retrospect, this first glimmering of dislocation seemed like an omen—if she'd known enough to recognize it—that this trip might be a mistake.

She glanced at the clock and did a quick calculation. It hardly seemed possible she'd been here less than nine hours. The thought of the Lowrys—and the fact that they'd soon be in L.A.—set off a new wave of anxiety. Hearing Alice's opinion of Freddy had altered Nicole's view of him and his family. They were no longer the respectable Brits who could be trusted with her property. *My God! What was I thinking?*

She tried to summon back the terms of the agreement they'd signed, whether it was possible to change her mind and toss the Lowrys out once they established themselves in the condo. She hoped the papers were upstairs in her remaining suitcase, but she made no move to go up and see. No matter how unreliable the Lowrys were, she wasn't about to give up her plans for the summer. If she let this opportunity escape, it would be gone forever.

At that moment, a clattering sound brought her to her feet. She rushed to the front door and looked out, but no one was there. She walked from room to room through the lower floor, but the house was silent and benign. Still uneasy, she made a second tour, inspecting windows and doors to make sure they were locked.

Outside, daylight had faded and early evening threatened rain. The house was quiet, and she decided the noise had been the building settling as the temperature dropped. Her nerves were shot; that was the trouble. It might be a while before the police arrived, and she was too jittery to wait down here alone.

As she tiptoed up to the second floor, she was aware of the creaking stairs and the fact that this was the same noise she'd heard while she was locked in the bathroom.

In the Lowrys' room, she felt better knowing that Alice was asleep just down the hall. Even so, her hands shook as she peeled off the green knit and dressed again, this time starting with the bra and panties she'd omitted in her earlier haste. As she was brushing her hair, she saw something she hadn't noticed before. The door to the closet that held the safe was slightly ajar. She was certain she'd closed it.

For a moment she debated whether to go down the hall and wake Alice from her nap. She told herself she was being silly, but her heart thumped as she walked to the closet and gave the door a pull. As it swung toward her, she saw that the door of the safe was open. Now she understood what the intruder had been up to.

She squeezed into the space in front of the safe and bent down to have a look. The main compartment held a medium-sized cardboard carton. On one of the shelves, a short stack of envelopes was secured with a rubber band. She pulled the carton out, unfolded the flaps, and peered in. It was filled with blue felt packets, the sort used for storing silverware. She untied the ribbon on one packet and unrolled it. Sure enough, it held a place setting of silver: a table knife, a butter knife, two forks (salad and main course), and two spoons (tea and soup).

The pieces were old and tarnished, but she could tell from their weight they were solid silver. The pattern was quite beautiful: a lush mosaic of flowers covered the entire handle. She rolled the felt up again and retied the ribbon. Then she opened a few others. More silver.

Judging by the size of the box, there were at least a dozen place settings, perhaps more. Silverware like this had to be worth several thousand dollars, and it struck her as odd that the intruder hadn't taken it.

She shoved the carton back then undid the rubber band on the stack of envelopes. The top one contained the deed to the house. It was in the names of Frederick H. and Muriel B. Lowry, dated a little over a year ago. It seemed a short time for the house to have such a settled look. She wondered if they'd bought the place furnished or had rented it first and lived here a while before buying it.

In the other envelopes were registration papers for the car and last year's Inland Revenue statement for Frederick Lowry. His occupation was listed as "financial consultant, self-employed." He'd paid £2,900 taxes on a reported income last year of £14,000. She did a quick calculation. Translated into US currency, that was less than $24,000—hardly enough to maintain a decent-size house in a good area of London. And they had a lot of rather nice furniture, including antiques, the set of sterling, and a number of original paintings. Well, she thought, there might be family money. Maybe Muriel Lowry had come with a dowry. Still, if they had additional income, wouldn't it appear on the tax form as earned interest or dividends?

It struck her that there should have been more documents, if these were the family's most essential records, worth keeping in a safe. Where, for example, were the Lowrys' insurance policies or their bank and investment records? Granted, she and Brad kept such things in a safe deposit box, but they didn't have a heavy-duty safe in their bedroom.

Taking a second look at the tax form, she wondered what a self-employed financial consultant actually did. It could be anything from managing investment portfolios to laundering money. She made a mental note to ask Alice. Surely she'd know that much.

She put the envelopes back in the safe and straightened up. As she squeezed her way out of the closet, she heard a loud click and realized—too late—that the door to the safe had swung shut. She rushed back and tugged at the knob. It was locked, and no amount of pulling would persuade it to open.

At least she knew what was inside. All she had to do was call the Lowrys and describe what she'd seen. They'd be able to tell her if anything was missing.

She placed another call, got the same recording, and left a message describing the break-in. "I don't think anything was stolen," she said. "But I won't know for sure until I speak to you. It's urgent that you call me right away."

She'd just hung up when she heard more knocking downstairs. This time the sound persisted, swelling to an insistent crescendo. As she hurried down, a cool rush of relief swept over her. This had to be the police. Here, at last, was someone who'd help her make sense of what had happened.

Instead of a policeman, she found Brad and Brenda waiting on the porch. Seeing them, Nicole felt a flurry of anxiety. It was as if something had disrupted a bees' nest in her stomach, and the insects—smaller and more excitable than the ones back home—were buzzing around in there.

"My God, Nicole," Brad said. "I've been half crazy. Where the hell have you been?"

"Oh, I've been right here." Even to her own ears, Nicole's voice sounded high and strained. Gazing at Brad and Brenda, she had a sudden revelation. It was as if she knew exactly what they were thinking. Perhaps it was Brenda's expression—that look of composed innocence—and the fact that it was identical to Brad's. Nicole could see that they were dissembling, pretending not to be in collusion against her. It wasn't only their faces, but something about the way they stood apart, leaning in opposite directions. Brenda (her tiny purse slung from one shoulder) had her arms folded across her midsection, as if to protect herself from a quick punch. Brad was holding his laptop in front of him, at crotch level.

As Nicole regarded them, her stomach gave another flutter. Something had happened between them, something irrevocable.

The seconds ticked away, with no one venturing to speak. Finally Nicole glanced at her watch. "You're late," she said. "What happened?"

Brad shot a quick look at Brenda. "I—uh—I'm really sorry. We got tied up. I kept trying to call you, only nobody answered. I think maybe I wrote down the wrong number."

While he talked, Brenda was blinking and fluttering her thick, dark eyelashes. She was dressed in a white silk suit that seemed more appropriate for dinner in Beverly Hills than a day at the office. The skirt was short and tight, and she wore no blouse under the jacket. Apart from her great cleavage, she was flat and elongated—like a teenager after a sudden growth spurt. With her widow's peak, shaggy lashes and Cupid's bow mouth, Brenda had the sort of face illustrators put on flowers in children's books. While it was pretty in its own way, it didn't quite work on a real person.

The odd thing was that everyone else seemed to think Brenda was beautiful. After meeting her, Nicole's sister had asked Nicole how she felt about Brad working with such a stunning woman.

Nicole had been incredulous. "Stunning?" she'd said. "Brenda?"

"You don't think so?" Stephanie had said. "Ask Brad what he thinks."

It wasn't in Nicole to do that. Instead, she kept an eye on Brad and realized Stephanie was right. Brad behaved differently when his assistant was around. Brenda had his complete attention. Even when he was speaking to Nicole, his eyes sought out Brenda as the audience.

Despite this, Brenda's personality, which was both bland and coy, allowed Nicole to dismiss her as a threat—that and the fact that, as Brenda's boss, Brad knew her limitations. He was always complaining to Nicole about Brenda's screwups, mistakes she made at the office because (in his words) she was too "sloppy" and "distracted," "immature" and "guy-crazy" to focus on work. Nicole thought it a wonder that he didn't fire her or, at the least, put her on probation. His putting up with her seemed to prove what a good person he was. Now, however, Nicole understood how completely she'd misread the situation.

"We sat down with the Brits and went into the whole morale thing," Brad was saying. "They got pretty steamed up, and I had to do some major negotiating. I'm really sorry we kept you waiting." As he talked, he kept looking around. "Is something burning?"

"Not anymore," Nicole said. It was an effort to keep her voice calm. While you were out there screwing Brenda, I came within a hair of being raped and murdered.

She took a deep breath. "I guess I'd better explain," she said evenly. "You did have the right number, Brad. I heard my cell and the Lowrys' phone ringing. Only I couldn't answer because someone had broken into the house and locked me in the bathroom."

Brenda gasped and said, "Oh, Nicole," in a strangled whisper. "How awful."

"Locked you in the bathroom," Brad repeated. "My God, Nick. Are you all right?"

"I'm fine," she lied. "Perfectly fine." And she went on to calmly describe her conversation with Reinhardt, the break-in, and, finally, Alice's arrival. As she neared the end of her story, she said, "We called the police. They said they'd send someone right out."

Brad stared at her for a long moment. Then her words seemed to sink in, and a look of panic crossed his face. "Wait a minute! What about our passports? The cash?" By now he was halfway up the stairs.

"It's fine. I checked," Nicole called after him. "Nothing's missing."

He turned and looked down at her, his face troubled. "This doesn't make sense," he said. "Why would someone bother to break in, lock you in the bathroom, and then leave without taking anything?"

"Maybe he did take something," she said. "After he left, the safe was open, and it was locked when we got here. We won't find out what's missing until I get in touch with the Lowrys."

By now, Brenda had disappeared into the living room. Nicole imagined her wandering around, looking at the pictures, running her hand across the backs of the damask-covered sofa and chairs.

She reappeared just as Brad reached the bottom of the stairs. "I hope I'm not butting in," Brenda said. "I mean, I wonder if I could make just one teeny little observation." Her voice was high and soft, like a little girl's, and she had a way of pausing between sentences. "Look, Nicole—isn't it possible you accidentally locked yourself in?" She stopped and cocked her head. "I mean, people are always doing that in strange houses." She smiled, "I've done it myself."

"Yeah," Brad agreed. He nodded his head, and his scowl relaxed. "That makes a lot of sense. The door stuck, and you sort of panicked. Hey, it's nothing to feel bad about. It could happen to anyone. You're jet lagged, alone in an unfamiliar house…"

"Listen—I know what happened," Nicole said. "Someone was in the house. He locked me in the bathroom. I wasn't imagining things, and I'm not hysterical." But her voice had gone all shaky again. And she did feel slightly hysterical, as if she were about to cry.

"It's all right, Nick. Just take it easy." As Brad said this, he reached over and gave her shoulder a squeeze. Nicole sensed Brenda's eyes on them and felt a surge of resentment. If Brenda weren't here, Brad would have taken her in his arms to comfort her. He wouldn't be doubting her like this.

"You had a bad scare," he was saying, "and you have every right to be upset. What you need is a good stiff drink. We could all use one. Listen, I noticed a great-looking pub a couple of blocks away..."

"We have to wait for the police," Nicole repeated, trying to hold on to her patience. "I was just having some tea. Why don't you fix some for you and Brenda? Then, after the policeman leaves, we can all go out for dinner."

It was another forty-five minutes before the policeman arrived. Nicole had expected to see a real Bobby, in full regalia—the black uniform with brass buttons and brass-trimmed epaulets and the tall, Victorian helmet with its big metal badge. But this man was wearing an unfamiliar costume that, she supposed, must be his summer uniform—black slacks and a white, short-sleeved shirt with nerdy-looking tabs on the shoulders. His hat was shaped like a helmet, but made of felt instead of metal.

When she invited him in, he carefully removed the hat and tucked it under one arm, as if he were carrying a basketball. With his freckles, pale blue eyes and fair curls, he looked like a very tall schoolboy.

Constable Browne, as he introduced himself, was nothing like the British law enforcement types Nicole had seen on PBS. He was neither sympathetic nor especially polite. Nor did he seem to be much of a listener. From time to time he jotted something in his notebook. Between jottings, his eyes strayed over to Brenda, drawn to the cleavage peeking from her jacket.

Nicole had been sure that when she told him about Alice, he'd insist on waking her from her nap to question her. But news of the tenant failed to produce even a squiggle in his notebook.

He didn't ask many questions, and those he did ask seemed calculated to cast doubt on Nicole's story.

"You got a good look at the person who detained you, then?" he said.

"Yes, I did. When I talked to him in front of the house, he was standing only a few feet away."

"I see, madam, but did you actually see him inside the house, this..." he paused to consult his notebook. "Reinhardt chap?"

"Of course not. That's why he locked me in the bathroom—to keep me from seeing him." As she said this, Nicole could feel their incredulity, which made her even more resentful and upset.

She led them upstairs to the bathroom, explaining how Alice had let her out with the key the man had left in the lock. It was still in the keyhole on the outside of the bathroom door, where Alice had left it. The police officer acknowledged the key with a nod but made no move to examine it.

Next, she ushered them in to look at the safe, explaining how she'd found it open but had accidentally let it shut. The whole time she was talking, she was aware of how unlikely her story sounded, the fact that she had no real proof any of it had happened.

When she finished, the policeman put away his notebook. "That's fine, then," he said. "I have enough for my preliminary report. Tomorrow one of our DCs—that's detective constable—will pop 'round to take a full report."

"Wait," she said. "Aren't you going to take fingerprints?"

"We have our procedures," the policeman said. "You said you touched the knob of the safe. And we haven't got the residents' fingerprints, so we couldn't sort them out from the intruder's, could we? We don't even know if anything was stolen. I don't mean to cast doubts on what you're saying, Mrs. Graves, but we can't make bricks without straw." His eyes wandered over to Brenda, and he winked. She flushed prettily and flashed him a smile.

Frustration and anger roiled in Nicole's head as she followed the others along the hallway and back down the stairs. At the door, the constable, who seemed to have lost track of who was married to whom, turned to Brad. "I'd strongly advise that one of you stays with her tonight. She's a bit overwrought after her—uh—experience. I don't think she ought to be left alone."

"I'll stay, officer," Brad said. "I mean—of course I'm staying. I'm her husband." He gave an embarrassed laugh, as if this small detail had slipped his mind.

The policeman stole one last glance at Brenda. "Well, that's all right, then. I wish you all good night."

By the time his car pulled away, it was 11:00 p.m., too late, they all agreed, to go out for dinner. Brad ordered a pizza delivered, then foraged through the cupboards for a bottle of wine.

They ate in the small dining room. Brad and Brenda didn't lapse into their usual shoptalk, nor was there mention of the tumultuous meeting that had supposedly kept them late at work. On the contrary, they were infuriatingly attentive to Nicole. Brenda, in her piping little voice, kept coaxing her to eat until Nicole finally snapped, "For God's sake, Brenda. I'm not hungry. Give it a rest."

Brenda's eyes grew very wide. After that, Nicole noticed Brad avoiding his assistant's wounded looks. A short time later, he sent her home alone in a cab.

Nicole didn't take any of this as a good sign. She had the feeling that Brad was going to use this incident as yet another argument to send her home.

She lay in bed a long time before she drifted off to sleep. A while later, she woke with a start. An unrelenting ache in her stomach reminded her how miserable she was, even before she remembered why. She turned to glance at the luminous face of the alarm clock on the night table. It was 1:30 a.m. She'd been asleep for less than a half hour.

She looked over at Brad. He was sleeping, his face relaxed and unperturbed. Her mind skipped back to the moment she saw him standing on the doorstep with Brenda. Now she knew why he'd been so inattentive, the reason he no longer seemed to like her much.

Brenda.

Over the last—how long was it? Six months? A year?—Brad had grown more and more distant, and this transformation had puzzled, distressed, and, finally, alarmed her. When she asked, he denied anything was wrong. She began looking for a reason outside their marriage. Perhaps it was something he didn't want her to worry about, trouble at work or some kind of emotional crisis.

She sat up and swung her legs over the side of the bed. She had to stop doing this to herself. She was tired and altogether too irrational to think. She remembered the sleeping pills she'd brought along. But if she took one this late, she'd be groggy tomorrow. She decided to try a glass of milk; if that didn't work, she'd take the Ambien and sleep late. She turned on her bedside lamp and found her robe. Then she went down to the kitchen.

As she was pouring the milk, she remembered her earlier call to the Lowrys. She looked at the clock. It would be 7:30 p.m. in Dallas now. Maybe they'd be in.

After she put in the number, the phone rang three times; there was a click, and the now-familiar voice came on: "Please leave a message," it drawled.

Nicole left another message, this one more desperate than the last. As she was hanging up, she heard a car slowing in front. Instinctively, she reached over and flipped off the light. Then she padded into the hall and looked out the small window in the front door. A battered white Renault coupe drove by slowly.

When it was gone, she went back into the kitchen, turned on the light and retrieved her glass of milk. In the cupboard, she found the open package of chocolate-covered biscuits. She munched on one, ears cocked for any new sound from the street. All was quiet.

She finished the milk and cookie and turned off the kitchen light. She was just starting up the stairs when she heard another car approach. Trotting back to the window, she was surprised to see the same white car, now heading in the opposite direction.

As she looked out, the car zipped over to the curb and parked. Then two men got out and started across the street toward the house. Under the streetlight, they were an odd pair, odder still by virtue of the fact that they were dressed almost identically in black leather jackets and dark pants. One was short and grossly obese with a ruffle of jowls that hung down over his collar. The other was tall and skinny with a long neck and small, narrow head.

They stopped on the sidewalk in front of the house and stared directly at the front door, where Nicole was cowering behind the little window. Then the fat one touched the other man on the arm, and both heads swiveled up toward the bedroom window where the lamp on Nicole's night table was the only light in the house.

She froze, her heart launching into a brisk percussion as the pair headed through the gate into the front yard. Only when they disappeared around the side of the house was she able to set her legs in motion and take flight up the stairs. "Brad," she hissed, when she reached the bedroom. "Oh God! There are a couple of guys sneaking around outside."

"Huh?" Brad said groggily. "Wha—?"

"They look like thugs. They went around back."

He got out of bed and went to the bedroom window.

"Out back," she repeated. "You'll have to go downstairs and look out the kitchen window."

Brad left the room and clumped noisily down the steps. She followed him as far as the top of the staircase, then waited while he walked around the lower floor, looking out the windows.

When she heard him open the back door, she dashed down after him, calling, "What are you doing? Don't go out there!"

The door slammed and, after a minute or so, reopened. Brad came in and, brushing past her, began trudging up the stairs.

"Did you see them?" she said, as she trailed after him.

"Nobody's out there, Nick."

She was filled with dread. "I think we should call the police."

"Jesus, Nicole. Everything's fine. Just try to get some sleep."

When they reached their room, he climbed into bed. Nicole turned off her lamp and went back to the window. The white car was still parked across the street. The sight of it chilled her.

She turned to look at Brad, now cocooned under the blankets. "They must be the ones," she said. "The ones who broke into the house."

He pulled the covers back and propped himself up to look at her. "You told the cop you were sure it was that guy Reinhardt."

She stared at him, suddenly filled with anger. He was doing it again, refusing to listen to her. "Look," she said. "I don't understand why you're acting like this. It's like you don't even believe there was a break-in—"

"Listen, Nick, I do believe you," Brad said wearily. "But those men you just saw out there? They're probably the neighborhood watch or something. Two guys picking up a third to go fishing, only they got the wrong house. Get some sleep, and in the morning, we'll both have a good laugh about it."

"You think I imagined the whole thing."

"No, I think..." he paused, reaching for the right phrase. "I think you're overreacting. You had a bad scare, and you're exhausted. That's enough to make anybody a little nuts."

With that, he lay down, turned toward the wall, and pulled the covers over his head.

Nicole stood at the window, staring down at the white car. The street was completely still. Finally, she climbed back into bed.

FIVE

WHEN NICOLE OPENED HER EYES, sunlight was streaming through the curtains. She threw the covers back and grabbed her robe from the chair, pulling it on while her bare feet searched the carpet for slippers.

From the silence, she could tell Brad had already left for the office. No matter how many time zones they crossed, Brad was always up and out early the next morning. Today he'd be especially anxious to get in and begin repairing the relationship between SoftPac and its new British subsidiary. This would require, as Brad put it, "a major effort in massaging bruised egos." Then Nicole remembered that Brenda would be there, too, no doubt eager to do a little massaging of her own.

On the kitchen counter, an envelope was waiting, covered with Brad's unruly scrawl. "Hope you had a good rest and feel more like yourself," it said. "Have fun shopping. We'll go out for dinner tonight. Just us two. Love, Brad." Inside the envelope was a stack of £20 notes.

She fanned out the bills to count them. At the current exchange rate, they added up to about $800. Stuffing the money back in the envelope, she let out a long, exasperated breath. He was treating her like a child. The money was especially galling after the flak he'd given her for taking the summer off.

And now, here he was, throwing money at her. He'd never been big on spontaneous gifts. And this, like his solicitousness of the night before, struck her as a sign of a guilty conscience.

She thought about this while she struggled with the coffee maker. It was a coffee press, which she'd seen in kitchen supply shops but had never actually used. She thought she grasped the basic principle: put in the coffee and boiling water, then work a plunger to pull the water through the coffee, or vice versa. But she didn't have a clue as to where to put the coffee, or whether to add the water first or last. She tried three different strategies, each producing the same muddy brew. Finally, she gave up and poured herself a cup.

She was still in her robe, sipping coffee and brooding about Brad and Brenda, when the detective arrived. She hadn't expected Detective Constable Keaton, as she introduced herself, to be a woman, but there she was, a slender brunette in her early forties wearing a fashionably cut dark-blue suit. She had an angular face, and her dark red lipstick and carefully penciled-in eyebrows made her look a bit hard. But she was polite, soft-spoken, and professional, a pleasant contrast to the rude young constable. Until this moment, Nicole hadn't realized how much she'd been dreading this interview. Keaton was a pleasant surprise.

Keaton murmured a polite, "None for me, thanks," to the offered coffee. "Tell me everything you can remember about this break-in, Mrs. Graves," she said.

Nicole started with her encounter with Reinhardt in the front yard. By now the detective had pulled a notebook from her tailored leather bag and began writing. "Please do go on," she prompted.

When Nicole was done with her story, Keaton brought up the possibility that Reinhardt wasn't the burglar at all. "You know, this man might really be your landlord's business associate. It wouldn't make good sense for him to put in an appearance and introduce himself if he was planning to break into the house." The detective smiled while she was talking. She smiled a lot, although as far as Nicole could tell, she didn't seem to have much sense of humor.

She pointed out that the intruder hadn't hurt Nicole—had, in fact, taken some care to wait until she'd gone in to bathe (the detective pronounced it bath) before he locked the door. "In his way, he spared you the trauma of a direct encounter."

"A real gentleman," Nicole said.

"Be grateful," Keaton said, with yet another smile. "Los Angeles doesn't have a corner on heinous crimes, you know. We see some terrible things.

"As for those two men you mentioned seeing in front of the house," she continued, "it's unlikely that they had anything to do with your break-in either. We find that most perpetrators stay away from the scene of a burglary for a while. Now, if you don't mind, I'd like to look around."

Methodically, she began examining the locks on the doors and windows. She had bright red nails and a dainty way of touching things that called attention to them. When she found the cellar door unlocked, she gave Nicole a smile. "You really should keep this secured," she said gently.

As she made her way down the stairs, Nicole was a step or two behind. In the cellar, the detective discovered yet another entrance to the house. It was a small trap door designed for delivering coal directly into the big bin next to the furnace. The padlock was missing. Keaton produced a handkerchief from her purse and, using it to protect her manicure, pushed against the trap door. It lifted easily and turned out to be not only unlocked but unlatched.

Nicole must have paled, for the detective reached out and gently gripped her shoulder. "Never mind about that," Keaton said kindly. "We'll lock it up now." She looked around until she found a cobwebby padlock lying on a window sill. The key was still in the lock. Still using the handkerchief, by now covered with cobwebs and soot, she carefully removed the key and handed it to Nicole. She dusted off the lock, slipped it into place, and clicked it shut.

"Don't worry," she told Nicole. "This wasn't the entry point for your intruder." She pointed to the coal bin, right under the trap door. "He would have landed there first. You don't see any coal tracks on the cellar floor, now do you?"

On the way back up the steps, Nicole remembered the Lowrys' tenant. When she mentioned Alice to Keaton, the detective immediately smiled. "I'd like a word with her," she said.

Nicole led the detective up to the second floor, then down the hall past the Lowrys' bedroom to Alice's room at the back of the house. She knocked on the door, but there was no response. "I guess she's out," she said. "Now that I think about it, I haven't heard her this morning. Maybe she already has another nursing assignment." Remembering Alice's offer to show her around London, she felt a pang of disappointment.

"I'll give you my number," Keaton said. "Ask her to give me a ring. I have a few questions for her."

She didn't ask if the detective was going to dust for fingerprints. The moment had passed. Aside from the unlocked cellar, Keaton was impressed with the amount of security in the house and admonished Nicole to take full advantage of it. "Even if it's broad daylight, and you're planning to go no further than the back garden," she said, turning on the full wattage of her smile, "for heaven's sake, lock the door and take the key with you."

As they were saying goodbye, Keaton produced her card and, still smiling, pressed it into Nicole's hand. "Now, I'd like you to keep your eyes open," she said. "Be aware of what's going on. If you notice anything out of the ordinary, please give me a ring. Even if it doesn't seem terribly important."

Despite Keaton's kindness, Nicole didn't think the detective bought her theory about Reinhardt being the culprit, nor was she much interested in hearing about the two men who'd been sneaking around in the middle of the night. On the other hand, Keaton did seem to accept Nicole's word that there had been an intruder who'd locked her in the bathroom. Keaton also seemed to respect her observations, listening to what she had to say and taking careful notes.

She still hadn't heard from the Lowrys but she'd remembered something that might explain this. In her last message, Mrs. L. had mentioned the possibility of doing some sightseeing while they were in Texas. She said they might go deep-sea fishing in the Gulf of Mexico and maybe drive to New Orleans or even Disney World in Florida.

On Nicole's last call, there was a beep and the phone cut off before she could leave a message. She took this to mean their voicemail was full. At that moment, the idea that the Lowrys might not be trustworthy was not as worrisome as the possibility they might not show up at all. What would happen to the condo? Her dog? The plants? Her sister could look after things for a few weeks, but it wasn't fair to expect her to spend the summer driving back and forth between Hollywood and West L.A, maintaining two households.

Nicole shook her head, trying to untangle her thoughts. Maybe Brad was right about her jet lag; it was making her crazy. After all the work the Lowrys had put into this house swap, why wouldn't they stay in the condo? Where else would they go?

While the phone was still in her hand, it struck her that she hadn't heard from the airline about her missing bag. She located the number and placed the call, asking for lost luggage.

"Ah, yes," the man said, after putting her on hold for several minutes while he located her in the database. "We have your claim form on file, but I'm afraid there's no sign of your suitcase yet. Don't be too concerned. Ninety-five percent of all lost luggage turns up in the first twenty-four hours."

"It's already been longer than that," she pointed out.

"Don't worry," he said cheerfully. "As soon as it turns up, we'll give you a call."

After she hung up, she took another look at the envelope Brad had left on the counter. Despite the airline clerk's confidence, she doubted she'd ever see her suitcase again. Why not use the money Brad had left to buy a few things to replace what she'd lost? It would be better than languishing around the house, obsessing about Brenda. Even if her suitcase eventually turned up, she could use another all-purpose outfit—something wrinkle resistant for sightseeing as well as for dinner and the theater.

She located her guidebook to London and flipped through the pages. "A good bet for the traveler on a budget," the book said, "Selfridges of Oxford Street carries quality merchandise that isn't as pricey as Harrods." This settled, she called a cab and spent several hours scouring Selfridges and the shops packed into the narrow streets behind the huge store.

She tried on dozens of combinations but couldn't seem to make a decision. It was hard to concentrate when her thoughts were constantly interrupted by flashbacks of yesterday's events—the sound of footsteps on the stairs, the realization that someone was in the house, her feelings of terror when she smelled smoke. And, even worse, this business about Brad and Brenda.

She tried telling herself that she had no evidence, no real reason to think anything had happened between them. Yet she knew something had, and this knowledge was eating at her

She took the tube to Harrods. By the time she got there it was almost 3:30 p.m., and she remembered she hadn't eaten since breakfast. She sought out the escalator and headed up to the enormous dining room. The sign read "Afternoon Tea: £29." Why not?

She was presented with a multi-tiered tray of cream-filled pastries, scones, and petit fours. She heaped her plate, then sat and stared at the food, unable to bring herself to take a single bite.

She got up, tossed her napkin on the plate and hurried out of the dining room, determined to finish shopping before the store closed. She settled on a slightly-flared skirt in a lovely shade of dark magenta, a white blouse, boots, patterned leggings, and a black linen jacket. She did allow herself a single extravagance: a wide-brimmed straw hat trimmed with roses in a lovely, delicate pink. In the mirror, she decided that the outfit (except for the short skirt, which ended well above her knees) made her look as if she'd stepped out of a painting by Renoir.

Later, getting dressed to go out with Brad, she did her best to put aside her bad feelings. Without proof, she knew, it would be a mistake to confront him. He'd repeat his mantra that she was being irrational. They'd have a fight, and her accusations would only strengthen his determination to send her home.

An intimate dinner offered the perfect opportunity to patch things up. She'd fought so hard to come to London for this very purpose. Now, she had to be strong and exert some self-control.

But when he came in bearing a corsage of white violets—a gesture quite unlike him—her suspicions came flooding back. Then, as he was pinning the flowers to her lapel, she noticed the way he kept glancing at her hat.

"What?" she said.

"Nice hat," he said, with a sardonic glance that communicated anything but approval.

"Great, isn't it?" she said with a tight-lipped smile. Well, she thought, she'd wanted him to notice her, and he'd noticed all right. She turned toward the mirror, flipping the hat brim into a straight line over her eyes. Until that moment, she hadn't been sure if she'd have much use for the hat. But now, in a wave of fresh indignation, she decided it would be the mainstay of her summer wardrobe.

The Indian restaurant that had come so highly recommended was more like the Taj Majal than the intimate bistro Nicole had pictured. It was housed in an enormous glass conservatory where the tables and chairs were overshadowed by gigantic ferns. All around them, green fronds seemed to slowly unfurl as dish after dish arrived at the table. The chairs were high-backed cane thrones, and a waiter stood on either side of the table, anticipating every need.

Conversation lagged between exclamations over the mulligatawny soup and chapattis, chicken tikka and puris, lamb vindaloo and saffron rice, the bowls of condiments, both cool and spicy. It had been so long since they'd shared an evening—just the two of them—that they no longer seemed to know what to say to each other.

Brad popped a bite of lamb into his mouth. Nicole watched the muscles in his cheek swell and bob as he chewed and felt a stirring of dislike. It occurred to her that this was merely a reflection of her own hurt and anger. She had an almost irresistible urge to blurt it all out—her suspicion, her feelings about the way he'd been acting toward her, and all the hostility she was feeling. But she managed to hold it in. Perhaps it was the rapt attention of the waiter hovering by the ice bucket that held their bottle of wine.

Brad was equally subdued. As the minutes ticked by, she began to resent the way his eyes kept wandering to her hat and then darting away, or maybe it was the fact that, all evening, he'd never once looked her in the eye.

The meal seemed to drag on forever. Yet even after dessert and coffee, Brad made no move to get the check. Instead, he ordered brandy. Then he pulled some folded sheets out of his jacket pocket and set them down in front of her.

She scanned the first page. It was a computer printout of an old news article, datelined Israel. She'd read it before, a story of international tourists who imagined encounters with Biblical heroes. Occasionally a case involved someone who thought he himself was Moses or Jesus, depending on religious orientation. According to the article, these were often people with no history of mental illness.

When she finished reading, she looked up at him. "What are you telling me, Brad—that I'm crazy?"

"Don't be ridiculous. I thought it would reassure you to know how common this sort of thing is. Travel is incredibly tough on the body. Jet lag can bring on all kinds of—um—reactions."

Nicole rattled the papers at him. "It's clear you haven't read this stupid article yourself. It's about tourists in Israel. And they didn't have jet lag; they were crazy. We're talking major breaks with reality. I'll bet Brenda searched the web to dig this up. Then she printed it out for you to bring home."

"For God's sake," he said. "That is a total crock of shit. Nick—what's gotten into you? I wonder if you should see a doctor or something."

"You mean a shrink."

"I mean, like, a psychologist. What's wrong with that? In fact, a guy I know is seeing a great therapist in Santa Monica. I'll get you his name."

"That's it, isn't it? You think you can use this as an excuse to send me home so you can do what you want."

"What I want? All I want to do is concentrate on…"

"You're having an affair with Brenda, aren't you?" The words were out before she could stop them. "That's why you're so bent on sending me home. But your little plan isn't going to work…"

"Are you completely out of your mind?" Brad said. Looking around, he went on in an angry whisper. "People are staring. Can we talk about this later?"

Nicole glanced around. Conversation at the tables nearby had ceased, and people did seem to be looking at them. She didn't care.

"I don't need a shrink." She didn't bother to lower her voice. "And I'm not going back to L.A." Instead of answering, Brad caught the waiter's eye and snapped his fingers for the check.

On the silent cab ride back to the house, Nicole wondered if their marriage was even worth saving.

Six

The next morning, when Nicole held the glass carafe up to the light, the coffee looked slightly less muddy than the day before. As she poured the steaming brew into a mug, she felt an inexplicable surge of happiness. Sunlight streamed into the little dining room, suffusing it with the promise of a new day—a fresh world of possibilities.

Thirty-six hours had passed since the nightmare of that first afternoon, and it seemed a lifetime ago. She'd even gained a fresh perspective on last night's fight with Brad. Now, after a sound night's sleep, she could see that he had been trying. He had, after all, planned an intimate evening for them. What was that but an attempt to make amends? Of course, that bit about travelers' hallucinations had been less than tactful. But she was at fault, too, for letting her sour mood get the better of her.

She understood clearly what had to happen next if she was to save the marriage. She'd have to swallow her pride, get him to admit whatever was going on, and forgive him. She wondered, in a momentary return of last night's anger, just how much forgiveness would be required. With this thought came a sudden vision of Brenda as she'd appeared two nights before, wearing her expression of feigned innocence. Nicole blinked and shook her head, but she couldn't seem to dispel the image. Was that night the beginning or had it been going on for months?

These thoughts were interrupted by a low rumble at the back of the house. For a brief, panicky moment, Nicole mistook it for an earthquake. She half rose from her chair and looked around for something to dive under if the shaking began in earnest.

Then she heard a door slam and realized the noise was someone entering the house. Heels clicked along the hall; a moment later Alice was standing in the doorway, beaming at her.

"My God—you're back!" Nicole said, "I was sure you'd taken another assignment."

"Oh, I've been 'round and about." Alice's smile grew wider as she waved her hand vaguely. "Visiting friends, attending to my chores." She looked happy, and her cheeks were aglow. "Oh, it's such a be-you-ti-fool day," she chirped. "Why don't we go for a dander 'round London?"

"I'd love that," Nicole said, before she had a chance to wonder what a "dander" might be. Then she remembered Keaton's request and went over to the message board on the kitchen wall to retrieve her card. "A detective investigating the break-in wants you to call her," she said, handing the card to Alice.

"I'll attend to that later," Alice said, dropping the card into her pocket. "It would be a crime to waste such a gorgeous morning. Come on. We'll take the bus and get in some sightseeing."

Nicole suggested taking the Lowrys' Renault instead, if Alice would do the driving. "I need some practice before I tackle traffic on the wrong side of the street."

Alice said, "You can't drive in central London these days. They have a congestion charge, and there's no parking." Instead, the two of them took the tube into central London. They hopped a series of double-decker buses that took them past Westminster

Abbey, Buckingham Palace, and the Houses of Parliament, then along the Thames to the Tower of London and back toward Trafalgar Square. At each site, great hordes of tourists waited in long lines, just as Nicole and Brad had done on their first trip to the city, several years before. At the time, Nicole had enjoyed the endless round of historic sites. Yet she'd been struck, even then, by the idea that there was more to this city than palaces, museums, and monuments. That had been another argument in favor of the house swap. It would give them a chance to see what it was like to live here.

The day's final destination was the National Gallery on Trafalgar Square. Alice guided Nicole into the pleasant coolness of the museum. Upstairs, the dining room was only half full. "It's only 11:30," Alice pointed out. "We beat the crowds."

The hostess seated them at a table next to the window. Below, throngs of people swirled through Trafalgar Square, disrupting the resident pigeons who fluttered out of the way. There were tourists being herded on and off buses and wholesome-looking couples with small children in tow. Hanging around the square's north edge were a number of tough-looking young men.

The restaurant was spacious, handsome, and sunny. Its focal point was a mirrored bar, surrounded by dozens of small round tables set with crisp pink cloths, sparkling crystal, and vases of summer flowers. In the background, the festive clink of cutlery was accompanied by a Chopin sonata, piped in by the sound system.

She gazed around the restaurant. Unlike the tourists outside, most of their fellow diners were well dressed. Alice had removed her lightweight raincoat, revealing a plaid sun dress in greens that made a nice contrast to her red hair.

Nicole felt a little drab in her skirt and white blouse. But the rose-trimmed hat was a nice touch, and she was glad she'd worn it. Looking around the dining room, she saw several other women wearing hats, although none as colorful as hers.

The hostess was leading two men into the dining room. They were in their early thirties and offered a perfect illustration of what would become of the young toughs in Trafalgar Square if they didn't pull up their socks. Despite the heat, they were wearing black leather jackets, black T-shirts, and black chinos. They had matching hairstyles, greased-up pompadours, and dark circles under their eyes, as if they were badly hung over. As they passed, Nicole caught a whiff of ripe body odor.

They made a very strange pair. One was tall and almost skeletal, while the other was short and hugely fat. The skinny one had no chin at all while the other had a lavish set of double jowls. As Nicole studied them, they reminded her of the men she'd seen at the house two nights before. It was their body types, the contrast between them. She told herself not to be crazy. It had been too dark for her to get a look at their faces.

The men were seated at the next table. They ordered beer, then sat in silence while the white-coated waiter trotted off to get it.

"You haven't told me much about yourself, Nicole," Alice was saying. "What sort of work do you do?"

Nicole hesitated. Since she'd left home, she'd barely thought about work. "I'm the office manager for a big law firm," she began. "When Brad found out he had to spend the summer in London, I decided to come along. So I took a leave and arranged the house swap with the Lowrys."

"That was crafty," Alice said.

"Oh, Brad didn't think so, and my boss was pretty upset. He said he'd try to hold the job for me, but he couldn't promise. To tell you the truth, I don't even know if I want it. I've never considered it permanent. I was looking for work, and my friend Norma—who had the job before me—needed back surgery. She asked me to cover for a few days until they found a long-term sub."

Alice listened intently, giving an occasional nod of encouragement. Despite the differences between them or the fact that they'd grown up on opposite sides of the world, Nicole had the feeling Alice knew exactly what she was talking about.

"They never did find a substitute," Nicole went on. "Once she was better, Norma decided that wild horses couldn't drag her back to Bascomb, Rice, Smith & Di Angelo. The atmosphere there is pretty frantic—constant pressure, a crisis a minute, very stressful. But I liked it. I mean, at first I did. I'm good at managing people, and I never knew that before. It was sort of an ego trip, having the paralegals and secretaries do what I told them and asking my advice."

Outside of work, she and Brad were busy getting married and nesting—buying the condo and fixing it up. Then all of a sudden, they were settled, both working ten, twelve hours a day, sometimes straight through the weekends. On Nicole's last birthday, she'd woken to a full-blown life crisis that made her job—her whole life—seem pointless and empty. There had to be more than getting up each day to the same routine—jogging, dashing off to work, coming home, eating take-out, going to bed.

Several of her friends had recently become mothers, and Nicole could see how fulfilled they were. For the first time, she began to think seriously about having a baby.

Brad had balked at the idea. "How can we start a family when we need two incomes just to make the payments on this place?" he argued. "Besides, we don't have room for a kid here. We don't even have a yard."

She brought it up more than once, prepared to argue that all these material things didn't matter to an infant. But Brad was especially adept at dodging the topic. Before Nicole could marshal her thoughts, he'd be starting up his computer, answering his phone, or on his way out the door.

His attitude surprised her. She'd always thought he was crazy about kids and imagined he would be eager to start a family as soon as she said the word. One of the things that had first charmed her about him was his relationship with his niece, Tiffany. Nicole loved watching him crawl around on the floor, making the little girl giggle. But now that Tiffany had grown into a wiry eleven-year-old, it was Nicole who had a relationship with her, not Brad.

On Brad's birthday, Nicole put a huge effort into a party, inviting his friends, coworkers, and bosses, many of them in a position to help his career. Looking around at the gathering, she realized there wasn't a single person there she cared about or even much liked. As for Brad, he was in his glory, working the crowd, talking sports, and making quips about the latest political flap.

Nicole stopped talking when she noticed her new friend's attention had shifted to the next table. The two men were staring at them, openly eavesdropping.

Alice threw Nicole a quick wink, then swung around in her chair. "Getting an earful, are we?" she said.

The fat one raised his hand and stuck two fingers up at her, shaking them for maximum effect. Alice returned the salute. "Scum," she said, in a tone loud enough to include the nearby tables.

People turned to stare, and Nicole felt her face go red. Unperturbed, Alice gave Nicole another wink. "Sorry about that," she said. "Please go on."

Lowering her voice, Nicole continued. She was trembling, and she couldn't seem to stop talking. Although she wasn't given to easy confidences, she found herself revealing her innermost thoughts to Alice. She even mentioned her suspicions about Brenda.

"You've got to have a word with that man of yours," Alice said in a low voice. "Ach, they're all alike." She made a sour face. "Always ready to make a fool of you, if you let them."

Nicole shifted uneasily in her seat. She wished she hadn't been so candid about Brad to someone who didn't even know him. "What about you?" she asked. "How long have you lived in London?"

Alice confessed she was a relative newcomer herself, from a small town in Northern Ireland. "I lived in Ballycastle all my life. I came to London a little more than a year ago because of my brother Sean. He got himself into a spot of bother here. I was hoping to straighten him out ..." Her voice trailed off.

The waitress had arrived with their orders, salad niçoise for Nicole and lasagna for Alice. The two men stared as the women began to eat. When Alice caught the fat one looking at her—his eyes small and mean—she made a face, bugging her eyes out, like a schoolgirl rebuking a rude boy. His stare continued; he didn't even blink.

Nicole was struck by the thought that these men might not be here, sitting at the next table, by accident. What if they were the same men who'd been prowling the backyard two nights ago? What if they'd followed her and Alice into the museum? She told herself to stop being crazy. It was the break-in. If she looked at anyone long enough, she'd start imagining they had something to do with it: Like the man eating by himself in the corner, who bore a slight resemblance to Reinhardt. If he didn't have that mustache, she'd probably be telling herself he was Reinhardt.

Meanwhile, Alice had gone strangely silent. Something about the way she'd spoken of her brother, Sean, had piqued Nicole's curiosity. She had the feeling he was in jail, living on the streets, or worse. But she understood enough about human nature not to push for more information. If she waited and moved the conversation back in that direction, she'd get the whole story.

As the waitress handed them the dessert menu, a cell phone went off in Alice's purse. She pulled it out and answered it, then listened intently for about thirty seconds. "I'll be right there," she said. Then she hung up and dropped the phone back into her purse.

"I'm so sorry, Nicole," she said. "It's my own fault—something I forgot to take care of. I—I really must go." She stood up, as if she were going to bolt, then remembered herself and sat down.

Opening her purse, she pulled out a couple of bills, pushing them across the table to Nicole. "This is for my share of the meal," she said. "Let me tell you how to get back to the house. The easiest way is by tube. There's a station down the road. I have a map. I'll mark the route."

"That's okay," Nicole said. "I'll take a cab."

Alice shook her head. "I hate to see you throw your money down the drain."

"Don't worry about it," Nicole said. "By the time I leave, I'll be too tired to deal with the tube. I'll just grab a taxi."

"All right," Alice said, pushing back her chair. "If you're sure."

After Alice was gone, Nicole paid the check and left the dining room. On her way down the stairs, she spotted Alice in the lobby, hurrying out through the double glass doors. As Nicole paused at the railing, she noticed the two thugs walk by. They were heading down the stairs in the direction of the exit Alice had used. Nicole thought of the alley they'd walked through on their way here. She pictured the men overpowering Alice, forcing her into a car. She debated running after her new friend to warn her. Then she realized how ridiculous that was. After all, it was broad daylight. This was London. And Alice was perfectly capable of taking care of herself.

When Nicole reached the lobby, she focused her attention on the list of exhibits. "British Impressionists in the Lake District." That sounded lovely. It was on the upper level.

She boarded an elevator and pushed the button for the upper floor. The door was starting to close when she heard the sound of running, and a man's voice shouted, "Hold it." (He dropped his "H," so it came out, "'Old it!") She punched the button, and the door sprang open.

There stood the two men from the next table. The fat one stared at her intently as if he had something to say. The door began closing again, and the skinny man stuck his arm in. With a snap, the door retracted and the two stepped inside. As they moved to the back of the car, the door closed and the air was filled with the smell of unwashed bodies.

Nicole drew in a breath and held it, wondering how long it would take to reach her floor. She noticed the men hadn't pushed a button for their destination. Maybe they were headed for the same floor and the British Impressionists, but she didn't think so.

The elevator was new and virtually noiseless, except for a vibration and a barely perceptible hissing sound. She began to wonder if it was moving at all.

As the seconds ticked by, she could feel them behind her, staring at her back. Her uneasiness grew, and it was hard to resist an impulse to punch the red emergency button. Take it easy, she told herself. Calm down.

At last the hissing sound stopped. After a jerk and a dull thud, the doors flew open. To Nicole's enormous relief, a cluster of tourists hovered by the door, waiting to get on the elevator. She shoved her way through and bolted off, leaving the two men to fight their way through the crowd. She didn't wait to see where they were headed. Only when she got to the end of the corridor did she look back. No one was there.

As she followed the signs leading to the exhibit, she wondered why she'd let herself get so wound up. Even if these men were serial killers, she reminded herself, the National Gallery was a public building with plenty of security guards. Even in L.A., with all its violence, the museums were safe.

She entered the exhibit and was soon lost in scenes of unimaginable tranquility—small boats gliding on deep-blue lakes, woolly lambs grazing in green-carpeted meadows, fluffy white clouds drifting over fairy tale villages.

An hour later, she put her glasses away and headed out of the exhibit, resigned to paying the cab fare home. She was much too tired to find her way back to the house on an unfamiliar subway.

Nicole saw them as soon as she entered the hallway leading to the elevator—the two men in leather jackets. They weren't doing anything, just waiting. The fat one was slouched against the wall under a no-smoking sign; the thin one crouched on his haunches, dragging on a cigarette.

Her heart froze. Their faces went alert when they saw her, and she could tell they'd been waiting for her. Although it made no sense at all, at that moment she knew her first instinct had been right. They had been following her.

She stopped. Both were now standing at attention, poised and ready. For what? She had no idea. She just knew she had to get away. She turned and headed back along the empty corridor. Now that she thought about it, she realized the exhibit had been deserted when she left. Earlier, she'd seen a guard. Where had he gone?

Just then she noticed a wooden sign. It showed a hand with its index finger pointing down a small sub corridor. Written on it were the words: WOMEN'S TOILETS.

She turned and glanced back. The men were moving toward her at a normal pace, not in any great hurry.

She darted down the sub corridor, walking quickly in the direction the sign had pointed. It was hard to keep herself from breaking into a run. At home, she was a devoted jogger, and these men looked anything but fit. On the other hand, their legs were longer than hers. Better to pretend she hadn't noticed them and was simply on her way to the ladies' room. When she got there, she'd lock herself in and scream for help.

She reached the point where the hallway turned at a right angle before it continued on, but there was still no door marked WOMEN'S TOILETS. It occurred to her that the sign might have been pointing in the wrong direction. Perhaps these men had turned it to confuse her.

As she entered the next section of corridor, her heart leapt. A WAY OUT sign, blinking red neon, was less than fifty feet ahead. Beneath it was an open stairwell.

She took a deep breath and started to run. The men behind her began running, too, their shoes slapping against the floor. She ran faster.

As she suspected, they were badly out of shape. After the first few steps, she could hear them grunting and panting as if they were ready to drop. Meanwhile, Nicole sprinted easily, widening the gap between them.

As she neared the exit sign, her body relaxed in the certainty that she was going to make it. But on the very next step, her foot came down wrong, twisting her ankle with a sharp, searing pain.

She managed to stagger on another few steps before the short man grabbed her by the shoulders and shoved her face-first against the wall. She gasped, trying to catch her breath to scream. He seemed to anticipate this and clapped his hand over her mouth. It stank of stale tobacco and another smell that didn't bear thinking about, sharp and repugnant. When she sank her teeth into the fleshy pads of his palm, he twisted her arm behind her back until it felt as if it were going to snap. The pain was excruciating.

"This is how it's gunna be." He spoke in a low voice, his mouth next to her ear. "Scream an' I break yer focking arm. Keep yer trap shut, and I let 'er go. You choose."

When she gave a nod, he released her wrist and took his hand away from her mouth. At the same time, he slammed his body against hers, pinning her to the wall. She could feel the weight of his great belly against her back. Against her left buttock, she felt the tip of an erect penis.

"Nothin' to get all aere-ated about," he purred into her neck as he ground himself against her. "We're just givin' you a frennly little worda warnin'. Cause we don't want nothin' happenin' to a nice little bit a skirt like you." His breath was foul, as if every tooth in his head were rotting.

"Tell yer old man he better pay the guv for that load a stuff. Cause Ben is ready to kill 'im. 'E's got 'til 6:00 tomorrow night.

You tell 'im. Maybe he gave us the slip, but you know where he is, and we know just how to find you." This last part was hissed—or, rather, sprayed—in her ear.

"Let's get outa here," came a second voice. "I hear someone coming."

"Remember wot I said," the first man hummed against her neck. "Or it's yore arse." As he said this, he gripped her rear with both hands.

Without warning, he took a step back, releasing the pressure of the great stomach that had pinned her to the wall. As she tumbled to the floor, the two men disappeared down the stairwell.

Seven

A long minute passed and then another. Nicole, still sprawled on the floor, propped herself on her elbows and listened hard. Beyond the thudding of her heart, there was only silence. It struck her that rescue wasn't on its way. The men had thought they'd heard someone coming, but they were wrong. How long before they realized their mistake and were back?

A fresh wave of panic forced her to her feet. Her ankle throbbed as she hobbled back to the main corridor. When she reached the elevator, she punched the button, stabbing it again and again. Her face was hot, and her breath came in quick gulps. The car was taking a long break two floors down. Finally, the floor indicator began moving almost imperceptibly as the car started its ascent. As she watched its progress, she kept looking back, but the corridor remained empty.

At last the elevator arrived, and there was another awful moment waiting for the doors to open. To her relief, it was empty. She got in.

As it started down and she began to catch her breath, she ran her fingers through her hair and tucked her blouse back into her skirt. Only then did she notice her hat was gone, lost in the scuffle. It was probably back there in the hallway, kicked into a corner somewhere. Remembering the lush pink roses on its brim, she felt a sharp pang of loss.

The doors opened, and she stepped into the warm, noisy confusion of the lobby. Tourists were everywhere—consulting in tight clusters, setting off for one display or another, heading in and out of the automatic glass doors. How normal they all looked, as if their biggest problem was finding their way to the next exhibit. That was what amazed her. Here, in the buzz and excitement of all these people, the violence she'd just experienced no longer seemed real.

She knew she should report the incident to someone in authority. Here in the lobby, guards were everywhere—flanking the front door, reinforcing the membership desk as well as the counter where coats and packages were checked. The need to stop and tell nagged at her, the voice of her fourth-grade teacher explaining the duties of good citizenship.

But the urge to bolt was stronger. Instead of stopping, she limped on past the guards, out the front door. Her only thought was getting back to the house. She'd double check the locks and put in a call to D.C. Keaton. After that, she'd take a bath. Then, remembering the break-in, she rejected that idea and opted for a quick splash in the shower. Once she got rid of that horrid man's smell, she'd get into her nightgown, pour herself a brandy, and climb into bed.

She'd have to call Brad, of course, and found herself dreading it. He'd be quick to portray the whole thing as another symptom of her deteriorating mental state. Again she remembered the fat one's threat, his preposterous notion that he knew Brad. But what if these were the same men she'd seen at the house? What if they were following her under the mistaken notion that she was someone else? She wondered if the English courts issued restraining orders, the way they did back home, to keep the crazies from stalking people.

Looking around, she spotted a taxi stand across the road from Trafalgar Square. Painfully, she made her way over to join a short queue waiting for the taxis that pulled up to the curb every minute or so. No one gave her a second glance. She took this as a good sign. Despite everything, at least she still looked fairly normal.

As the line moved forward, she glanced at her watch. Two o'clock. Something was happening at two. But what? Then it came to her, and her heart sank. At that very moment, Brad was catching a train for Liverpool to carry out his first official order of business, a two-day junket inspecting SoftPac's Northern England operations. She didn't even know where he would be staying. He said he'd call her when he got to his hotel.

He hadn't asked Nicole to come. But at least she had the satisfaction of knowing Brenda wasn't going either. He'd made a special point of mentioning it.

In the back of her mind, she heard the fat man's threat. "We know just how to find you." She realized she couldn't go back to Chiswick. She had no idea when Alice would return, and facing the house alone was unthinkable. It occurred to her that she could ask the neighbor, Mr. McGiever, to go in with her, but he'd be useless if there were any real danger. Besides, all that British politeness made her skin crawl. She could imagine how appalled he'd be if she told him about the fat man's assault, the way he'd threatened her. No, she decided, she didn't have the strength to put up with it.

By now, she'd reached the head of the line. A cab was standing there, waiting for her. The driver, a nice looking man in shirtsleeves and a visored tweed cap, looked at her quizzically. "You all right, miss?"

"I'm sorry," she said, stepping out of line. "But I've changed my mind. I won't be needing a cab after all." She felt his puzzled stare as she turned and limped back across the square and into the museum.

In the administrative office, she told her story to the young woman behind the counter, bracing herself for the same incredulous reaction she'd gotten from Brad, or the dubiousness of the young constable. But the young woman seemed genuinely appalled. She was a pale-eyed, mousy looking girl of perhaps twenty, who emitted squeaks of horror as Nicole described the assault.

She assured Nicole that violence of any sort was all but unheard of in the National Gallery. "Although we do have our pickpockets and bag snatchers. Oh, I'm so dreadfully sorry, miss." She whispered this in a strangled tone, as if the whole thing were her fault. Then she picked up the phone and called the museum's security office. As she hung up, she said, "It will take him a few minutes to get here. He's over in the east wing. He'll take your report, and then I'll call an ambulance. I can see how much it's hurting you to walk. Your ankle might be broken."

"I don't want an ambulance," Nicole insisted. "And my ankle couldn't be broken, or I wouldn't be able to walk. Anyway, it's feeling better now." In truth, her ankle was throbbing painfully. But she couldn't bear the thought of being turned into a disaster victim, strapped to a gurney and whisked off God-knew-where.

"The rules require it, miss." She paused to pull a small booklet out of her desk and open it to an earmarked page. "Medical personnel must be summoned in all cases of injury," she read, "whether serious or not." The young woman looked so stricken that Nicole agreed to wait, at least until someone arrived from security.

Meanwhile, Nicole pulled out her phone and called Brad's cell. When he didn't pick up, she called his office. The woman who answered promised to track him down when he arrived in

Liverpool and have him contact her. After they hung up, Nicole sent Brad a text. He rarely responded to her messages, but it was worth a try.

Then she fished out Keaton's card and, when the detective didn't pick up, left a message describing her recent encounter. Once these calls were out of the way, Nicole allowed the girl to help her into the museum administrator's office. The administrator himself was out, and the girl steered Nicole into a big leather chair that made a soft, swooshing sound as she sunk into its cool caress.

She inspected her ankle. It was starting to swell but didn't seem quite as painful, as long as she didn't put her weight on it.

Really, she was all right. If only she didn't keep hearing that man's words, the menace in his voice: "Tell yer old man he better pay up. 'E's got 'til 6:00 tomorrow night. Or it's yore arse." She thought of his hands on her, his horrid smell.

He seemed to think he knew her "old man." That was impossible, ridiculous. Brad would never have anything to do with a lout like that. Then something occurred to her. Was it possible he and his pal were after Lowry? If Reinhardt was looking for him, maybe other people were, too.

She remembered SoftPac's labor problems, Brad's reason for coming to England, and felt a flicker of doubt. Maybe these men were involved with Brad's company. But this seemed unlikely, too. She'd heard of union goons, but these two were a couple of low-class criminals who assaulted innocent bystanders in public. For all their buffoonery, they reminded her of the villainous biker types featured in sci-fi films, patrolling the ruins of civilization.

On the other hand, something had been bothering Brad these last few months. She wondered if he might actually be mixed up in something illegal. It was an old worry of hers, relating to a period before she knew Brad, when he'd gotten into serious trouble with the law.

It had started out as a prank, the kind of mischief young people get into because it presents a challenge. As college freshmen, Brad and his best buddy had used the school's computer lab to break into the mainframe of a big credit card company. All they'd meant to do was leave a harmless virus. Their program was designed to show an image of a man in a raincoat, a flasher, who exposed himself to the person operating the computer. The raincoat whipped open and shut too quickly for anyone to see he was actually wearing a fig leaf. After the flasher appeared a few times, the virus erased itself.

By some unlucky fluke, the virus was incompatible with the credit card company's software. The whole system crashed and was down for the good part of an afternoon.

Brad and his friend were tracked down and arrested. The DA tried to make an example of them. The boys got off with a few months community service, but the trial received a great deal of media attention. Nicole herself had followed the story, although she hadn't even known Brad at the time.

She wanted to believe he'd never do anything like that again. Yet there was something in him that couldn't resist pushing the limits of authority. Even though his more recent trespasses had been minor, they worried her. On their return from a trip to Paris the previous year, he'd insisted on sneaking several bogus designer watches in through customs. Although they weren't of any great value, knockoffs like these were considered contraband, and it was illegal to bring them into the U.S. Nicole, who'd seen several news stories about a government crackdown, was certain he'd be caught and arrested.

Brad himself was the picture of cool. "I can't understand what you're so freaked out about," he whispered as they approached the customs inspection station. "This is nickel-and-dime stuff, Nick. A couple of fifty-buck watches. Nobody cares about chicken shit like that."

And he was right. The customs officer placed stickers on their luggage without inspecting it, motioning them on. As they walked away, Brad laughed. "They always do that. I could be carrying a suitcase full of diamonds, and they'd just wave me through." He didn't even bother to lower his voice.

Her thoughts were interrupted when a museum guard walked in, a gray-haired, bespectacled man in a navy blue uniform and visored cap. Right behind him were two London bobbies. They looked no older than the officer who'd come to the house. The one who did most of the talking had bad skin, and the bobbing of his Adam's apple did not inspire confidence. But at least he was courteous.

She repeated her story, and when she mentioned the break-in at the house and her contact with Detective Keaton, the policeman noted down Keaton's name. Then he said, "Did the assailant give any indication what he meant by 'the load of stuff' he expects your husband to pay for?"

"No," she replied. "I told you everything the man said before they ran away."

"Did you get any impression at all as to what it might be?" he persisted. "Drugs or guns, for example—or explosives?"

"Really—I have no idea what he was talking about."

"Has your husband ever mentioned this individual named …" His eyes dropped to his notes, "Ben or that he owes someone money?"

"Of course not." Nicole was starting to lose her temper. "My husband's a business executive. These people were common criminals."

"Does Mr. Graves make frequent trips to the U.K?"

"He's come here four or five times in the last year and a half for his company," she said. "We came once on vacation, and now he's here for the summer. I suppose you might call that frequent." She could see where these questions were headed. He had the idea Brad might really be mixed up with these people. Even though she'd had the same thought herself, she found his suggestion insulting.

The young officer asked a few more questions about Brad's company and his position with them. Then he said, "I wonder if you'd be kind enough to give me your husband's mobile number. We'd like a few words with him."

"He's in Liverpool for a couple of days," she said. "I just called and he didn't pick up. His office said they'd track him down and get back to me."

The two officers exchanged glances. Then the more talkative one said, "That sort of follows what your assailant said, then—doesn't it?—that your husband had given them the slip, but he knew where to find you?"

"My husband only left town this afternoon," she said. "He's been staying with me in Chiswick since we arrived."

"When your husband contacts you from Liverpool, please have him give me a ring," the policeman said. He jotted a number on a page of his notebook, tore it out, and handed it to her. "Now, just a few more questions. Did you hear either of these individuals make demands or express threats against members of the government?" He went on in this vein, as if he were reciting from memory. "Did they say anything about the making or planting of bombs or incendiary devices?"

She found the questions puzzling. She stared at him. "Surely you don't think these men are terrorists," she said.

"Can't be too careful, madam, as I'm sure you know. We receive threats against public buildings like the National Gallery almost every day. You'd be surprised. Now, may we offer you a lift home?"

Nicole was grateful for the ride, especially when the two officers assisted her to their patrol car without once mentioning doctors or ambulances. On the way to Chiswick, Nicole felt a certain amazement at finding herself riding in the back of a police car. Just two days in England, and she'd had more contact with law enforcement than in her entire life.

When they reached the Lowrys' street, Mr. McGiever was out in front of his house, astonished to see her delivered by the police. While the officers helped Nicole out of the back seat, McGiever paced about the sidewalk before following them up the path with the eagerness of a stray dog.

She could see he was eaten up by curiosity, but after all she'd been through, she wasn't about to explain. Instead, she faked a smile, gave a little wave and did her best to act as if she were used to arriving home accompanied by officers of the law.

While the policemen checked around the house, Nicole glanced out of the front window. A small crowd of neighbors had gathered in front, and McGiever was talking to them excitedly. She wondered what he could possibly be telling them. She felt disappointed in him; what an old busybody he'd turned out to be.

As they left, the more talkative of the two officers said, "Don't forget to ask Mr. Graves to get in touch with us. I don't think you're in any danger, but I wouldn't stay here alone tonight if I were you."

Even Nicole, in her somewhat numbed state, could see that. She explained there was a tenant, a nurse, who would be staying with her. Yet even as she said this, she remembered how silent Alice's room had been at night. It occurred to her that Alice might be sleeping somewhere else.

A few minutes later, as she watched the police car drive away, she was assailed by fresh doubts. What if those men had mistaken Brad for someone else? Worse yet, what if they really were after him?

She thought of what the fat one had said. "Tell yer old man he better pay for that load a stuff. Cause Ben is ready to kill him." At this moment, they might be tracking Brad down, determined to carry out their threat. My God, she thought. She had to warn him.

She pulled out her phone and checked for messages. Nothing. She called Brad's office. As it rang, she glanced at the clock on the wall over the stove, surprised to see it was already past 6:00 p.m. At the other end, the phone rang perhaps twenty times before someone finally picked it up. "Ryan here," he said.

She told the man about her earlier call from the museum, the fact that someone in the office had agreed to track Brad down and have him call her.

"Sorry, luv," he said. "I don't know anything about that. Best you call back in the morning."

"Is Brenda Ferraro there?"

"I seem to be alone here at the moment, and I'm a bit pressed for time. Want to leave a message? Just say the word, luv."

"If she comes back, have her call me."

The man took her number.

She put down the phone and then stood there, feeling anxious and vaguely guilty, as if she'd brought all this trouble down by insisting on coming to London. But that was ridiculous. These men were after someone who owed them money and, through some crazy mistake, had focused on her and Brad. It could have been anyone.

At that moment she thought of the message she'd left Keaton earlier. If she could reach her now, maybe she could help locate Brad. Nicole fumbled through her purse until she found the detective's card with her number.

When the call went directly to Keaton's voicemail, Nicole glanced at the clock and realized Keaton probably had left for the day. She left her name, number, and a message describing the assault.

As Nicole hung up, her eyes fell on the morning paper, still lying on the kitchen counter. As soon as she saw the date, she realized it was the day the Lowrys were scheduled to arrive in L.A. This meant she'd be able to reach them and let them know about the break-in. And maybe—just maybe—they'd be able to shed some light on what was going on. She wished they'd left her a better means of getting hold of them. Mrs. Lowry had told her they were turning their cell phones off because they didn't want to run up a big phone bill using them in the States. It was a mystery to Nicole how they'd manage without some kind of telephone or email service. Didn't the U.K. have overseas calling plans like hers with AT&T?

She dialed her home number and waited while it rang. There was a click and then voicemail kicked in. The message was in her own voice: "We aren't available right now, but please leave a message … " She hung up.

At that moment, she heard rumbling from the back of the house. She limped down the hall to catch Alice on her way upstairs.

"Why, Nicole," Alice said. "Whatever is wrong?"

Hearing the sympathy in her friend's voice made Nicole want to cry. Her story tumbled out in a torrent of pain and anger.

As Alice listened, her face grew very pink. "Well, what bastards!" she said, "The bloody bastards!"

When Nicole finished, Alice ushered her into the living room and insisted Nicole lie down on the couch. Then Alice proceeded to pack Nicole's ankle in a pile of ice-filled plastic bags.

Nicole protested. The bags might leak on the upholstery—the expensive-looking beige damask—and ruin it.

This seemed to infuriate Alice. "Don't you worry your head about the property of Freddy damned Lowry. Let the Freddy Lowrys of the world look after themselves." She was quiet a moment, then she said, "I have something I need to tend to. I'll be right back."

Nicole lay back on the couch, closed her eyes, and tried to relax. But the ice pack made her ankle hurt more, and she kept hearing the man's threat, repeating in her head.

Several minutes passed before Alice was back, carrying a small, battered overnight bag.

Nicole's heart sank. "You're not leaving, are you?"

Instead of answering, Alice set the bag down, went to the kitchen, and came back with a glass of water. She handed it to Nicole along with two white pills. "Here we are, dear," Alice said. "I'd like you to take these. They'll help the pain a little and stop the swelling in your ankle." She pulled a tiny white box from her pocket, rattled it, and set it down on the lamp table. "These are stronger pain killers. But you shouldn't take any just yet. They'll make you drowsy, and you mustn't nod off while you're alone here. Now I want you to promise something."

"All right," Nicole said. "But first, I want to ask you a question. Why did you rush away from lunch? Was it because of the men sitting at the next table?"

"No, Nicole," Alice said. "It was the phone call. A friend of mine is having some troubles. But if I'd had any idea you were in danger, I'd never have left."

"But you do know something, don't you?" Nicole said. "You know what's going on."

Meeting Nicole's gaze, Alice said, "No, Nicole, I truly don't. But when scum like that follow you around and threaten violence, you have to take them seriously." After a pause, while she seemed to consider this, she added, "My gut feeling is that it's something to do with Freddy. Maybe they think you're Muriel, you know—his wife."

Nicole sat up. "How could they possibly think that? Mrs. Lowry is English. I'm American."

"No, Nicole. That's not so. She's American, like you. Oh, she's lived here for years, but anybody can tell. You people never lose your accent. Of course, she's older and not nearly so pretty." She reached out and brushed the hair from Nicole's forehead.

"Now about that promise I mentioned," she went on. "I have to go away for a few days. If you reach your husband, perhaps he can catch a train back tonight. But if he can't, I want you to promise you won't spend the night here by yourself. Why don't you let me take you to a wee hotel I know? The owner's an old friend. It won't be very dear."

Nicole's ankle throbbed, and she felt a wave of overwhelming fatigue. "I need to rest for a bit," she said. "You go ahead."

"Nicole," Alice said sternly. "You're in danger. I won't have you staying here by yourself."

"Okay," Nicole said. "Give me the name and address of the hotel. In a little while, I'll call a cab. I promise."

This seemed to satisfy Alice. "That's all right, then. I'll see you in a couple of days." When she gave Nicole a hug, she said, "Goodbye, Nicole. You'll take care of yourself, won't you?"

"You are coming back?" Nicole said, suddenly worried. "I will see you again, won't I?"

Alice gave a laugh. "Now what are you on about? Of course you'll be seeing me. Saturday at the latest. We'll have afternoon tea at Fortnum and Mason. It's time we started putting some flesh on those bones of yours."

After she left, Nicole watched through the front window. Alice walked down the front path, turned right, and made her way past the Lowrys' car, which was parked at the curb.

When she was out of sight, Nicole pulled out her phone and called Brad's cell again, then his office. The same man answered. "Sorry, luv," he said, before she had a chance to ask. "Haven't seen a soul. Just heading for the door myself." His accent was even more clipped than before. Clearly, he was in an enormous hurry, eager to get rid of her.

"It's urgent I reach Brad," she said. "Brenda is sure to have some idea where he is. I wonder if you might have her phone number."

There was a brief silence at the other end of the line. Then the man said, "Hang on a mo. I just remembered—old Bren's gone to Liverpool herself."

"That's impossible!" Nicole said, unable to hide her distress. "Brad said she wasn't going."

There was a long pause. Then he said, "I'm sorry, luv. You know, I think I was mistaken. Yes, that's right. Brenda didn't go at all. Now, why don't you call back bright and early in the morning. She's sure to be here, and she'll help you find him."

From the way he said this, his sudden patience, Nicole could tell he was trying to placate her. He knew Brenda was in Liverpool, just as he understood exactly why Nicole would be upset about it.

Her thoughts were spinning. If Brenda was on that trip… But no. The man had to be wrong. "Listen—this is an emergency," she said. "My husband's life may be in danger. Is it possible Brenda left a number where she can be reached?"

"Haven't a clue. Awfully sorry, luv. Really must run. Ring back tomorrow." There was a click, and he was gone.

Nicole went to the front window and stared out. Then she limped into the dining room. As she stood in front of the painting, she realized she'd been avoiding it since that first day. Sure enough, there they were: the same nude, androgynous creatures engaged in their eternal struggle.

Since she'd last seen it, the picture seemed to have acquired a message—something to do with the trouble between her and Brad. Even beyond that, it symbolized the war between men and women that she witnessed daily in her office's legal practice; the huge gap between their needs and desires; the hopelessness of either side achieving any satisfaction.

The idea was too complex, or perhaps too muddled, to sort out. But as she pondered it, she felt the most enormous lump of anger growing inside. It grew until she was trembling almost uncontrollably. Finally she shook her fists at the picture and screamed at the top of her lungs, as if it were to blame for everything.

Despite the protests of her ankle, she hobbled upstairs. In the bedroom, she systematically tore Brad's things out of the closet and went through his pockets. Then she started going through his dresser. In the top drawer, at the very back, she noticed a red velvet drawstring bag. The sight of it made goosebumps rise on the back of her neck.

She pulled it from the drawer, untied the cord and dumped out the contents. Half a dozen watches clattered onto the dresser top. They were crafted of soft glowing gold with black faces. Each had a ring of diamonds around the dial. If they were fakes, they were masterfully done.

As she stared at them, it struck her that this might be even worse than she'd imagined. He wasn't just involved with Brenda, but in some crooked deal. Who knew what trouble he might be in?

After a moment, she scooped the watches back into the drawer and began looking through the rest of his things. She reached in every pocket, shook out each garment, scanned notebooks and bits of paper until his possessions lay in a great disordered heap in the middle of the room.

On her second run through the pile, she wore her glasses and went more slowly. This time, she recognized some notebook-sized pages that were stapled together. It was a printout of the address book he kept on his computer.

She found Brenda's number and called it. A recorded message came on. "This is Brenda Ferraro. I'll be out of town on business until Friday. If this is an emergency, please call my office and ask them to get in touch." She gave the number. "Otherwise, leave a message, and I'll call you the moment I'm back." There was the sound of her high, tinkling laughter. "Can't wait!" Then: "Ciao!"

Nicole hung up and took a few deep gulps of air. She knew what she was going to do.

She threw a few things into an overnight bag and called a cab. Then she went to the desk and took out a brand new credit card, one of two that Brad had brought along. It was impressive-looking—shiny and black—and it had her name on it. He'd ordered the cards for the trip, in case of an emergency.

Well, this certainly was an emergency.

EIGHT

AT THE LAST MINUTE, NICOLE DECIDED against the hotel Alice had recommended. Instead, she directed the cab driver to take her to the Dorchester, one of London's most expensive hotels. She would install herself in a top floor suite and charge it to their brand-new credit card.

Anger and the busy work of packing kept despair at a distance, at least until she climbed in the cab and told the driver her destination. Grief and misery caught up with her as the cab pulled up in front of the Dorchester. Then, as she stepped into the plush gilt and burgundy of the lobby, the enormity of Brad's betrayal hit her full force.

It occurred to her that the notion of a broken heart was invented by someone who'd never had one. It wasn't her heart that hurt but her stomach, with a continuing visceral ache that made it impossible to think of anything but Brad and Brenda, the two of them together.

While she was busy signing the registration form, tipping the bellboy, unpacking her overnight bag, the ache in her stomach was a constant reminder. If anything kept her from breaking down completely, it was the thought that once she started to cry she'd never stop.

She tried to focus on her surroundings, for the suite was truly lovely. The bedroom featured a four-poster bed bedecked with a yellow organza canopy. The mattress sat perhaps three-and-a-half feet from the floor. A stepstool had been placed beside the bed, an invitation to climb up and try it out. At any other time, Nicole would have hoisted herself up for a few bounces. If she were in a better frame of mind, if she were here with Brad. The thought sank to the bottom of her stomach where it combined with anger and sorrow into a great molten mass.

She wandered back into the living room. It, too, was done in shades of yellow with silk textured wallpaper and matching swag drapes. The cherry wood furniture, with its ornately-carved panels, belonged to a period she thought was Jacobean, although she wasn't quite sure.

She went over and stood at the bank of windows looking out over London. At 8:30 p.m., it was not yet dark. Mile upon mile of rooftops stretched out to the east: peaked Victorians with chimney pots, along with more modern structures dotted with squat, louvered cooling ducts. To her far right, a huge expanse of rolling green treetops marked the location of an enormous park.

As she settled on the love seat facing the window, she thought of the men who'd threatened her. In the face of Brad's betrayal, the two hoodlums seemed irrelevant and almost laughable. Yet she knew they were still out there, a threat she'd eventually have to deal with.

If these men continued stalking her and the police still did nothing, she'd have to take steps to protect herself. Returning to L.A. was one option.

But she knew she wasn't going back. That was exactly what Brad wanted: the summer alone with Brenda. Well, he wasn't going to get it.

Glancing at her watch, she realized that the two of them would have checked into their hotel by now. They'd register separately so each would have a room for expense account purposes, but that would be purely for show. At this very moment, they were probably in bed together.

God, if she could only stop thinking about it. She got up and paced the length of the room a few times. Then she noticed the remote control for a TV on the coffee table and began looking around for the set itself. Eventually, she found it, concealed in a cabinet on the far wall.

When she turned on the set, a newsman with a long face and bushy, worried-looking eyebrows was talking about the latest terrorist threat. It had closed the London rail and underground stations. "Police suspect it may be a hoax, but they are looking for possible explosive devices. This is the third such alarm since a bomb at Victoria Station killed twelve people on the fifth of May." The man's voice deepened as he recounted that incident. "No organization has come forward to take credit for that attack, but police believe it was the work of ISIS, al Qaeda, or one of the other groups that have stirred up violence throughout Europe and the Middle East."

Gloomily, the man described the likelihood of railway stations instituting new security measures. He suggested they might even put in baggage scanning devices and metal detectors, like those used in airports. "If you're planning a train journey," he said, "pack along an extra measure of patience and be prepared for possible delays."

She turned the set off and closed the cabinet. Outside, daylight was beginning to fade. She couldn't stay in the room another moment, alone with her terrible thoughts. She'd noticed a restaurant on the main floor of the hotel. Maybe she'd head down for a glass of wine. Yes, that was exactly what she needed. Later, if she felt hungry, she could have something to eat.

A few minutes later, she paused outside the suite, trying to get her bearings. She decided the elevator must be hidden beyond the large columned archway at the other end of the hall. As she strolled toward it, she thought she heard something creak, and her body gave a quiver of alarm. She picked up her step and looked around. No one was there.

Only as she reached the columned alcove did she realize that it wasn't the elevator lobby but the entrance to a posh suite. The elevators were at the other end.

There was another creak, this one louder than the first. At the sound, her heart began to thump, her scalp to tingle. Again she looked around, but the corridor appeared as deserted as before. She told herself she was being silly. Old buildings always made strange noises.

On the wall next to the door was a tapestry. She paused a moment to gaze at it, trying to work up the courage to head back to her room. The hanging was lit by soft spotlights that brought out the colors: radiant teals, chartreuses, roses, and pinks. She recognized it as a rendering of Hieronymus Bosch's hellish Garden of Delights. Across the crowded landscape, nude, tormented-looking figures struggled with one another while flocks of giant birds dashed hither and yon. In these images, she found the same message she'd seen in the painting in the Lowrys' dining room: It was something she understood but couldn't articulate. It involved the shattering of her dreams; the charade of her marriage; the impossibility of love.

For a short while she stood staring at the hanging, lost in thought. At last, she pulled herself away and turned to face the silent corridor. Taking a deep breath, she began to walk back.

She was halfway back to her room before she spotted him, standing in the shadow of a small alcove at the corridor's midpoint. It was someone she'd never seen before—a conservatively dressed, stern looking man in his late thirties. He wasn't doing anything, just standing there.

For the briefest moment, their gazes locked. Then he averted his eyes, focusing on a point somewhere beyond her. He made no move in her direction, nor did he retreat toward the door behind him. Instead, his body took on a statue-like stillness, like a guard at Buckingham Palace.

She came to a stop, then stumbled past him, ignoring the renewed pain of her ankle as she rushed to her room. She was determined not to run. She knew from experience what a bad idea that was.

My God, was this man following her, too? Watching her room and waiting for her to come out? The odd thing was that her appearance seemed to have startled him almost as much as his had startled her.

Fumbling with her key, she let herself back in her room. Once inside, she slammed the door, slipped the chain lock into place and picked up the house phone. "There's a strange man loitering on the tenth floor," she told the operator. She was switched to security.

"The tenth floor?" the man repeated calmly. A paper rattled, as if he were looking something up. Then: "Yes, well, one of our guests is a person of some celebrity. He brings his own security staff with him. Not that there's any need here, of course. I hope this person hasn't disturbed you in any way."

She assured him he hadn't and hung up feeling foolish. She wasn't a coward, and yet the idea of that man outside her door was so unsettling that she no longer had any desire to leave her room.

Instead, she called room service and ordered a small bottle of wine, along with—why not?—baked salmon en croute and a small green salad. When it arrived, she took only a bite before the now-familiar sick feeling took over, making it impossible to eat. She put the silver dome back on the tray and stared out the window again, sipping from her wine. The bottle only held a glass and a half. When it was gone she put on her nightgown, swallowed two of the painkillers Alice had given her, and got into bed.

The pills made her groggy but refused to grant the release of sleep. Instead, she lay there for hours, tormented by her thoughts. At her lowest point, life without Brad didn't seem worth living. She fantasized about giving up her job and joining the Peace Corps so she could devote whatever miserable years she had left to good works in West Africa, perhaps, or the Middle East.

At other moments, she was ready to do whatever it would take to get him back. She visualized herself getting dressed and catching the next train to Liverpool. She'd burst in on them and break up their little love nest with a scene so ugly that neither Brad, nor Brenda, nor anyone else staying at that hotel tonight would ever forget it.

Fresh doubts would assail her, and she'd wonder once again if their marriage was already doomed. Looking back over the last few months, she could see that she and Brad had become more like business partners than husband and wife, always discussing arrangements, the direction of their investments, the structure of vacation plans. Between his business trips, they'd sit down at the dining room table with the entertainment section of the paper and their calendars. Then they'd negotiate which movies, plays and other events they'd attend. Sex was scheduled, too—subject to cancellation when preempted by another obligation.

Yet she could remember when things were good between them. When they were first together, Brad had found her a source of endless fascination. He'd been charmed by everything about her, from her crooked baby toe to the tiny birthmark just below her left breast that he swore was shaped like a perfect heart. He'd respected her then, listening solemnly to her opinions and laughing at her jokes.

She wondered if that was simply a phase men went through when they were first in love. Her sister swore that once the glow of novelty wore off, men (like hunting hounds) began sniffing around for fresh prey. As Stephanie put it, "They're led around by their little divining rods. Can't even help it, poor things. It's programmed into them."

Nicole had laughed, but it worried her that Stephanie was so cynical. She feared that her sister, at the age of twenty-eight, was becoming a man hater. Now, as a steady procession of tears slid down her face and onto the pillow, Nicole decided that Stephanie was right.

The pain in her stomach was still there when morning came. Even before she awoke, she recognized it as grief and understood its source. She told herself that this, too, was a sign of progress.

She picked up the phone and ordered a breakfast of croissants and strawberries. She still couldn't eat, but the coffee was good. As she sipped it, she decided the best thing would be to get away from London for a while. Why not take some time to see the English countryside? She wouldn't even leave a note. When Brad came back to the house and didn't find her there—well, that would give him something to think about.

She decided against taking a train. With the bomb scare, it would be too much of a hassle. Instead, she'd go back to the house and get the Lowrys' car. She hadn't forgotten the fat man and his ultimatum, but she'd pick up the car in the afternoon, well before 6:00 p.m.

She took a hot bath, soaking the remaining soreness out of her ankle in water laced with jasmine bath oil provided by the hotel. When she was finally dressed, she went downstairs, asked for directions from the liveried concierge, and headed for the tourist information center at Victoria Station, a half dozen blocks away. It was already almost 1:00 p.m., cool and threatening rain.

By the time she was talking to the clerk at the tourist center, she was feeling considerably stronger, more resolute. On the way back to the hotel, she stopped at a coffee bar and browsed through the travel brochures she'd picked up. She returned to her room and finished packing a little past 3:00 p.m. At checkout, the bill came to a staggering £620. There was a snag with the new credit card because she hadn't called to activate it. She had to talk to the credit card company then wait nearly an hour for the charge to clear. She was starting to feel uneasy about the time.

As she got in the cab and gave the driver the address, she wondered if it would be better to avoid the place altogether—to forget the Lowrys' car and simply rent one.

No, she thought. Maybe she couldn't do anything about Brad, but she wasn't going to let that pair of clowns frighten her away from the house. Auto rentals here were expensive, and she had every right to use the Lowrys' car.

She'd stay out of London five days, maybe even a week. Then she'd show up at Brad's office and have it out with him.

Another worry flickered at the edge of her thoughts. What if Brad really is in danger? But no—he wouldn't be returning to the house until the day after tomorrow. By then, those men would have given up and moved on. Besides, even if she stuck around to warn him, he'd refuse to believe her.

The minute she walked into the house, she knew she'd made a mistake. The place felt spooky and haunted, as if there were someone hiding in the shadows, waiting to jump out at her.

She paused at the foot of the stairs, staring up at the dim hallway. On second thought, she decided, there wasn't any need to pack a bag. The new credit card had a $50,000 limit. If she felt like it, she could spend a couple of weeks being more extravagant than she'd ever been in her life and not exhaust the line of credit. She deserved it. Besides, what was the point of worrying about their credit cards when their marriage was falling apart? She knew only too well what a divorce would do to their savings.

She didn't have much cash left, though, and she remembered the £20 notes in the bureau upstairs. She stood with one foot on the bottom step, debating whether to run up and get them.

The chime of the cell in her purse went through her like an electric shock. She pulled it out and answered.

"Hello, hello? Is anyone there?" The voice on the line was familiar.

"Stephanie?" Nicole said.

"Nicole, is that you? You sound weird."

"I'm fine," Nicole said. "What's going on?"

"Those people still haven't showed. They were supposed to get here yesterday, right? I tried phoning this morning. No answer, so I drove over to feed Arnold. And there's still no sign of them. I mean, no suitcases, nothing. Do you think something might have happened?"

"They probably were delayed for some reason and didn't bother to call us." As Nicole was saying this, she remembered the stories she'd read about carjackers who preyed on foreign tourists. She wondered if the Lowrys might be dead, lying in a ditch somewhere.

"Nicole?" Stephanie was saying. "Are you there?"

"I'm sure they'll turn up," Nicole said. "Could you just look after Arnold another day or two? Then we'll figure something out."

"Okay, let's give it two days."

"Look, Stephanie, I'm going to be out of London for a few days sightseeing, but I'll check in with you. If they don't show, you can board the dog."

There was a silence while Nicole debated whether to tell Stephanie about her troubles. Stephanie was a good listener, one who could be relied on for sympathy. But Nicole always paid a price for that sympathy later. Once in possession of Nicole's problem, Stephanie would make it her own, fretting and stewing until she decided what should be done. In the next frame, Stephanie would be insisting that Nicole follow her advice, which she invariably saw as the only solution. Nicole, of course, would want to do things her own way, and there would be a fight. At that point, Stephanie would turn on Nicole with a litany of I-told-you-so's and hard, hurtful truths. Remembering the fallout from her last confidence, Nicole decided she had enough trouble without the burden of her sister's sympathy.

"Okay," Stephanie was saying. "I'll take Arnold home with me tonight, but he'd better not poop on my rug. You hear that, Arnold?" She paused to let the dog take this in. Then: "If those people don't turn up by Saturday, he goes into one of those boarding kennels over on Sepulveda. Look, this is your nickel, and it's costing you a fortune. We'd better hang up."

"Wait," Nicole said. "How's Daddy?"

"Don't ask," Stephanie said. "He's spending a lot of time outside—digging. This time it's the front yard."

"Oh, no," Nicole said. There was a silence while she considered their father's behavior.

For any other seventy-year-old widower, digging in the garden might be a healthy sign. But this was different. Their father wasn't gardening but tearing up the flowerbeds in a futile search for a cache of gold coins he thought their mother had hidden somewhere. She'd once told him she was collecting the coins, one at a time, on her cruises and tours abroad. The trips were financed by her salary as a filing clerk at the federal building, a job she'd come to at an age when most people were ready to retire. She'd taken it out of rebellion, after a lifetime of railing at her husband's tight-fistedness.

After the funeral, when their father told Nicole and Stephanie about the missing coins, they were certain that their mother had been lying. Travel, clothes, and the payments on a flashy red convertible had kept her perennially broke. The gold coin story had been her final revenge on their father for his unrelenting cheapness.

When they tried to explain this to him, he was indignant. "That old lady wouldn't lie to me," he said. "She didn't know how to lie."

This was news to her daughters.

Since then, their father had exhausted himself searching the house. It was like a sickness. The idea of that treasure, hidden just out of reach, was eating him alive.

"Don't worry about it, Nick," Stephanie said. "Even if you were here, he wouldn't listen to you. He won't listen to anybody, for God's sake. There's nothing we can do."

"I know," Nicole said. "Credibility. That's always a problem for the women in this family."

A long silence, then Stephanie said, "Is everything all right, Nick?"

"I'm fine," Nicole said, a little too quickly. "That was a joke."

There followed a verbal scuffle, with Stephanie insisting something was wrong and Nicole denying it. At last, Nicole managed to extricate herself from the conversation and hung up.

She was hurrying into the front hallway to get the car keys when she remembered Alice and their Saturday date for tea. If Alice got back and found Nicole gone, she'd be concerned, especially in light of the fat man's threat. And, while Nicole didn't care if Brad was frantic over her disappearance, she didn't want her new friend to worry.

She rushed back into the kitchen, grabbed the pad of paper and dashed off a note. Clutching it in her hand, she hurried upstairs. The door to the Lowrys' bedroom was closed, just as she'd left it. She paused, remembering the money. She had no idea where the nearest ATM was, and she couldn't embark on an automobile trip without cash in her purse. She glanced at her watch. She had barely enough time to leave the note and get out.

As she bent down to slip the note under Alice's door, it gave a creak and slowly swung open. Alice's room was smaller than she'd expected, sparsely furnished with scuffed, mismatched pieces that looked as if they'd been gleaned from garage sales. Limp, ruffled tieback curtains hung at the windows. The only new item of decor was a cheap-looking bedspread in shiny aqua polyester.

The closet door was standing open. Nicole was surprised at how empty it was. Just two garments were hanging inside: a dress and a skirt. There were two extra hangers, as if Alice never hung more than four garments at a time. Surely she had more clothes, but where were they? Her overnight bag had been just big enough for a nightgown and an outfit or two at most.

Nicole walked over to the dresser and opened the top drawer. It was immaculate, devoid of even a crumb or a speck of dust. At the back of the second drawer was a pair of cotton bikini underpants, pristine white, as if they'd never been worn. Other than that, the dresser was empty. She looked under the bed—nothing, not even a dust ball. It seemed odd when Alice had insisted she'd be back.

Nicole glanced at her watch, startled to see it was now 5:52 p.m. The note was still in her hand. She tossed it on the bed and, in sudden panic, dashed for the stairs. Her ankle was beginning to protest.

The car keys were on the hall table. She grabbed them as she opened the front door. This time she slammed it shut and hurried down the steps, not bothering with the deadbolt. As she slid behind the wheel of the car, she felt disoriented, almost dizzy. It was the unfamiliar position of the driver's seat, the fact that the steering wheel was on the wrong side of the car, the car on the wrong side of the street. It occurred to her that she might not be able to pull this off.

She thought of the two men and their deadline. There wasn't much time. She had to get away, put some distance between herself and the house in the next few minutes. She reached out and turned the key in the ignition, but nothing happened. She tried again, pumping the gas pedal. Still nothing.

Then she remembered what Muriel had explained in one of her messages. The car had a choke she was supposed to pull out as she started the engine. Or was she supposed to push it in? She stared at it a moment, then jumped at the sound of someone tapping on the car window.

It was Mr. McGiever. He smiled at her, pointing to himself and then to the driver's seat. She hesitated only a moment before opening the door and hopping out. "It won't start," she explained breathlessly. "I'm in the most enormous hurry. If you could just ..."

Even before her words were out, he was stiffly easing himself behind the wheel. He was such a sweet man, really. His eagerness to please made her sorry she'd been so unfriendly. He always seemed to be hanging about, trying to make small talk. Lately, she'd even taken to peeking out the window to make sure he wasn't there before stepping outside.

He turned the key and worked the choke button until the engine sprang to life. Then he opened the car door and began to slide out.

She gave him a smile. "Thanks a lot, Mr. McGiever," she said. "I don't know what I'd have done without you." She glanced around at the house again. Now that he'd turned up, she thought, why not go back and get the money? "You know, I just remembered something I left inside," she said. "Would you mind ...?"

"By all means, Mrs. Graves," Mr. McGiever beamed at her. "Feel free to go take care of it. I'll keep an eye on the car. We'll just leave the engine running to warm it up." He settled back behind the wheel and shut the door.

She'd just opened the front door when she heard, or rather felt, a rumble that made the front steps tremble beneath her feet and then rocked the whole house. A sound accompanied it, a loud swoosh that filled her head with a strange ringing sound. A moment later, she was blown into the house by a ferocious wind that was as hot as dragon's breath. The phrase, which she'd once read in a fairy tale, popped into her head as the wind tossed her into the entry hall on her hands and knees.

Then the whooshing sound stopped or, rather, everything went silent. A brilliant light made her turn her head and look out. There, framed perfectly in the open doorway, the car where she'd just been sitting was now a fireball. As she watched, flames leapt from the car to dance along the Lowrys' rosebushes, reducing them to a few charred twigs.

Nine

From the floor of the entry hall, Nicole stared out at the inferno. She could feel its heat, its ferocious hunger as it consumed the small black Renault. The hot point of the blaze, its very source, appeared to be the spot where Mr. McGiever had been sitting. There was no longer any sign of him. The fire had taken over the driver's seat. The explosion had blown out the car's windows, and brilliant streamers of flame reached through them to flap against the roof. It was inconceivable that anyone inside could have survived.

That poor, sweet old man.

People began to gather across the street. They kept their distance but seemed to be drawn to the blaze, as hypnotized by it as she was. She wondered if anyone would approach and try to pull him out. Clearly, it was too late. Beneath the acrid smell of burning metal and plastic was a more organic stench she knew instinctively as death, the reek of burning flesh.

Oh, God, she thought. It's all my fault. If only I hadn't asked him to start the car.

Then she realized what would have happened if he hadn't taken her place at the wheel, if she hadn't chosen that very moment to go back into the house. A dull numbness took over. She was sprawled in the entry hall, lying on one side with her knees drawn up. From this vantage point, she stared through the open doorway, no longer taking in the scene before her. Although she felt the heat of the fire, she couldn't seem to stop shivering.

Eventually police cars, fire trucks and an ambulance arrived, their approach heralded by a shrieking chorus of sirens. As men in uniforms appeared and began to dash about, she stirred and struggled to her feet. The movement made her vision crack and break into hundreds of tiny pieces. When they slowly reassembled themselves, the floor was tilted at an unfamiliar angle, and she had to lean against the wall to keep from falling.

Then two ambulance attendants were standing there. They had a compact bundle that unfolded into a stretcher. After they set it up, one of them turned and spoke to her, his words lost against the ringing in her ears. From his gestures, she could guess what he was saying. He seemed to be under the impression that she was hurt and should go to Emergency. She explained that she was fine. She had no intention of being carted off like a dead horse. It was Mr. McGiever who needed help.

Perhaps she wasn't making sense, for the two exchanged a glance, an almost imperceptible nod. Then they refolded the stretcher, linked their arms in hers and, with gentle insistence, led her down the steps. To avoid the fire, they cut across the yard to a far corner; they hoisted Nicole over the low picket fence before climbing it themselves. The ambulance was several doors down, parked in front of a neighbor's house.

The firemen swarming around the blaze, the ever-arriving police cars, the curious onlookers, the row of houses—all tilted and swam as the paramedics pulled her along. Nicole took stock of herself. She was somewhat surprised to discover that she had her purse, its strap slung over her shoulder. She didn't think she was bleeding anywhere, and her arms and legs seemed to work. Yet she felt injured in some indiscernible way. She seemed to remember hitting her head; perhaps that explained why she was so dizzy. The dizziness and the loud ringing in her ears made it hard to think. Even so, she felt the need to protest. "I'm not hurt," she told them. "You can't take me to the hospital without my consent. Not even if I'm dying."

Neither attendant answered. They seemed to think they had every right to carry her off whether she agreed or not.

As they were opening the back of the ambulance, a battered Volkswagen careened around the corner and screeched to a stop a few feet away. The door burst open, and a rather objectionable looking young man jumped out and pointed a camera at them.

"Looky 'ere," he said.

But they were already looking. The ambulance attendants and Nicole gawked opened-mouthed as he snapped a few pictures, then continued clicking the shutter, approaching them in a practiced zigzag that seemed calculated to vary his camera angle.

One of the attendants waved dismissively. "Aw, it's just the bloody tabloids." He and his partner gripped Nicole's arms and lifted her into the ambulance. By now, she'd given up any thought of resistance. It was a relief to lie down on the narrow cot that occupied the rear of the vehicle.

While they were strapping her in, the man with the camera stuck his head in the door. He had greasy hair and needed a shave. "Wot's your name, lady?" he said. Then, when there was no response: "Know who bought it over there?" Shrugging and raising his hands in a conciliatory gesture, he added, "I've got me job to do. Doesn't cost noffink to be civil." The questions stopped when the paramedics pulled the man away from the door and slammed it shut.

As the ambulance started up and the siren began to wail, Nicole's indignation resurfaced. Being dragged away in an ambulance with its siren screaming was humiliating and unnecessary. Then she remembered Mr. McGiever, and a wave of terrible grief swept over her. She was aware of the siren and the motion of the vehicle as it maneuvered through the traffic, yet her mind was quiet, utterly empty of thought.

At some point the ride ended and, after a long wait on a gurney in a crowded hallway, someone examined her. She was given a couple of pills and a glass of water. A nurse helped her out of her clothes into a short white gown and into bed. The smooth, cool sheets felt unimaginably good against her skin. She slept.

She opened her eyes, and Brad was there. He was sitting forward in his seat, resting his chin on the backs of his hands, staring at her. She'd never seen him look so miserable.

When he saw she was awake, he came over to the bed and put his arms around her. "Oh, God, Nick," he said. "I never dreamed… If anything had happened to you, I couldn't… I just…" His voice trailed off.

She could feel him tremble. His cheek was hot against hers, almost feverish. Only when he made a funny gulping sound did she realize he was crying. She'd never known him to cry, and his grief mystified her. She herself felt nothing.

As he held her, she remembered about Brenda—the fact that Brad had taken her to Liverpool. And yet the terrible emptiness she felt rendered Brenda, and even Brad, irrelevant.

She had the most dreadful feeling that nothing mattered, nothing at all. Then it all came rushing back. The car, the explosion, the fact that it could have been her.

"Mr. McGiever? " she said.

"Dead, poor old buzzard," Brad said. "I heard about that bomb threat on the news. But I never dreamed it could—that you…" His embrace tightened, and he made another gulping sound.

She wondered what he was talking about. Then she remembered the newscast she'd heard in the hotel room, the bomb threat that had closed the railway stations.

She pulled away from him and said, "Listen, you've got it wrong. It wasn't terrorists." As clearly as she could, she explained about the two men who'd followed her, the way the fat one had insisted he knew her "old man" and had threatened him.

As he listened, Brad shook his head. She could tell from his expression that he didn't believe her. Her voice trailed off and—to her own surprise—she began to cry in great, heaving sobs of frustration and anger. As she wept, she had the feeling of observing herself from across the room and wondering why she was making such a fuss.

Just then a nurse walked in carrying a tray with miniature paper cups lined up in rows. She handed Nicole one of the cups. It held two white pills that looked like aspirin.

While the nurse poured water into a glass, she turned to Brad. "We mustn't sit on the bed, sir. And we mustn't upset the patient. She's had a bad shock. In fact, it might be better if we came back later." She spoke in a sharp tone, like a parent upbraiding a naughty child.

"No, no! I'm not upsetting her." He stood up and backed away from the bed, patting the air as if to demonstrate how agreeable he was.

The nurse propped the door open and shot Brad a warning look before rushing off.

The rebuke was lost on Brad, who immediately sat on the bed again and renewed his argument. "Look, Nick, it's natural for you to be a little mixed up—I mean, after all you've been through. But the cops think it was terrorists. It's got terrorist written all over it."

Although she hadn't asked, he went into detail about the way he'd heard about the explosion. "I called the house and your cell a number of times from Liverpool," he said. "I was getting pretty worried because you didn't answer."

He paused and looked at her, as if expecting an answer, but Nicole glanced away. He was lying about the phone calls. If he'd called her cell, she would have seen the missed calls. But she wasn't going to point this out. Nor was she going to tell him she'd gone to a hotel. He'd want to know why, and she didn't have the energy to explain. The rage and jealousy that had driven her out of the house had completely evaporated.

"This morning," he went on, "when I was getting ready to catch the train back to London, I decided to give it one more try. You can't imagine how I felt when a cop answered the phone and told me about the bomb. He said they'd taken you to the hospital. He paused before continuing, "The bottom line is London's too dangerous for tourists right now. They've even got a cop stationed outside your door. Oh, man—the minute you're on your feet again, I'm putting you on the first flight to L.A."

Still trembling, he took her hand and planted a kiss on it. His emotion seemed real enough. Yet Nicole could see he was taking advantage of the situation, using it as an excuse to send her home. She understood there was a flaw in his logic, but her dizziness made it hard to sort out. Then it came to her. If the bomb was a random act of terrorism, as he insisted, that would mean she was no longer in danger. In the whole history of terrorism, who'd ever gotten in the way of two car bombs?

He was just trying to get rid of her so he could pursue his sordid little affair. It was what he'd wanted all along. The odd part was that she no longer cared. What did it matter if he spent the summer sleeping with Brenda?

There was a tapping sound, and, from the doorway, a woman's voice called out, "Pardon me!" D.C. Keaton, the lady of smiles, was standing in the doorway. Today, she was wearing a red and black print dress with a red linen blazer, a black silk carnation in the lapel. The red of the jacket, combined with the dark lipstick, gave her a brittle, sallow look.

"I apologize for bursting in like this, but I wonder if I might come in," she said. Without waiting for a reply, she headed directly for Brad, smiling broadly and reaching out to shake his hand. "I'm Detective Constable Keaton," she said. "You must be Mr.

Graves." She released his hand but held onto the smile. "Would you mind if I speak to your wife in private? Later, perhaps you'd be kind enough to answer a few questions."

Clearly puzzled, Brad stared at her for a moment before nodding his assent. As he made his way to the door, Nicole studied the way his shoulders sagged, the rumpled state of his suit. The curls he always took so much care to straighten with the blow dryer were in complete rebellion. He threw Nicole a last unhappy glance, before Keaton shut the door and sat down next to the bed

"I know you're not well," she began, "so I'll only take a moment. I just want to assure you that we're searching for the men who accosted you at the National Gallery."

"Then you heard..."

"Indeed I did," Keaton said. "I've read the police report. I also received your telephone messages, and I did try to reach you. But there was no answer." She looked at Nicole a long moment and shook her head. "Then, sometime before yesterday evening someone planted a bomb in the Lowrys' car. It was on a timer, apparently set to go off at 6:00 p.m. A terrible coincidence, the way everything hit you at once."

"But it wasn't a coincidence," Nicole said. She explained about the assailants' threat and their 6:00 pm deadline.

"Oh, I see," the detective said. "You think those men were responsible." The detective was silent for a long moment, chewing the inside of her lip. "Well, I can understand why you might come to such a conclusion, and it is a possibility—but not the only one. We've received a rash of bomb threats in the last few days. We have a bomb squad that makes a science of this sort of thing, and they have reason to believe the explosion was the work of a terrorist group—although we're not entirely sure which one." She shook her head. "Yes, it's a bit of a muddle, I'm afraid. We're looking at Al Qaeda tie-ins, but other groups as well, such as ALF."

"ALF?"

Keaton nodded. "The Animal Liberation Front. Opposed to blood sports and any animal testing. They often go after large corporations. I wonder if your husband's company might be a target."

Nicole thought of the animal rights groups at home. They were crazy all right, but she'd never heard of them throwing bombs around. "SoftPac is a computer software firm," she said. "They don't use laboratory animals."

"I see. That makes it all the more puzzling, doesn't it?" Keaton gave another of her smiles. "Well, no one has ever accused these people of being very precise in picking their targets. But the truth is that it might not have been terrorists at all. That's why we have to keep an open mind and look into all the possibilities."

Keaton paused before continuing, "May I be completely candid?"

Nicole nodded, but her stomach had gone funny. She didn't want to hear what the woman had to say.

"We've spoken to several people who work in your husband's London office." Keaton's face was sober. No hint of a smile now. "Someone told us, that is, he mentioned certain rumors that have been circulating about your husband..." Her voice trailed off. For the first time, she seemed at a loss for words.

"Just say it," Nicole said.

"This person said your husband appears to be having an affair with a young woman who works for him. I'm dreadfully sorry to bring this up when I have no way of verifying it. But I must ask."

Nicole hesitated. She could see where this line of questioning was headed, but it was ridiculous. "Even if it were true," she replied, "I don't see what it could possibly have to do with the car bomb."

"Forgive me," the detective said. "But in the vast majority of murder attempts, the perpetrator is the spouse or a close relative.

So, when an apparent attempt is made on a woman's life, the first person the police question is the husband."

Nicole stared at her. "You can't possibly imagine he's trying to kill me."

"Well, I'm terribly sorry," Keaton said. "But you must see that we have to look into it. And one last thing; Several people, not just the one individual but three or four others, mentioned that your husband has a criminal record back in the U.S."

"That was a computer prank when he was a kid, and he paid dearly for it," she said. "I know who planted that car bomb, and it wasn't Brad or any terrorist organization." Tears of anger filled her eyes. She blinked them away. "Only, you've made up your mind, haven't you? You aren't the least bit interested in what I have to say."

Keaton reached out and took Nicole's hand. "Oh, Mrs. Graves, nothing could be further from the truth," she said. "As soon as I get back to my office, I'm going to ask for an increase in the number of officers searching for the men who are stalking you. Now, I thought you might want to see this ..." She pulled the neatly-folded page of a newspaper from her purse and, unfolding it, placed it on the bed. "Of course, the paper misidentified you. Perhaps one of the neighbors told the photographer that the house and car belonged to the Lowrys."

It was an inside page containing several photos. Nicole picked it up, her eyes drawn to a picture of a blackened, burned-out hulk she recognized as the Lowrys' car. Next to it, another photo showed paramedics hustling a rumpled-looking blonde into the back of an ambulance. It was a dreadful picture. Her mouth was hanging open; she looked dazed and slightly demented.

She read the caption: "Mrs. Muriel Lowry, Chiswick resident injured in yesterday's bomb blast, shown as she was taken to hospital."

As Nicole reread the words, trying to make sense of them, her eyes kept closing. She remembered the pills the nurse had given her and realized they must have been some kind of sedative.

"Now, I'm afraid I must take your husband away to ask him some questions," Keaton said softly. "We'll bring him back to you presently."

With enormous effort, Nicole opened her eyes. "You can't hold him," she said. "The American Embassy ..."

She couldn't complete the sentence, but Keaton seemed to understand. "I'm afraid your embassy won't be much help," she said gently. "With a bombing like this, we have a right to hold your husband up to seven days for questioning under the Prevention of Terrorism Act."

Nicole's eyes opened then closed again, "You can't possibly ..." she managed to say.

"Don't worry. We'll release him later today, tomorrow morning at the latest. Look at it from our point of view: Mr. Graves might have heard or seen something."

Nicole wanted to argue, but sleep was already carrying her away.

Ten

Nicole woke up with a dull headache, feeling exhausted. It was too much effort to move, so she simply lay still, staring at the ceiling. It was light green, crisscrossed with an intricate network of pipes that, like the ceiling itself, was coated with thick layers of paint. The pale color made a perfect backdrop for the image that kept replaying in her head—the fireball that had once been the Lowrys' car.

Then a gray-haired nurse was standing over her, popping a thermometer into her mouth and taking her vital signs. Nicole was handed over to a nurse's aide, a plump, brown-skinned girl, who guided her to the shower and waited just outside the door while she washed and shampooed. When she was done, she was handed a fresh gown of blue-striped cotton, slightly faded. It was of the same design used by hospitals everywhere, open at the back with two frayed ties—positioned near the neckline—to hold it closed.

At the aide's suggestion, Nicole's purse was taken out of a small overhead cupboard where it had been stowed and her makeup retrieved. Carefully, the girl lined up Nicole's cosmetics and their respective brushes on the tray table. "A little color," she said in a singsong accent, "and you are looking better already."

Nicole held still while lipstick and blush were applied, although it was beyond her to take much interest in the process. Not that she was as dizzy as she'd been the day before, nor did she seem injured, at least in any obvious way. Her problem was a deep sense of malaise accompanied by a crippling numbness like nothing she'd ever experienced. It was as if a great part of her emotional core had been obliterated by the explosion.

A little later, the girl who delivered Nicole's breakfast urged her to eat. Rather than argue, she picked up a triangle of toast and took a tiny bite. Once the girl disappeared along her route, Nicole put the remains back on the plate and lay down again. After a while, she grew tired of watching the fireball dance on the ceiling and closed her eyes.

She had no idea how long she slept, but when she woke up, she was no longer alone. A man was sitting in the chair by the bed. He was nicely dressed in a charcoal suit with a dazzling white shirt and blue striped tie. He was good looking; in fact, this was the most striking thing about him. Beyond that, Nicole had a strong sense of recognition, the feeling that she'd met him somewhere before.

Perhaps thirty seconds passed before she realized who this was—and she was sitting upright with her heart pounding in her ears.

Reinhardt—for it was Reinhardt—was instantly on his feet, taking a few steps backward. "Sorry," he said. "I didn't mean to startle you. You see, I'm with the police, and I need to ask you a few questions. Here," he said, pulling his wallet out. "My identification."

She stared while he flipped the wallet open and held it out for her inspection. The ID bore a police insignia and a photo that identified him as Ronald H. Reinhardt, Detective Inspector, London Metropolitan Police.

Looking from the ID to the man standing before her, she could see that this was definitely the man in the picture.

"Mrs. Graves," he said, returning the wallet to his pocket, "Do you feel well enough to answer a few questions?"

"I guess—yes—all right." Her voice was barely more than a whisper. Only now, as he sat down and pulled out a notebook, did she decide she wasn't dreaming. Another realization followed.

"Wait a minute," she said. "I just spoke to the police. Inspector Keaton is investigating the explosion and a break-in that happened just after you stopped by."

"I'm aware of D.C. Keaton's involvement. My inquiries involve a separate matter. We're still looking for Mr. Lowry," he went on. "We haven't had any luck finding him, and we urgently need to do so. Perhaps you've had word from him and can tell us where he is."

"That day you came to the house," she said, "why didn't you say you were with the police?"

He gave a nod. "Good point. But I didn't want to cause you or any of Mr. Lowry's neighbors undue concern. The truth of the matter is that Mr. Lowry wasn't the object of our investigation. We were simply hoping he could assist us in our inquiry. That being the case, I'm sure you understand why it was simpler for me to introduce myself as Mr. Lowry's business associate." He gave a smile—lots of nice, even white teeth—as if he were pleased to have cleared up this matter.

"Okay," she said. "Now, let's see if I understand this." She paused to plump up her pillows, then leaned back. "The fact that you're here, asking questions about Lowry—does that mean the police now believe there's a link between Lowry's disappearance and the car bomb?"

His smile faded. "I'm sorry," he said, "but I'm afraid I wouldn't be willing to make that leap." For a moment, he gazed across the room, as if carefully considering his next words. Then he cleared his throat. "As I said, our main interest is another case we've been working on for some time, the one in which Mr. Lowry might be of help."

"I see," Nicole said. What she saw was that Reinhardt was trying to avoid explaining any more than he had to. Yet she had the feeling he knew perfectly well what was going on, that he could explain the whole mess.

"Now," he said, "Do you have any idea where Mr. Lowry is?"

She explained that the Lowrys had failed to show up in L.A., and she had no idea what had happened to them. She did give him the phone number in Texas, which was now firmly committed to memory. Once he'd entered this in his book, she said, "Can you tell me about the other case you're working on?"

"I'm afraid I'm not at liberty to discuss that," he said. "Believe me, I wish I were. Unfortunately…" He smiled and gave a shrug. "I wonder if you could put that question aside and tell me what you do know about Mr. Lowry. Unless you're too tired."

"No, really," she said, "I'm fine." In a way, this was true. The conversation had revived her with the hope that she might learn something.

"If you don't mind then," he said, "I'd like you to start at the very beginning—how you came to occupy the Lowrys' house."

She explained how Brad had found the Lowrys through someone in his company's London office.

"Can you give me the name of the person who recommended them?" Reinhardt asked.

"I have no idea," she said. "But I'll ask and get back to you." She had the feeling that Reinhardt didn't know that Brad was in police custody, and this was something she wasn't going to volunteer.

As she told her story, Reinhardt listened attentively. He was a good audience. Perhaps it was the way he sat forward in his chair with his eyes on hers. There were moments, however, when his gaze made her uncomfortable. She found herself omitting certain details, such as Brad's betrayal.

When she was done recounting the events leading up to the explosion, she mentioned her recent conversation with Detective Keaton and the fact that she'd rejected the theory that the two thugs had planted the car bomb.

Reinhardt nodded. "I'm afraid I would have to agree. It's unlikely those men could pull off a bombing like that. They're rank amateurs, acting on impulse. Assaulting a woman in a public place—what a very foolish and risky thing to do."

"But they got away with it," she said, wondering at his logic. "No one stopped them, and they haven't been caught."

"Forgive me," he said. "I'm afraid I put that rather badly. I wasn't discounting the menace of their behavior—the way they assaulted and threatened you. But it takes a great deal of professionalism to plant a bomb and walk away free. I'm talking about planning and advance work, discipline and coordination. I haven't spoken to D.C. Keaton, but I'm sure she's putting all the resources she can spare into apprehending them."

Nicole frowned. "If you haven't talked to Keaton, how did you know I was here?"

"I read the police report," he said. Then he regarded her a moment, before adding, "And, of course, your picture appeared in the paper.

"They misidentified me."

"So I noticed." He smiled slightly, as if acknowledging what an awful picture it had been. "Now, I just have one final question," he went on. "The Lowrys' tenant seems to have disappeared. Do you have any idea where she might be?"

Nicole felt a great weariness. "Alice hasn't disappeared. She told me she was going away for a few days. She left just before I went to the hotel. It was the day before ..." Her words trailed off as she remembered the bareness of Alice's room, the empty dresser and closet.

"Did she mention where she was going?"

Nicole shook her head.

"According to the police report, this woman represented herself as a nurse. Do you have any idea of her employer?"

"No." Nicole went cold, and it was an effort to keep her teeth from chattering. "She told me she worked for an agency, but she never said which one. Are you saying she's not a nurse?"

"There is some question about it," he said. "We've called every nursing agency in London as well as the Royal College of Nursing, but there's no one of that name." He put his notebook away and stood up. "I think that's enough for today. I don't want to overtire you."

"Wait," she said, "I want to ask you something. Do you think those men mistook me for Mrs. Lowry—like the paper did—because I'm staying in her house?"

With a sigh, Reinhardt sat down again. "Anything is possible," he said. "After fifteen years in police work, I'd be a fool not to admit that. But I've also learned not to jump to conclusions before all the evidence is in. At this point we have no idea who those men are or what they're after."

He was quiet for a long moment, staring at the opposite wall. "I will tell you this much," he finally said. "There are times when a member of the public—a tourist like yourself, for example—becomes inadvertently involved in an ongoing investigation. Perhaps she's witnessed something strange or disturbing and reports it to the police. If the investigation is very hush-hush, then she might not receive a satisfactory explanation. As you can imagine, she might go away feeling confused."

Nicole nodded, although she wasn't sure she understood. "Are you saying I stumbled into an undercover investigation?"

For a long moment, he stared at her, then got to his feet. "I'm afraid I've already said more than I should," he said. "I just want you to know that we're doing everything in our power to ensure your safety. I don't think you'll be hearing from these individuals again.

"Sorry, I almost forgot," he added. "If you do remember anything or hear from Mr. Lowry or the tenant, please give me a ring." He pulled his notebook out again and, after jotting something down, tore out the page and handed it to her.

After he was gone, Nicole remained sitting up in bed, studying the sheet of paper he'd given her. The name, "Reinhardt," was written in a loose, masculine scrawl. Beneath it was a phone number.

Replaying their conversation, she remembered things she hadn't consciously noticed at the time—the heady musk of his aftershave, the dimple in his chin, a scar over his right eye that made that eyebrow slightly irregular.

He had a nice smile, and there had been moments when she'd felt drawn to him. But there were other points in the conversation when his expression had turned grim and he had all the warmth of a hired killer.

She still rankled at the things he'd said about Alice, hinting that she wasn't who she said she was, that she had, in fact, lied about everything.

Nicole remembered that Alice was from Northern Ireland, a place called Ballycastle. She strained to recall what else Alice had said. The strife of the IRA, the Protestants, and the British government must have been part of her life when she was growing up. Nicole wondered which side her family had been on and how she felt about the use of violence. These were things they hadn't discussed.

Not that it made any difference. The trouble in Northern Ireland was history. Of course, there were occasional incidents. If Reinhardt had evidence that Alice was connected with terrorists, he hadn't mentioned it. Besides, no matter what he thought, Nicole was sure Alice would never engage in a wanton act of violence like booby-trapping a car.

She thought again of the moment Reinhardt had said goodbye, the way he'd lingered over their parting handshake, holding onto her hand until she'd withdrawn it. She found herself wondering if he'd actually come for some other reason than to ask about Lowry. Maybe he wanted to let her know the police were watching out for her. But that didn't make sense. If she were actually at risk, he would have said so; he'd have a moral obligation to warn her. Yet both Reinhardt and Keaton denied she was in any danger at all.

She thought about Reinhardt again—her initial alarm at seeing him here and the ID he'd been so quick to produce. She wondered about his credentials. Surely such things could be forged.

Thinking about it made her head hurt. The terrible feeling of numbness rendered all questions irrelevant. What did it matter if he was a policeman? What did anything matter?

She grabbed the extra blanket and, getting into bed, pulled it up to her chin. After a while, when her teeth stopped chattering and her feet no longer felt like ice, she drifted off to sleep.

ELEVEN

SINCE NICOLE'S CELL PHONE was dead, Brad's call came through the nurses' station. He had to shout to make himself heard over the roar of static. "I'm calling from the Paddington Green Police Station," he said. "You know, that's where they toss us terrorists."

"Are you all right?" As she said this, she realized how silly the question was. Of course he was all right, or he wouldn't be at the other end of the line, making lame jokes. She was also aware of the nurse leafing through papers on the other side of the counter. Although members of the staff had been scrupulously polite in avoiding the subject, Nicole could tell they knew about the bombing. She also suspected they knew the police had taken Brad away.

"Don't ask," he was saying. "The good news is they've given me my walking papers." A loud blast of static cut in, and it was a good fifteen seconds before his voice cut in again. "... contacted every agency in the civilized world trying to get more dirt on me. Some asshole at the office told them about my criminal past."

"I know," she said. "Keaton told me."

"She did?" He was quiet, then: "Listen, Nick, that business about me and Brenda. It's a complete crock."

"We'll discuss it later. Okay?"

"Right. Sorry," he said. "Stupid of me to bring it up on the phone. Twenty-four hours in this hole, and you lose all sense of privacy. Look, I'm on my way to the hospital."

"That's not necessary. I'm being released," she said. "I've asked them to call me a cab."

"No, no," he said. "You stay put. I'll get a cab here and swing by for you." As he went on, his voice gained enthusiasm. "So—you're well enough to come home. That's great! I'll be there as soon as I can. I love you."

Without responding, she set the phone in its cradle. "Don't bother about the cab," she told the nurse. "Someone is picking me up."

Back in her room, the bed had been stripped, the sheets and blankets cleared away. She lay down on the bare mattress, glad of the chance to rest before making the trip back to Chiswick. She wondered if the house was even habitable. Had the explosion blown the front door off? Still, they'd have to go back to the house, at least to get their things.

The numbness she'd felt since the blast made it hard to think. Worse yet, the flashbacks had become more vivid. For the hundredth time, she heard the deafening blast, felt the heat and fury of the flames. With it came the odor of the explosion—the chemical reek of the burning car, the rank, sweet smell of roasting flesh.

She kept thinking of Mr. McGiever, that poor old man. She wondered if he had family. He seemed to live alone, and she had the impression he was a widower. She was sorry now that she'd never thought to ask if he had any family. If he did, what must they be going through?

She thought of the men who'd planted the car bomb. What kind of people would leave loaded explosives in a well-populated area like Chiswick? What had been their intent—to kill someone or simply frighten her husband (whoever they thought he was) into giving them what they wanted?

Not that their intent mattered. They'd killed Mr. McGiever, and it was unthinkable to let them get away with it. Despite Keaton's reassurances, she wasn't convinced that the police were treating them as serious suspects. But maybe this was something she could do for McGiever—make sure the right people were brought to justice.

Then, Brad was standing over her, his hair wet and slicked back. He reeked of unfamiliar aftershave, a pungent mix of musk and spice. His suit—the same summer-weight tweed he'd been wearing when Keaton took him away—was even more rumpled. But his shirt looked fresh and crisply ironed. She took all this in without asking how he'd managed to shower and shave or where he'd found a clean shirt. Had he come directly from the police station or had he stopped somewhere on the way? These questions took shape and slowly fluttered away, but she lacked the energy to pursue them.

As he leaned forward to kiss her, she pulled away, swung her legs to the other side of the bed, and stood up.

"Look," he said. "I hope you don't believe any of that crap Keaton fed you. I mean, even she ended up admitting it was a pack of lies. Man, when I find out who was spreading that ..."

"Whatever you say." She busied herself gathering up her things.

"Hey, you don't believe me." His tone was wounded, calculated to make her feel guilty.

Instead of answering, she went to the mirror and began to apply her last touches of makeup while silence hovered between them like a malevolent spirit. When she was done with her lipstick, she turned and met his gaze. "I'm ready," she said.

"Fine." His voice had a funny catch in it. "Let's get out of here. We can't go back to that house. I think we should move to a hotel."

She could see through his thinking. The hotel. Then, as soon as she felt better, he'd put her on the next plane home. "No," she said. "All my things are at the house, and I'm just too wiped. I can't move anywhere today. If the front door needs fixing, you can get someone to do it. Because that's where I'm staying."

"Nick ..."

"It's settled," she said.

On the ride, he kept sneaking looks at her, chewing the inside of his cheek. Nicole rested her head against the seat and closed her eyes, hoping to discourage any attempts at conversation. She told herself that she was too numb to feel anything; a sick sensation in her stomach gave evidence to the contrary. In addition to the caustic mix of outrage and hurt, she also felt a deep ache of loneliness, the sense of having no one to turn to, no one who cared.

As the cab turned into the crush of traffic on High Street, Chiswick's main business drag, Brad reached forward to close the partition between them and the driver. "I just want you to understand," he said, "there's absolutely nothing between me and Brenda."

"Look, Keaton didn't have to tell me," she said. "I already knew you took Brenda to Liverpool."

His shoulders sank, as if the air had gone out of him. "Listen, Nick—it isn't like you think. I'm sorry I didn't let on about her going to Liverpool, but there was no way you could come, and I was afraid you'd get all weird about it. It was wrong to lie, but that doesn't mean I..."

"It doesn't matter."

"What are you talking about? Of course it matters."

She stared out the window a while before she answered. "I can't stop thinking about Mr. McGiever," she said quietly. "I can't get him out of my head. He was starting the car for me. Did you know that?" She turned to look at him. "If he'd showed up a minute or so later, it would have been me sitting in the car. And now it's like—this business between you and Brenda?—it just doesn't seem very important."

"I swear, Nick …"

"Please." She turned to stare out the window again. "Don't."

"She's nothing to me." He glanced at the driver on the other side of the partition and lowered his voice. "I love you. You know that."

Traffic had come to a halt while an ambulance, its siren wailing, tore past them along the center of the road.

Brad put his hand under her chin and turned her face until she had to look at him. "Give me another chance. I'll make it up to you."

To her surprise, a tear welled up and spilled down her cheek. "It's not just this business about Brenda," she said, "or that you lied about Liverpool. Remember the two men I told you about—the ones you refuse to believe blew up the Lowrys' car? When they first threatened me, I thought it was a case of mistaken identity or that they might be after Lowry. But now I'm wondering if you really do know them, and they're after you because of some shady deal you're involved in."

"Here we go again," Brad said. "That's totally…"

She studied him. His distress looked genuine. It was possible he was telling the truth, but she was convinced he was lying.

She wondered if they'd reached the point in their relationship she'd observed in several couples while their marriages were coming apart: It was that moment when all communication broke down because neither believed anything the other said. It marked the end of all trust and respect, the end of the marriage.

The cab had just entered a vast park with broad, curving roads. They continued on for a while before Brad broke the silence. "There's something I don't get," he said. "If you're so worried about those men following you, why won't you go back to L.A.? I mean, you'll have to be alone all day while I'm at work, and sometimes I've got to be out of town. I wish I could stay with you, Nick, I really do. But I can't."

As she listened, she wondered how he could say such things without an inkling of how insincere it sounded.

"I haven't made up my mind about what I'm going to do," she said. "But just suppose I did go back to L.A.? If those men would blow up an innocent bystander with a car bomb, they're capable of getting on a plane and flying to California. They're capable of anything."

"Did you tell Keaton your theory about who blew up the car?" When she didn't answer, he said, "She doesn't think it was those guys either, does she?"

"I don't care what she thinks."

The cab pulled up in front of the house, and they both sat forward to stare. The Lowrys' car was gone. On the spot where it had been, parked midway between the Lowrys' house and Mr. McGiever's, the pavement was marked with a sooty Rorschach splotch. The Lowrys' rosebushes had been reduced to charred sticks, but McGiever's property had taken the real force of the blast. Chunks of burnt debris were scattered everywhere, and scorched earth replaced the old man's carefully tended lawn and flowerbeds. The hedge that had once separated the two yards was a blackened skeleton.

Brad paid the driver then helped Nicole out of the cab. Walking through the front gate, they both stopped, mesmerized by the war zone that had once been the two front yards. Then Brad took her arm, and she noticed he was shaking almost as much as she was.

The Lowrys' front door was blackened from the explosion, but it was closed and turned out to be locked. Inside, the house was filled with the lingering stench of scorched metal and chemicals. Brad opened some windows then followed her upstairs. His things were still heaped in the pile where she'd thrown them before leaving for the hotel.

"Christ," he said. "We've been burglarized."

"No," Nicole said quietly. "It was me."

Brad stared at her in consternation. "My God, Nick! What on earth?"

"The afternoon you left for Liverpool," she said. "I was looking for Brenda's number."

He stared at her a moment longer. Then, without a word, he began picking up the mess. Nicole changed from her street clothes into a nightgown and got into bed.

It seemed as if she'd only closed her eyes for a moment when she heard him say, "Wake up, sleepyhead. Careful—I'm putting this on your lap."

She sat up as he placed an old-fashioned white wicker breakfast tray in front of her. Besides the mug of coffee, it held a newspaper, a vase with daisies from the back garden, and a shrunken looking grilled sandwich on a large white china dinner plate. The sandwich had been quartered, the crusts trimmed, but all other exposed surfaces were charred. It had a squished appearance, as if he'd used a very dull knife.

She took a sip of the coffee and grimaced. It wasn't coffee at all but tea—black and thick and bitter.

She put down the cup and glanced over at Brad, who was sitting backwards on the chair at the desk. He was gazing into space, absorbed in his own thoughts. Her glance seemed to rouse him, for he immediately got up and moved the phone from the desk to the bedside table. "Well, I'd better shove off and face the music downtown," he said. "There's a nice obit for McGiever in this morning's paper. I put it on your tray. Look, you're not planning to go anywhere, are you? I mean, just promise you won't. Okay?"

"I'll be right here," she said. "All day."

"If you get it in your head to take a walk or something, pick up your phone and let me know. Because if I call the house and don't get an answer..." He let his voice trail off, then added, "Damn it, Nicole, you don't understand what I'm going through. This car-bombing thing absolutely scared the shit out of me. I guess it made me realize just how precious you are to me. There's just one reason I want you to go home: I know you'll be safe there. And I don't have any nefarious motive …"

"What kind of an idiot do you think I am?" Her voice was almost a shout. "You lied about taking Brenda to Liverpool. Why should I believe anything you say?"

He put his hands up, as if to ward off a blow. "It's over." His voice was barely audible. "I'll tell her."

For a moment, her mind refused to take this in. Then understanding came, striking her with the force of fresh betrayal. Despite all evidence to the contrary—some part of her had hoped that she was wrong.

"I'll tell Brenda we're through," he said. Then he added in a small, cracked voice, "I'll make it up to you, Nick. You'll see."

She ignored this, grabbing the newspaper and rifling through until the pages fairly rattled with anger. Meanwhile, Brad hovered in the doorway. She could feel him staring, as if he had more to say.

She refused to look at him. By the time she found the article about the old man—among the obituaries on page twenty-six—Brad had clumped down the stairs and slammed the front door.

BOMB BLAST VICTIM RESPECTED CIVIL SERVANT

The victim of yesterday's bomb blast in Chiswick, Edgar McGiever, 67, was a retired manager of the maintenance department of the Greater London Council's Board of Public Works.

McGiever, a veteran of the British Army, had been a widower for several years. He is survived by two sons and six grandchildren. He was an active member of St. Bethany's Church and leader of their choir. He was also a luminary in the Chiswick Thespians, a local amateur

> theatrical group that performs children's plays to benefit a hospital for children with AIDS and cancer.
>
> "He was a quiet man, except when he appeared in one of our little theatricals," said the Rev. Wilford Roland, vicar of St. Bethany's. "He was a true good Samaritan..."

Nicole closed her eyes and, once more, the flames rose up, engulfing the car. She could feel its ferocious heat, hear its roar. She wondered if there had been much pain, or if the blast had snuffed him out instantly.

At that moment, the sound of knocking at the front door made her jump. She pushed the tray away, scrambled out of bed, and grabbed her robe. It couldn't be Brad. He was supposed to take the Lowrys' extra key and engage the deadbolt from the outside. Had he forgotten? My God, she thought, whatever had possessed her to think she'd be all right alone?

She tiptoed to the bedroom door and looked out into the hall. Barely daring to breathe, she padded softly to the top of the stairs and peered down. Nothing. As she crept down the steps, the front door came into view. She caught sight of a pile of envelopes lying on the floor and felt a cool flush of relief. The noise she'd heard had only been the postman delivering the mail, the clattering of the mail slot cover as it dropped back in place.

When she reached the front hallway, she picked up the envelopes. She checked to be sure the deadbolt was engaged—sure enough, Brad had locked it from the outside, just as he'd promised.

She put the letters on the front table and began walking around the house, checking the windows, the back door, the door to the basement. Everything was locked up tightly.

In the kitchen, she was fixing some herbal tea when something occurred to her: Why not call Keaton and ask her to find out more about Reinhardt. Maybe she'd refuse, but on the other hand...

She located Keaton's phone number and, somewhat to her surprise, the switchboard put her right through. After describing Reinhardt's visit, Nicole said, "I wonder if you could find out if he's really a member of the police force. His credentials looked authentic, but I'm no expert. I thought it was strange that you hadn't mentioned him. Don't you people usually work as a team?"

"The visit you describe is a bit unusual," Keaton agreed. "And I'm not acquainted with Inspector Reinhardt. But you have to keep in mind that the Metropolitan Police is a very large organization. Let me check into this. I'll give you a ring as soon as I have some information. Meanwhile, if you happen to run into him again, ask him to give me a call."

"Of course," Nicole said. After they'd hung up, she realized that she was going to do her best to avoid any more conversations with Reinhardt, at least until Keaton checked him out.

She went back to the hall table, grabbed the mail, and carried it into the living room. There, she flopped down on the couch and began to sort through the stack. There was a flyer from a plumbing firm and another offering reduced rates on treatment for "rising damp," whatever that was. An oversized postcard featured half a dozen photos of heaping platters of food, printed in aggressively unappetizing colors. On the other side, the card offered a twofer coupon for an Indian restaurant.

More intriguing was a cream-colored envelope hand-addressed to Mr. and Mrs. F. H. Lowry. The letter, as it turned out, was a mass-mailed invitation to invest in a time-share resort in an area described as the "British Riviera."

She picked up the final envelope and, turning it over, was surprised to see that it was addressed to her. There was a London postmark but no return address.

She tore it open. The letter seemed to be typed on an old-fashioned typewriter. Nicole wondered where one of those could be found in working order:

Nicole:

> I'm taking a terrible chance sending this, but I want you to know I had nothing to do with the car bomb that killed the neighbor. I know the police are looking for me. I had my own reasons for dropping out of sight, but now I'm afraid they think this is proof I'm guilty when I'm not. I am against all violence and killing. You must believe me.
>
> I have to talk to you, Nicole. Please get in touch with me through the people I told you about. I don't dare say more in case someone else finds this.

The letter was unsigned, but she had no doubt who had written it. She read it a second time. For the life of her, she couldn't remember Alice talking about anyone except her brother, and she hadn't mentioned where he was. All afternoon something tugged at the edge of her memory, something she couldn't retrieve.

Twelve

Afternoon faded into early evening, and still Nicole remained on the couch, gazing through the double French doors. As the shifting light deepened the greens of the foliage, swathing it in shadow, she pursued her thoughts.

At last the silence was broken when the jingling of keys and slamming of the front door announced Brad's return. He came in balancing two big bags of groceries and an armload of long-stemmed red roses.

She stared at the bouquet. The roses were exquisite—a deep pinky red with long stems and buds just beginning to unfurl. The extravagance of the gesture—its patent transparency—made her both sad and angry. "Thanks," she said. "There's a vase in the hall closet."

He went away and, after a few minutes, came back with the roses stuffed into a bulbous white china vase. Even before he set it on the lamp table nearby, her thoughts had moved on.

She'd done nothing about dinner. But when she heard the clank of pots and utensils, she realized dinner was taking care of itself. Eventually, Brad reappeared in the doorway, "Do you want a tray so you can eat in here?" he said.

His voice had a false heartiness, and she could tell he was cowed by her silence, by where it might be leading.

"Nope," she said. "I'm perfectly able to get up." Until this moment, she hadn't been able to imagine sitting down to dinner with him. But somehow the fear she seemed to have inspired in him lifted her spirits. As she followed him into the little dining room, she rather enjoyed thinking of herself as a volcano about to erupt.

Dinner looked surprisingly good. There were grilled lamb chops with bacon and sausages, and the bacon was hardly burned at all. To go with the meat, he'd made instant mashed potatoes puddled with butter. The canned spinach, lukewarm and unseasoned, was less of a success.

For the first time since the explosion, she felt hungry. But when she sampled the food, her sense of taste was still tainted by the metallic stench of burnt car, and she couldn't eat more than a few bites.

While she toyed with her food, Brad did his best to fill the silence. For Nicole, it was too much effort to listen, much less respond. Her numbness had deepened into something more paralyzing. The CAT scan at the hospital had detected nothing wrong, but she wondered if she'd been injured in some way the machine couldn't detect.

After his attempts at conversation sputtered and died, Brad began to describe his afternoon at work. As he explained, he'd been afraid the arrest would ruin him with the company, perhaps even get him fired. But Bud Cooper himself, SoftPac's CEO, had personally called him from the company's limousine somewhere on the Ventura Freeway. After asking about Nicole, Coop had gone on to express outrage about Brad's overnight detention. He said he'd called the American Embassy, and Brad could expect an apology from the police.

As he talked, Nicole noticed that he was no longer pale and drawn as he'd been earlier in the day. Despite a certain tension when he glanced in her direction, his face was relaxed, his cheeks rosy. She had the feeling his transformation was due to this recent vote of confidence from SoftPac's top boss.

She thought of Brenda. The prospect of ending the affair didn't seem to have upset Brad much. Was Brenda really of such minor consequence, or had he postponed his talk with her? Perhaps he was simply waiting for Nicole to go home; then he wouldn't have to do anything about Brenda at all.

At that moment Nicole heard her cell phone chime.

It was Stephanie. "My God, Nick," she said. "Brad told me what happened. You weren't seriously hurt, were you? You must be in shock though, right? When are you coming home?" She spoke in a rush, not waiting for an answer to one question before hurrying on to the next.

"I'm fine," Nicole said quietly. "It was upsetting, but I'm okay. Really. Except for a couple of bruises and a bump on the head. Actually, it's amazing how all right I am."

"You don't sound all right," Stephanie said.

"Well," Nicole said, reaching for an explanation. "I do have a little headache, and I took a pain pill." Even to herself, her voice sounded strained. It was the effect of swallowing back an avalanche of unshed tears, brought on by the sound of her sister's voice, the weight of all the things she couldn't tell Stephanie. The degree of anxiety this tale would inspire in her sister was too much to contemplate.

"Look," Nicole said. "It's my first day out of the hospital, and I'm wiped." Then she added, "But I'm fine. Really. I'll call you tomorrow, and we'll talk."

"Oh, no," Stephanie said. "You're not hanging up until you tell me when you're coming home."

"I'll have to think about it," Nicole said. "Tomorrow. We'll talk. Okay?" Then, without waiting for the argument that was sure to come, she said, "Bye," putting the cell back in her purse.

About thirty seconds passed before the cell started ringing again. Nicole handed it to Brad, signaling that she was on her way to bed. Brad, who was listening to Stephanie, rolled his eyes and nodded that he understood.

On her way upstairs, she could hear his voice rise as he tried to interrupt Stephanie's harangue. Nicole couldn't help smiling. Her little sister was giving him hell. He was in for at least fifteen minutes of castigation for not insisting strongly enough that she go home.

Entering the quiet bedroom, she was profoundly grateful to be alone and fell asleep almost immediately.

She awoke around midnight when Brad tiptoed into the room and slipped under the covers next to her. Oddly enough, she didn't mind him lying there—as long as he didn't touch her. This she managed to avoid by settling at the edge of the mattress, as far away from him as possible. Meeting no resistance, Brad invaded the unoccupied territory in the center of the bed.

Later, unable to go back to sleep, she realized who Alice had been alluding to in her letter: her friends who ran the little hotel. She'd even written its name, address, and phone number on a slip of paper. Once Nicole decided to go to the Dorchester, she hadn't given Alice's hotel recommendation another thought. Now she couldn't even think of its name. What on earth had she done with the note? She sat up and hugged her legs to her chest, trying to remember.

Brad stirred and turned over. "Wha…?" he muttered groggily. "What's wrong?"

Nicole pushed back the covers and got up. "Can't sleep," she said. "I think I'll go downstairs for a glass of milk."

He flopped back on the pillow. She waited until his breathing grew slow and regular before ducking into the closet, closing the door behind her, and switching on the light.

Her skirt, blouse, and jacket, which she'd been wearing at the time of the explosion, had been wadded up and tossed on the closet shelf.

She checked, but the pockets were empty. As she was putting the clothes back on the shelf, the bed gave another creak. "Nicole?" Brad called. "Is that you?"

"Just looking for my slippers." She turned off the closet light, grabbed her purse from the dresser, and hurried downstairs. In the kitchen, she sat down at the table and dumped out the contents of the purse—her wallet, makeup case, a few loose coins, a pack of Kleenex. Next, she emptied the wallet, pulling out her dwindling supply of pound notes, receipts, credit cards. No slip of paper.

She went to the counter and opened the phone book to the hotel listings, slowly running her finger down the columns. None of them was familiar.

As she sat there thinking, she was aware of the darkness beyond the kitchen window, the fact that while she couldn't see out, anyone who might be outside would be able to see in.

She flipped off the light, pulled a kitchen stool to the window and opened it, then perched with her elbows on the sill, gazing out. In the glow of the full moon, the shrubs that lined the fence were still except for an occasional breeze that set them trembling.

The night was surprisingly mild. The stink of the explosion had finally cleared from her nostrils, and she caught a sweet scent on the breeze that might have been orange blossoms or honeysuckle. It took her back to the most magical evenings of her childhood, Santa Ana nights when she and Stephanie would play outside long after dark.

On special occasions—the Fourth of July, Labor Day, the arrival of houseguests who needed the beds in the girls' rooms—the two sisters were granted permission to sleep outside in their little pup tents. It was the late eighties, early nineties, an era when the threat of violence in their own backyard was still unimaginable.

Free of supervision, the two of them plotted their own crime wave. Using Nicole's telescope, they'd spy on the neighbors and dream up escapades that involved climbing into adjacent yards.

Stephanie was the one with the wildest ideas, but she'd quickly lose courage. Not only would she lack the nerve to carry out a dare; she'd end up begging Nicole to abandon dares that she herself had issued. But Nicole, once challenged, could not be dissuaded. She'd set off on her quest while Stephanie stayed behind, weeping with fright.

There was almost no dare Nicole wouldn't accept, like the time she'd climbed through a neighbor's open kitchen window to steal ice cream bars for the two of them. The mission failed, however, when the neighbor, a famous crosspatch named Mrs. Gilles, heard the rattle of the screen and came downstairs to investigate. Nicole had escaped detection by ducking into the broom closet, where she had to remain for a good fifteen or twenty minutes, while the old lady finished clumping around in search of a burglar.

Remembering, she wondered what had possessed her. Even into adulthood, her quiet impulsiveness, her willingness to act after the briefest reflection, persisted. Since the explosion, however, her sense of invincibility had evaporated. That blast, the moment when the hot wind swept her off her feet, had brought an epiphany—the understanding that she wasn't immune to failure and disaster, that no one goes on winning forever.

The breeze had turned chilly, and she was actually shivering. As she was closing the window, she remembered it had been chilly the night Alice had left, cool and cloudy enough to warrant wearing a raincoat. She found it hanging in the front hall. Sure enough, in the right hand pocket was the scrap of paper. Under the word "Cartwright," were the address and phone number.

Nicole hurried to the front hall table to get her cell phone from her purse.

"Cartwright Hotel?" The desk clerk sounded sleepy and confused, as if he wasn't quite sure.

"I'm looking for an Alice McConnehy," she said. "I wonder if someone there might know how I can get in touch with her."

"Just a minute, miss," he said. After a brief pause, he was back. "Sorry, we've no guest of that name."

"She's not a guest. She's a friend of the people who run the hotel."

"I'm afraid I can't help you much there. But the proprietor will be in tomorrow around 9:00 a.m. Would you like to ring back then?"

Nicole hesitated, struck by the idea that someone might be able to listen in on her cell phone. With so many people looking for Lowry, and the police now searching for Alice as well, this seemed like a real possibility.

"Maybe I'll just drop by," she said. "Thanks for your help."

In the morning, after Brad had left the house, she got dressed and called a cab. Traffic grew dense as they approached the neighborhood surrounding the hotel, Marble Arch. She reached into her purse and turned off her phone. She didn't want her mission interrupted.

The cab ground to a halt a few blocks from the great triumphal arch that gave the area its name. She could see it through her window, straddling the street and looming incongruously over the buildings nearby. When, after a few minutes, they still hadn't budged, she asked the cabby to let her out. "I think it would be faster if I walked."

"You're probably right, ducks," he said, as she handed her fare though the window. "But I'd advise you to keep an eye on your handbag."

As she started toward her destination, she looked around and decided that, despite what the cabby had said, the neighborhood was safe, if slightly shabby. She felt better this morning. It was good to be out walking in the brisk morning air, to have a sense of purpose.

Before long the neighborhood began to change, taking on a Middle Eastern flavor with exotic lettering in the store windows. Black-veiled women perused crates of fruits and vegetables displayed in front of the many small food shops. Men in red-and white-checkered kufiyas sipped coffee at sidewalk cafes. They had a clear division of roles, she noticed, with no women in the cafes and no men shopping at the markets.

Glancing at herself in a store window, she noticed a man walking about thirty feet behind her. A minute or so later, as she'd paused to recheck the hotel's address, she looked around and noticed that he'd stopped, too. He was standing in front of an abandoned shop and appeared to be studying something in the window.

She was surprised when she realized it was Reinhardt. He was dressed differently—this time in a tan windbreaker, Levi's, and a baseball cap that made it hard to see his face—but she would have known him anywhere.

Why, she wondered, was he following her? And why on earth was he so obvious about it? Weren't police inspectors trained to avoid being spotted by the people they were following?

As these questions occurred to her, she realized he must be following her because he thought she would lead him to Alice.

She resumed walking again, this time more quickly. She slipped through a group of veiled women, all pushing baby carriages, who were congregated in front of a butcher shop. Once past the crowd, she ran for the next corner and darted into the side street.

She took refuge in the first doorway she came to and waited, looking around and trying to catch her breath. There was no hope of retreating into the building. Attached to the door was a heavy lock box and a FOR LEASE sign. At any moment, she expected

Reinhardt to come hurrying around the corner looking for her. She would have no choice but to confront him, ask him what he thought he was doing. Then, of course, she'd have to give up her plan to stop by the hotel.

Seconds and then minutes passed, but Reinhardt did not appear. She checked her watch and waited another full minute before she peeked out. Cautiously, she made her way to the corner and looked up and down Edgware Road. The local population was still out in force, but there was no sign of Reinhardt. She began to wonder if she'd been mistaken.

She pulled the slip of paper out of her pocket, studied it and—after a last glance around—hurried the two remaining blocks to the address she was looking for, 346 Penfold Place. It was a modest, glass-fronted building that looked more like a bank than a hotel.

In the small, overheated lobby, several veiled women were packed onto two small sofas with a horde of young children. The little ones, who ranged in age from toddler to five or six, crawled, slid, and climbed about on the sofas and over the women. They rarely dropped to the floor, and when they did, they instantly hopped back up again. Nicole's guess was that they'd been forbidden to run around the lobby, and this was the only game left. She couldn't imagine it was much fun for the women. Their faces—all but the eyes—were covered with veils, making it impossible to guess what they were thinking.

When Nicole explained she'd come to speak to the manager, the desk clerk lifted a section of the counter and led her back to a small, untidy office where a gray-haired woman was working at a computer. She stood up and gave Nicole a tentative smile. She was slightly built with deeply-lined skin and eyes of startling blue. Hearing her voice, Nicole felt a sudden surge of hope. The woman's accent was identical to Alice's.

"I'm Mrs. Hall," she said when Nicole introduced herself. "Timothy left a note about your call. I wish I could help. But I'm afraid I don't know—what did you say your friend's name was?"

"Alice McConnehy," Nicole said. "She told me she knew the people who own this hotel."

Mrs. Hall looked puzzled. "There's only me. I'm the proprietor."

"Maybe you'd know her by sight," Nicole said. "She's about my size and has red hair and rather prominent blue eyes."

"Is she in some sort of trouble?" the woman said.

Nicole shrugged. "She hasn't done anything wrong. I'm sure of it."

Mrs. Hall slowly shook her head. "I'm afraid I don't know anyone answering that description. I hope you don't mind me saying so, but you look all in. Why don't you have a sit down and let me bring you some tea."

"No, thanks," Nicole said. "But I would like to call a cab."

The woman insisted on making the call herself then asked Nicole to wait in her office. "It will take ten or fifteen minutes. The driver will know to come in and ask for you. Now make yourself comfortable, and I'll bring you some tea."

This time Nicole said, "That would be nice. If it's not too much trouble."

"No trouble at all."

As soon as the woman left, Nicole began to wander around the room. She studied pictures on the wall—colored photos of woodland lakes—and glanced over stacks of papers on the desk. It occurred to her that the woman might be lying, that she might have her own reasons for not admitting she knew Alice. She took a more careful look around, as if something in the room might yield up a clue, but all she saw were hotel bills and invoices for goods like detergent, toilet paper, bath soap, and paper towels.

She was behind the desk, reading the information displayed on the computer screen—room charges for someone named Hazzan Abduhl—when Mrs. Hall walked in carrying a small tray. Nicole moved quickly away from the computer, but if the woman was annoyed, she gave no sign of it. She glanced at the displayed record and said, "They're all Arabs, every one of them. The whole of Kuwait moves up here for the summer. Not that I'm complaining, mind you."

While Nicole drank her tea, Mrs. Hall asked where she was from and what it was like living in L.A. Looking into the woman's earnest blue eyes, Nicole decided that Mrs. Hall was probably telling the truth about not knowing Alice. It must have been someone else who Alice wanted her to contact. But try as she might, she couldn't remember Alice mentioning anyone except the people who owned this hotel.

The woman appeared to be in no great hurry to return to her work. Nicole, on the other hand, was beginning to feel tired and anxious to get back to the house; it seemed an eternity before word came that the cab was waiting in front.

"I wish you luck finding your friend," Mrs. Hall said as she showed Nicole back to the lobby. Then she added, "Take care of yourself, Mrs. Graves. We have a lot of crime in London, pickpockets and robbers. They like to prey on tourists. The people who stay here—poor things—they're like lambs to the slaughter."

Nicole was on her way back through the lobby, past the veiled women and their children, when Mrs. Hall came dashing out carrying her raincoat. "Wait! You left your mac."

By the time she climbed into the cab, Nicole was exhausted. Her head and, in fact, her whole body ached. The morning had been a complete waste of time.

She asked the cabby to let her off in front of a pharmacy on Chiswick's main shopping street so she could buy some aspirin. She planned to take a couple before walking back to the house. Maybe the fresh air would do her good.

She got out of the cab, pulled some money out of her purse, and, after checking to be sure it was enough, thrust it into the cabby's waiting hand.

The wind was brisk. When she put her hands in her coat pockets to warm them, she noticed a piece of paper in the right one. She took it out and stared at it, a folded sheet. On one side, a message had been printed in large block letters. It read, "Do not open until you are alone." She glanced at the warning, then shoved it, still-folded, back in her pocket as she hurried into the pharmacy.

While she waited in line to pay for the aspirin, she kept reaching into her pocket to touch the folded paper, fingering its edges. Once she was outside again, she paused and glanced around. Except for a small crowd waiting for the bus, the street was almost empty. At the bus stop, the people appeared harmless and preoccupied—two plump women who might have been twins carried string shopping bags; a small cluster of girls giggled; a dirty-faced, disheveled old man dozed on one of the benches. A few yards away, a teenage boy with long greasy hair slouched against the wall, his face buried in a book.

None of them were paying the least bit of attention to her. She was taking one last look around before pulling out the note, when she spotted Reinhardt. He was half a block away, standing at the end of a line waiting at an ATM. At that very moment, he glanced in her direction, and their eyes met; for Nicole, the impact of that eye contact was like an electric shock.

She turned and, after a quick glance to her left, started across the street. The bleat of a horn and the screech of tires nearby almost made her heart stop. On her right, coming at her from the wrong side of the road, a car screeched to a stop a few inches away. A man stuck his head out of the window and screamed something she couldn't understand. Blindly, she ran the rest of the way across the street. She hurried through the first open doorway, finding herself in a tiny grocery store.

Her heart was still pounding as she made her way around crates of apples, tomatoes, grapes, lettuce, and squash to peer through the front window. Across the street, there was no longer anyone in line at the ATM. The sidewalk in front of the bank was empty.

She killed a few minutes cruising the aisles. She settled on some items she thought she could use—a loaf of bread, milk, and cereal. She used her last £10 note to pay for her purchases and hurried out of the store. Only when she reached the Lowrys' corner did she allow herself to look back. The street was empty.

She ran the rest of the way home. Once inside, she slammed the front door and locked it. Leaning against it, she pulled out the note:

Nicole:

Sorry to send you chasing all over London, but I have to be very careful. I want to talk to you, Nicole, and I wonder if you would bring something I left at the house. It's an envelope I hid under a loose floorboard in the upstairs hall by the door to the bathroom. The carpet is tacked down, so you'll have to rip it up. You'll find more tacks in the linen cupboard.

It's just some money and a key to a storage locker. If it isn't there, the police will have taken it. I don't think this is likely, but even if they did, please come anyway.

Meet me tomorrow morning at 11:30 at the Pig and Whistle Coffee Shop at Canary Wharf. Don't come by taxi because someone might follow you. The tube is best: Take the District Line to Edgware Road Line at Earl's Court, then to the Central Line at Notting Hill Gate. Get off at Bank and follow the blue signs (down two flights of escalators) to the Docklands Light Rail. Get off at Canary Wharf. The trip will take about an hour.

If you think you're being followed, turn around and go back. If you don't come, I'll know what happened.

Take care, Nicole. There is something I must talk to you about. You are in danger.

Locating the loose floorboard was easy. She had, in fact, noticed it creak the first time she walked through the house. Once the carpet was rolled back, she pulled up the board and found the envelope.

She was just opening it, when she remembered she'd turned off her phone. She pulled it out and turned it on. It rang almost immediately.

"Where were you?" Brad said. "I must have called a dozen times. If you hadn't answered just now, I was coming home."

"I was reading a book in the yard," she said. "I guess I fell asleep."

He was quiet a moment. Then, in a gentler tone, "Please—just stay in the house 'til you're better. I'm really worried about you. Look, about tonight—I've got to meet with some people, and—well—I don't want to leave you alone."

"Don't worry about it." She'd opened the envelope and was staring at the contents. Just as Alice had said, it held a half dozen £50 notes and a key.

"So I invited them over to our place," Brad was saying. "There will be six of us. I'm having food delivered. You don't have to worry about a thing. We can meet in the dining room, so we won't be in your way. We'll be there around 7:00, 7:30. I mean, is that all right?"

"Sure," she said absently. "Fine."

As she hung up, she thought of Brenda and wondered if he'd have the nerve to invite her, and if she'd actually have the chutzpah to come. Had Brad told her yet that their romance was over? Had he told her anything?

She tacked the carpet back down, using the hammer and nails she found in the linen closet. Then she put the envelope in her purse. Before Brad and the others arrived, she fixed herself an omelet, ate it, and washed the dishes.

The knocker on the front door sounded, and there they were—Brad, three disgruntled-looking Brits, and Brenda, hanging back at the edge of the porch. From the anguished expression on Brenda's face, Nicole decided that, indeed, Brad had spoken to her.

Nicole smiled and greeted the men as Brad introduced them. When he was done, she turned to Brenda and said, "It's so good to see you again." She was careful to insert just the right degree of warmth she'd be expected to bestow on her husband's administrative aide.

Before the food arrived, Nicole made her excuses and retreated upstairs. From the spare bedroom, she located a small black and white TV, which she moved to the night table in the Lowrys' room. She got into bed and flipped channels until she found something that looked mindless enough to suit her mood. The show turned out to be a sitcom about a cabinet minister, a man perennially in trouble with his wife and his mistress, who also happened to be his administrative assistant. The sound of the TV had to compete with the hum of voices floating up from the meeting. Despite the noise and her awareness of Brenda's presence downstairs, it wasn't long before Nicole was asleep.

Thirteen

As Nicole entered the station, she expected a long, steep escalator to plunge her into the depths of the London Underground. But Turnham Green, with its small station, offered no such drama. Passing through one of the turnstiles, she walked down a short flight of stairs into the brightness of an outdoor station. True, it was below street level but hardly worthy of being called a subway.

She kept looking around. So far, there was no sign of Reinhardt. He hadn't followed her to the station; she was sure of that. And now, with the exception of a few old ladies and herself, the terminal was empty.

It was a good five minutes before a train roared in. At the front of the car, she chose an empty seat in a row facing backward so she could keep her eye on the door. Once settled, she reached into her purse for Alice's note and reread her instructions. At the first stop, she studied each new passenger, noting height and gender, then looking closely to be sure Reinhardt hadn't managed to assume a new size and shape. She took note of who settled in for a long ride and who remained standing, poised to depart after a station or two.

After a few minutes, the train entered a tunnel that took it beneath the city. She leaned back and closed her eyes, trying to relax.

Breakfast that morning had been stressful; she thought Brad would never leave. He'd lingered over his coffee, dawdled over his laptop, and hurried back upstairs several times for things he'd forgotten. Clearly, he was hanging around, hoping for forgiveness. He had the same cringing aura of remorse she'd seen in Arnold, their terrier, when he was punished for chewing something up—a pair of shoes, an eyeglass case complete with glasses, and, on one occasion, the electric razor Brad had left lying on the edge of the sink.

Rather than inspiring sympathy, Brad's demeanor reinforced her suspicion that he was hiding something beyond the now-admitted affair with Brenda. Nicole couldn't stop wondering how much trouble he might be in.

The train slowed and pulled to a stop. When she looked around, she realized it was Earl's Court, where she had to change trains. This was easily done, and the new train waited while more people poured in. By the time it started up again, the car was packed, and Nicole could see nothing beyond the man standing in the aisle next to her.

At last the train began to slow again, and the sign outside the window told her this was her stop, Notting Hill Gate. As she got to her feet, a man at the rear of the car caught her eye. He wore a Panama hat and was a couple of inches taller than the people around him. She couldn't quite see his face but there was something familiar about him—his posture, the set of his shoulders.

For a long moment she stood frozen to the spot. As soon as her initial shock passed, she had an irresistible urge to run, to bolt from the train. She'd just begun to push her way down the aisle when a bell rang. The doors trembled, then snapped shut, and the train was on its way again.

It was too late to resume her seat; someone had taken it. She made her way through the crush of passengers to a spot near the door. There, she hung onto a pole and chewed her fingernails, trying to figure out what to do. She was aware of the man's reflection in the window. He seemed to be edging closer while studying the subway map on the opposite wall.

A plan began to hatch. As they pulled into the next station, she remained facing away from the door, as if she had no interest in getting off. The signs identified the stop as Paddington, which was an intersection of major subway lines. As passengers filed off, and more got on, Nicole waited.

At last the bell rang, and the doors made their first trembling pass at closing. At that moment, just before they closed in earnest, she bolted from the train and sprinted along the platform toward the exit sign.

As she passed through the archway into the stairwell, she heard an alarm go off behind her—a loud, excited oinking sound. She couldn't resist looking back. All the waiting passengers had shoved their way onto the train, which was now sitting on the tracks with its doors closed. All doors but one, that is, which was wedged slightly ajar by the arm and shoulder of someone inside.

If there was a mechanism that made the doors spring open when an arm or leg became stuck in its jaws, it wasn't working. The man—Reinhardt or whoever he was—was using his free arm in a desperate attempt to pry the doors open. She turned and ran.

The shriek of the alarm followed her up the escalator until she reached the top. When the sound was no longer audible, she glanced back, but the only people behind her were travelers like herself, standing at ease while the moving staircase carried them to the top. There was no one in pursuit.

Her stomach still churning, she hurried on. After checking the subway map again, she realized she had to transfer to the Central

Line at Oxford Circus. That was what fascinated her about the underground. You could get from any point in Central London to any other point through dozens of different routes, using a network of trains that crisscrossed the city.

She made her way down to the platform and waited less than a minute before the next train came. Once she found a seat and got herself settled, she noticed that the sick feeling in her stomach was gone, although she was still wary, on the lookout for Reinhardt. She checked the map again and realized she'd boarded the wrong train. She was on the Victoria Line, not the Central Line. She'd have to get off and figure out a new route.

When the train pulled into Victoria Station, she got off and followed other passengers and through a series of connecting passages. She was about to ask directions when she noticed a tourist information sign pointing to the enormous escalator up ahead. The escalator carried her up, up, up, into the roar of a building large enough to hold several airplane hangars. At the top was a huge glass dome, made up of thousands of small panes of glass like a Victorian exposition building. A warren of shops had been constructed inside, converting the structure into a modern shopping mall.

Like an airline terminal, the place was packed. Impatient commuters stood in disorganized rows, staring up at a huge black and white electronic board, which was constantly being updated with the latest train arrivals, departures, and track assignments. Others fidgeted in long lines, waiting to buy tickets or get information about train routes and times.

The line in front of the Tourist Information kiosk was especially long. As soon as she saw it, she realized it would be a mistake to get in line to ask directions. If Reinhardt somehow did manage to pick up her trail, he'd spot her the moment he walked into the station.

On the opposite side, she noticed a coffee shop, its interior too dim to make out the faces of the people inside. She headed toward it, glancing back over her shoulder. Her plan was to walk into the coffee shop and ask one of the employees how to get to the right platform for the next leg of the journey. Then she'd spend a minute or two scanning the station from the other side of the darkened glass before exiting back into the teeming hub of commuters.

As she walked in and saw the buffet table, the smell of food made her realize she hadn't eaten much in days. She felt lightheaded. Why not grab a quick snack? She could use the time to take a careful look around the station. She picked up a tray and selected a Danish pastry with thin apple slices on top and a small assortment of cheese. From the cashier, she ordered a pot of tea. After glancing around, she chose a table near the window.

She ate quickly, keeping an eye on her watch while scanning the station for Reinhardt. Hidden away in the safety of the coffee shop, she began to realize how unlikely it was that he'd turn up. Even if he'd managed to get off at Paddington, he wouldn't know what line she'd taken or in which direction. Nor would he have any way of anticipating this stop at Victoria.

At that moment, a tall man in a Panama hat emerged from the corner of the station where the escalators were located. He was too far away to make out his face, but the sight of that hat brought her to her feet.

Taking a desperate look around, she darted through the nearest doorway into a tiny, overheated kitchen. The air was heavy with the smell of onions being chopped by a young man in a chef's hat. He turned to look at her. "You can't come in, miss. This 'ere kitchen's closed to the public." His eyes were red and running from the onions, and he needed a shave. A cigarette dangled from his lips.

Nicole fixed him with a look of desperation. "Oh, please don't make me go back out there," she gasped. "I was looking for the rear exit. My ex-husband is following me." She paused to look around, making sure no one had followed her into the kitchen.

"He has a violent temper." This didn't seem to get much reaction. The man simply stood and stared at her, as if he didn't quite get what she was saying. Finally, she added, "I think he might be carrying a gun."

He froze, gaping at her in a way that made her wonder if she'd overdone it with that bit about the gun. She'd forgotten that people here weren't allowed to carry guns.

That did it. A look of panic crossed his face, and he pointed toward a rear corner. "There's a back exit that brings you right out at the head of the escalator," he said. "Go down, and you can get the tube. Or slip back round to the train line and get away like that." He nodded his head vigorously, as if he thought getting out of London altogether was her best option.

He moved around the table, took her arm, and propelled her toward a large metal door. At close proximity, the reek of onions made her eyes sting. As she dug through her purse for Alice's note, the young man shot the bolt, yanked the door open, and pushed her into a dimly-lit corridor.

"Wait," she said, consulting her directions. "How do I get to the Docklands from here?"

"You go right along the corridor." He pointed vaguely into the distance, where it faded into semi-darkness. "Keep on to the end. There's a door opens right by the escalator. Then you go down and turn right. You'll see the sign." With that, he disappeared back into the kitchen and shut the door. A moment later he opened it a crack and peered out at her. Nicole was still standing in the same spot, trying to adjust her eyes to the dim light. He waved her on, making a loud hissing noise, as if shooing a cat. Then he slammed the door.

At the sound of the bolt sliding into place, she turned and began walking down the warm, airless corridor. It smelled of mold, and the walls were scarred with water stains. Every forty feet or so was a bare bulb, but the wattage was low and some of the bulbs were burned out. The light grew even dimmer as she turned corners and burrowed deeper into the passage. At one point, it forked in two directions, and she had to decide which way to go. As she trudged along, she fought a growing panic, the fear that she'd never find her way out. She could imagine someone years from now, exploring a forgotten passage and stumbling across a pile of bones that would be all that remained of her.

She walked for what seemed like miles but was probably several long city blocks, the length of the terminal, before she reached the end of the passage and found a metal door identical to the one that led from the kitchen. She was afraid it might be locked. But to her enormous relief, it opened, and the escalator was a few steps away.

She held her breath as the escalator carried her down into the depths of the system again. She was afraid to look around, afraid she'd find Reinhardt behind her. At the bottom of the escalator, she studied the subway map, figured out a new route, and boarded a train.

Once it was on its way, she began to wonder if she was making a mistake. Alice had said to turn back if she even suspected she was being followed. But she had given Reinhardt the slip, and he was rather bad at staying out of sight. If he was still on her trail, odds were that she'd see him. Then she could go back to Chiswick.

This question settled, she began to feel calmer. The rest of the subway ride went without a hitch. She transferred to the Central line and headed down another long escalator to catch a train to the Docklands. It was a light rail system constructed several layers below the regular subway. In contrast to the dark and grotty corridors of the Underground, the light rail was clean and quiet with high-ceilings and walls of white tile. The silence gave Nicole an eerie feeling, as did knowing how far she was below ground.

Only three others boarded the train with her—none of them Reinhardt—and she had a car to herself. Suspended in the smooth-running hum of the new train, she knew that she really had managed to shake him. She not only felt good but was also exhilarated, almost like she was laughing out loud.

Several stops before her destination, the train ascended from the tunnel to run along the ground then rose to an elevated track. At Canary Wharf, when she finally got off, she had to descend two steep flights of stairs to reach the street. Her only company was a swarm of German tourists armed with cameras.

Checking her watch, she realized she was twenty minutes late. She walked fast, resisting the urge to run, afraid of attracting attention. The Pig and Whistle Coffee Shop, where she was to meet Alice, was only a half block away. She dashed in, breathless, and glanced around. The place appeared to be empty until a figure emerged from an alcove, a woman wearing a black turban, sunglasses, and dark red lipstick.

The woman pulled her glasses off, then rushed toward Nicole and pulled her into a hug. Close up, Nicole noticed that Alice had done an amazing job with her makeup, using light and dark shades to create a new structure for her face. She looked like a completely different person.

"Oh, Nicole," Alice said in a tremulous voice. "I've been so worried about you." Then, relaxing the hug, she looked around the restaurant. "Let's take the table over in the corner," she said. "We'll ask the waiter to bring us coffee, then we can talk. I want to tell you everything. But I don't want to put you in danger, Nicole, and I'm frightened that bringing you here has done just that."

"I didn't have any problems getting here," Nicole lied. "And I'm certain no one followed me."

"You're sure?" Alice asked.

"Positive. That was a good idea, meeting out here." As Nicole said this, she felt uneasy and a little guilty. What if her own stubbornness—her refusal to turn back when she saw Reinhardt—had put Alice in danger?

They settled into the table and summoned the waiter, who also appeared to be the proprietor, to bring coffee. He was a small, plump Indian, whose white turban provided the perfect counterpoint to Alice's black one. "Perhaps you would like to order a meal." His high, soft voice was almost a whine. "At this time of day, there is a minimum of ten pounds per head. We must have this policy to keep the tables for our regular patrons."

"That's fine," Alice said, without a glance at the empty tables around them. "Just leave the menus, and we'll order in a bit."

As the man padded silently away, Alice said, "I want to be sure you know I didn't have anything to do with that bomb."

"Of course not. I know who it was," Nicole said quickly. "Those men who accosted me in the museum. Listen, Alice, I think you may know more about what's been happening than you've told me."

Alice hesitated. "It's a long story, Nicole," she said. "And the only way I know how to tell it is from the beginning."

She was quiet for a moment while she pulled a pack of cigarettes from her purse. After offering one to Nicole, who refused, Alice lit hers and took a long drag. "About two years ago," she finally began, "my younger brother Sean told my parents that he had an offer of a job in London making good money. He was nineteen and hadn't had work since he left school at sixteen. There's an awful lot of unemployment in our little town, Nicole. Young men leave school, marry, raise children, grow old, and die without ever having a real job. They live by casual work. Or, if they have a bit of land, they grow vegetables to sell on market day.

"Sean was a wonderful, jolly boy," she went on. "Everyone loved him. He could make the whole room light up, set people laughing just like one of those comics on the telly."

As Alice spoke in her low musical voice, Nicole could almost see Sean. Soon after he left, Alice went on, the family began to wonder where he would have met anyone who could give him such a job. They were even more troubled when, after a few months, he visited home with a suitcase full of gifts and new clothes. He also had plenty of money to spend, and this, above all, worried them.

As time went by, they began to accept his prosperity. They even bragged to the neighbors about how well Sean had done for himself. But early the previous May, Sean failed to make his usual Sunday afternoon call home. For days they tried to reach his apartment, but there was no answer. Finally, Alice bought a ticket and flew to London. When she went to his place, no one was there. A neighbor told Alice that Sean had been arrested for drug trafficking.

At this point in her story, Alice nodded and gave Nicole a long, sorrowful look. "That was the kind of work he'd been doing—transporting drugs, driving a car for people who smuggle cannabis and cocaine from west Scotland onto Liverpool and then London."

After making a few phone calls to locate Sean, she understood why they hadn't heard from him. He was in the hospital, unconscious from a beating he'd received in his cell the night of his arrest. Although the police said they had no idea who was responsible, Alice was convinced they knew and might have even played a role in it. She believed his beating had been arranged by the people Sean worked for to make sure he didn't turn them in. He lingered, unconscious, for a few months and then died.

As Nicole listened, she fought a growing sense of panic. It was impossible to imagine Brad having anything do to with drug smugglers. The idea was ludicrous. And yet he had been in the U.K. during the period of Sean's involvement with drug running and his arrest.

At this point in the story, Alice pulled off her sunglasses, wiped her eyes, and snuffled into a Kleenex. Her hands were shaking, and it was perhaps a full minute before she could go on. "After my brother was hurt, I stayed on in London so I could be near him. As the weeks went by, I found work through a nursing agency. Then when Sean died..."

Tears spilled down Alice's cheeks, and her mascara began to run. She pulled another Kleenex from her purse, dabbed at her eyes, and put her glasses back on. "I couldn't let it go. I couldn't let the people responsible for his death walk away free, the drug runners and dealers who profit on people's misery. I had to do something. Do you know…"

Alice's voice trailed off and she looked up. The waiter had silently appeared beside her and was waiting to take their order. Alice picked up her menu and said, "I'll have plaice and chips." She bit her lip and contemplated the menu again. "And a Coke."

After scanning the list of entrées, Nicole ordered curry and a Coke, and the waiter scurried off. Meanwhile, Alice had pulled a compact from her purse and was dabbing at her makeup. "Jesus, what a mess." She stood up. "I've got to make a trip to the loo and do my face. Excuse me, Nicole. I won't be a minute."

After the waiter left, Nicole sat staring out the window, thinking about Alice's story, the tragedy of her brother's death.

She couldn't wait for Alice to come back and tell her the rest. She was convinced that Alice could explain a lot of the things that had been happening—why, for instance, those men were following her and whether it was Brad they were looking for.

Just then, the waiter returned with the Cokes they'd ordered. Nicole glanced at her watch. Five minutes had passed since Alice left the table. With a shiver of foreboding, she got up and hurried to the back of the restaurant. The door marked WOMEN'S TOILET was standing open, revealing an empty room, barely big enough for a sink and toilet. Nearby was a swinging door. Pushing it open, she saw that it led into a small, cluttered kitchen where a woman in a sari and a teenage boy looked up from their work.

"Did you see a woman in a black turban?" Nicole asked.

The boy looked puzzled, and from the way the woman shrugged, Nicole gathered neither of them spoke English. Looking around, she spotted another door at the end of the hall.

She opened it, and a cold wind rushed in. Outside was an alleyway where a row of sagging garbage cans stood against a wooden fence. The gate was latched but didn't appear to be locked.

The waiter materialized beside her. When she looked at him, he pointed to a sign she hadn't noticed. It was posted on the door and said, THIS DOOR IS TO REMAIN CLOSED.

She stepped back while he struggled against the wind to close it. "I don't know where my friend is," she said. "Did you see her leave?"

He finished latching the door and shook his head. "I am sorry, madam," he said in his careful English, "but we have already prepared the dishes you ordered. Even if your friend could not wait, you must still pay for her meal."

"Of course," she said, trying to hold on to her patience. "But, please. That gate—where does it lead?"

He shrugged. "To the alley."

"And where does that go?"

"To the street, madam."

She made her way back through the restaurant to the front door and out to the sidewalk, the man a step behind her. People in business garb hurried by, along with a few tourists, but there was no sign of Alice. Nicole went back inside; still dogged by the waiter, she sat down again. A feeling of dread rose in her throat.

She waited while her curry, still untasted, cooled and congealed. Every few minutes she got up and went to the front window. Sometimes she walked to the rear of the restaurant and, ignoring the sign, opened the door to look up and down the alley. Finally, she motioned for the waiter to take the food away and bring the check.

Only as she was putting her change away did she notice that she still had Alice's envelope. She hadn't had a chance to give it to her.

On the walk back to the station and while she waited for the train, Nicole felt sick with remorse. If only she'd turned back when she saw Reinhardt. She'd ignored Alice's warning in her need to find out what Alice had to say.

As she thought about it, she realized something. Reinhardt might be responsible for Alice's disappearance, but he certainly hadn't arrested her. What policeman would arrive on foot, make an arrest, and whisk the suspect away without attracting notice? At the very least, the scene would have included a squad car and a bit of drama. The few arrests Nicole had witnessed back home had been high public spectacle with suspects spread-eagled on the ground or against the car, a policeman standing a short distance away with gun outstretched while a second cop conducted a search.

If Alice hadn't been arrested, there were plenty of other possibilities. She might have been kidnapped, or worse. On the other hand, she could have spotted Reinhardt or someone else she thought was following her and bolted. Sufficiently frightened, she might have disappeared without a word.

Yet, no matter how hard Nicole tried to convince herself otherwise, she had the feeling that something terrible had happened to Alice and that she was to blame.

FOURTEEN

WAITING FOR THE RETURN TRAIN, Nicole kept picturing Alice being dragged, fighting and kicking through the back door of the restaurant and down the alley. There would have been no witnesses, no one to help. Her teeth began to chatter, and the sour taste of bile rose in her throat. She got up from the bench and paced up and down the platform.

After a minute or so, a train was there on the track next to her. As she stepped aboard, she noticed the car had one other passenger—a derelict sprawled across a rear seat. It was impossible to tell if he was asleep or unconscious.

She eyed him warily and for the briefest moment toyed with the idea that this might be Reinhardt in disguise. But this man was genuinely disgusting. His clothes were filthy and ragged, and his skin was a sick, grayish color. No, she thought. No one would go to that much trouble to follow her.

The train started up, slowly at first. She made her way forward. The next car was empty. She took a seat toward the front.

She considered what to do. Detective Keaton had urged her to call if she saw anything suspicious. But, for all of Keaton's professed sympathy, the detective hadn't been of any help.

The train slowed to a stop and she glanced out the window. Here, the track was still above ground, offering a skyline of tall buildings against the gray sky. When her eyes focused on the platform next to her, she felt a sudden jolt of alarm. Not twenty feet from her window were two familiar figures, one short and fat, the other tall and thin.

They were looking into the train as if searching for someone. When the fat one spotted her, their eyes met, and he gave a little smile.

For a moment she was too stunned to move, but when he headed toward the open door at the rear of her car, she jumped to her feet and rushed forward. She understood that these men had followed her to the Docklands. They must have seen her boarding the train at Canary Wharf and had somehow raced ahead to intercept her.

Then she had another thought. If these men had been following her, they must be the ones who'd taken Alice. If so, where was she? What had they done with her?

Just as she reached the door to the next car, it opened, and the second man, the skinny one, was standing in her path. She turned to run away, but the fat one was right behind her, sliding his arm around her neck and pressing something hard against the side of her head. "This 'ere's a gun," he said. "Now you're gonna to do what I say, nice and quiet. That way, I won't have to hurt you."

He marched her back down the aisle, shoved her into a seat and squeezed in next to her. The other man sat across from them and rested his elbows on the seat back in front of him, staring glumly ahead.

The fat one pushed the gun into her ribs just under her left breast and edged his bulk closer. The smell was overpowering.

"That's the girl," he said. "We're gonna have ourselves a nice little trip. A couple of stops up we got a car waiting. We all get off, real friendly and co-op-er-a-tive like. You scream or try anythin' silly, you're dead. You got it?" He poked her with the gun. "The guv'nor wants to talk to you. You answer a couple a questions, we drive you home. That's all there is to it. In't it, Kevin?"

Instead of answering, Kevin turned and stared at him.

"That's right," Fatso muttered to himself. "Just tell him what he wants to know an' you're off the 'ook."

Nicole's eyes were scanning the walls and ceiling of the car. Even if the train was completely automated, she reasoned, there must be a system that monitored the cars for muggings and other emergencies. Just then she spotted a small, glass-fronted red box labeled FIRE ALARM. It was across the aisle and several rows up, too far away to be of any use.

"About the other day," the fat one breathed into her ear. "We jus' wanted to give you a message. Nobody was supposed to get..."

"Chazz!" Kevin said in a low, warning voice.

The fat man was silent for a few seconds. Then he said, "Never mind about that. Now we have a chance to get ac-quain-ted." As he spoke, he relaxed the gun and ran his knuckles over her breast.

When she batted his hand away, he used the gun to poke her hard in the ribs. The pain made her eyes sting, but she was determined not to cry. "You've made a mistake," she said. "I'm not who you think."

He was silent, his small, dark eyes regarding her attentively.

"You say you know my husband," she went on. "But you're wrong. I'm married to Brad Graves. He's an executive with a software company. He doesn't know you."

The man smiled, as if amused by the anger in her voice. "Brad Graves," he repeated in a high, mocking voice. "'E's an executive with a soff-air company." He wagged his head in exaggerated imitation. Then he turned to the second man, the one he called

Kevin, and repeated Brad's name with a derisive snort. "That's the bloke, innit?"

"No, it isn't!" She was almost shouting now, as if by insisting loudly enough, she could force him to admit his mistake. "You're looking for someone else," she went on. "Tell me—it's Frederick Lowry, isn't it?"

Instead of answering, Chazz gazed at her with amused interest, a look not dissimilar to the way a butterfly collector might regard an especially exotic specimen before applying chloroform. He seemed entertained by the fact that she could not only speak but was challenging his judgment. It was useless trying to reason with him.

The train had reached another station where several people were waiting on the platform. His grip on her arm tightened, and he pressed the gun into her side. Surely, as more passengers boarded, someone would enter their car. That would be the time to scream and put up a fight. She doubted the fat man would use his gun. At the museum, the pair of them had behaved like cowards, quick to run away when they thought someone was coming. The very act of leaving a car bomb was cowardly.

She held her breath, watching the door, but no one appeared. Soon the train would start up again, and it would be too late. Summoning all her strength, she jerked away from him in an attempt to get up. She had nothing in mind, except a vague plan to hurl herself over the back of the next seat, scramble to her feet and run.

She managed to rise only part way before he yanked her back and twisted her arm behind her. The pain was excruciating. "Stop!" she screamed. "You're breaking my arm!"

At last, Kevin said, "The guv' told us we wasn't to hurt her, Chazz. Get her and bring her along, but don't hurt her. That's what he said."

"Shut yer face, Kevin," Chazz said. "It's not my fault if she won't do what she's told." Despite the words, his grip on her arm relaxed.

As the pain subsided, Nicole swallowed a deep gulp of air. The car seemed unbearably hot. Her clothes were sticking to her, and a trickle of sweat ran down her face. She thought of her self-defense class, but the techniques she'd learned had abandoned her. Dimly, she understood there was something she was supposed to do, a trick that might persuade them to let her go. For the life of her, she couldn't remember what it was.

Already the train was underway again, hurtling toward the next station. She had a sudden vision of Alice, limp and lifeless, sprawled in a deserted alley or stuffed into a dumpster. Her stomach contracted, and she felt as if she was going to be sick. She closed her eyes and took a few deep breaths, in an attempt to fight it off.

If she was going to save herself, she had to do something now. By the time they forced her from the train it would be too late.

It wasn't long before the train slowed and came to another stop. The men stood up. "This is it," Chazz said, his voice loud in the sudden quiet. He pulled Nicole out of her seat. Then he and the other man began to herd her toward the exit. "No funny stuff," Chazz said. To emphasize his point, he poked her again with the gun.

Just then, she heard something at the back of the car, a whooshing sound she recognized as the door opening. Kevin must have heard it, too, because he looked around and released her arm. She turned to see what he was staring at.

A man wearing a conductor's hat was observing them from the shadows of the doorway to a short passage leading to the car behind theirs. He was holding something that resembled a baseball bat.

By now, Chazz had turned to look. His body was angled slightly toward her, and his hand still gripped her left arm. The sight of him standing like that brought it all back—the hand-to-hand exercises they'd practiced with the instructor. Chazz was in the perfect position. She heard movement behind them and sensed the conductor heading toward them. This was her chance.

She turned toward Chazz and quickly slammed her knee into his groin with every bit of her strength. When they'd practiced in class, the instructor had been wearing a padded body suit, with a specially designed codpiece for protection.

This time, instead of the rigid armor, she felt a soft pouch of flesh that flattened as her knee collided with the bone beneath. The impact sent a shock of pain through her kneecap and down her leg. But this was nothing compared to its effect on Chazz. He let out a high-pitched scream like the cry of a wild animal. Then he doubled up, clutching his crotch, and crumpled to the floor.

Meanwhile, Kevin took off, bolting from the train. Through the window, she saw him streak along the platform toward the exit.

Only when the train began moving again did Nicole realize she was free. Inexplicably, she felt a fresh wave of panic. She bolted for the door to the next car, jabbed the button to open it and ran. Although the danger had passed, she couldn't seem to stop running. As if pursued by demons, she tore through the rest of the train, passing a handful of passengers who stared as she ran by.

When she reached the front car, she stopped; panting for breath, she dropped into a seat. The car held four other passengers sitting in a cluster, Asian men in business suits. For the briefest moment, they regarded her curiously then averted their eyes.

As she sat there, sweating and trying to calm herself, she remembered the conductor, the man whose sudden appearance had saved her. Still trembling, she wondered why she'd run away without stopping to explain what had happened or even to thank him for saving her. It occurred to her that Chazz might be seriously wounded. From what she'd learned in class, however, the pain she'd inflicted was only temporary. No doubt the conductor and whatever crew was onboard would detain Chazz and, presumably, summon law enforcement to meet them at a station down the line. She had the feeling the conductor would soon send someone in search of her. She'd be asked questions for some form they'd have to fill out.

The train continued along its route, stopping at each station, but no one came looking for her. As far as she could tell, the police weren't waiting to meet the train at any of these stops, nor did anyone get off who remotely resembled Chazz. At last they reached her station; she stood up and got off. Eventually, she'd have to report the incident to Keaton or someone else. At the moment, however, it was a relief to walk away without having to face another round of questioning.

The train had disappeared down the track, presumably carrying Chazz and her unknown rescuer to stations beyond. She rode the escalator from the depths of the system up to the street and hailed a cab. On the way back to Chiswick, she checked her phone for calls or messages. It was dead; she'd forgotten to recharge it. As the cab traveled on, she tried to remember what the conductor had looked like. In her mind's eye, he bore a striking resemblance to Reinhardt. This she recognized as a trick of memory. She'd been too frightened, her glimpse of him too brief to register any detail of his face.

The Lowrys' phone was ringing when she reached the front porch, but by the time she unlocked the door, it had stopped. She was certain the call had been from Brad. He'd probably been trying to reach her on her cell and couldn't get through. Although she and Brad hadn't spoken much at breakfast, she had mentioned that she was planning to spend the day at the Victoria and Albert.

He'd done his best to dissuade her. "Why are you running all over London?" he said. "The doc told you to take it easy for a few days. And I worry about you."

She told him she'd be back around 3:00 p.m., and now it was past 5:00. He'd probably been calling her for the last two hours and was now arranging to leave work so he could come home and check on her. Perhaps he'd even called the police.

She turned and went into the kitchen, picked up the phone, and called his office.

"He's not in, luv," the man told her.

Nicole's stomach tightened. "Is Brenda there?"

"Uh-h-h. Seems to me I saw her a while back. Hang on. We'll have a look."

It was a minute or two before Brenda came on the line. "Hi, there," she said. Her voice was throaty and flirtatious, as if she thought she knew who was calling.

"Brenda, it's Nicole," Nicole said, "I want to leave a message for Brad."

"Brad?" Brenda repeated. "But I thought…"

"What?" Nicole said. "What is it?"

"I'm sorry," Brenda said slowly. "I mean, I thought he was with you." She paused, and her voice grew more anxious. "He said he was taking you to the doctor." Then she added in a small voice, "You mean you don't know where he is?"

After they hung up, Nicole fought a growing sense of dread. Any satisfaction she might have drawn from Brenda's discomfort was overshadowed by the larger question of Brad's whereabouts—how he'd spent the afternoon.

One thing was undeniable. Whatever Brad was up to, he was now lying to both her and Brenda.

Fifteen

By the time she reached the upstairs bedroom, the phone was ringing again. It was Brad. "I hear you've been looking for me," he said.

"I wondered where you'd gone," she said, "that required making up a story about taking me to the doctor."

"Oh, yeah, well…" He gave a quick, frustrated laugh. "Look, I just got back to the office, and it's a mad house. I'll tell you all about it when I get home."

She was silent.

"Nick?"

"Why can't you just give me a straight answer?"

"I've got people in my office, waiting to talk to me." He lowered his voice again. "Come on, honey, it's something good. You know—for us, for our future. Have some faith. It's not what you think."

She sighed, wondering if he could possibly imagine what she was thinking. "Alright."

"Look, I'll be a little late. Seven thirtyish. Maybe quarter to eight."

"Whatever."

"Come on, Nick. Don't be like that…"

Before he could finish, she hung up. She went over to the window and stared out, recalling the events of the afternoon, the fact that Brad had been missing when Alice disappeared from the restaurant.

For the first time, it struck her that Chazz and Kevin might have had a third partner, someone to drive them from Canary Wharf to where they intercepted her. The driver would have then raced ahead to a prearranged stop where the two men planned to take her off the train. It was crazy to think Brad was part of this. Whatever his failings, he'd never associate with criminal types like Chazz and Kevin, much less drive their getaway car. Yet the events of the last few days had created a new reality where anything seemed possible.

She was still standing at the window when the phone went off again. She picked it up on the second ring.

"Oh, Nicole, thank God!" It was her sister's voice. "I couldn't reach you, and I was getting really worried. Are you all right?"

"I'm fine," Nicole said. "I hope you're calling to say you heard from the Lowrys."

"No such luck," Stephanie said glumly. "Listen, I have a bit of bad news. But there's no real harm done, so don't get upset, all right?"

"Just say it."

"Right," Stephanie said. "Someone broke into your condo last night. When I got here a little while ago, the place was a mess. Some of the drawers were dumped out in the bedroom and study. Fortunately, nothing seems to be missing, so maybe they were scared off before they had a chance to take anything. I checked your jewelry, Mom's silver service, the TV, and speakers. It's all here." Then she added, "Oh, except for Brad's laptop, but he took that with him, didn't he?"

"Of course," Nicole said. "Well, everything's all right then." She did her best to sound calm.

"I'm not sure," Stephanie said. "Something weird is going on with your phone. Like, when I'm here watering your plants and it rings? As soon as I say hello, they hang up. Just now, while I was checking around to see what was missing, it happened again."

"My God, Steph," Nicole said. "Are you telling me you're alone there? Didn't you call the police?"

"Of course I did. They'll be here any minute. Look, Nicole, after all that's happened, don't you think you should come home? We can't leave this place unoccupied. It's an invitation for the burglar to come back and finish the job."

Nicole was silent for a moment. Then she said, "I'm afraid I can't leave London just yet." Bracing herself for her sister's reaction, she described her troubles with Brad, including a somewhat amended account of his strange secretiveness.

There was a long silence. Then Stephanie said, "I'm really sorry, but I can't say I'm surprised or that I didn't already have a pretty good suspicion ..." The phone crackled, and Stephanie's voice cut out, a reminder of the thousands of miles of ocean and land that separated them. The link was reestablished in time for Stephanie's summation: "... they're all alike, every one of them."

It wasn't necessary to ask Stephanie to repeat herself. Instead, Nicole said, "So I'm sure you understand how important it is for me to stay here long enough to straighten things out."

"I can't imagine why you think you can straighten it out," Stephanie sighed. "Or why you want to stay in a city with terrorists planting car bombs. I mean, did they ever catch those guys?"

"Listen, Steph, getting involved in a random act of terrorism is like being struck by lightning. It isn't going to happen again—at least not to me. Really. That's one thing you don't have to worry about."

"I'd feel better if you were home," Stephanie said. "And what are we going to do about the condo?" She was quiet a moment, then, "Hey, I know! I'll close up my place and stay here until you get back."

"That's not necessary," Nicole said quickly. "Just let the police know we're out of town and leave a note for the Goodmans. They have the unit next to ours. They can keep an eye on things."

"But if we leave it empty, you'll get ripped off."

"I don't care about the condo. I care about you," Nicole said. "Promise me you won't stay there, okay?

"Fine," Stephanie said. "It's a free country. If you want to support the criminal underclass by donating your household valuables, that's your right." She was quiet for a moment. Then she said, "I think I'll keep Arnold at my place. I feel better with him around."

After they hung up, Nicole felt shaken, unable to take in this new development; the situation was spinning out of control, involving more and more of the people around her. It was possible, of course, that this new break-in was a coincidence, but her instincts told her that the people hunting for Lowry were behind it.

She wondered if Stephanie might be in danger. Half a world away, it was impossible to assess the situation. Yet she had the feeling Stephanie would be all right—as long as she didn't take it into her head to stay at the condo.

She walked back to the window and stood gazing out at the quiet street, her mind abuzz. She remembered something Reinhardt had said about Lowry—that the police wanted to talk to him because someone he knew was under investigation. Now that she thought about it, this seemed odd. The law firm she worked for rarely handled criminal cases. But in cases she'd read about, the police never went to this much trouble to track down anyone who wasn't party to the crime under investigation. Sure, they made an effort to find key witnesses, but these were usually people who needed immunity to testify, as well as protection from their former associates.

This raised new questions about Lowry. She decided it might be worthwhile taking another look around the house. Maybe there was something she hadn't noticed before, a clue about what was going on.

The bedroom closet, where Freddy and Muriel's clothes were jammed in around the safe, seemed a good place to start. When she opened the closet door, she was hit by the musty smell of mothballs, cigarette smoke, and stale perfume. She pushed her way past the safe and tried to part the wall of hanging garments, but they were jammed in too tightly. So she began pulling armloads of clothing out of the closet and tossing them on the bed.

She found only a few items that belonged to Freddy—a worn navy blazer with dull brass buttons, a pair of mustard-colored pants with a sprung elastic waistband, and a plastic bag containing a dated-looking pin-striped suit with wide lapels. The pockets held nothing but a sprinkling of tobacco crumbs.

Most of the clothes seemed to be Muriel's—sweaters and dresses, a few pairs of shoes lined up neatly in a built-in shoe rack. On the shelf was a box holding a hat and some handbags.

When it was all in a big pile on the bed, she began sorting through it, item by item, shaking out each piece before she put it back in the closet. At the top of the stack was a beige wool knit vest, apparently belonging to Muriel. It was in bad shape, stretched almost to dress length, its texture shaggy with pilling; next came a navy suit, baggy and covered with lint, but otherwise resembling a policewoman's uniform. The suit, she noted, was about her own size, the vest large enough to accommodate two of her. No pockets in either.

Next came four shapeless rayon dresses, all in a similar granny-dress style. They ranged in sizes, she noticed, from one that would fit her to one that was size eighteen. Other than a few petrified Kleenexes, the pockets yielded nothing. She quickly made her way through the rest, an endless stack of separates—blouses, skirts, slacks—none of them matching. At the bottom of the pile was an oversized gray jogging suit that might have belonged to either Lowry.

The shoes were ancient and lifeless—a pair of cracked white plastic high-heeled boots, several pairs of caved-in black pumps. The purses were not only old, but covered with dust, as if they hadn't been used in years. They were empty. She unfolded a black knit cap, and a small winged insect flew out. Sure enough, when she held the cap up to the light, it was dotted with tiny holes.

When the clothes had been inspected and returned to the closet, she felt more puzzled than before. True, Mrs. Lowry might be a thrift shop addict. But the items hanging in the closet didn't appear to be a functioning wardrobe.

She went over to the bedroom's second bureau, the one still filled with the Lowrys' things, and started going through it. In the bottom drawer, she found a moth-eaten sweater vest, a faded blue nylon nightgown, and a couple of pairs of mismatched men's socks. In the next drawer were two pairs of women's underpants of the pre-bikini variety, and a hopelessly tangled ball of leggings and pantyhose. Another drawer contained a cache of junk jewelry—cheap beads, tarnished bangles, and snap-together pearls—all tangled together.

As she closed the last drawer, she realized she hadn't yet come across any winter coats or jackets in the Lowrys' wardrobe. This was strange, given London's harsh winters. Except for a single pink poplin raincoat—lightweight and unlined—there were no coats at all, no boots, mufflers, or mittens. But surely they wouldn't take their winter things to L.A., not in June. She dragged a stool into the hallway and poked her head through a trap door in the ceiling. The light shone through the side vents of the attic, revealing bare rafters but no provision for storing clothes. She pulled the door shut and climbed down.

Next, she worked her way through the rest of the closets and even braved a quick foray into the basement, but she found no winter attire.

Back in the Lowrys' bedroom, she began to rummage through the drawers of the night table. Here, she found a pair of sunglasses with cream-colored plastic frames, a key ring, assorted small change, a packet of embroidery needles, and a plastic bag filled with a rainbow assortment of sewing thread. In a side storage compartment sat a phonebook. When she lifted it out, she discovered a stack of magazines, notable in being the first and only reading material she'd encountered among the Lowrys' possessions. She set them down on the night table and flipped through them. They were travel magazines, well-worn and dog-eared.

She sat down on the bed to take a closer look. The top magazine was folded open to an article entitled, "Off the Beaten Track in South America." The piece talked about the lonely beauty of the Guyanan highlands, the pristine beaches of French Guiana, the remote villages of the Peruvian Andes. Below that, several other magazines were dog-eared on articles about exotic and isolated places: Australia's great outback, the New Zealand Bush, the vast savannas of South Africa, lost ashrams in the Himalayas, the stark landscape of India's Malabar Coast, the surprising beauty of springtime in Siberia.

Next came some pamphlets offering real estate, in some cases whole islands, in Uruguay, Chile, Venezuela. A more elaborate brochure contained color photos of plantations for sale in Colombia, Honduras, and Nicaragua, although no specific crops were mentioned. At the bottom of the stack was a booklet with full-color spreads of estates in Ecuador. A paragraph in the introduction described Ecuador as a popular spot for foreign settlers because of the country's very low taxes and "even more importantly, the privacy Ecuador offers as a nation beyond the reach of most extradition laws." This passage was underlined in pen.

Nicole studied the page for a long time, digesting its implications. Clearly, this wasn't describing a vacation spot, but a hideout for people with enough money to make sure they weren't found by those who could launch a worldwide search—the law or the mob.

This suggested the Lowrys never intended to occupy her condo at all. Perhaps they planned the house swap as a diversion, a way to keep their house occupied so they could buy a few days' time and disappear. "Gone to ground" was a phrase that occurred to her, like a spy who's blown his cover or someone in the witness protection program.

A sudden banging on the front door brought her to her feet. Then the mailbox cover rattled and Brad's voice called, "Hey, Nick, I forgot the key. Let me in!"

She glanced at her watch. It was 7:30 p.m. She hurried down to the front door and, after peeking out, opened it. Brad was standing there. The expression on his face infuriated her. After everything that had happened, he actually looked pleased with himself.

"My God," he said, "do you realize how ferocious you look? Like some babe in one of those old comic strips, ready to hit the old man on the head with a rolling pin."

At that moment, she came close to truly hating him. It was almost as if she were seeing him for the first time, getting a glimpse of the real Brad.

In response to her stare, he held his hands up in mock surrender. "All right," he said. "I'm going to come clean about everything. I'm working on a special project for Coop." His smile broadened, as if he thought she'd be happy to receive the news.

"This is something really big, my first real chance to show what I can do."

He took her hand, and before she could pull it free, steered her into the living room. "I was planning to tell you, but first I wanted to make sure things were working out."

She took a seat on the couch and, against all reason, willed herself to keep an open mind. What if he was going to tell her the whole truth, she asked herself. What if he had dumped Brenda and was determined to be a better person? At the same time, she feared that nothing could save their marriage.

He sank into the blue wing chair opposite her, stretching his long legs out in front of him. "It's a new venture," he said. "A firm that uses electronic trading to invest in currency futures. You know, of Third World countries."

"I don't get it," she said. "How could you be working on something for Bill Cooper if you were out of the office all afternoon?"

He was silent, as if gathering his thoughts. "Look, this project I'm involved with—it's top secret. Nobody at SoftPac is supposed to know. Coop doesn't want me working on it down there. We're, like, doing the whole thing through another company, out of their offices." He paused and gave a smile, earnest and imploring. "Nick, I need to ask a favor."

"A favor," she repeated.

"Right," he said. "I have to go back there tomorrow morning, so I told Bren' I was bringing you in for more medical tests. And, well, I want to be sure you don't call the office looking for me. You know, like you did this afternoon. If anyone calls here before noon, just don't answer the phone. Got it?"

She stared at him, thinking what a liar he was. SoftPac had sent him to England to solve a serious management crisis at Britcomp, which was their first big investment abroad. While he was on this assignment, they'd never saddle him with a huge task like setting up a new business. Yet she knew how useless it was to confront him. He'd only embellish the lie, trying to make it sound more plausible, and she couldn't bear to listen.

"Nick?" he said. "Can I count on you?"

"All right. I won't answer the phone. That's easy enough." This said, she quickly moved on to tell him about the call from Stephanie, the news of the condo break-in, and the fact that the Lowrys still hadn't showed up.

"Jesus," he said. "What about our new sound system?"

"Stephanie checked. She says nothing's missing."

He put his hands over his face and was silent for a long moment before he looked at her again. "You know something?" he said, shaking his head. "This house swap was the stupidest idea …"

"Right," she said crisply, cutting him off. "One more question. What exactly did you tell Brenda?"

"Pardon me?"

"How did you explain what happened this afternoon? You know, you're supposed to be taking me to the doctor, and then I call the office, looking for you."

He flushed slightly. "Promise you won't be mad?"

She waited.

"I told her it was because you got knocked on the head when that car blew up," he said. "You know, it sort of blitzed your short-term memory. I explained that I really had taken you in for your medical appointment. I brought you home and had just gone over to the pharmacy to get your prescriptions."

As she stared at him, her anger—already simmering—erupted into a boiling rage closely resembling the fireball that had consumed the Lowrys' car. "You told her I forgot that you'd just been here?" Her words came out in a low shout.

"Come on, Nick. You promised you wouldn't get mad," he said. "I mean, I told her it was temporary; the doc said you'd get over it."

"How could you imagine I wouldn't get mad," she ranted, "when you portray me as some kind of amnesia case who loses hours at a time?"

"I swore her to secrecy," he said. "Don't worry. She's good at keeping her mouth shut."

"I'll bet she is." She gave him one last angry look and began leafing through the newspaper, pretending to read.

Brad was determined to finish describing his new project. As he launched into the details, she realized there was something familiar about the idea. Then she remembered. Brad had mentioned it before. It wasn't Bill Cooper's brainchild, but Brad's own, one of the get-rich-quick schemes he was always hatching. At the time, Nicole had pointed out to him that Third World countries had laws against foreigners messing around with their currency. And to flaunt such laws was to risk being tossed into a filthy, toiletless cell in Africa or Central America.

"What a Cassandra you are!" Brad had scoffed. "Our government never allows foreign countries to extradite Americans for chicken shit like that." He hadn't denied that the scheme was illegal, she noticed, nor had he brought it up again, until now.

Rumor had it that Cooper was planning to make SoftPac a publicly traded corporation. If that were true, he couldn't afford to be involved in anything even remotely shady. No, she decided, this was exactly the kind of thing Brad was always daydreaming about—the fortune that could be made if only he had the guts to take a few risks. The more she thought about it, the more convinced she was that this scheme had Brad's name written all over it.

Sixteen

THE NEXT MORNING, when Brad called goodbye from the bottom of the stairs, Nicole was waiting in the bathroom, already dressed. As soon as the front door slammed, she hurried down the stairs. She reached the front window in time to catch a glimpse of his departing figure heading in the direction of the subway.

She was wearing the pink poplin raincoat she'd found in the Lowrys' closet. It had a fake fur collar and matching rain hat. To give herself a slightly different shape, she'd padded her middle with an old sweater from the same source. Completing the ensemble were her white Reebok running shoes with cuffed white socks.

She'd also done some work on her face, using pancake makeup she'd found in the medicine cabinet. Pale pink lipstick created a monotone that helped blend her face into the shadow of her hat. The clunky-looking sunglasses from the Lowrys' night table provided another good touch, although the lenses slightly distorted her vision.

Opening the hall closet, she glanced in the full-length mirror and gave a laugh of surprise when she saw the stranger looking back at her—short, pudgy, and rather dim. She looked like a woman of limited intelligence who, at thirty-two, would still be living with her parents. She'd be employed as a box girl at the market and have a hopeless crush on one of the checkers.

Taking stock of her appearance, she decided the disguise was convincing enough to fool Brad, which was the point. If she was going to find out what he was up to, she couldn't risk being recognized.

She made a face at herself in the mirror and then, after closing the closet door, cut through the kitchen and left by the back door. She cracked the gate and peered into the front yard. No one in sight. On reaching the sidewalk, she ran for the subway.

At the station, she was relieved to find Brad still on the platform, waiting for the train. She kept her distance, stationing herself behind a wide, freestanding column covered with advertising posters. From here, she watched him pace up and down the platform. Once in a while, he would stop and peer into the distance for the train. He seemed oblivious to her presence.

Just then a young woman entered the station, and Brad turned to look. At the sight of her, his eyes widened, and his mouth went slack. Even Nicole had to admit the woman was stunning. Dressed in a black stretch minidress, she had a tiny waist, narrow hips, and a bosom that was out of proportion to her body. As her high heels clicked down the stairs, her breasts bounced. She didn't look in Brad's direction. But her lips were parted in a smile that indicated she was completely aware of the effect she was having on him.

Brad edged toward the woman and murmured something to her that Nicole was too far away to hear. In response, the woman smiled up at him. She had full, pouty lips, the sort achieved with the help of a dermatologist and repeated injections of collagen. Still, Nicole had to admit, they did the job, endowing her with an expression of smoldering sensuality. When Brad leaned forward to hear the woman's reply, the expression on his face was something to behold.

Nicole's throat constricted. Despite all the anger she'd been feeling toward Brad these last few days, her eyes now stung with the threat of tears. He'd never looked at her that way—not when they met, not on their wedding day, not ever.

The disguise she was wearing no longer seemed quite so outlandish. It was almost as if the persona she'd assumed that morning had become the real Nicole—unloved, unlovely, and completely pathetic.

At last a train rolled into the station, pulled to a stop. and opened its doors. The three of them boarded the same car. The woman was first. Her body seemed to glide along, the narrow pelvis thrust forward, leading the way. Brad was next. Nicole plodded along behind, unnoticed in her bubble-gum coat and white tennis shoes.

The woman found an unoccupied pair of seats. When Brad slid in beside her and resumed the conversation, she smiled up from under her eyelashes, as if surprised to find him sitting next to her.

As she watched, Nicole couldn't help remembering the Brad she'd first met. Outgoing and sunny, he possessed a certain charisma, and yet he was completely unconscious of his own attractiveness. Although Nicole sensed his interest, she had to make the first moves. Now, to her disgust, she saw that he was very smooth at picking up women. When and where had he acquired this skill? Another question presented itself: How many had there been besides Brenda?

After a few stops, the woman disembarked. As she walked toward the exit, she turned and waved at Brad. He nodded and raised his hand in a little salute. Gripped between his fingers was a business card.

As the train hurtled on, Nicole had an overwhelming urge to get off at the next stop, go back to the house, and book the next flight back to L.A. Not yet, she told herself; she was going to see this thing through.

It couldn't have been more than a minute before they pulled into another station, and Brad got up. She stood up and followed him off the train.

He led her on a brisk walk five or six blocks, while attractive window displays gave way to open bins of cut-rate goods. Here, the side streets were occupied by lofts for clothing manufacturers. As they walked—Nicole half running to keep up—the area grew shabbier. Debris littered the gutters. Occasionally, a cluster of raggedy men stood smoking on the sidewalk. They appeared to be at that phase of economic decline where they'd given up any pretense of looking for work.

Brad turned down an alley, walked quickly up the steps of a run-down brick office building, and disappeared inside. After a moment's hesitation, Nicole followed him in. A man was already waiting for the elevator. He and Brad exchanged nods; they stood two abreast in companionable silence while Nicole hovered behind them in the shadow of the entry hall.

At last the elevator arrived, and all three of them crowded into its narrow constraints. Although Nicole had a certain amount of faith in her disguise, she didn't want to risk allowing Brad a close look at her face. So she stationed herself in the rear of the car, staring intently at her shoes.

Under the thick coat of makeup, she'd begun to sweat, and it seemed an eternity before the elevator stopped on the second floor. When Brad and the other man filed out, Nicole punched the button for the next floor. She figured it would be prudent to ride up the extra floor, then reverse the elevator and come back. In such a small building, it wouldn't be hard to figure out where Brad had gone.

When the door opened on three, she could see the floor was unoccupied. The windows were covered with tattered brown paper that admitted little light. The hallway was clogged with debris—old packing boxes, wads of paper, and a thick layer of dust littered with nails, paper clips, and wood shavings. Panes in the doors of nearby offices were dark.

She took all this in before pushing the button for the second floor. The door remained open, but the humming of the elevator stopped. She stabbed the button again and again to no avail. She reached out and tried to pull the door shut, but it wouldn't budge. Finally she decided to find the stairs and walk down.

In the hallway, she pulled off the dark glasses and, after sticking them in her pocket, began to maneuver her way through the clutter, jumping over cartons and dismantled light fixtures. She'd worked her way almost to the rear of the building, where the corridor turned at a right angle, when she heard a noise and looked around. Behind her, the door of the elevator had shut. The mechanism began to hum, and the floor indicator shivered into movement as the car started down.

She stumbled back through the debris and punched the button to summon it back. After a moment or so, the asthmatic rattle of the elevator stopped; there was a loud thud, then silence. According to the indicator, the car was stuck between the first and second floor.

The place was unimaginably hot; rivulets of sweat trickled down her face. She gave the call button another stab. Was it broken? Disabled by a power outage? She hit the button again and waited. Nothing.

At last, she turned and gingerly began working her way along the hallway again. Just as she turned the corner at the rear of the passage, she heard movement up ahead and something that sounded like a small animal skittering away. In a panic, she wheeled around and bolted back to the elevator.

She'd just reached it and was about to try the button again when the door flew open. She got in and punched the button for her floor. The car slowly lumbered downward. When the door opened on the well-lit hallway of the second floor, she could hear the reassuring sound of voices and the distant ringing of a phone.

The first office door bore the sign, APEX JEWELRY. She kept walking. Another company, Levinson & Levinson, occupied two suites but gave no clue to the nature of its business. Around the corner was a door that said SITVACK HOME MORTGAGES.

The lettering on the next door read, FINANCIAL VENTURES NETWORK. After studying the name, Nicole tuned in on a low murmur of conversation, in which she could distinguish Brad's voice. He and several others seemed to be discussing a system crash. This was the place, all right.

She forced herself to pause just long enough to note down the name of the company and the suite number. Outside the building, she stopped and wrote down the address. This done, she quickly walked a few blocks, stepped into a doorway, and pulled out her cell. She searched the web for the company and found the phone number.

"I'm calling from ABC Credit Company," she told the man who answered the phone. "I need some programming done, and I'd like to have your company bid on the job."

"Sorry, miss," the man said. "We don't do programming."

"Oh," Nicole said. "What do you do?"

"That's a bit difficult to explain. We work in electronic trading of—uh—equities. But we don't work for other companies."

"Are you a subsidiary of SoftPac?"

"Never heard of it." He sounded puzzled.

"It's a software firm owned by an American named Bill Cooper."

"Sorry," he said. "Never heard of him either."

"Who does own your company?" As she said this, she could hear Brad's voice in the background. "Who is it?" he was saying. "Here, give me the phone."

She hung up. As she made her way back to the tube, she thought about the tiny bit of information the man had revealed. He'd confirmed at least part of Brad's story: This business dealt in electronic trading. But if Bill Cooper wasn't involved, did that mean Brad was the sole proprietor? Where had he found the money?

It was true that they had some savings—about $20,000, mostly in mutual funds, plus a somewhat larger amount in Brad's 401k. But even if he cashed it all in, that wasn't enough to sustain a business that needed capital to rent an office, pay employees, and buy equipment.

By the time she arrived home, her growing sense of outrage had strengthened her determination to find out the truth. Never mind about his messing around. Today had revealed a much greater betrayal. He'd been living a lie, leading a double life: as the hard-working, married computer executive and as the smooth operator who picked up beautiful women and managed some kind of dubious financial scheme on the web.

Seventeen

Nicole washed her face and changed her clothes. Feeling no better, she went downstairs and turned on the TV. She spent a few minutes browsing channels, flipping from one talking head to the next. They were all reporting the same story; a bomb had exploded that morning at a coffee shop in a quiet residential area of London. "According to authorities," a woman with a sleek helmet of blonde hair said to the camera, "this incident appears unrelated to the car bombing that took place in Chiswick on Thursday. But many wonder if this recent rash of violence might signal a new wave of terrorism in the U.K."

Nicole knew, of course, that the car bombing in Chiswick hadn't been the work of terrorists. Watching the footage that appeared next, she could see another difference between the two incidents. Today's explosion had been a direct hit, killing two people, injuring four others, and reducing the cafe to a smoldering heap of ashes. Under ordinary circumstances, it was the kind of story she always felt compelled to follow, riveted by a mixture of horror and fascination. Today, she couldn't bear to watch.

She turned off the TV. Opening the sliding glass door, Nicole let herself out into the backyard. There, she began to stroll up and down, taking deep breaths. It wasn't just the gut-wrenching news that had upset her, but the morning spent following Brad—what it revealed about him. Eventually the cool fresh air of the garden had a soothing effect, as did the tranquility of its rectangle of lawn and neat border of shrubs.

She was just walking back into the house when she realized that she still hadn't called Detective Keaton about the attempted kidnapping. She pulled out her phone and put in the number, debating whether to say anything about Alice's disappearance. Alice herself despised the police and would no doubt be appalled at the idea of enlisting their help. Even so, Nicole was worried enough about her friend to consider asking Keaton's assistance.

"I'm sorry, madam," said the man who came on the line. "Detective Keaton is out. Would you like to leave word?" He had a flat, neutral voice that reflected a polite but resolute disinterest.

At that moment an insistent tapping made her look around. A young man was standing just outside the kitchen window, knocking on the glass. Nicole let out a little cry and almost dropped the phone.

"I say, are you there?" said the man at the other end of the line.

Nicole didn't answer. She was too busy staring at the stranger at the window. He was dressed in a windbreaker, jeans, and a soft, visored cap; he was carrying a backpack. When she met his eyes, he put his finger to his lips, gesturing for silence. Then he pulled off his cap. A mop of red hair tumbled out, and Nicole saw that it wasn't a stranger at all. It was Alice.

The sight of her, the realization that she was safe and well, gave Nicole a cool rush of relief. Meanwhile, Alice beckoned silently and disappeared from view.

"Hello? Hello?" the voice on the phone insisted.

"I have to go," Nicole said. "Just tell Detective Keaton to call me."

She was about to hang up when the man said, "Wait! You haven't given your name and number."

She reeled the information off then had to repeat the number slowly and spell her last name. When she was finally able to get away, she hurried outside.

At one side of the yard stood a small shed, a prefab structure of light green aluminum. The door was slightly ajar.

Nicole gave a quick look around at the surrounding houses; the windows were dark and unrevealing. She hesitated only a moment before slipping into the shed. The interior was dark, the air heavy with the damp, moldy smell of potting soil. Nearby, she heard a creak, a popping of knee joints. Then Alice's voice: "Nicole!"

The two of them stumbled together and embraced.

"Oh, Alice," Nicole said, "Where have you been? I've been so worried about you."

"Sorry to run out on you like that, Nicole," Alice said. "But I hadn't any choice. I spotted a man watching the restaurant. It was the same one I'd seen earlier, behind me on the train. What was I to think but that he was following me? So I ducked into the loo and left by the rear door."

Nicole wondered if it might have been Reinhardt. "What did he look like?" she said.

Alice was quiet a moment. Then she said in a rush: "He was heavy set with a red face and a bald head—and a wee bit of gray hair showing at the sides. Oh, Nicole, I've been wanting to let you know I was safe. But I didn't have your mobile number, and I couldn't give you a ring, could I? Not with the house sure to be bugged."

"You mean the police have the house bugged?"

"Shhh," Alice whispered. "I wasn't talking about the police. Although you're more than likely right. The police must have their own bugs." She let out a sudden whoop of laughter, then clapped a hand over her mouth. "Sweet Jesus," she whispered. "Will you listen to me, now. It's the strain—pushin' me over the edge." She shook her head as if to clear it. "Alexander Hayes is the one who'd have bugged the house. He's looking for our friend Freddy. He must think you know where he is."

"Who is Alexander Hayes?" Nicole said.

"Have you not heard of him? He's a drug trafficker who gets more publicity than the royals. He calls himself the "King of Cannabis". But the truth is he's into dealing the hard stuff, too." Alice paused and patted some sacks of potting soil stacked against the wall. "Here, why don't we have a seat?"

As Nicole's eyes adjusted to the light, she took a closer look at her friend. Somehow, this masculine attire suited Alice better than the femme fatale outfit she'd worn to their last meeting.

At Alice's insistence, Nicole went first with an account of what happened after they parted ways at the restaurant. As briefly as she could, she described her encounter with Chazz and Kevin.

"The bloody bastards," Alice said. "I wish I'd been there. But it sounds like you taught them a thing or two." Alice paused and studied Nicole carefully. "So, how is your other problem?" she said. "The husband and his assistant?"

"Don't ask," Nicole said. "But Alice, why would a drug smuggler want to bug the Lowrys' house?"

Alice was silent, as if she were sorting out her thoughts. Then she said, "It has to do with what I found out after my brother died. When I was clearing out Sean's things, I discovered a journal he'd been keeping. That was how I learned he'd been carrying drugs for Freddy."

Something clicked in Nicole's head. This explained everything. "Are you saying Lowry's a drug dealer?" she said.

"He is that. Not the kind you'd find on streets, selling little packets of the filthy stuff. He's a few notches up— the drug ring's operative in London. The real king pin is Freddy's governor,

Alexander Hayes. Hayes brings drugs into the U.K. by private yacht. Does it through a posh estate he owns on the west coast of Scotland. They've got hundreds of miles of lochs and inlets on that coastline. HM customs can't keep track of all the drug shipments."

Alice went on, "My brother wrote it all in his journal. He first ran into Freddy when he came through our little town. He was in Northern Ireland, trying to negotiate a deal. But my brother didn't know that. He didn't find out about the drugs 'til later," she continued. "At the time, Freddy gave a big story about owning an import-export company. Oh yes, he was looking for cottage crafts—handknit sweaters, crocheted tablecloths and the like—to sell abroad. He tells Sean, 'Come to London and I'll give you a job.'

"Sean jumped at the chance. At first, he rented a room with the Lowrys—the very room I have now. They treated him like one of the family. Soon they have him smoking pot regularly. Then Freddy makes Sean a drugs courier and gives him a big pay rise. So Sean moves to his own digs. The work is easy. He drives up to Hayes' estate near Oban and brings the drugs back into London."

Nicole let out a long breath, and Alice said, "Yes. It's beginning to make sense now, isn't it? Imagine how I felt when I read my brother's journal. That's when I found out Freddy lured Sean into the drugs trade and killed him."

"You're saying Lowry murdered your brother?" Nicole said.

"As good as. My brother was beaten to death to make sure he didn't turn informer. I don't know who did it. But the beating was meant to kill Sean, and Freddy must have arranged it. I was determined to get him. I gave Sean's journal to the police, but they did nothing. Months went by, and Freddy, that—that filthy murderer, still walking around a free man, dealing his …"

Alice broke off and stood up. "Wait." She moved over to the door and peered out. "Shhh."

Now Nicole heard it, too—the crunch of footsteps in the gravel by the house. She squeezed in next to Alice and looked through the narrow opening of the door. Less than twenty feet away, Detective Keaton, dressed in a natty black-and-white checked suit, was standing by the kitchen window, peering into the house.

The two women watched, barely daring to breathe, while the detective tried the back door and, finding it unlocked, disappeared inside.

"Oh, Nicole," Alice whispered. "She must have rung the front bell. Nobody answered. So she thinks it's a license to start snooping around. You'd better go after her or she'll be looking back here."

Nicole hurried toward the house. "Detective!" she called from the back door. Then, on her way through the kitchen, "Hello?"

By the time she reached the front hall, Keaton was halfway up the stairs. When Nicole called her name, the policewoman turned and looked down at her with a sheepish expression that morphed into her customary smile. "Mrs. Graves!" she said, as she started down the stairs. "Forgive me for walking in like this, but I found your keys in the front door. I rang the bell, and when you didn't answer, I was afraid something might have happened to you."

As Keaton handed the keys to her, Nicole felt herself flush. "My God," she said. "I can't believe I did that. I guess I was pretty rattled… "

"I heard you were trying to reach me," Keaton said, with another of her broad smiles. "I was in the neighborhood when I checked my messages. I thought it would be best to drop by. Why don't you tell me what happened?"

Nicole let out a long breath. It was clear she'd have to take time to sit down with the detective for a chat, a prospect that made her itch with impatience. Would Alice wait, or would she panic and bolt like she had before?

When they were settled—Keaton on the couch with Nicole across from her on an overstuffed chair—Keaton pulled out a notebook and pen. "Now, then," she said. "What's this all about?"

Nicole took a deep breath, trying to gather her thoughts before launching into a description of the incident on the train. She decided not to admit she was on her way to the Docklands. Since it wasn't exactly a tourist attraction, she couldn't think of a reason to explain why she'd be going there. Instead, she placed the incident on the Victoria line, explaining that she was headed for the Victoria and Albert Museum. But after she said this, she realized that a line as busy as the Victoria would never be deserted at midday. And while the light rail had doors allowing riders to pass from one car to the next, this didn't seem to be the case on underground trains, at least not the ones she'd seen.

As she spoke, Keaton was busy writing in her notebook. If she noticed any inconsistencies, she gave no sign. Nicole hurried on, emphasizing her point that Kevin and Chazz, the pair who'd accosted her on the train, were the same men who'd threatened her and then planted a car bomb set to go off at 6:00 p.m., the time of their deadline. She also mentioned that someone broke into her condo in L.A.

Then she gave Keaton her theory about Lowry's disappearance, working in what Alice had just told her about his drug dealing. She presented the information as a theory she'd worked out from something Alice had mentioned earlier. "I think Kevin and Chazz really are after Lowry," Nicole went on. "According to the Lowrys' tenant, he owes Hayes a lot of money. Since I'm staying in the house, maybe they mistook me for Mrs. Lowry and thought they could get to Freddy through me." Now, after hearing Alice's story, Nicole was beginning to think this might be true. Maybe Brad wasn't involved with these people at all.

"It's an interesting theory," Keaton said. "But I'd be happier if we had some real proof. Evidence, for example, that Lowry is hiding abroad or of his connection with these men."

"Why won't you listen?" Nicole said hotly. "I've been telling you those two men are responsible for the car bombing, and you don't seem to be trying very hard to find them. You..." She stopped herself. Why keep arguing, prolonging the discussion when her real goal was to get the detective out of the house?

"My dear Mrs. Graves," Keaton said. "Of course we're listening to you. As for these individuals who accosted you on the train—why, we are indeed searching for them."

"Great," Nicole said, although it was hard to keep the sarcasm out of her voice. "Oh, and by the way, did you ever find out anything about Inspector Reinhardt?"

"Yes," Keaton said slowly. "I did make some inquiries, and we do have an Inspector Ronald Reinhardt. He works in ..." There was the slightest hesitation, while she seemed to grope for a word. "another division, which is why I didn't recognize the name."

"I see," Nicole said, waiting for the detective to say more about Reinhardt.

Instead, Keaton stared at her for a long moment, then said, "I wonder if I might offer you some advice. I hope you won't take offense."

Once Nicole had nodded, Keaton went on, "You must give yourself some time to recover from these terrible experiences. When it's a deliberate act of violence, the victim is always fearful the perpetrator will return to finish the job. In a case like this, where you were an innocent bystander, that virtually never happens. Yet people go through a period of—I don't want to say paranoia. Let's just call it acute sensitivity to anything out of the ordinary in their daily lives. It's easy to interpret any unusual event as a threat or sign of conspiracy. Believe me, if you were in any danger whatsoever, we'd give you protection or advise you to go home."

It was a struggle for Nicole to remain silent. She had the most terrible urge to point out that she was being stalked by two dangerous criminals and that the police—London's finest in general and Detective Keaton in particular—were doing nothing to protect her.

"As for the break-in at your condominium," Keaton continued, "you tell me that nothing was taken, and your sister has turned the matter over to the Los Angeles police. You're in capable hands."

She reached out and gave Nicole's shoulder a reassuring squeeze. "As for the incident on the train," she went on, "it's true that things like this occur every day on our transit system—bag snatching, robbery, and even murder. Of course, it's a different matter since these men seem to be stalking you. You have my word that we're sparing no efforts to apprehend them."

"I don't mean to rush you," Nicole said, getting to her feet, "but I do have an appointment."

Keaton followed her to the front door, and they said their goodbyes. The detective was starting down the front steps, when she turned back. "Oh, Mrs. Graves, there's something I'd like to ask of you, a small favor that might help us find these men. We'd like you to come down to headquarters, look at some photographs, and see if you can identify them."

"All right," Nicole said quickly. At this point she would have agreed to anything to get rid of her. "How about tomorrow morning?"

"Fine," Keaton said. "I'll be by around nine to pick you up. We won't keep you more than an hour or so. By the way, if the Lowrys' tenant contacts you, please let us know."

Nicole regarded her through a narrowing crack in the door. "Is she in some kind of trouble?"

"Oh, heavens no. We just want to ask her a few routine questions." She smiled brightly and gave a wave. "Until tomorrow, then. Look after yourself, Mrs. Graves. And please be more careful with those keys."

Nicole watched from the front window until Keaton got into her car and drove away. Then she waited another two minutes by her watch—an eternity—before she felt it was safe to return to the yard. To her enormous relief, Alice was still there.

This time they left the door of the shed open. Once they were settled, Nicole stationed herself in a spot where she could keep an eye on the gate. Then she said, "Listen, Alice, before you go on, I have to know something."

When Alice nodded her head, Nicole said, "What about my husband? He found this house for us. He said he'd run into Lowry in his company's office here, but how likely is that? Do you know anything that would make you suspect Brad is mixed up with Lowry and Hayes?"

"That I don't know, Nicole. But you say your husband works with computers, and I once overheard Freddy talking about a chap who launders Hayes' drugs money. He said the man was a computer expert who could move money around on the Internet."

Nicole's blood froze. Brad's electronic trading scheme would be the perfect vehicle for laundering money. And Hayes' profits would give Brad the capital he needed to keep his business afloat. Part of her thought it was hard to believe he'd get involved in something that was not only illegal but also dangerous; on another level, it made perfect sense.

"Now, where was I?" Alice said. "Oh, yes, about Sean's diary. Well, I gave it to the police, but they never did follow up. There wasn't anything for me to do but get the goods on Freddy myself, was there? I thought I'd turn it over to someone I know with the tabloids. With that publicity, the police would have to go after him. So I came to the house and said I was looking for a place. Of course, I didn't give them my real name.

"I told the Lowrys I'd heard they sometimes let rooms," she went on. "At first they said they didn't want another tenant. But when I told them I'd help in the house, Muriel's ears pricked up. They invited me in. Next thing I know, Muriel is saying she needs someone in the house, seeing as Freddy is gone all the time. He says they don't know if they can trust me. Muriel says she has a good feeling about me, and she'll keep an eye on me." Alice chuckled.

"They were always doing that, talking about me as if I was deaf or something," she went on. "Of course, I spread the Oirish on so thick I sounded like a foreigner. They think we're all stupid Paddies anyway.

"So I move in and keep my ears open. My bedroom is just down the hall, so I hear more than I want. They don't have much of a marriage. That's for certain."

She got up and stretched. "Stuffy in here," she murmured, raising her arms over her head and yawning.

After a minute or two, she resumed her seat. "So one day Freddy tells Muriel the police are onto him. I don't know, maybe it's Sean's journal that started them watching him. In any case, a couple of detectives corner Freddy, and soon they're saying they have enough to convict him of drug dealing. They give him a choice: They'll put him away for fifteen years. Or he can rat on Hayes and help build a case against him. If Freddy did that, they said, they'd turn a blind eye to what he's done himself.

"So Freddy, willing lad that he is, promises to cooperate. But the whole time they're meeting with him, putting together a case against Hayes, Freddy must have been laying his own plan. It isn't until the night before they leave that I overhear him and Muriel discussing something that makes me think they're about to pull a runner. The police have begun a big crackdown on street dealers, so Hayes is stuck with a huge shipment of cocaine. Freddy had talked Hayes into letting him have it on credit. This is highly unusual, Nicole. Hayes always makes his distributors pay up front. It was a real windfall for Freddy."

As Nicole tried to digest what she'd just heard about Brad, she was having trouble concentrating on Alice's story. But the account of Lowry's windfall did catch her attention. "I guess that means the Lowrys never intended to stay at our place," she said. "They arranged the house swap so they'd have someone occupying their house while they disappeared."

"You may be right," Alice said. "It gave them a chance to get out of the country. Freddy's money worries were over when he got his hands on the new load of drugs. Imagine how I felt at the idea of that bastard walking away free, a rich man, after all he'd done. And Sean only twenty when his life was taken. I wasn't going to let Freddy get away with it. So I found Hayes' number and rang him up. I told him that his trusted associate, Freddy Lowry, had cut a deal with the police.

"But Freddy and Muriel were out of the house the next morning before dawn. It's my guess that Hayes' men couldn't get here in time to stop them," she said. "The last I saw of Frederick H. Lowry, he and Muriel were pulling away in a taxi. I've been trying to track him ever since.

"And I won't give up," she added. "That's for certain. The only clue I have is in the envelope I asked you to bring to the Docklands. You still have it, don't you, Nicole? It's one of the reasons I came back."

"Sure," Nicole said. "Wait here. I know just where it is." She hurried back into the house and retrieved the envelope from where she'd hidden it, behind a plate in the china hutch. As she removed the envelope she noticed the china and figurines on display, a colorful collection of Delft, Wedgwood, and Lladro worth hundreds, perhaps thousands, of dollars. It all made sense now: the expensive furniture, the antiques, the big-screen TV and state-of-the-art sound system in what was basically a very modest house. These were things that could be purchased on the cash economy, without attracting notice from tax authorities.

Back in the shed, Alice extracted the key from the envelope and examined it in a shaft of sunlight before closing her fingers on it. She explained that she'd found the key taped in Sean's journal, along with a rental receipt for a storage locker in Glasgow.

This locker, Alice said, was where Sean kept the drugs he was transporting to London. "First he'd bring the whole load to Glasgow in a rented lorry. Then he'd transfer it to his car, because it's less suspicious than the lorry. Since there wasn't that much space in the car, he'd leave some in storage and then make several trips. I think he must have put some of his own things in the locker as well.

"I found only one of his journals at his place. He'd been keeping them even before he left home, and he always saved the old ones. He kept the used journals in a leather case our da gave him when he went down to London. It wasn't in his flat, and I'm thinking he must have put it in the locker for safekeeping. These journals are just what we need to put Hayes and his whole filthy operation out of business.

"I know you want to see Kevin and Chazz punished for killing the Lowrys' neighbor. But Lowry and Hayes have blood on their hands, too. It would be a travesty if they walk away free. Someone has to go to Glasgow and take a look in that locker."

"I have an idea," Nicole said. "The police are looking for Lowry. Why don't I turn the key over to Keaton? I'll say I found it in the house."

Alice gave a disgusted cluck. "Don't be so bloody wet; the police can't be trusted. I've got a better plan. If Sean's journals have the evidence we need, my friend will write it up for her paper. That will force the police to hunt down Lowry and Hayes, won't it? Meanwhile, if we find Freddy's whereabouts, we'll put in a call to Hayes, and he'll call his dogs off."

"What do you mean? He'll still be looking for his money."

"Yes, but he'll know just where to find Freddy then, won't he?" Alice said. "If Freddy can't cough it up, that's his problem. Meanwhile, Hayes won't have any call to be following you, will he?"

Nicole stared at Alice, trying to digest this plan. It made sense, and yet something still bothered her. "What if you found drugs in that locker?" Nicole said. "What would you do?"

"Not hand it right over to the police. That's for certain." Alice was quiet a moment. "First I'd get a laboratory to weigh and authenticate it. I'd call my reporter friend and ask her along as witness. Then I'd turn it in to HM Customs."

"What if you found the money?"

"Money?" Alice repeated.

"Whatever money Lowry got for the drugs, if he was able to sell them."

Alice paused, as if the possibility hadn't occurred to her. "If Freddy left the U.K.," she said slowly, "you can bet he'd take every penny."

"Well, sure," Nicole said. "He'd try. But it's not so easy walking out of the country with a suitcase full of cash. With Hayes and the police closing in on him, maybe he didn't have time to launder the money, or whatever he'd have to do. Just for the sake of argument, Alice, suppose you did find it?"

"Don't know," Alice said. "A bit like winning the Irish Sweepstakes, isn't it? I mean, drugs money doesn't belong to anyone. The government hasn't any more right to it than you or me." She was silent for a long moment, absorbed in her thoughts as she twisted her hair into a topknot.

"I suppose I'd catch a flight to Switzerland and deposit it in a bank," she finally said. "Then I'd take my own sweet time finding a use for it. I'm thinking I'd like to set up a charity in Sean's name—some kind of anti-drug trust." She was quiet again. Then she said, "So I was wondering, Nicole. Can you help me out?"

"Help you out?"

"Go up to Glasgow and see if Sean's journals are there. You wouldn't have to touch anything else. Just get those journals." Before Nicole could answer, Alice added, "I can't do it myself. Not with the police looking for me."

"Keaton told me they just want to talk to you," Nicole said. "They're not looking to arrest you."

Alice snorted in disgust. "What bloody difference does that make? They'll lock you up in a heartbeat and say you have information about terrorist activities. That's what they did with your husband, isn't it? Look, Nicole, it wouldn't even take you the morning once you're up there."

When Nicole didn't reply, Alice said gently, "No need to give an answer now."

"No. It's okay," Nicole said. "I'll go. It probably would do me good to get out of London for a bit. I want to see those men punished."

"It will do you the world of good to get away from this filthy city," Alice said, her tone growing more enthusiastic. "Have a look in the locker; then you can book one of those posh motor coach tours. A trip up the Scottish coast—just the thing to put the color back into your cheeks. The scenery is gorgeous. The Outer Hebrides and the Orkney Islands—and the Isle of Skye. They say that Skye is one of the most glorious spots on earth.

"The Isle of Skye," Nicole repeated. She pictured a cool, wooded island floating in a vast blue ocean. Then she realized how impossible it was. "How can I go off on a pleasure trip right now?" she said, "Especially if I find evidence against Lowry and Hayes. I'll want to get right back to London and see it through."

"No, Nicole," Alice said. "You'll be shipping the journals to me, and I'll take care of them. You bloody well need some relief. All we're talking about is a few days."

"I don't know," Nicole said, shaking her head. Under the circumstances, she couldn't imagine herself setting off on a sightseeing trip. "But tell me where you're staying, so I can ship the journals if I do find them."

"I can't tell you that," Alice said. "Believe me, it's much safer if you don't know. Safer for both of us. But I'll give you a post office address that belongs to someone who knows how to get in touch with me. You can ship the case with the journals there." She pulled a pencil and a notebook from her backpack and wrote out the address of the storage facility and the PO box where Nicole was to send the journals. Then she tore the page out and handed it to Nicole, along with the key to the storage locker.

"If you don't mind," Alice said. "I'll just leave my rucksack here a bit while I take care of something." She leaned her backpack against the wall. "Don't worry," she said. "We'll be in touch. Take care of yourself."

Alice stepped out of the shed, and once again they embraced. Nicole watched as Alice put on the cap. Then she hopped the fence into Mr. McGiever's yard and disappeared.

Eighteen

Silently, Nicole eased herself out of bed, acutely aware of the slow rhythm of Brad's breathing. His computer was on the desk, no more than six feet from where he was sleeping. Before turning off the light, she'd memorized the machine's position. In the dark, it was relatively easy to disconnect the electric cord; a firm yank pulled it free.

Next, she put his cell phone on top of the computer, picked up the computer and tiptoed across the room. The phone was where he kept the passwords needed to get into his computer and run the software. Brad had explained about this several months before, after a food-poisoning episode incapacitated him. While he was alternately moaning in bed and dashing for the bathroom, his office had called with an urgent need for information kept only on his computer. The job of retrieving it had fallen to Nicole.

She was just walking out of the room when Brad stirred and called out.

"It's okay," she said. "Go back to sleep."

The light snapped on. "Nick—that you? What's wrong?" He sounded a little less groggy now; she wondered how long it would be before he glanced over at the desk and noticed that his beloved laptop was gone.

"Nothing," she said. "Can't sleep. I'm going downstairs to read. Night."

"Night," he mumbled. The lamp went out, and she could hear the bed creaking as he worked to get comfortable again.

In the kitchen, she went through half the passwords before she found one that admitted her to the hard drive (password: Hercules, in honor of a Doberman Brad's family had once owned). That was how Brad's system worked. A password began with the same letter of the alphabet as the program or online service it opened. Not written down were the numbers appended to the end of the name. It was 1984, Brad's birth year, sometimes reversed to 4891. Walter, which was Brad's father's name, opened Westcom Financial Network. Peggy, his mother's name, went with Points West Data Management, and so on. Then she got to an application called GlobalTrader—password Georgia. Who was Georgia? She decided it merited closer inspection.

After tinkering for a while, she figured out that GlobalTrader was a database for tracking financial transactions made through an online service of the same name. The files had two letter names followed by the extension .ACCT. The largest and most extensive file was AH.ACCT. Staring at it, she wondered if AH stood for Alexander Hayes and AH.ACCT for the Alexander Hayes account.

The file contained hundreds of transactions documenting the movement of money around the globe through a series of banks. Although no clue was given about the nature of the initial deposit, subsequent transactions were made electronically, as the money moved from bank to bank, often across international boundaries.

Columns in each row were headed, alternately, Money In and Money Out with the last column marked Commission, F.V.N., which she surmised, was Financial Ventures Network, Brad's new venture.

Each entry showed a date, the amount of deposit or withdrawal, the name of the bank, and an account number. For example, on March 22, £44,910 was deposited in an account at the Federated Bank of the Seychelles Islands, which seemed the hands-up favorite for money-in transactions. On April 1, it was withdrawn and shifted to the National Bank of Nassau. Movement of the £44,910 continued for two rows—a total of eight transfers—until June 3, when it made its way to the Hibernian Bank of Scotland. The Scottish bank, she noted, was where most of the deposits eventually ended up. At this point, £1,796 was deducted from the total and entered in the final column, headed Commission, F.V.N. The £1,796 went into a numbered account at Bank Lucerne.

A web search for Bank Lucerne showed it in Switzerland. Arriving at the bank's website, she consulted the organizer again. The password for this account was Nicole. With some disgust, she wondered why on earth he'd used her name when it didn't even match her initial. But she knew. In some twisted way, he told himself he was doing this for her.

She followed the instructions on the web page, pulling down the menu options to get information in English, amounts in U.S. currency. Then she typed Nicole1984 into the password box, and the balance came up—a whopping $512,000.

Oh, Brad. What have you done?

Just then she glanced at the clock and noticed that it was a little past 5:00 a.m. The sun would rise soon, and Brad would be up. She had to get the computer back.

When she reached the bedroom, the sky was already beginning to show light. This made it easy to put the computer back and plug it in. Even so, she had a few bad moments when Brad stirred and seemed on the verge of waking.

She climbed into bed just as the first rays of sunlight slanted through the window; Brad's eyes fluttered open. He didn't get up right away, but lay there with his hands behind his head, his elbows forming wings on either side.

Neither spoke. Brad was fairly uncommunicative at this hour. As for Nicole, she was stunned by the weight of her discovery. There was no longer any question that Brad was laundering money. He wasn't a small-time chiseler, but a full-fledged criminal. He'd gotten himself in so deep that he'd put her life—both of their lives—in danger.

Even so, it was clear to her—at least from Alice's account—that Chazz and Kevin's campaign of terror hadn't been directed at Brad but at Frederick Lowry, who'd absconded with a sizable shipment of drugs. This suggested that the two men had mistaken her for Muriel Lowry, just as she'd first suspected.

Mistaken identity or not, Nicole thought, Brad was to blame for getting involved with these people. For that she couldn't forgive him. The part that really staggered her was the way he'd disregarded the risks. How could he possibly imagine that he'd get away with this?

What was going to happen when Lowry, Hayes, and the others were caught? Would they bring Brad down with them? This, she decided, was no longer her concern—if Brad was determined to destroy himself, there was nothing she could do.

When Detective Keaton came by the next morning, Nicole was still in a state of shock. Perhaps Keaton misinterpreted this as the lingering effect of the explosion, for she was especially solicitous. As they walked out to the car, she inquired about Nicole's health and the progress of Brad's work. From there, she moved into polite chitchat about the traffic, the weather, the merits of shopping at Marks and Spencer compared to Selfridges or John Lewis.

Only as they sped away from Chiswick did Keaton change the subject, her voice crisp and official. "I'm afraid we found the young woman you knew as Alice McConnehy."

Nicole stared at the woman as goose bumps rose on the back of her neck.

"A man walking his dog along the Thames Embankment last night spotted a woman's shoe among some flotsam," Keaton went on. "On closer inspection, he saw it was a body and called us. Although the woman had no identification, we were able to identify her as the Lowrys' tenant."

"She isn't ... You don't mean ..." Nicole's voice trailed off. Somehow, she couldn't form the words.

"Dreadfully sorry," Keaton said gently. "It appears to have been foul play."

Nicole swallowed hard. "How did it happen?"

"We're not sure, but we have reason to believe she was killed elsewhere before being dropped in the river. We'll have more information when the medical examiner completes his report. That may take several days."

As hot tears began to spill down Nicole's cheeks, Keaton pulled a white, lace-edged handkerchief from her purse and handed it to her.

After the first jolt of shock, Nicole began to feel guilty she hadn't done more to help Alice. At the very least, she could have found her friend a place to hide. The Lowrys' house would have made an ideal hiding place: so obvious no one would think of looking there.

They rode for a while without speaking, the detective intent on negotiating a traffic snarl while Nicole snuffled into the handkerchief. Over and over, she replayed the moment the previous afternoon when Alice disappeared into Mr. McGiever's yard, as if there were a way to summon her back.

At last the car jostled over a curb and they entered a parking lot. Keaton maneuvered the vehicle into a tight space next to a tall iron fence. Getting out of the car, she bustled around to take Nicole's arm. "This is it," she said with a smile. "Our local headquarters."

Nicole gazed vaguely around at the unpretentious office complex; she followed Keaton into the main building. Inside, the corridors were buzzing with activity. About half the people they passed were in uniform, the others in casual business attire. Keaton, in her beige suit and peach silk blouse, looked somehow dated and out of place, a relic from another era when women tried to dress for success.

Keaton led Nicole up several flights to a small room furnished with several chairs and a table holding a computer. Keaton sat down and went through several screens until a database of mug shots popped up. Then she turned the computer over to Nicole who began looking through the photos, one by one.

Nicole was amazed by the number of people who resembled Kevin with his thin face and shaggy, dark hair. Even so, Kevin himself wasn't among the mug shots. As for Chazz, he seemed to be one of a kind, for she saw no one with his beady pig eyes and ruffles of chins.

The whole time she was going through the mug shots, Nicole was thinking of Alice. Finally, she turned to Keaton and said, "How can you be sure that body really was Alice, if there was no ID?"

"Before the body was found, we received a tip about the killing—informants, that sort of thing," Keaton said. "The body had deteriorated somewhat, but . . ."

"Wait," Nicole said. "How long had she been in the water?"

"The coroner estimated two or three days, maybe longer," the detective said.

"But . . ." Nicole caught herself. She had been on the verge of blurting out the truth—that it couldn't have been Alice; she'd seen her the previous afternoon. "That's terrible," she finished lamely. Then she took a deep breath; feeling enormously relieved, she turned her attention to the photographs.

When a couple of hours had passed, Keaton asked if she was getting tired. Nicole had to admit that the faces were all looking alike. They agreed that she'd come back the next morning to finish.

Only as they were on their way back to Chiswick did Nicole begin to wonder if Keaton's story about the dead woman might have been a deliberate lie, something the detective cooked up in hopes of squeezing more information out of her. If so, it had almost worked.

Nicole took precautions before going out to check on Alice's backpack, first making sure Keaton's car was gone, then pretending to take out the garbage before nipping into the shed.

The backpack was leaning against the wall, just as Alice had left it. Nicole quickly thrust the pack into a trash bag she'd brought along for the purpose.

A minute or so later, she was in the Lowrys' bedroom, unbuckling the flap on the backpack. Carefully, she removed each item and placed it on the bed.

On top was the envelope Nicole had returned to Alice the previous afternoon, still holding the same £300. It seemed odd that Alice hadn't returned for the money. The other contents didn't amount to much—a change of underwear, a T-shirt, a toothbrush, toothpaste, and a comb. She found another £20 note, tightly folded into a tiny square inside of a cheap plastic wallet that lacked photos, credit cards, or any sort of ID.

She returned everything to the backpack. After a moment's thought, she hurriedly selected a few basic toiletries and a couple of items from the closet and threw them into a plastic shopping bag. Putting on her jacket, she gathered up the shopping bag, her purse, and Alice's backpack and carried them downstairs.

From the kitchen, she called the railway information number; while she was on hold, she decided to leave a note for Brad to explain her absence. Not that he deserved an explanation, but if she didn't leave one, he was sure to call the police, and that was the last thing she needed

"Brad," she wrote, "I've decided to see a little of the English countryside while I make some decisions about the future. I'll be gone a couple of days, maybe more. Don't worry about me. I'll be all right."

She'd almost forgotten the phone propped against her ear when a woman came on and said brightly, "Rail services information." It didn't take long to get the information she needed.

Nicole left the note for Brad on the dinette table, anchored under a bottle of Worcestershire sauce. Then, after returning the backpack to its spot in the shed, she was on her way.

When she reached the Turnham Green Station, she paused in the gloom of the entryway and looked around. Spotting the sign, WOMEN'S TOILETS she headed purposefully through the swinging door.

The restroom was clean, although the lighting was a bit on the anemic side. The ancient black-and-white tile floor looked freshly scrubbed, and the air was filled with fumes of an especially noxious disinfectant. Placing her shopping bag on a shelf, she pulled the pink raincoat out of the bag and put it on. This time she didn't bother altering her makeup, except to blot off her lipstick.

When she was done, she put on the white-framed sunglasses and the pink hat. After inspecting herself in the mirror, she decided she would do. If anyone had followed her here, he probably wouldn't recognize her. She checked her watch, noting with satisfaction that she'd allowed plenty of time to get to Euston Station and catch the train to Glasgow. She wasn't planning to get there by tube but had only stopped at the Chiswick station as a diversion, in case she was being followed. Her plan was to return to the street and hail a cab.

As she walked back through the station lobby, she spotted Reinhardt. He was leaning against the wall, talking on his phone. Her heart began to pound as his eyes swept over her without a flicker of interest. Not too fast, she cautioned herself, although it was hard to keep from running. As she reached the exit, she couldn't resist stealing a backward glance. Still engaged on the phone, he now had his back to her and was leaning with one elbow propped against the wall.

From that moment on, everything seemed to click. As soon as Nicole stepped out on the sidewalk, a cab pulled up, and she climbed aboard. They made it to Euston Station with over an hour to spare. Despite the recent bomb scare, the station seemed to be doing business as usual. Joining one of the long ticket lines, she fidgeted, nervously watching the clock as the queue inched forward. When she reached the window, she handed over her credit card for a first-class round trip to Glasgow. From there, she stopped at the tourist information booth and then headed for the train.

Once onboard, Nicole made her way directly to the lavatory, a coffin-sized compartment where a rank, organic stench competed with the reek of chemicals. Over the toilet, a sign warned, DO NOT USE WHILE TRAIN IS STANDING AT A STATION. As Nicole eyed the message, trying to sort out its implications, the train began to move.

Bracing her feet against the motion, she struggled out of the pink coat and hat and did her best to cram both items into the room's only trash receptacle, a small wire wastebasket. She looked in the mirror, gave her hair a final fluff, and reapplied her lipstick.

She walked unsteadily along the swaying corridor, past a series of unoccupied compartments toward the front of the train. She chose the second compartment and, once inside, locked the door. Here, she reasoned, she'd be undisturbed. It seemed unlikely that many passengers would walk this far forward in search of a seat.

Nicole sat back and watched as the bleak apartments on the outskirts of London gave way to open countryside. Fences of thickly grown shrubbery sectioned off the rolling fields into a patchwork of neat green squares.

She had the most delicious feeling of release as the wheels clickety clacked, carrying her away from her troubles—away from Brad and Brenda, Chazz and Kevin, and Detective Keaton. She'd even managed, at last, to shake Reinhardt. All she had to do for the next few hours was relax and enjoy the Scottish countryside.

NINETEEN

THROUGH THE FOG OF SLEEP, Nicole could hear the sound of someone tapping. At first she thought it was Alice knocking at the kitchen window. When she opened her eyes, she remembered she was on the train to Glasgow. The conductor was tapping on the window of her compartment. "Train's in, miss," he called, as he moved along the passage. "Time to wake up."

Apparently the train had been in for a while. Except for Nicole and the conductor, it appeared empty. Above, through the station's vaulted glass ceiling, daylight had almost vanished, and she could see a faint sprinkling of stars. Below the glass, a bright array of flags announced an upcoming exhibit at a local museum.

Earlier, at Euston Station, the woman in the visitor's information booth had explained that the Glasgow train station featured a hotel on top. "It's a very convenient location for a woman traveling on her own," she had said. "Would you like me to make a reservation for you?" Without giving it much thought, Nicole had agreed. Now, groggy from the long nap, she was grateful she wouldn't have to hunt down a cab and look for a place to stay. She easily found an elevator that carried her up into the hotel; the desk clerk was expecting her. The hotel wasn't up to the standard of a Hyatt or a Doubletree. Her room, on the second floor, was a dismal combination of brown and yellow that seemed to match the lingering smell of Pinesol and old cigarette smoke. Okay, she told herself. It's only for one night.

She locked the door and checked the small clock radio on the night table. It was just past 9:00 p.m., which meant it would be around 1:00 p.m. in L.A. She thought of her burglarized condo and decided to put a call in to her sister. Reaching Stephanie's voicemail, Nicole left a message, along with the number of the hotel and her room. "Don't worry," she said. "Everything's fine. But please call me back."

She was up and dressed before 8:00 a.m. Before leaving the room, she called Keaton's office and left a message canceling her appointment to finish looking at the mug shots. She didn't give a reason but promised she'd call soon to reschedule.

Remembering that Stephanie hadn't returned her call, she checked her phone for messages or email. Nothing. She reminded herself that her sister was always overextended, running late, neglecting messages.

The dining room offered the complete Scottish breakfast (included with the price of a room). The huge buffet spread featured warming trays of scrambled eggs, kippers, bangers, thick slices of what she'd always regarded as Canadian bacon (but was just called bacon here), hot oatmeal, and dark unappetizing slabs of something a waiter identified as blood pudding. There were also trays of small Danish pastries, soft rolls, and whole grain bread. There was cold cereal, too, and bowls of figs, cooked prunes, orange and grapefruit sections. She drank lots of hot coffee and sampled everything but the kippers and blood pudding.

In front of the hotel, the sun was no match for the chilly breeze. Waiting for a taxi, she buttoned her jacket, pulled up the collar, and considered the task ahead. Now that she was here, she had a feeling this excursion was a waste of time. On the other hand, if she did find Sean's journals, it would be an easy matter to ship them to the address Alice had given her. What worried her was the possibility that, despite all her precautions, she was being followed.

She kept turning around to check the rear window as the cab headed toward the outskirts of the city and began to pick up speed. The buildings grew seedier by the block. Even though she didn't see anyone following her, she couldn't seem to shake her uneasiness.

They turned onto a street where shabby Victorians alternated with newer two- and three-story brick structures in an equal state of decay. The cabby stopped at the address she'd given him. The building was in slightly better shape than its neighbors and appeared occupied; even so, it had a strange anonymity, lacking any signs or placards to identify the businesses inside.

The lobby was chilly and deserted. To locate the building directory, Nicole had to walk down the hall and turn a corner. The MacLowe Removal & Storage Company occupied floors four through seven. When the elevator opened on the fourth floor, the dim hallway gave her a feeling of déjà vu. She held down the "open" button and called a wary, "Hello!" into the gloom. Then louder, "Is anyone there?"

"Come all the way down the corridor and then turn left!" a man shouted from the distance.

The owner of the voice was a thin, balding man with red-rimmed eyes. He looked frail, and his skin had a pallid glow that suggested a lifetime avoiding the sun. He pulled out a ledger and slapped it down in front of him. When Nicole reached the counter, he twirled the book around to face her and thrust a pen into her hand.

The page contained only a few signatures, the most recent dated two days earlier. Nicole had already decided to sign it as

Alice and explain that she was Sean's sister. When she finished, she handed back the pen.

Without a glance at what she'd written, much less any questions, the man slammed the ledger shut and shoved it back under the counter. Then he produced a dented metal flashlight and passed it to her. As he started toward the door behind him, she said, "I've forgotten exactly where the locker is. Could you...?"

"Here, show me your key," he said. After giving it a cursory glance, he gestured toward a dark alcove about twenty feet away. "You can use the stairs," he said. "Your unit is one floor up. At the head of the stairs, turn right and walk along the corridor." He gestured with a wag of his head. "Then left. Number's on the door." He turned and disappeared through the doorway.

Nicole climbed the stairs; using the flashlight to read the numbers, she passed dozens of storage spaces that resembled small rooms rather than lockers. At last, she came to 571, which appeared to be the number on the key. She attempted to unlock the door, but the key didn't work.

Back in the hallway, she trained the flashlight on the key and took a closer look. This time, she saw that the etched numbers were so worn they might as easily be read as 577 or 517. She tried 577. No luck. Finally, at 511, the key fit.

The room was small, lit by a single dim bulb. An attaché case was sitting on the floor and three cartons were stacked against one wall.

Nicole squatted down and took a close look at the attaché case. It was brown leather, new, and well made. It might have been the one Alice had described except for a distinguishing feature she hadn't mentioned. Dangling from its handle was a solid-looking brass chain with a manacle meant to be worn around the wrist to prevent theft. Why, she asked herself, would anyone go to such lengths to protect some old diaries? Obviously, Alice hadn't given her the whole story.

After determining the case was locked, Nicole picked it up. It was surprisingly heavy. When she gave a gentle shake, it didn't rattle; the solid weight told her it was full. She set it down and went over to the cartons. Two were empty, and the third was sealed with heavy strapping tape.

Nicole knew she should simply take the attaché case and walk away, but there were too many unanswered questions. Before she decided what to do with it, she'd have to find out what was in it. And what about the sealed box?

She gave the carton a shake, and several objects rolled about, like a pair of tennis shoes. Next, she tried peeling off the tape. When this failed, she dug around in her purse; finding nothing equal to the job of cutting the tape, she left the room and went down to the desk.

The man was nowhere in sight. She hesitated a moment, then went behind the counter and knocked on the door. After a brief pause, it opened, and the man peered out. Behind him, she caught a glimpse of a room lit only by the flicker of a small TV.

His eyes were even redder than before, and his breath so reeked of whiskey that it forced her to step back. "I wonder if I could borrow a letter opener or a pair of scissors," she said.

He emerged from his room as she retreated back into the hallway. Without a word or even a glance in her direction, he began rifling through drawers and cupboards. At last he produced a pair of scissors, which he slapped down on the counter before disappearing back into his room.

"Thanks," she called after him. Scissors in hand, she hurried away, taking the stairs two at a time. Once inside 511, she relocked the door and began on the sealed carton, using the scissors to slit the tape and pulling back the flaps. Once it was open, she sat back on her heels and stared at the contents.

The box held three clear plastic bags of white powder. They were about the size of two-pound sacks of powdered sugar. In fact, the contents might have been powdered sugar or flour or cornstarch, but something told her it wasn't. As she closed the box, she wiped it with the inside hem of her skirt, in case she'd left fingerprints.

Next, she turned her attention to the attaché case. Crouching beside it, she jammed the point of the scissors into the lock, then tried to force it with a quick twisting motion. When nothing happened, she did it again. This time, the scissors jerked away from the lock with a loud snap. Taking a closer look, she saw that the tip of the blade had broken off and was now wedged in the keyhole. It took considerable pulling and tugging to extract the piece of metal, but the case still wouldn't open.

She stood up again and considered what to do. One possibility would be to take the attaché case back to the hotel where she'd have the time and resources to deal with the lock. But this might present other problems. What would she do, for example, if the briefcase contained more of the incriminating white powder?

On the other hand, she felt an enormous need to see justice done in the deaths of Alice's brother and poor old Mr. McGiever. If there was a chance Sean's journals were in the attaché case, how could she just walk away and leave it?

With the attaché case and broken scissors in hand, she headed back down to the desk and was somewhat relieved to find it still unattended. She left the scissors on the counter, along with a £10 note to cover the cost of replacement.

Outside, no cabs were in sight. After walking a block and a half in search of a taxi, she noticed a hardware store. Inside, she placed the attaché case on the counter and explained to the clerk that the lock was broken. "I'm leaving for the airport in an hour," she said, "and my plane ticket is inside. I need something to pry it open."

The clerk, a burly man with a beard, stared at the attaché case with its gleaming chain and manacle, then gave her a funny look. "That's a job for a locksmith, young lady," he said. "Or a luggage shop."

"I don't have time!" She was running out of patience. *How hard can this be?* "I'll miss my plane if I don't leave soon. You must have some kind of pick or chisel I could use on the lock."

"It would be a crime to ruin a fine piece of luggage like that." He gave her the odd look again, then reached out and picked up the attaché case. "Why don't you let me try to coax it?"

"I've already tried everything," she said. "Look, my husband is waiting out in the car. We're in a terrible hurry."

The man shrugged and pursed his lips. Then he reached into a cubbyhole behind him and pulled out a gadget that looked like a cross between a small crowbar and a medium sized screw driver. "Here," he said. "You may be able to do something with this." He came from behind the counter to get a hammer out of a bin. "If the lock still won't give, you could do this." He demonstrated, wedging the tool under the lock and waving the hammer at it. Then he shook his head and turned down the corners of his mouth. "It would be a sin to ruin such a fine leather case." His expression was so doleful it almost made her want to apologize.

Back in her room, Nicole lay the attaché case on the bed, stuck the tool in the lock and went to work with the hammer. The lock was stubborn, requiring half a dozen blows before it broke open.

She lifted the lid of the attaché case and then stood there, gaping. There were no journals, no bags of cocaine. Only money: banded stacks of lavender-colored bills. They were a currency she'd never seen before. Nicole pulled one out so she could read the print. It said "1000" and, in smaller letters, "Banque National Svisse."

She studied it a long time before she reached out and ran her hand over the cool, flat surface of tightly packed bills. There were ten stacks. She pulled out one of the stacks and counted. It held 100 notes.

She returned the bills to the case, then got out her phone to look up the currency exchange rate. The phone was dead—the battery drained again. She'd left her charger at the house and made a mental note to pick one up.

She went over to the phone on the night table and dialed 0. "Can you connect me with a bank?" she said.

"What bank, miss?" the operator said.

Nicole stepped to the window and looked out. Scanning the surrounding buildings, she spotted a sign and read it aloud. "The Bank of Caledonia."

At last she was connected to the foreign currency department. "Can you tell me how much a 1,000 Swiss francs is worth in dollars?" she asked.

After a pause, a man at the other end of the line said, "Approximately $1,108, minus our commission. That's the fee we charge for changing one currency into another."

After she hung up, she counted the stacks and calculated the total number of notes: 1,000 in all. When she did the math, the sum came to $1,108,000. How could it be that much? she wondered. It fit in a briefcase and seemed to weigh no more than seven or eight pounds, counting the case.

As much as the amount terrified her, she knew she wasn't going to return it to the storage space, or ship it to Alice, as she'd promised. Alice had lied to her. She'd known all along what was in the attaché case. Besides, the money was evidence in a murder investigation. It had been the motive behind the car bombing, and she had a duty to turn it over to the police.

Nicole also understood that the police would ask her a lot of embarrassing questions. They'd be especially interested in her secret meetings with Alice. Even so, she doubted they'd make any real trouble for her. Keaton herself had said the police didn't have a warrant out for Alice. More recently, of course, the detective had even told her Alice was dead.

One thing was clear. She couldn't carry this huge sum back on the train, nor was she willing to hand it over to the authorities in Glasgow. She'd read about too many cases in which the LAPD had mishandled evidence. In a number of instances, they'd lost the evidence altogether. Her recent experience with the British police made her suspect they weren't much better. She decided that if she wanted the car bombing case resolved, she'd have to turn the money directly over to Keaton or, better yet, to the team investigating the case.

She had an idea: There wasn't any reason she and the attaché case couldn't make their way back to London separately. She could ship it overnight by Federal Express. She remembered seeing a FedEx office on her cab ride that morning, just a few blocks from the hotel.

Then something else occurred to her. Someone had left over a million dollars, along with a sizable stash of cocaine, in that locker. It had to be Lowry's profit and leftovers from the drugs Hayes had given him on credit. For the first time, she began to wonder if he'd made it out of the country after all.

Twenty

The mini bar was too small, even after Nicole took out the little liquor bottles and removed the shelf. Under the bed was too obvious, as were the closet and shower.

Yet she couldn't bring the money with her. For one thing, the lock on the attaché case was broken and refused to stay closed. Even if it would, she couldn't imagine walking around a place as public as Glasgow's Central Station, toting $1,000,000 in cash. Her only option was to find a good place to stash it while she went downstairs and found what she needed.

For a moment, Nicole studied the drapes—pleated panels of a homely brown-and-beige tropical print that hung to the floor. Placing the attaché case under the window, she pulled the drapes shut and decided this would do. As long as the drapes remained closed, no one would guess something was hidden there.

As the elevator began its descent, she had fresh misgivings. She'd left the DO NOT DISTURB sign on the door. Only now did she think of experiences she'd had at hotels back home where staff often ignored DO NOT DISTURB signs. She pictured what would happen if a maid arrived to clean her room. She'd knock; when no one answered, she'd go right in. The maid would open the drapes first thing. When she saw the hidden attaché case, she wouldn't have to be a genius to figure out that it held something of value.

Still deep in thought, Nicole glanced at the other passenger. He was tall and beefy with graying sideburns. It seemed to her that she'd seen him before; as she breathed in the heavy smell of his aftershave, she remembered. The same man had been in line behind her when she checked into the hotel. My God, was he following her?

In a sudden panic, she reached out and jabbed the button for the hotel lobby, a floor above street level, where she'd been headed. The elevator jerked to a stop, and she bolted out, pursued by the heady reek of aftershave. It took enormous will power not to look back to see if he got off, too.

At the desk, she asked for her messages, her thoughts shifting briefly to her dead cell phone and her failed attempt to reach her sister. The clerk told her there was nothing in her box. When she ventured a glance around, the lobby was deserted. The elevator door had closed, and the man was nowhere in sight.

Turning back to the desk clerk, she asked directions to the nearest stairwell. Upon finding it, she scurried down two steps at a time.

This morning the station was alive with travelers—commuters, tourists, shoppers. The sun, streaming in through the glass dome, made the heavy stone structure seem light and airy. Like highflying kites, the bright banners suspended from the rafters lent a festive touch, as did the rich fragrance of coffee from an Italian-style coffee bar. She passed it and went into the bookshop next door. Just as she'd hoped, it had a reasonably well-stocked stationery department, where she selected two rolls of brown wrapping paper, heavy-duty strapping tape, and twine.

At the checkout stand, she asked if the shop had an empty carton she might have. The clerk was dark and compact with bushy eyebrows that met in the middle. He eyed her in a way she didn't like, as if she were the merchandise, and he was considering a purchase. "Afraid not, luv," he said. "You can ask at the gift shop. That old lady sometimes has a box or two, but she'll make you pay a pretty penny."

"Thanks," she said, rankling under his gaze. As soon as he counted out her change, she hurried away.

Two doors down, the window of a gift shop sparkled with crystal glassware. As soon as Nicole stepped into the shop, the salesclerk bustled over. She was a sizable woman in a red challis dress, tucked and gusseted to fit like a slipcover. "May I help you, dear?" she said.

Nicole smiled. "I'm looking for an empty carton—you know, so I can pack something for mailing."

"Oh, my dear, I'm afraid I can't help you there. Each item we stock is packed at the factory in its own special carton. We haven't any to spare." The woman had a flutey voice and a cultivated accent with only the slightest hint of a Scottish brogue.

"All right," Nicole said, trying to hold on to her patience. "What can I buy that comes packed in a box about this size?" She held up her hands and outlined a box big enough to accommodate the attaché case.

The woman turned and pointed at a large cut glass vase in a display case. "What about this absolutely gorgeous vase?" She pronounced it vaaze.

Nicole studied the vase for a few seconds. It was a Victorian design of cut glass, heavy and bulbous. "I'll take it," she said.

"You have exquisite taste," the woman said, plucking the vase from the shelf and holding it up to read the tiny sticker on its stem. "This piece is only £140," she said. "And you can save over £20 when you recover the VAT. You fill out a form at the airport…"

As the woman went into detail about this process, Nicole reached into her purse and silently produced her credit card. For the briefest moment, she considered reimbursing herself out of the bills in the attaché case before rejecting the idea. The money was dirty; she didn't want anything to do with it.

As the woman rang up the sale, Nicole said. "Don't forget the box."

"Of course not," the woman said. "Would you like us to send it for you?"

"No." Nicole said, feeling another surge of irritation. Couldn't the woman see that she was only buying the vase so she could have the box? "I'll take it with me."

Once the vase was paid for, the woman retreated into a rear storeroom to look for the carton. Nicole, left alone by the cash register, paced up and down, her thoughts alternating between the money hidden upstairs and the man she'd seen on the elevator.

A minute passed, then two, and still the woman didn't return. At last, Nicole made her way to the back of the shop and through the doorway where the woman had disappeared. As soon as Nicole stepped into the cluttered storage room, she noticed a pile of empty cartons against one wall. Then, looking up, she spotted the saleswoman. She was perched on a ladder at the back of the room, poking into the upper reaches of the top shelf.

"Excuse me," Nicole called up. "But I'm in a dreadful hurry. Any of these empty cartons will do."

"Oh, those cartons are for other merchandise we have in the shop," the woman said. "We save each one until the item is sold."

"But you'll always have extra cartons—as long as you have merchandise on display," Nicole pointed out. "Look, I'll give you £50 for an empty carton—£50 cash. You can keep the vase."

The woman looked down at her. "Why, my dear," she said, as if she were deeply offended. "I couldn't possibly do such a thing. This won't take a minute. I know I saw that carton up here just the other day. "

After what seemed an eternity, Nicole was finally heading for her hotel room with the boxed vase in her arms. When the elevator stopped on the second floor, she used the button to hold the door open while she looked up and down the hall. It appeared empty, and yet she felt a sudden tug of alarm, the sense of someone watching her.

She felt an almost irresistible impulse to leave, to simply punch the elevator's down button and walk out of the hotel. Nicole pictured herself calling the police from the train station to tell them where she'd left the money. Even if it never made its way to the London police, at least she'd have tried.

The elevator began to make a loud, buzzing protest; she released the button and hurried to her room. She had to set the box on the floor to find her key. As she fumbled with the lock, her hands shook.

When the door swung open, the room was just as she'd left it. Once inside, she fastened the chain lock. Then she tossed the box on the bed and pulled the attaché case from behind the drapes. She lifted the top; the money was still there.

She removed the vase and plastic popcorn from the carton and put in the money from the attaché case. The box was a little bigger than she needed, but she had plenty of packing material to fill the empty space. She used the brown paper, tape, and twine she'd bought to wrap the box.

By the time it arrived at the house in Chiswick, she'd be there to receive it, but she couldn't help imagining what would happen if Brad were to get a look at this money. One thing was certain: a million dollars wouldn't intimidate him the way it had her. He'd instantly know what he wanted to do with it. She could almost hear him trying to persuade her to deposit it in an offshore bank account so the IRS wouldn't find out about it. Then he'd want her to invest it in some screwball scheme he'd cooked up.

When the package was ready, she pulled out her phone. Remembering her cell was dead, Nicole used the room phone to call her sister again, hanging up when she reached voicemail. Where had Stephanie disappeared to? If there was no answer next time, she promised herself, she'd call her sister's best friend and have her track down Stephanie.

Before Nicole unlatched the chain, she opened the door and peeked out. The hallway was empty. She went back to the bed to get the package and hurried out. This time, she headed toward the rear exit sign where a narrow, uncarpeted staircase delivered her into the alley behind the hotel.

Nicole headed east, where she'd seen the FedEx office. The box was fairly heavy, and she was sweating from the effort. Besides the weight, walking down the street with so much money in her arms was terrifying. She was suspicious of every person she passed. Those approaching from the opposite direction seemed to stare knowingly at the carton.

Up ahead, a crowd had gathered around a store window where a soccer game was in progress on a huge TV set. Just as she reached the gathering, there was a sudden screech of brakes and a loud crash as an old white American-made sedan—an Oldsmobile, she thought it was—smacked into the side of a new red Hyundai hatchback, which was parked in front of the store. Nicole's heart dropped to her shoes as the hatchback lifted briefly in the air and hopped onto the nearby curb. The white car paused only a moment before speeding away.

No one was hurt, but the crash was enough to pull the crowd away from the TV set to gather around the Hyundai.

A man—his face nearly as red as the car—came dashing out of a nearby barbershop with a towel draped around his neck. "The bloody bastard!" he screamed, whipping off the towel and flinging it to the pavement. "Did anyone get his bloody license number?" No one had. Heads were shaken, and several people turned and moved away, as if they were afraid the man might blame them. After circling the car to assess the damage, he raised his arms toward the sky in an almost biblical gesture. "Will you look at that?" he shouted. "The bloody sod! Me brand new motor, and see what he's done!"

For a minute or so, Nicole stood at the edge of the circle, staring. At last, she pulled herself away. Only as she resumed her trek toward FedEx, did she fully understand what had almost happened. If the little red Hyundai hadn't been parked there, the car would have driven right up onto the sidewalk. She or someone else could have been badly hurt, or even killed.

She couldn't help wondering if this incident, too, had something to do with her. My God, Nicole thought. The money is making me crazy. She had to get rid of it before she completely lost her grip.

FedEx was crowded. She got into line and then, setting the carton on the floor, filled out the mailing form. She put down herself at the Chiswick address as both sender and addressee.

At last, Nicole reached the head of the line and made her way to the window. With a sigh of relief, she surrendered her burden into the hands of one of the uniformed clerks, an auburn-haired woman with a furrowed brow, who looked as if she took her job very seriously.

"My word, that's heavy," the woman was saying. "What do you have in here?"

"Just some books," Nicole said.

"Why don't you send it along at our third-day rate, then? It won't be nearly so dear, although will take a little longer..."

"No, thanks," Nicole said. "I want to be sure it gets there tomorrow."

The woman's smile faded. "Well, suit yourself," she said. "That'll be fifteen pounds, thirty seven P." She sounded cross, as if the money were coming out of her own pocket.

Once Nicole was on the sidewalk with the shipping receipt in her hand, she felt an enormous sense of relief. She let out a deep breath and, for the first time, began to look around at her surroundings. Many of the buildings were quaintly Victorian, constructed of sand-colored stone. The one across the street had elaborate gingerbread trim that included garlands of leaves and flowers as well as angels, serpents, and gargoyles. She strolled along at a leisurely pace, gazing in shop windows. They were filled with tantalizing goods—smart clothes, lush woolens, hand-knit sweaters, fuzzy toys, fine china.

Nicole couldn't remember when she'd last felt so light hearted. What a relief it was to be rid of that awful burden. There was no reason to hurry back to the hotel, none at all.

As she strolled along, she spotted a travel agency and stopped to look in the window. A poster promoted a U.S. tour of astounding geographic scope—from the New York skyline and Disney World to the Grand Canyon, Santa Fe, and the Golden Gate Bridge. Another poster advertised a luxury coach tour up the West coast of Scotland and out to the islands of Mull, Skye, and the Outer Hebrides. It was, in fact, the very tour Alice had recommended. A large color photo showed majestic stone ruins sitting on a promontory overlooking a rugged ocean. Sea and sky were both the same impossible shade of blue. "Exclusive tours from central Scotland to unhurried, unspoiled places," the poster read. "Small groups, fine hotels."

Nicole had always avoided group tours. Part of it was a fear of getting stuck for days, even weeks with people she had nothing in common with. Nor did she like the idea of being herded around twelve hours a day by a tour guide. But as she gazed at the photo of a large, well-appointed bus filled with smiling tourists, she realized how safe she'd feel among these solid, respectable companions.

Once she went back to London and handed over the money, maybe she would take this tour. She certainly wasn't going to spend any more time in Chiswick. And it would be stupid to return to L.A. without seeing something of the U.K.

Starting back to the hotel, Nicole entered a street of fashionable shops, separated from the main flow of traffic by planter boxes.

The shops were housed in a block-long building of the same sandy stone she'd noticed before. This particular structure had bright gold awnings and deeply-inset arched windows. She stopped in front of a shop with two mannequins in the window. One wore a long, flowing print dress with lace trim. Next to it, the second figure was dressed in a smart, short-skirted dress of mauve linen. A sign, leaning against the stand of the mauve-dressed mannequin, read, WE SPECIALIZE IN SMALL SIZES. After a moment's hesitation, Nicole went in.

An hour later, she emerged with a substantial load of goods. She'd acquired some lacy lingerie, a nightgown and matching robe, a sweater set, a hooded sweatshirt, several knit shirts, and jeans. As she was leaving, the girl directed her to a leather shop a few blocks away where she bought comfortable walking shoes and a suitcase to replace the one she'd lost.

By the time her shopping was complete, she was so loaded down that she had to take a cab back to the hotel. She instructed the driver to go around to the alley; she had him wait while she transferred her new things into the suitcase. She left the empty shopping bags on the floor of the cab. She paid the driver, adding a generous tip, and then hurried in the back door of the hotel. It was only a few steps to the stairs.

The maid seemed to have skipped her room. The DO NOT DISTURB sign was in place, the bed unmade. The crystal vase and empty attaché case were still where she'd left them.

She took her things out of the suitcase and neatly refolded them. Then she changed into jeans and a sweater, tossing the rumpled jacket, skirt and blouse into a plastic laundry bag, which she also placed in the suitcase.

The vase was relegated to the wastebasket with the attaché case on the floor next to it. On each, she placed a note saying, "Trash. To be thrown away. Thanks!"

She checked the train schedule and looked at her watch. The next train to London left in eighteen minutes. Maybe she could catch it. If she used instant checkout, she wouldn't even have to go downstairs to settle the bill.

In her rush, she neglected to check the hallway before unfastening the chain. Perhaps it wouldn't have made any difference. The lock was flimsy, and there were two of them waiting in the hall, one on either side of her door.

As she emerged from the room, Chazz grabbed her right arm, and Kevin seized the left. She dropped the suitcase and tried to scream. By then Chazz, who seemed to know what to expect, had clamped his hand over her mouth.

There was a long moment while she resisted, trying to wrest herself free. But the harder she fought, the tighter he grasped the lower part of her face, until she was gasping for breath. Then his grip loosened, and she was able to turn her head away.

That's when she spotted Reinhardt hurrying toward them with a gun in his hand. "Police," he said, motioning with the weapon. "Release the woman and step back against the wall."

Instead of releasing her, Chazz shoved her forward, cupped one hand under her chin, and twisted her head sideways at a painful angle. "Drop the gun," he shouted, "or I'll break her neck."

Reinhardt did as he was told, tossing the weapon behind him, Then he hurled himself at them. The three men began to struggle, with Reinhardt trying to force Chazz to let go of her.

In the confusion, she saw someone approaching from the rear hallway. It was the bald, portly man she'd seen on the elevator, the one with the overpowering aftershave. For a moment she thought help had arrived. But when he began sneaking up behind Reinhardt, she understood that he, too, was in league against them.

She struggled to call out, but Chazz's hand was over her mouth, and he had his other arm wrapped around her neck. All she could do was watch helplessly while the newcomer took a gun from his pocket, raised it in the air, and brought it down on the back of

Reinhardt's head. The blow made a sickening, hollow sound, and Reinhardt crumpled to the floor.

Before Nicole could see what happened next, Chazz shoved her against the wall and jabbed a needle into her shoulder. She heard a dull popping noise somewhere behind her, and everything went dark.

Twenty-One

At first Nicole was aware only of pain. It centered in her jaw, a vibrating sort of ache that grew to a crescendo and then retreated before starting in again. She half imagined herself in a dentist's chair, sitting under the drill. Drifting closer to consciousness, she realized she was lying face down on a hard surface that was shaking violently against her lower jaw. It was dark and bitterly cold.

She put her arm under her chin to cushion it. The ache began to subside, and once more she dozed. The next time she opened her eyes, the ache had spread to her entire body. Her mind was clear enough to grasp that she was in a moving vehicle. Either its shocks were gone, or it was traveling on a badly pitted road. As it bounced along, the movement pummeled her body against the hard floor.

She shifted to her other side. But as one set of discomforts eased, others surfaced—the cold, the stiffness of her muscles, and, worst of all, the complete and unremitting darkness.

She made an attempt to sit up but only managed to bump her head. Scrabbling her hands around, she discovered a low ceiling immediately above. Lying next to her was a large rounded object with jagged grooves that identified it as a tire. Now she understood why it was so dark. She was in the trunk of a car.

Once again, she ran her hands across the surface above, this time more carefully, searching for a latch. All she could feel were smooth, rounded walls.

As her desperation grew, Nicole heard someone crying. She stopped and listened, trying to pinpoint where the sound was coming from. When she realized the sobs were her own, an enormous wave of despair washed over her. She knew they were going to kill her. They planned to abandon the car in a remote place, leaving her to suffocate in the trunk, or they'd take her out and shoot her. She was completely at their mercy, and she was doomed.

Dimly, she understood that allowing herself to give up would seal her fate. Her self-defense course had provided a number of strategies to use in a situation like this. Once again, she could remember none of them. In any case, her options were limited while she was locked up in here. She had to rest and conserve her strength. Hopefully, by the time they came for her, she'd be ready.

On the floor of the trunk, Nicole discovered a pile of blankets and, after some tugging and twisting, managed to cocoon herself somewhat against the cold. She tried to visualize what she was going to do when they opened the trunk. She'd come out fighting like a wildcat—punching, kicking, biting, anything that would take them by surprise so she could get away.

Her thoughts flashed back to the struggle in the hotel corridor and Reinhardt's brave, failed effort to save her. She recalled the muffled thud she'd heard just before she lost consciousness. Could it have been the sound of a gun equipped with a silencer? Had they shot him? Was he dead?

Obviously, they were after the money. If they thought she knew where it was, their next step would be to force her to tell them.

But even if she did, they'd kill her. That was the way it worked. They had too much to lose if they let her go.

Nicole's thoughts shifted once again, this time to her family, and she felt an almost unbearable wave of grief. She'd never see them again. They'd never even know what had become of her.

She wept for her sister, for her father, and for herself. Then, remembering her broken marriage, Nicole wept again—not for Brad, but for all the years she'd wasted on him. In a sudden flash, she saw him the way the world would see him, as a sad, even tragic figure—the young widower whose wife had met an untimely end. He'd be sought after by friends and relatives who'd work tirelessly to ease his loneliness by fixing him up with their single women friends. Then she realized Brad wouldn't be lonely at all—not with Brenda to console him.

That was enough to dry her tears. She wasn't going to let these people kill her.

There had to be a way out of this.

The car slowed, lurching and bumping, then—after a noisy shifting of gears—came to a stop. The vehicle rocked a bit, doors slammed. Before Nicole fully understood what was going on, she was hit by a rush of cool air as the trunk was pulled open. When she sat up, she saw Chazz and Kevin silhouetted against the moonlit clouds. They peered down at her in surprised silence, as if they hadn't expected to find her awake and alert.

Now that she was actually facing her captors, the only part of her self-defense instruction she could summon up was a film about a carjacking that ended rather badly for a victim who'd been stupid enough to wind up in the trunk of a car. Then she recalled a point the teacher had mentioned several times: Even in the worst scenario, there might be something to be gained by addressing the assailant firmly, as if she expected him to obey her.

She fixed her gaze on Kevin, who seemed the less malevolent of the two. "You can't leave me in the trunk," she said. "There's no air in here. I'll suffocate." She reached out and spoke again in a very stern tone, "Now, give me a hand out."

Kevin hesitated and glanced at Chazz. Then, to her amazement, both men reached out to her. But instead of helping her out of the trunk, Chazz grabbed her arms and held them while Kevin tied her wrists in front of her. She struggled, but it was useless. They worked quickly and efficiently in coordinated movements that reflected a certain experience with this sort of thing. When they were done, Chazz pulled out a large white square of cloth and twisted it into a narrow band. When he stretched it between his hands and reached for her, she began to throw her head about, trying to resist.

"It's only a blindfold, you silly cow," he told her. "Stop fightin' or it's around your neck, in't it?"

Once the blindfold was in place, they lifted Nicole out of the trunk and set her on her feet. After stumbling a bit, she managed to get in step. It occurred to her that the blindfold might be a hopeful sign. It suggested that they expected her to survive long enough to be a threat to them.

As they walked, she tried to take in what she could about her surroundings. There were no traffic sounds, which meant they weren't near a main road. Once in a while a bird cooed or hooted in the distance. The air smelled damp, like the woods, and the ground beneath her feet was sometimes rocky, sometimes covered with soft debris that felt like decaying leaves.

As they hurried her along, Nicole pretended to stumble and turn her ankle, then cried out as if in pain. The men stopped and waited with a patience that surprised her, supporting her arms while she hopped up and down on the other foot.

"I can't walk. It hurts too much," she said. "Just let me …"

Before she could finish, they hoisted her up so her feet no longer touched the ground, then started off, faster than before. They walked for several minutes before stopping and setting her down again.

"What we 'ave 'ere," Chazz said, "is an old petrol station. There's a toilet you can use."

Her mind reeled. Here she'd been afraid they were going to kill her, and they were simply escorting her to the nearest ladies' room. But why the blindfold? Presumably, this service station wasn't their final destination, and they weren't going to stay long. My God, these men were even stupider than she'd thought. "How can I use the toilet," she said, "when my hands are tied and I can't see?"

She heard them confer in whispers. Then one of them untied her. "The two of us is goin' in with you," Chazz said, "so don't try nothin'."

They untied her hands, and she reached up to pull off the blindfold. One of them snatched it away. She blinked and rubbed her eyes.

They were standing in front of a derelict gas station next to a deserted two-lane road. The men marched her through an open doorway into a small room with a sink and two toilet stalls. There didn't seem to be a bulb in the fixture, but moonlight drifted in through the open door and several high windows.

The door to the stall had a crude latch, which she hooked. But it was too flimsy to hold out against them. From the condition of the place—the stale, moldy smell, the layer of debris on the floor—she could tell the service station was long abandoned. This wasn't the sort of place where a good Samaritan was likely to happen by and rescue her.

As she undid her jeans and perched on the icy toilet seat, she was acutely aware of the two men right outside the stall. Finally, she called out, "This would be a lot quicker if I could have a little privacy. Could you step out of the room for a minute?" When no one answered, she added, "There's only one exit, you know. I can't escape."

After a moment's hesitation, Chazz said, "We'll be right outside. Don't try to be clever or you'll be sorry." And she heard them make their way to the door.

Once again, she considered their behavior, which was rather strange, given the fact that they were kidnapping her. Obviously they were under orders to make sure she came to no harm. And, in their own clumsy way, they were making an effort.

For the moment, Nicole didn't seem to be in any great danger. As she saw it, her best option would be to pretend to cooperate. At some point, these men would let down their guard. And that would be her chance.

When she was done, she went to the sink. There was no soap, but the tap released a flow of icy water. She rinsed her hands and dried them on her jeans.

Walking out to join the two men, she pretended a calm she didn't feel. Chazz handed her a can of Coke. It was cool, but not chilled. She pulled off the tab and drank greedily. When she was done, he took the empty can from her and tossed it on the ground. Then they retied her wrists, replaced the blindfold, and began the trek back.

As she stumbled along, Nicole strained against the rope around her wrists. There was a bit of slack, she noticed, and it seemed to give slightly when pulled. Encouraged, she worked at the rope as they walked, repeatedly flexing her hands against it.

She had no idea they'd reached the car until she heard the trunk open. Before they had a chance to lift her in, she said. "I can't breathe in there. You'll open it up and find me dead. Is that what you want?"

"There's air," Chazz said. "'e told me there's plenty." But there was a hesitation in his voice, as if he weren't sure.

"I'm telling you, I'll suffocate," she insisted.

The two men exchanged whispers, then led her a short distance where they stopped, and she heard the car door open. "All right,"

Chazz said. "You can sit in the back. But we're keeping you tied up. You try anything, you're going in the boot, suffocate or not."

"Sure. Anything you say. Could you get the blanket from the trunk?"

Instead of answering, Chazz told Kevin, "Hold onto 'er." Someone grabbed her arm; boots crunched off, presumably around the car. The trunk opened, then shut.

They pushed her into the backseat and spread the blanket over her. Then one of them slid in next to her, closing the door while the other got in the front. "Can I have my purse?" she said. "Where's my purse?"

Neither man answered. The motor started up, and the car began to move. Reminded of her purse, she thought of the lovely new things she'd purchased that afternoon and realized, with a pang of regret, that all of it was gone, even the new leather suitcase. The loss of her purse troubled her the most, for it contained her driver's license, passport, credit cards, cell phone—everything that could identify her should the worst happen.

Then something else occurred to her. She kept a card with emergency numbers in her wallet. She'd even remembered to update it with Brad's office number in London. Whoever found it might contact him. If he heard that her purse, wallet and passport had been found, abandoned in a hotel room, he'd call the police, and they'd start looking for her.

Even as she was thinking this, she knew how unlikely it was. These men might be dumb, but not dumb enough to abandon her purse in an empty hotel room where it was sure to raise questions. They had no doubt taken her things and, if they hadn't already gotten rid of them, would soon do so, probably by selling them.

They drove for a long time, perhaps an hour or more, while she feigned sleep and continued working on the rope. At last she managed to slide one hand part way out, although she couldn't get her knuckles past the knot.

Without warning, the car screeched to a stop, and she was almost thrown to the floor. From Chazz's swearing, she gathered that another car had appeared around a bend, and they'd nearly collided head on. She could make out the other car's headlights through the blindfold.

There was a loud altercation of horns while Chazz shouted more curses. Finally, he backed up and appeared to be waiting for the other vehicle to pass. As the lights grew brighter, she figured the moment had come. She moved quickly, snatching off the blindfold with her partially freed hand and pushing her way past Kevin to press her face against the window on his side of the car. The glare of the other car's headlights was blinding. She couldn't wave her arms, but she screamed as loudly as she could.

"Bleeding Jesus!" Chazz shouted. The car bucked forward, and Kevin pulled at her shoulders while another pair of hands yanked her hair, wresting her away from the window. The pain brought tears to her eyes.

At that moment, the car gave a lurch, and began rolling downhill. The men both screamed and released their hold on her, causing her to tumble to the floor.

Next came a loud thump, as if they'd struck something, and the car seemed to push off in a new direction. Wherever they were headed seemed to put them in great peril, for both men began to shout things like, "Bugger me," and "Sweet Jesus." The brakes screamed again, this time even louder. The car came to a stop, but they were now tilted at a strange angle. After a moment of silence, someone groaned.

"You all right, Chazz?"

"I'm talkin' aint I? Where's that bloody bint?"

"I don't know. I can't ..."

Nicole felt someone poke her in the side.

"Yeah, here she is—on the floor."

"She breathin?"

"Dunno." Kevin poked her again, then ran his hand over her face. She attempted to bite it, and the hand withdrew. "Yeah, she'll do," he said. Then, after a moment: "Listen, Chazz—that other car. Did it stop?"

The car creaked with movement, and Chazz said, "I don't see no lights."

"Kind of funny, in't it?" Kevin said. "I mean, here we go off the side of the road. We could of got killed or something, and they don't even bother to stop."

"You idiot," Chazz pronounced it idjit. "We don't want 'em to stop. That's all we need, in't it? Hold tight, and I'll get a look at the damage." The car gave a sickening lurch as he shifted his weight toward the passenger seat.

"What the bloody hell?" he yelled. "Me front wheel is gone off the edge of a cliff." His voice dropped to a whisper, as if he thought the sound might send them into the abyss. "Don't move," he hissed, sliding over to the passenger's side and opening the door. "I'll climb out. Then I'll hold it steady an you get out."

"What about her?"

"Leave her. We'll push the car back on the road. Then we won't have to worry about her, will we?"

"What if it goes down and her with it?"

"If we all get out, it's going down for sure, in't it?" Then he added, "All her fault anyhow. Sticking her bloody face to the glass, screaming, trying to make trouble."

The car had barely stopped swaying from Chazz's exit when Kevin opened the back door, and the rocking began again. This time the motion was even more violent, but it stopped when Kevin gently closed the door behind him. After a moment or so, Nicole could feel jerks and twitches from the front end of the car, accompanied by grunting and groaning from the men. They seemed to be trying to push the vehicle into a less precarious position. As far as she could tell, they weren't making much progress.

Nicole, still lying on the floor, took stock of herself. In half disbelief, she realized that the rope around her wrists was loose. With a little effort, she pulled her hands free. Slowly, taking care not to rock the car, she opened the door on the side of the car where Chazz and Kevin had made their exit. It was too dark to see. She had the feeling that if she got out, she'd find herself plummeting to the bottom of a ravine. This possibility frightened her, but not nearly as much as the prospect of remaining at the mercy of Chazz and Kevin.

She gave a final push, slipping into the dark void and landing, seconds later, in a pile of soft dirt. If she'd set the car rocking, the two men didn't seem to notice. She could still hear them grunting and straining against the weight of the car.

The moon had disappeared behind some clouds, but she could see a cluster of lights some distance ahead, the only brightness in a wall of thick darkness. She scrambled to her feet and headed toward the lights.

As the trees got thicker, she realized the velvety blackness ahead was a forest. Working her way through the trees, she lost sight of the lights. Beneath her feet, a thick layer of leaves and pine needles crunched despite all her efforts to tread lightly. The moon peeked in and out between the clouds, providing just enough light to keep her from bumping into trees.

Shouts rang out: "She's pulled a runner." and "Over there!"

Looking back, she could tell by the beam of their flashlight that they were heading toward her. The path began to slope downward, and she felt a surge of hope as she picked up speed. But soon it grew so steep that she found herself stumbling and then sliding downhill. In an attempt to slow herself, she grabbed branches of the trees and bushes in her path as she skidded unsteadily down the incline, noisily breaking the lower branches of the small fir trees in her path.

When she paused to glance back, the beam of the flashlight had vanished. Was it possible she'd managed to shake them?

As she turned back to resume her flight, the ground before her dropped away into blackness. She found herself tumbling down a rocky incline.

"Over there!" Chazz shouted, and she could hear them scrambling after her.

It wasn't long before the ground leveled out, and her fall ended. But there was no time to get up and run. They were already upon her, dragging her to her feet. Chazz raised his flashlight as if he were about to strike her. She braced herself for the blow, but Kevin reached out and grabbed the raised arm.

"The guv said …" Kevin murmured.

"She's a real hellion, this one," Chazz growled, but he let his arm drop to his side.

"You got the stuff to keep her quiet?" Kevin said.

"Nah, I left it in the car. We'll drag her up there, hit her with everything we've got, and chuck her in the boot."

"You don't want to give her too much," Kevin said. "He said be careful."

"He can't have it both ways," Chazz said. "He tells us bring her, don't let her escape, and then says don't hurt her. But she's a right little bitch, in't she. We don't knock her out, she screams bloody murder at the first car 'at goes by."

This time they didn't bother with rope or blindfold. Instead, they gripped her upper arms and dragged her roughly along. At the crest of the hill, the car was waiting. The moon was out from behind the clouds, allowing Nicole her first real look at the vehicle. It took her a second or two, to remember where she'd seen it before. It was the same ancient white Oldsmobile that had narrowly missed her on her way to the FedEx office in Glasgow. It was off the road, sitting at the edge of the cliff. But it was no longer at a tilt; all four wheels were firmly planted on the ground.

Chazz opened the car door, rifled around in the glove compartment and brought out a plastic box resembling a first-aid kit. He opened it and pulled something out. "Here," he said to

Kevin. "Put the chloroform on this rag and stick it over her face, while I give her another jab of the needle."

"He said don't give her both ..."

"You know something, Kevin? It'll go easier if you keep your bloody mouth shut."

She struggled and held her breath against the sweet, sickening chemical smell. But she was already sinking when she felt the needle go into her arm. It seemed no more than a second or two before everything went black.

Twenty-Two

She heard a voice and opened her eyes. "Here, I can see you're tryin' to wake up." The woman leaning over her smelled faintly of lemon and disinfectant. She rearranged the pillows and helped Nicole sit up. "You missed breakfast, but I've got some nice soup for you. There now, I'm putting the tray across your lap. Careful—it's hot."

Other than the fact that she was in bed, Nicole had no idea where she was. The room was bright and welcoming with sunlight streaming through the windows. Wooziness made it hard to think, to integrate the comfort of her surroundings with the terror she'd just lived through. Yet it hadn't been a dream. Her body still ached from the violence of the ride. Her wrists were chafed and raw from the rope.

She remembered the near collision on the narrow road and realized what must have happened. When she pressed her face against the window and screamed, the other motorist must have called the police. Somehow they'd managed to catch up with Chazz and Kevin in time to save her.

"Where am I?" Her voice came out hoarse and unfamiliar.

"You're on the Isle of Benbarra. It's a wee island on a loch along the coast of Scotland." The woman's voice had a soft Scottish burr.

"How did I get here? Is this some sort of hospital?"

"Now let's not be tiring ourselves with questions. You're safe here. Everything is being taken care of—everything you could ever want or imagine wantin'. All you have to worry about is taking some nourishment."

"I'm not hungry."

"That's all right. Let's just start with a wee bit of water."

Nicole picked up the water goblet and took a sip. A wave of nausea hit her. She put the glass down, lay back, and closed her eyes.

The woman went away and was immediately back with a cool, damp cloth, which she pressed against Nicole's forehead.

At last the wooziness passed. Cautiously, she propped herself up and gazed around. If this was a hospital, she thought, it was in a completely different league than the one where she'd been treated after the explosion. Her room was large and handsomely furnished. The bed featured a canopy of white eyelet lined with gauzy pink fabric, and the dark wood furniture looked expensive.

The night table held a large vase of fresh flowers, a cheery arrangement of roses: zinnias, carnations, marigolds. The sight of them stirred an idea, a question that vanished before she could put it into words.

On the opposite wall, she noticed a vanity table with a flounced skirt made of the same white and pink as the canopy. Here were more flowers, baby pink roses mixed with lacy fern. This time the thought took shape: Were these flowers from someone in her family? Did they know about her ordeal? The thought made her eyes fill with tears. "My family..." she said. "Has someone called them?"

"I'm sure they have," the woman said in a soothing voice. "But I wouldn't know the particulars." She gave Nicole's hand a pat, as if comforting a child. “Don’t worry, dear. You’re safe here,” she went on. “Now, why don’t we just take a look at what I’ve brought you.”

The woman lifted the dome from a steaming bowl, which held a thick broth floating with vegetables and chunks of meat. “Why don’t you try some of this nice lamb and barley soup?”

The smell brought back Nicole’s queasiness. “I don’t think I can eat.”

“Just a wee bit, and you’ll feel stronger.”

“Please,” Nicole said. “I can’t.”

“Very well, then.” The woman put the cover back on the bowl and returned it to the serving cart. “Try to take some water whenever you think of it. I’ll put the pitcher and glass right here on the table. Now, if you need to use the toilet, you’d better let me help you. You might be dizzy, and we don’t want you falling down.”

Nicole shook her head. “Not now.”

“Well, if you’re sure.” The woman looked at her doubtfully. “The important thing is to call me when you feel the need. Just give this a wee tug.” She gestured toward a braided pull hanging on the wall nearby. “I’m only a minute away.”

When the door clicked shut, Nicole pushed the covers back and swung her legs around to the side of the bed. As she got to her feet, she realized the woman was right. She was so dizzy she had to sit down again. When the feeling passed, she got up more slowly and went to the window.

Her room was on the third floor of a big old building. Another wing jutted out to the left, fortress-like in a homely combination of large gray stones and small red ones. Below, a garden the size of a small park was divided into neat geometric segments of lawn and flowerbeds. The grounds ended at an impenetrable wall of trees that appeared to mark the beginning of a woods.

In the mirror over the vanity, she was startled by her own reflection; she looked like a ghost from another century. Perhaps it was the unfamiliar nightgown. It was white batiste with vertical rows of lace and tucks and tiny buttons down the front. Her face was pale, and she had dark circles under her eyes. She gave a little cry when she saw the raw marks on her wrists. No wonder they hurt. On her upper left arm was an enormous bruise where Chazz had stuck her with the needle.

She stared at the black and blue mark, wondering if he'd managed to inflict some real harm. What would a man like that know about hygiene, much less administering shots? As soon as a doctor turned up, she'd ask for an antibiotic. She was lucky he hadn't given her an overdose.

Her attention shifted to the vase of baby roses. At first, she'd assumed the flowers in the room had come from a florist and that someone had sent them—her sister perhaps, or Brad. Up close, she saw that the blossoms, irregular in size and shape, were homegrown. Perhaps they'd come from the garden below.

Her eyes strayed to the drawer in the vanity table. After a moment's hesitation, she pulled it open. Inside was an extensive assortment of makeup—lipsticks, pots of rouge, eye shadow and the like, arranged in neat rows.

Someone lives here, she thought. This isn't a hospital but someone's home. She thought of her missing purse with her own makeup, and it struck her that the housekeeper had been lying. The people who ran this place—whoever they were—couldn't have notified her family. Without her purse, they didn't have her ID, much less the card with her emergency numbers. They wouldn't even know who she was. It struck her as odd that the woman hadn't asked any questions, hadn't shown any curiosity about her at all.

Nicole had begun to feel dizzy again, and it was hard to pull her thoughts together. She turned; leaning against the wall, she made her way to the huge armoire standing near the entryway and tried the handle, but it seemed to be locked.

In the entryway, which was more of a short hallway than an alcove, she opened a door to her right. It led to a huge, old-fashioned bathroom, an immaculate expanse of peach and white tile with an enormous tub that sat on little clawed feet. After a quick look, she walked unsteadily to the last door, the one by which the housekeeper had left.

She tried the doorknob. It was locked.

She stood there a moment, confused and alarmed. Why would they lock her in? What kind of place was this?

Something else was bothering her, but her head was spinning too much to sort it out. Her knees went weak, and she staggered forward, grabbing the bathroom doorway to keep from falling. It occurred to her that she'd feel better if she could lie down. She took a step and tumbled, rather than sat, on a fluffy peach rug. Then she stretched out and rested her cheek against the cool tile floor.

When she woke, she was back in bed. Although she was still exhausted, her head was clear, and she knew exactly where she was. This house belonged to Alexander Hayes. He'd arranged for Chazz and Kevin to kidnap her and bring her here. She was his prisoner.

What she needed was someone on the outside to negotiate her release. If only she hadn't been so clever about covering her tracks. In the note she'd written Brad and the message she'd left for Detective Keaton, she'd taken care not to let on where she was going or when she'd be back. Now the joke was on her. By making all that effort to keep people from looking for her, she'd sealed her fate.

She thought of the way she'd dodged Reinhardt at the Chiswick tube station. That was a fatal mistake—for both of them. She tried to imagine what would have happened if, instead of sneaking away, she'd simply walked up to him and asked him why he was following her. What would he have said?

Reinhardt had managed to track her to Glasgow, but now he was completely out of the picture. Even if he'd escaped serious injury, he'd have no idea where to find her.

Somewhere in the house, the loud mechanical hum of an elevator started up and after fifteen seconds or so, came to a stop. Alarmed, Nicole sat up and listened. It wasn't long before a cart began to rattle along the hall.

With a jangling of keys, the door opened and the woman pushed a tea cart into the room. She glanced over at Nicole and smiled, "Good morning."

"Morning?"

"That's right, dear. You slept straight through supper." The woman turned to lock the door then wheeled the cart over to the bed. Tall and plump, she was at the point in life when her chin was dissolving into the folds of her neck. Her thin, graying brown hair was done in a frizzy perm that she wore tucked into a hairnet.

As she placed the tray on Nicole's lap, the woman glanced up and smiled. She seemed kind, and it was easy to imagine that she had no idea what sort of a man her employer was.

When the woman was settled on the chair next to the bed, Nicole said, "You haven't told me your name."

"It's Catherine."

"Listen, Catherine. This house—it belongs to Alexander Hayes, doesn't it?" She waited for the woman to nod, then said, "Do you know why he's holding me prisoner?"

Catherine straightened up and leaned forward in her chair. "No one's holding you prisoner, you foolish girl. You've been ill. We're looking after you until you're well enough to go home."

Nicole held up her chafed wrists. "How do you think I got this?"

Catherine gave the marks a cursory glance and looked away. "Why, you did that yourself."

"That's crazy," Nicole said, her voice rising. "How could I possibly do this to myself?" She rotated her wrists so the woman could see the extent of her injuries. "I was tied up, dumped in the trunk of a car, and brought here against my will. My life is in danger. You've got to help me."

Catherine stood up. "Well, I realize it's your sickness talking," she said, with some indignation, "but I won't put up with that sort of thing. Mr. Hayes is doing your family a great favor letting you stay here. You can't imagine the bother he's gone to."

Nicole tried for a more reasonable tone. "If I'm not a prisoner, then why did you lock me in my room?"

"Because of your illness," Catherine said. "We don't want you wandering off and doing more harm to yourself. And let's not be getting out of bed without help or we'll have to restrain you. Lucky you didn't crack your head."

Nicole stared at her. "They told you I'm crazy to make sure you don't listen to me. But you've got to. Alexander Hayes is an international criminal, a drug smuggler. Someone stole a large amount of money from him, and he thinks I know where it is. I'm in terrible danger."

"I won't have any more of this," Catherine said. "I haven't worked in this house long, but anyone can see that Mr. Hayes is a good man. Look at all the expense he's gone to, bringing me in to look after you."

She got up, grabbed a thick, woolly cloth from the bottom of the cart and began polishing the dresser as if to extract revenge from the glossy wood surface.

As Nicole watched, a great weariness came over her. If only she could find the right words to make this woman believe her.

Her attention shifted to the breakfast tray across her lap. It contained two plates, covered with clear glass domes. On the larger plate were fried eggs, sausages, and a broiled tomato. Next to it, a smaller dish held buttered toast. Despite the artful arrangement of the food, the sight of it repelled her; she couldn't imagine ever feeling hungry again. She was thirsty, though, and coffee seemed like a good idea. She reached for the tall carafe and poured herself a cup. It smelled good—strong and rich.

As Nicole began to sip the coffee, Catherine left off dusting and came over to the bed. "Try to eat a wee bit of your meal," she said. "You need your nourishment."

"I can't," Nicole said.

"Well, it doesn't do any good to sulk. Here, at least take a bite of toast." She pressed a piece into Nicole's hand.

Nicole took a bite and, when Catherine went into the bathroom, returned it to the plate. After a brief silence, she heard the sound of water filling the tub.

After Nicole finished her second cup of coffee, she was hustled out of bed and into the bath. Then, when she was settled in the tub, Catherine explained that she had to change the sheets and disappeared into the bedroom.

The water was billowing with fragrant bubbles. Lying back in the tub, she felt drowsy and relaxed. She was drifting in the water, half dozing, when Catherine touched her shoulder and motioned for her to get out. The woman helped her up and wrapped her in a giant towel. Being pulled into a crisp, fresh nightgown made Nicole feel like a child again. She lay down on a chaise lounge and watched dreamily while Catherine finished making the bed.

"I can't imagine why I'm so sleepy," she said as Catherine helped her back into bed.

"Your body's telling you something, isn't it?" the woman said. "You need all the rest you can get. That's how you heal yourself. Sleep and good, wholesome food."

Back in bed, Nicole dropped off immediately, waking only when she heard the cart rattling up the hallway again, announcing it was time for another meal.

By the time afternoon tea arrived, Nicole had figured out the pattern. After each meal, the same thing would happen: She'd drink her coffee and nibble at the food. Then an irresistible drowsiness would take over and she'd sleep until the next meal.

They were drugging her, putting something in her food.

Then she remembered that she'd eaten nothing at some meals, but had taken coffee each time—lots of it, hoping it would wake her up. That, she decided, must be where they were putting the drugs.

Why would they want to keep her asleep? It suggested some kind of holding action, a way of keeping her quiet while they waited for something to happen. But what?

From the tray, she ate a piece of toast, reasoning that they wouldn't risk weakening a drug by putting it in food that had to be baked. She poured herself some coffee. Instead of drinking it, she dumped it in the vase on her night table while Catherine was straightening the bathroom.

When she was alone again, she got up and wandered around. She still felt tired and a little foggy, but no longer dizzy and confused. The door remained locked. The transom was open, but it was too high for Nicole to reach, even standing on a chair. The bedroom window appeared painted shut, and in any case, she was too far from the ground to consider jumping.

Nicole was still at the window when she heard voices in low conversation somewhere down the hall. A vacuum cleaner started up, grew louder, and stopped near her room.

When the machine was silent, the women resumed talking. Nicole moved closer to the door, trying to make out what they were saying. Then keys rattled on the other side, and she froze.

A woman's voice said, "No—not that one. That's where they put her."

"The loony?" a second woman said.

There was a loud shushing noise, some giggling, and the sound of a cart being hurried past the room. Nicole pressed her ear to the door.

"They have to lock her up," the first one said. "If we open the door and she runs off, we'll get the sack, won't we? No one goes in there unless Catherine is watching her. They say she went after a bloke with a razor."

"Why don't they put her away then?"

"They don't do that anymore, do they?" the first one said. "They dose them up with tranquilizers. Her relations are thick with the guv. He tells them she can stay 'til they get her medicine right. Old Mr. Heart of Gold. You know what he's like."

"I wish I didn't," the other one said.

They seemed to find this very amusing. When they stopped giggling, one of them gave a sniff. "It's all very well for him to play the lord of the manor when the work falls on us. Just the thought of her in there …"

"Wait …" the second woman interrupted. "Don't you hear something? It's that airplane of his, isn't it?"

Then Nicole heard it too—the buzz of a small plane overhead. It was growing louder.

"Oh, God! Hurry! We've got to freshen up his room before he gets here."

Their footsteps began to retreat while Nicole, her face resting against the door, considered screaming for help. But what good would it do if they thought she was crazy?

With a doomed feeling, she climbed back into bed. She lay there for what seemed like a long time, drifting on a tide of memory and regret.

Then she heard the elevator start up again. Next came the approach of hurried footsteps and the sound of someone unlocking her door.

Twenty-Three

Catherine burst into the room. "Get dressed," she said, placing a stack of neatly folded clothing on the bed. "The master wants you." Nicole recognized the clothing as the outfit she'd been wearing when she was kidnapped. Clean and freshly ironed, her jeans and sweater looked like new. The walking shoes, freshly polished, were barely scuffed at all.

Catherine gestured impatiently at the clothes. "Here now, put your things on and be quick about it. We mustn't keep him waiting."

As Nicole pulled on her jeans, she considered ways to disable the woman—a palm thrust to the nose might do it or a thumb in the eye. But her instincts told her the timing was all wrong. First, she had to map out an escape route. It would be useless running away if she had no idea where she was going. She'd end up cornered; they'd lock her up again, and she'd never have another chance.

Although her mind was clear enough to consider these matters, her hands were shaking so much that she was having trouble fastening her jeans. With a grunt of impatience, Catherine leaned forward and did it for her.

Outside the room, Catherine pulled her along, firmly gripping her arm. Meanwhile, Nicole was looking around, taking careful note of each corridor they passed, the location of doors and windows. On the way back to her room, she told herself, an opportunity would open up, and she'd make a run for it.

At the bottom of the stairs, they entered a large, wood-paneled vestibule, then stepped through an open doorway into a room that was almost dark in the waning afternoon. Once inside, Catherine pulled Nicole to a halt.

The room's only occupant was a man leaning against the fireplace, his head bent in thought. He had narrow shoulders and graying brown hair gathered into a ponytail at the nape of his neck.

Only when Nicole heard the door click behind her did she realize that Catherine had left the room. At that moment, the man looked up and noticed her. There was something repellent about his appearance—the thin, bony face and protruding eyes. With his thick, rimless glasses, he had the look of an intelligent lizard.

But when he saw her, his face lit up with a boyish smile that transformed him. He hurried over and held out his hand. Nicole didn't offer hers, but he took it anyway, shaking it enthusiastically. Then, instead of releasing her hand, he turned it over to examine her bruised wrist. "My God," he said, "look what they've done to you." He picked up her left hand and studied that wrist, too. Then he released her, and his eyes met hers. He looked stricken.

"I want to apologize for the way my people treated you," he said. "Their behavior was unforgivable." His British accent was soft and pleasing, the unmistakable product of a good education. "I gave my people strict orders to make sure no harm came to you, and they— well—they completely botched it."

Nicole stared at him, astonished not so much by the apology as by the assumptions behind it. He seemed to think it was all right for his goons to kidnap her, as long as they watched their manners and avoided leaving bruises.

She didn't say anything. It's his move, she decided. Let him do the talking.

Hayes was silent, too, apparently waiting for her response. Finally, he said, "I hope you'll find it in your heart to forgive us…" He hesitated. "What would you like me to call you?"

The question caught her by surprise. Who did he think she was? She still had the feeling Chazz and Kevin had mistaken her for Muriel Lowry. It was anyone's guess what Hayes was thinking; his expression told her nothing.

If he did think she was Muriel, he'd try to get her to tell him where the money was. But he could see that Freddy had left her behind. She could say he deserted her and left her with nothing. That she was a victim, as much as Hayes, of Lowry's greed. She decided to take a gamble. "Why don't you call me Muriel?" she said.

"Excellent," he said. "Muriel, then. Can you put all this unpleasantness out of your mind so we can make a fresh start?"

"All right."

He motioned for her to sit down. She chose a comfortable-looking overstuffed chair, one of a matched pair in front of the fireplace. By now, her eyes had adjusted to the gloom. As she got settled in the chair, Hayes went to the table and reached into a cut-glass bowl for a piece of candy.

"Like a mint, would you?" he said.

"No, thank you."

He stood there, munching and regarding her with an enigmatic smile. The man was certainly creepy, and yet he seemed to be on his best behavior, even eager to please.

His appearance was anything but threatening. He was slightly built and hunched his shoulders in a way that was almost self-mocking. His manner of dress was odd and, in Nicole's opinion, a little pathetic for a man pushing fifty—a bolo tie, Indian tapestry vest, and faded Levis. His white shirt, which appeared to be silk, had full, oversized sleeves gathered into large cuffs. The vest was adorned with heavy gold embroidery and appliqués inset with mirrors.

He tossed the candy wrapper into the fireplace, helped himself to another piece, and headed for the chair opposite hers. Meanwhile, Nicole glanced around the room. Books were everywhere—jammed untidily into shelves that ran from floor to ceiling. An overflow of volumes was stacked on the great library table, on the small round one next to her chair and on the floor. There was no desk in sight, nor any phone, fax, or computer. Clearly, this wasn't the kind of study that doubled as an office, but a real library, a quiet place devoted to reading. Now that she thought about it, she hadn't seen any surveillance cameras on the way downstairs. For an international crime ring, this was definitely a low-tech operation.

By now, Hayes was seated. "I want you to know that Chazz and Kevin will be punished," he said. "Suspended from their duties and sent down to London. If we do take them back, we'll never trust them with any real responsibility. I abhor the idea of violence—won't employ anyone who uses it." He considered this for a moment, then added, "Except, of course, in self defense."

She wondered about the disclaimer. Perhaps it explained the attack on Reinhardt, but what about Mr. McGiever? Or was Hayes even aware of the car bombing?

"Freddy seems to have vanished," he was saying. "I was hoping you might be able to tell me where he is."

"Don't you know?" she said. "I mean, I thought you'd sent him away on business."

"I have no idea where he is. Believe me, Freddy could fly to the moon and stay there, for all I care. Unfortunately, he's gone off with a fair sum of my money. My people think he may not have succeeded in getting it out of the country. I want it back." He paused to stare at her, head cocked. Nicole's attention was diverted. On the other side of the fireplace, something she'd taken for an untidy pile of animal skins trembled into life. She watched in alarm as a huge canine head rose out of the heap, and a pair of yellow eyes stared out at her. It was an enormous, shaggy dog, she realized—no, two dogs—snoozing next to the fire.

She looked back at Hayes. "Maybe he hid it somewhere in the U.K.," he was saying. "I was hoping that you, Muriel, might be able to fill us in on the details."

"I'm afraid I can't," she said quietly. "As a matter of fact, he emptied out our bank account. Left me without a cent. You can imagine the position that puts me in." She was improvising, making it up as she went along.

He gave a smile. "Then you understand it's in your interest to cooperate."

"Honestly, Mr. Hayes ..."

"Alex," he said. "Please."

"Look, Alex ..."

"Excellent." He nodded encouragingly.

"I really wish I did know something," she went on. "Then I'd tell you and you'd let me go." She licked her lips, then couldn't help adding, "When are you going to let me go?"

"All we want is a little information," he said, ignoring the question. "If Freddy didn't confide in you, then we can put our heads together and work out where he might have put it. After all, you're married to the man, and we men are such creatures of habit."

Again, he paused to study her. "Perhaps you're in need of pecuniary assistance. Well, I'm a very soft touch, always have been. It's just that Freddy took a little more than I can afford to lose at the moment."

"Really?" she said. "May I ask how much?"

"Nearly a million pounds."

"A million?" she repeated, as if this were news to her. "Well, that is a lot of money to lose, even for someone like you."

He stared at her. "Someone like me?"

"An international..." she hesitated a moment, then added "um—dealer."

The word hung in the air. Then he gave a whoop of laughter. "What a load of rubbish," he said. "I'm just a little pot peddler, and they insist on portraying me as an international bogeyman. I never sell hard drugs, you know, only cannabis, which isn't nearly as lucrative as you might imagine. But at least I can live with myself. Cannabis has never hurt anyone in the 8,000 years that men..." he paused and gave a quick nod in her direction, "yes, and women, have been using it."

The moment he said this, Nicole recognized the source of the odd herbal smell she'd noticed. It was marijuana. This explained the man's garrulousness and his odd behavior. He'd been smoking weed.

"And look at the huge police effort they're putting into apprehending me." He chuckled. "Forgive me. You're not amused, but it's quite a joke. I suppose I should be flattered. They claim I have billions tucked away in banks all over the world when all I am is a glorified cashier. Money comes in, but it goes out." His smile disappeared. "Believe me, it does go out. My overheads are staggering. And your Freddy..."

He got up and walked over to the window to stare out, his mood gone sour.

Time passed, and Nicole began to wonder if he'd forgotten her. "Look," she finally said, "none of this makes sense. If Freddy really did take that money, why would he leave the country without it? Isn't that what you think? That he went abroad?"

"That's our best hunch." He still had his back to her and was gazing out the window.

"Alex, I really don't know anything. Why can't you just let me go?"

He turned and looked at her. "Of course I'll let you go. What did you think? That I was planning to sell you into white slavery?"

When she didn't reply, he let out an exasperated laugh. "Christ, that look on your face. You really do think I'm some sort of monster. I assure you, I'm extremely nonviolent. Just look at this shooting lodge. Since I bought it, I've never permitted a single person to fire a gun here. I'm a bloody vegetarian, for heaven's sake."

He stared at her a moment longer, then shook his head. "Never mind, Muriel. Your opinion of me isn't important. But you will have to cooperate. Otherwise I'm afraid I'm going have to take steps we'll both find extremely unpleasant.

"If you choose not to be helpful," he went on, "well, that's your prerogative." He said this reproachfully, as if it certainly wouldn't have been his choice, or the choice of any reasonable person. "Now, I want you to go back to your room and think this over very carefully."

He reached over to push a buzzer on the wall and then resumed his vigil at the window.

He didn't speak again. Nor did he look around, even when she got up and made her way to the door. As she was turning the doorknob, she paused to look back. Hayes, still staring out the window, didn't seem to notice she was leaving, but over by the fireplace, one of the dogs was rising to its feet.

Hastily, she stepped out into the hall and shut the door. Before she had a chance to turn around, someone grabbed her. Her heart dropped to her shoes as he shoved her against the wall, then pulled her around to face him. It was the man from the hotel, the one who'd struck Reinhardt with the gun. She drew in a big gulp of air and screamed.

The library door opened. "That's all right, Ben," Hayes said. "Catherine will see her back to her room."

"Catherine isn't here, sir," the man said.

"She's on her way. Just give Mrs. Lowry a seat out there. Oh, and Ben ?"

"Yes, sir?"

"While she's waiting, I strongly suggest you keep an eye on her."

On the way back to the room, Catherine walked beside Nicole with a firm grip on her arm. As they climbed the stairs, Nicole stopped, resisting Catherine's determined pull, for a look at something she hadn't noticed on the way down—the skin of a leopard that was hanging like a tapestry on the staircase wall. The creature had been slit down the belly and hung to display its luxuriant, spotted back. The legs were splayed outward, the tail sadly flattened and drooping toward the floor. The animal's large, majestic head, the only part that remained three dimensional, pointed upward. Nicole couldn't see its eyes, and for that she was grateful.

Once again, she thought of Hayes' disavowal of violence. Even if she'd believed him, the creature's remains were proof that he was lying. No self-respecting vegetarian would leave something like this hanging on the wall, even if it had come with the house.

As they reached the third floor, she heard voices. The door to her room was standing open; inside, two young women were busy cleaning. They were dressed in matching cotton dresses of the same gray fabric as Catherine's smock. One girl was vacuuming the rug while the other pulled fresh towels from a cart. They both looked up and stared as Catherine steered Nicole into the room. Then, after a nervous exchange of glances, the two returned to their tasks.

As Catherine helped her back into her nightgown, Nicole's eyes fell on the cleaning cart, parked near the foot of the bed. A set of keys dangled from the handle.

Once she had Nicole changed, Catherine busied herself folding up the jeans and sweater. Nicole could see the woman planned to take the clothes away. This was another way of controlling her, making sure she didn't escape.

Nicole concentrated on the keys, trying to think of a way to get her hands on them. Then it came to her. She turned to Catherine and said, "I have a terrible headache. Could I please have some aspirin?"

Catherine patted the pockets of her smock and, finding nothing, turned and went into the bathroom, where a cleaning girl had just disappeared with fresh towels. Now only one girl remained in the room.

Nicole made an anguished face at her, silently mouthing, "Help me, help me," over and over. The girl's eyes grew very wide. She gaped at Nicole for a moment, then turned on the vacuum cleaner and steered it into the opposite corner, where she busied herself running the machine back and forth over the same spot.

As soon as the girl's back was turned, Nicole moved to the supply cart, grabbed the keys and tossed them under the bed. Just as she'd hoped, the roar of the vacuum cleaner covered any noise they might have made hitting the floor.

She'd just straightened up when Catherine reemerged from the bathroom, carrying a glass of water. She handed the glass to Nicole along with two white pills. Then she stood and waited for Nicole to swallow them. Nicole prayed they were nothing stronger than aspirin.

Catherine and the other two gathered their cleaning gear onto the cart and wheeled it out of the room. The door closed behind them, and there was a long silence. Nicole held her breath, picturing the three of them searching the cart, then going through their pockets for the missing keys.

Then a key turned in the lock, and Nicole realized that the job of securing the door would have fallen to Catherine, since Catherine was in charge. Even when the cleaning crew noticed their keys were missing, they might not report it for fear of being fired.

When the hallway was quiet, Nicole retrieved the keys under the bed. She worked her way through them until she found one that unlocked the door to the hall. She opened it a crack, peered into the empty hallway, then closed and relocked it.

She remembered Hayes' threat: "If you choose not to be helpful, that's your choice." What would they try next? Torture? Putting a gun to her head?

She had to get away before they came back for her. But first, there was the matter of clothes. She couldn't leave the house dressed only in a thin nightgown.

Nicole went over to the armoire; after trying several keys, she found one that worked. Inside, an assortment of garments was neatly arranged on hangers. The clothes, mainly black evening wear in a number of sizes, seemed intended for the use of houseguests who might have forgotten something essential for a weekend in the country. This, she realized, also explained the cache of makeup in the vanity table.

She pulled out the most promising item: a lightweight wool jersey jumpsuit studded with rhinestones. It was too big, a size eight, but after rolling up the sleeves and pant legs and cinching the middle with the belt from a cocktail dress, she decided it would do. Draped over a hook was a royal blue maillot swimsuit, plain and utilitarian, the sort of thing a channel swimmer might wear. Hanging beneath it was an aqua terrycloth beach coat. This, she decided, could be worn over the jumpsuit as an extra layer against the chill. She pulled it down and put it over her arm.

On the bottom of the armoire sat several pairs of black kidskin pumps with impossibly high heels; she decided against them.

As she closed the armoire, she noticed the light reflect on something on top. She had to stand on tiptoe to get a look. When she saw it was a black purse, she felt a surge of hope. Could it be the one she'd lost? She grabbed the chair from the vanity and climbed up to get it.

To her disappointment, the purse was an unfamiliar black clutch, worn but of good quality, with an oversized gold clasp. Among the items inside was a passport. With a sense of foreboding, she opened it and stared at the photo.

A headshot of Alice stared back at her, the face framed with an unfamiliar blonde pageboy cut. The name under the picture read, "Muriel B. Lowry."

Twenty-Four

Nicole stared at the woman in the passport photo, and her heart froze. What could this possibly mean? That the woman she'd known as Alice was really Muriel Lowry? That everything Alice—or Muriel—had told her was a lie?

She remembered, suddenly, the body the police had identified as Alice McConnehy. At the time, Nicole had thought Keaton was lying; how could Alice have been dead for several days when she herself had seen Alice the afternoon before? Now it struck her that Keaton might have been telling the truth. The real Alice was dead, and Muriel Lowry had taken her identity for reasons of her own. Nicole wondered how she could have been so gullible. She'd believed Muriel's story—every word of it—even the overblown melodrama about her dead brother.

As she stared at the passport, other questions presented themselves. Had Muriel been in this house, this very room? When? And what had become of her? The purse didn't appear to be dusty, which suggested it hadn't been here long. She took it to the bed and dumped out the contents. Inside was a wallet, in which she found a £100 note. It was tightly folded into a square, just like the £20 note she'd found in the backpack.

She picked up the passport and examined it more carefully. The dark blue cover was stamped with the familiar gold eagle and the words United States of America. This confirmed at least one part of Alice/Muriel's story: that she was an American and not a Brit. Then she remembered the musical pattern of her speech, the heavy Irish accent. My God, even that had been fake.

When she studied the photo more closely, she could see a slight resemblance between herself and the other woman. With her hair blonde, as it was in the picture, Muriel's coloring was similar, and there was something about her mouth and the shape of her face. This made it easier to understand why Chazz and Kevin might have confused her with Muriel.

She walked over to the window and stared out, still struggling to understand. Okay, she thought, maybe Muriel had been in this house as a guest or a prisoner. But since Chazz and Kevin were part of Hayes' London operation, maybe they weren't here at the same time.

She thought of the implications of her own attempt to pass herself off as Muriel. Hayes would know she was lying, and this lie compounded her problems. But what did it matter? Hayes already had a pretty good hunch that she might know where his money was.

Nicole took another look at the items from the purse. Aside from Muriel's passport, there was a checkbook with her name and address, a driver's license, and a Barclay's' Visa card. These weren't the sort of things a person easily left behind.

She glanced at her watch. She couldn't afford to waste any more time.

She returned the purse to the top of the armoire, shoving it all the way to the back. Then she unlocked the door to the hall and leaned out. The corridor was empty, and she still didn't see any sign of a surveillance camera. Reassured, she left the room and relocked the door.

At the rear of the house, Nicole found an alcove leading to the back stairs. This area hadn't been modernized like the rest of the house, and it was easy to imagine the armies of servants who must have used the steep, winding staircase when the place was new. The walls of the stairwell were done in ceramic tiles: the lower half in a checkerboard of maroon and mustard, the upper part in faded yellow and dull, metallic blue. Dominating all was a narrow window of multicolored glass that appeared to reach all the way to the bottom floor.

She gripped the rail at the top and looked down. Below her, the wrought-iron staircase spiraled in a sharp, dizzying descent. She carefully placed her bare feet, one at a time, on the cold metal slats. As she descended, a man's voice floated up from a lower floor. He spoke in a harsh tone that suggested an argument, but she couldn't catch enough to make sense of it.

Abruptly, on the second landing, the spiral staircase became a broad, carpeted one. She was almost down the next flight when a door opened below. She hesitated, then retreated a few steps before turning to scramble back up the stairs.

Reaching the landing, Nicole opened the door, entered a dim hallway, and pressed herself against the wall, her heart racing until the footsteps hurried on up the stairs. A door slammed above, and the house was quiet again.

When she decided it was safe, she continued down the stairs to the bottom. Here she encountered two closed doors. The one directly ahead, where the staircase would logically continue downward, was locked.

The other door opened into an enormous laundry room. It was warm and steamy, the air charged with the chugging and churning of several industrial-size washers and dryers. Passing through, Nicole caught sight of an impressively-equipped workbench in one corner, complete with lathe and electric saw.

She headed for a large alcove on the other side of the room that appeared to lead to an exit. Sure enough, the door to the garden was only a few steps away. Outside, daylight was fading. Through the slightly warped glass, she caught a tantalizing glimpse of neatly manicured lawn.

Next to the door, a rack held rows of rubber rain boots in a variety of sizes and colors. She grabbed a yellow pair that seemed about her size and tucked them under her arm.

Just as she'd expected, the back door was locked. She was reaching into her pocket for the keys when she noticed the lock, which appeared to date back to the original construction of the house. The keyhole was perhaps triple the size of a modern one, far too large for any of the keys on the stolen ring. She didn't even bother trying them.

If this door was locked, the other exits probably were, too. To get out, she had to find the right key or get her hands on a tool that could be used to pick the lock.

She paused, standing first on one leg and then the other to pull on the rubber boots. Then she made her way back to the laundry room. All manner of tools were hung on a pegboard over the corner workbench. She located an awl that appeared the right size and shape, as well as a small screwdriver. In a drawer, she found a small folding knife and a leather pouch for carrying the tools.

Nicole put these things in her pocket and was checking around for a flashlight when she heard footsteps. In a panic, she looked around for a hiding place. Her eyes fell on a small closet with panels of blue and white checked fabric hanging over the doorway. She darted inside where she had to fight for space among a forest of brooms and mops.

Two men walked in and headed for the workbench. She couldn't see their faces, but between the curtain panels that covered the door, she caught a glimpse of two sets of black-trousered legs—one pair skinny, the other wide. Right away, she knew who they were. So much for Hayes' claim that he'd sent Chazz and Kevin away.

The owner of the wide legs took a set of keys from a drawer and unlocked a small cupboard on the opposite wall. As he opened it, Nicole parted the curtains slightly to get a better view. The cupboard held several rows of keys in assorted sizes and shapes, hung neatly on cup hooks. Chazz removed a key, relocked the cupboard, and put the original set of keys back in the drawer. This done, he started going through the other cupboards, removing an occasional item and tossing it on the floor. Meanwhile, skinny legs lounged nearby.

For a while, neither man spoke. Then Kevin leaned down and picked up a sack that Chazz had tossed on the floor. Kevin weighed the sack in his hands then wagged it at Chazz. "How do we know it'll keep the body from floating to the top?" he said.

"Because it's concrete, stupid," Chazz said. "You put a great lump of it round the feet and let it set. Then the body sinks to the bottom of the loch, doesn't it?"

"Don't see how," Kevin said, tossing the sack in the air and catching it. "This don't weigh hardly noffing."

"You mix in water," Chazz was saying. "The water makes it heavy. Now, put that down and make yourself useful. Get a couple of those great black rubbish sacks from the store room."

"He wants us to knock her off tonight, then?"

"I already told you. The guv don't know what he wants." From Chazz's tone, he was supremely impatient with Kevin, Hayes, and perhaps the whole world. "Be prepared," he went on. "That's all he tells me. If you ask me, he thinks he's going to make her talk by treating her like one of the royals. I don't know why he doesn't let me have a go at her."

"You know how he is about women. He made Ben go easy on the other one, and she pulled a runner."

Chazz gave a derisive snort. "You think she got away?"

"I don't know. They says ..." Kevin's voice trailed off.

"Nobody gets away from Ben," Chazz said. "Nobody."

The pair stood in reflective silence until Kevin stirred himself and left the room, presumably to get the trash bags. Chazz resumed his search through the cupboards, tossing more items on the pile.

At last Kevin returned. "Put that whole load a stuff in the sacks," Chazz said. "Then we slide off to my room with a couple a beers."

"He told us no drinking," Kevin said. "That shipment's due in around 3:00 a.m., and he says meet him in the library at 2:00."

"There's beer in the larder," Chazz said, holding up the key he'd taken earlier. "It's eight at night. Nobody tells me I can't have a pint or two at the end of me day. Not even the guv."

The moment they were gone, Nicole hurried over to the drawer where Chazz had put the keys and took them out. It was hard to keep her mind on what she was doing. She kept hearing Chazz and Kevin, casually discussing whether or not they were going to kill her.

She had to get away—now.

Nicole unlocked the small cupboard and studied its contents. Only one key was large enough to fit the back door. She took it out and relocked the cupboard.

A moment later, she was at the back door, trying the key. It fit.

Slowly, she unlocked the door and opened it. She fully expected to hear the clanging of an alarm, but to her enormous relief, the house remained silent. Was it possible these people felt so removed from the outside world that they didn't bother with any real security?

She stepped out onto a large, screened back porch then carefully closed and relocked the door. The sun had set, but it wasn't quite dark. It was a good moment to slip away, before the house's external lights came on. She had already decided on a route: She'd head for the rear of the house and the woods she'd seen from her window.

The moment she set her foot on the top step of the porch, a siren went off, and lights flashed in her face. The ear-splitting wail was like a physical assault. For a long moment she was stunned, rooted to the spot.

Then Nicole began to run. She got about twenty feet along the garden path before she heard footsteps thundering after her. When she glanced around, she saw that it was Ben. "Come back, you stupid cow!" he shouted. "We're on a bleeding island! You'll never get away!"

She kept running—across the broad lawn between the house toward the woods. Her ankle had begun to ache, and she was gasping for breath. She almost reached the fountain in the center of the lawn before he caught up with her. She struggled, but he twisted her arm behind her and half pulled, half dragged her back along the path and up the steps.

Inside the back door, he stopped to use his key to turn off the siren. The control was in a small white box attached to the wall. Then he waved away two scruffy-looking men who came running in response to the alarm. Neither Kevin nor Chazz were anywhere in sight.

"You're hurting me," Nicole said, as he hurried her through the kitchen. Ben didn't answer, nor did he relax his grip. Instead, he marched her into the big central hallway and down the corridor that led to the library.

Twenty-Five

Hayes was waiting at the door to the library. His eyes lit up when he saw Nicole, and he let out a low laugh. "Oh, there you are, my dear. For a moment, we were afraid you'd taken leave of us. What a shame that would have been when we have a visitor waiting to see you. I understand he's an old friend of yours."

He made an extravagant bow. Gesturing for her to follow, he disappeared through the doorway. Ben gave Nicole a shove, and she stumbled into the dim recesses of the library.

This time there was no mistaking the smell of marijuana. As Hayes guided her toward the fireplace, he wandered rather than walked. Nicole felt a wave of disgust. Here was a man who sat around smoking dope while others did his dirty work.

At that moment, she noticed someone standing against the wall by the fireplace as straight and still as a suit of armor. It was Kevin, looking thinner and paler than before. His eyes were fixed on a chair in front of the fireplace.

Nicole followed his gaze and froze.

As the man in the chair turned to look at her, she saw that it was Reinhardt. Recognition flashed in his eyes, along with a warning she couldn't read. She wondered what he was doing here. Was he undercover, pretending to be part of Hayes' operation?

Then she noticed the way he was sitting, slumped slightly forward with his arms behind him. She realized that his hands were tied. He was a prisoner, too.

Hayes broke the silence. "Am I getting the impression that the two of you aren't exactly thrilled to see one another?"

"You've made a mistake," Nicole said. "I don't know this man."

Hayes looked at her, his shoulders shaking in mirth. "Well, that's gratitude for you. Our friend here went through all manner of heroics to break into the house in a misguided effort to rescue you. Just like—what was it they called her? Oh, yes—Rapunzel." His entire body quivered with silent laughter as he began to chant, "Rapunzel, Rapunzel, let down your golden hair."

From Rapunzel, he went into a talking jag, his attention skipping from topic to topic—his adventures as a drug dealer, his duty to challenge the law and all "bureaucratic despots," and bits of religious credo. His monologue included a drug-skewed mishmash of reincarnation, existentialism, and man's God-given right to smoke marijuana. Meanwhile, Reinhardt regarded him with a weary impatience, as if he'd heard it all before.

While Hayes rambled on, Nicole took a long look at Reinhardt. He wasn't wearing a jacket, and his white shirt was torn and splotched with blood. His dark hair was tousled, and she could see a shaved spot of scalp with a red, puckered line of stitches. She knew it was from the blow he'd received in the hotel corridor.

Hayes had stopped talking and was staring at Nicole. When he saw that he had her attention, he glanced over at Reinhardt and assumed a long face. "I'll be very disappointed if what she says is true—that the two of you have never met and you've thrown your life away on a stranger. Perhaps I'm a hopeless old romantic, but

I'd like to think there was some kind of grand passion between you, or at least a spark. Well, no matter ..."

His voice faded, as if he were running out of steam. After glancing back and forth between his two guests, he rested his gaze on Reinhardt. "Your fate is entirely in this good lady's hands. I'm giving her one last chance to tell us where the money is."

She already understood the situation. If she told Hayes what he wanted to know, he'd have no more use for either of them. He'd kill them both. "I told you," she said to Hayes. "I have no idea."

"We'll see about that," Hayes said. "Ben!"

Instantly, the man appeared in the doorway.

"I don't care how you do it," Hayes said. "Find my money."

Ben stepped forward and grabbed Nicole by the arm. Then he pulled out a small, snub-nosed gun and pressed it to the side of her head. He looked at Reinhardt and, with a nod, motioned for him to stand up. "Start for the door," Ben said. "We'll be half a dozen steps behind. I'll tell you which way to go. And I warn you. Do exactly as I say. I won't hesitate to use this gun."

As they filed from the room, Kevin stepped forward, ready to join the procession, but Ben shook his head. "Stay here. I don't want you tagging along, mucking things up."

Ben and Nicole followed Reinhardt out of the room. Ben kept the gun pressed to Nicole's head, gripping her arm with his other hand. When they entered the alcove at the bottom of the rear staircase, Reinhardt was ordered to stand with his forehead against the wall, legs spread. Meanwhile, Ben got out some rope and tied Nicole's wrists behind her. The job required two hands, and he had to let the gun dangle from his fingers. As he secured the knot, he kept looking up to make sure Reinhardt hadn't moved. Nicole tried to keep her hands flexed, but Ben tied the rope tightly enough to kill any hope of working her hands free.

When he was done, Ben wrapped one arm around her neck and unlocked the basement door. He ordered Reinhardt to lead them down the stairs.

As they neared the bottom, Ben released Nicole and sent her stumbling down the last few steps. Then he hurried to the top and pointed his weapon at them. "I'm afraid I have to leave you," he said. "But don't get any ideas. I'll be right back." He went out, slamming the door. They heard a key turn; a second or two later, the lights went out, and they were in darkness.

After Ben's footsteps faded, Reinhardt said, "Let's see what we can do to get these ropes off. We don't want to be here when he comes back."

"I've got a knife," she said. "It's in a little bag in my pocket."

"Brilliant!" he said. "Move closer. If we stand side-by-side, I can get to it and cut your rope. Then you can cut mine. "

In the darkness, it was all very awkward. Nicole held her breath while he fumbled to get the pouch, remove the knife, and hand the pouch back to her. He opened the blade, felt for the rope around her wrists, and placed the blade in a favorable spot for cutting. Then, before the rope was completely severed, he dropped the knife. As it clattered to the floor, he hissed, "Rotten luck!"

"Wait. My hands are almost ..." She gave a last pull, and the rope dropped to the floor. "I'm free," she said. "Don't move. I'm going to look for the knife." It took only a few seconds to locate it. When she stood up, she found the rope around his wrists, slipped the knife under it, and cut.

Reinhardt withdrew his hands with a sharp intake of breath. "That does it! " he said. "Hang on while I pick up those bits of rope. They might come in handy." She stood still while he retrieved them.

A moment later, he said, "Give me your hand." And when she did, he placed it on his shoulder. "Follow me," he whispered. "I have a plan."

He turned and began patting his way along the wall. Nicole followed, her hand anchored to his shoulder. It was going to be all right, she told herself. Reinhardt knew what he was doing. This was what he'd been trained for.

He stopped and seemed to be trying a doorknob. "It's locked," he said. "I'll see if I can force it with the knife."

"Wait," Nicole whispered. "I've got something better." She opened the pouch, removed the awl, and pressed it into his hand.

"I must say—you've certainly come prepared," he said. "This might just do the trick. I'm fairly handy with locks."

She drew in a quick breath. "Was it you who broke into the Lowrys' house that afternoon?"

He make a soft tsking sound. "Yes. Sorry about that. I do owe you an explanation, but I'm afraid that will have to wait." He paused for a moment while the lock made a faint click, as if he'd almost managed to turn it. "Come on," he murmured under his breath. "Come on."

On the floor above, she heard pounding footsteps. Then a door slammed, and all grew quiet except for the sound of Reinhardt's breathing and the tool rattling in the lock.

"Don't worry," he said. "We're almost there."

There was a solid click as the lock released. He opened the door, and after some fumbling, flipped on a light switch. Nicole was disappointed when she saw that this was the furnace room, not the way out of the house. Directly before them, a dim bulb revealed a great, old-fashioned furnace. To their right stood several large water heaters and a coal bin. The temperature was warm, and it was difficult to breathe, as if the boilers had sucked out all the air.

Noiselessly, Reinhardt closed the door and led her over to the furnace. "I want you to lie on the floor directly in front of the furnace as if you're unconscious." he said. "When he comes down the stairs, he'll notice the light, open the door and there you'll be. I'll hide behind the door. Once he steps into the room to investigate, I'll jump him from behind."

The floor was dusty and smelled powerfully of mold, but Nicole did as she was told. Reinhardt knelt beside her and wrapped the rope around her wrists so it would appear they were still tied.

"That's the way," he said. "Now turn your head toward the furnace." Then, as he stood up again, he added, "Whatever you do, you're not to move or look around."

Despite the admonition, she turned her head long enough to watch him walk away and flatten himself against the wall. On the floor above, a door opened, and footsteps started down the basement stairs. As Nicole turned back toward the furnace, she began to see weaknesses in Reinhardt's plan. Ben had a gun. What if he started shooting as soon as he walked in, before Reinhardt can disarm him? There was also the possibility that Reinhardt was no match for him.

She heard the door to the next room open. Then Ben's voice said, "What in blazes?" Then, he shouted, "Reinhardt! Reinhardt! Where are you? Don't be a fool, man! Show yourself!"

There was another silence, and he called Reinhardt again, this time in a less certain voice. He opened the door next to her and, after a brief hesitation, stepped into the room. "All right, woman," he said. "What …"

There was a loud grunt as Reinhardt jumped him from behind. Nicole was instantly on her feet, trying to scramble out of the way. For fifteen seconds or so, she was trapped in front of the furnace while the two men grappled nearby. Reinhardt pressed the point of the knife into Ben's throat. Ben let out a guttural croak and dropped the gun. Reinhardt attempted to kick it toward Nicole, who by now had retreated into the corner. She did her best to catch it, but the gun hit the base of the coal bin and skittered away, disappearing into the shadows.

By the time she straightened up, the two men were struggling over the knife. Ben grabbed it away, but a moment later Reinhardt kneed him in the stomach. The knife hit the floor, and it, too, spun into the darkness.

At the start, Reinhardt had the advantage of surprise; he was also younger, more agile, lighter on his feet. But Ben was strong and solidly built, and he seemed to have experience with this sort of combat. He kept hitting Reinhardt in the face, occasionally striking the injured side of his head. In the dim light, Nicole could see dark blood dripping from Reinhardt's wound.

If Ben kept hitting him like that, it was only a matter of time before he knocked Reinhardt down and moved in for the kill. Looking around, she spotted a tool lying on the back ledge of the coal bin. It was a lethal-looking contraption, a cross between a sledgehammer and a pick ax, probably used to break up large chunks of coal. She dashed around the outside of the bin and picked it up. It was heavy, perhaps sixteen or seventeen pounds, but solid and well balanced.

The thrashing and grunting on the other side of the room stopped. Looking out from behind the coal bin, she saw that Reinhardt had Ben on the floor, face down. Using his knees to pin Ben's arms to his sides, Reinhardt began to slam the man's head against the cement floor—once, twice, three times.

On the third blow, Ben went limp. After a moment, Reinhardt got up and knelt beside him to check his pulse.

There must have been a noise, for Reinhardt looked around. Instinctively, Nicole shrank back into the shadows.

Kevin was standing in the doorway, holding a gun. "Step away from 'im," he said in a tremulous voice. "On the floor. Face down."

Reinhardt did as he was told, and Kevin advanced toward him. Neither man glanced in Nicole's direction.

When he reached the two prone figures, Kevin bent over to check Ben. Then he stood up and pointed his gun at Reinhardt. "You bastard!" he said. "You rotten bastard! You bloody well killed 'im."

As he spoke, Nicole ran up behind him. It took all her strength to raise the heavy tool in the air and bring it down on his head.

Her aim was perfect. The blow made a horrible sound, loud and hollow, while blood and soft globs of something else spattered everywhere—on her face and clothes, on the wall behind her. In what seemed like slow motion, Kevin folded up and sank to the floor.

The tool slipped from Nicole's hands and the sour taste of bile leapt to her throat.

"Good girl." Reinhardt was already on his feet, going through the pockets of the fallen men.

Nicole stared for a moment, then ran over to the coal bin to be sick.

Twenty-Six

As they left the house, Reinhardt disabled the alarm next to the back door, using one of the keys he'd taken from Ben's pocket. Outside, it was completely dark except for the moon, shining through a thin layer of clouds.

They took the path leading to the rear of the house, then cut across the damp grass. Reinhardt reached the rose garden first, easily hopping the short hedge and zigzagging his way through the bushes. Gasping for breath, Nicole struggled to keep up. At one point, she was forced to a stop by thorny branches that latched onto her jumpsuit and refused to let go. Almost at once, Reinhardt was beside her, seizing the branches and—after a couple of distinct ripping sounds—she was free.

He held out his hand. "Let's go. They'll soon have the dogs on us."

With Reinhardt pulling her along, they quickly reached the fountain at the center of the rose garden. She glanced back and felt a fresh wave of alarm. "The basement light," she said. "We forgot to turn it off."

"It doesn't matter," Reinhardt said. "They know where Ben took us. The basement is the first place they'll look."

The rose garden ended, and they started across the last stretch of open lawn. Nicole, now getting a second wind, pulled her hand free and ran easily beside him.

She took another look, but the house appeared to be asleep. Other than the basement and a few dim lights on the first floor, the place was dark. Even so, she had the feeling that, any moment, Hayes' troops would burst out the front door and come tearing after them.

Reinhardt grabbed Nicole's arm and pulled her along. "It's best if you don't look back," he said.

They passed through the opening in the hedge and onto a wooden footbridge leading to the woods. When they reached the trees, the darkness was all but impenetrable. Once again, Reinhardt took her hand. "It's all right," he said. "I've already scouted the route. Just follow me."

As the path sloped uphill, she caught glimpses of the house through the trees, her first real look at its exterior. The structure, lit by a series of spotlights, was a squat baronial manor of granite and red sandstone. It was the sort of thing that might have belonged to a turn-of-the-century industrialist, built with money made on the backs of women and children working long hours in their factories.

On the other side of the house, a van was parked at an odd angle. The door stood open, as if the driver hadn't expected to be gone long. She had a hunch it was Ben, that he'd locked them in the basement so he could get the van and take them away from the house. Hayes wasn't the sort who'd want dirty work done under his own roof.

The path took them back and forth across the face of the hill, crisscrossing a wandering stream on a series of small wooden footbridges. The moon had moved out from behind the clouds, casting a glow on their surroundings. On either side of the path, flowerbeds were crowded with exotic plumes of foliage while dense banks of shrubs covered the slopes. Silhouetted against the sky were giant ferns and distinctive tree-sized shrubs she recognized as bird of paradise plants. They were as common as hibiscus back home, but she'd never seen any this large.

Her injured ankle, which she'd almost forgotten, had begun hurting again. After they crossed the fourth footbridge, she paused and looked at Reinhardt. "My ankle," she said, "I have to stop."

"That's all right," he said. "I have to stop here for something I left earlier. Rest a bit." He gestured in the direction of a stone bench just off the path. She limped over to it and sat down.

Reinhardt retreated into the bushes, then reappeared a minute or so later carrying a backpack. After removing a flashlight, he slung the bag over his shoulder and held his hand out to her. "Do you think you can get back on your feet?" he said. "We haven't much time."

Her ankle felt a little better. She stood up, taking his hand.

As they resumed their trek up the hill, he said, "It's all a façade, you know—this patch of rainforest. Hayes had some bulldozers carve up the hill. Brought trees over from the mainland. The big tropicals are plastic. Rather good imitations, if you fancy that sort of thing.

"He even smuggled in tropical birds," he went on. "Parrots and the like. They didn't survive. The harsh winter and the hawks..."

As Nicole glanced around, she understood her feeling of déjà vu. The place reminded her of the Jungle Boat ride at Disneyland, the perfect outdoor component of the dream world Alexander Hayes had created for himself. She was especially indignant about the parrots. What a rotten thing to do.

At the top of the hill, the path ended at a thick hedge of oleander, covered with blossoms. Well before they reached it, Nicole noticed something nauseating in the sweet heaviness of its perfume. Then she realized it wasn't the oleander. Mingled with its scent was the unmistakable stench of something dead and rotting.

As if he'd read her mind, Reinhardt said, "I smell it, too. Wait here. I'll have a look." He was back almost immediately, pulling her in a new direction, away from the stand of shrubs.

As the stench began to fade, he said, "I saw signs of a shallow grave. Maybe it was here when I passed through before but hadn't started to …" he hesitated and seemed to grope for the right word, "decay."

They continued along in silence until they reached the hill's crest. Here, Reinhardt turned on his flashlight and pointed the beam down a gently rolling slope. A narrow stream, no more than a couple of feet wide, meandered down toward the loch, which appeared as a vast stretch of darkness.

After locating the stream, Reinhardt snapped off the flashlight. There was a creaking nearby, a wild rustling of leaves, and a dark shape burst from the branches of a tree. Nicole's heart leapt to her throat and seemed to stick there, as Reinhardt turned the flashlight on again. He swung the beam in an arc, catching the culprit—a large owl in flight. As it flapped away, the bird's head swiveled around and stared back at them, its eyes iridescent in the light.

After it disappeared, Nicole couldn't shake the feeling that the creature was some kind of omen—a warning. Reinhardt, unruffled as ever, tucked the flashlight in his backpack and pulled out a square bundle of dark cloth, which unfolded into two ponchos. He handed one to Nicole, "Here," he said. "we won't have much cover going down. This will us give a bit of camouflage."

When she had put hers on, he reached over to pull up her hood. "Now," he said. "Let's go. To put the dogs off our scent, we'll walk in the streambed. Mind your step. It's slippery."

They were just starting down, Nicole a few steps behind him, when she heard excited barking in the distance. She looked around. The hill behind them was still deserted, but the implications were clear. Their absence had been noted. The search had begun.

Nicole tried to remember how long it had taken them to climb up the hill. Seven minutes? Five? Surely it wouldn't take that long to get down the slope and out of sight. From the top, it looked like an easy walk, but the rocks were indeed slippery, and maneuvering the creek bed was tricky.

Reinhardt tackled the terrain more easily, walking at a brisk pace and reaching the trees near the water's edge well ahead of her. As he turned to look back at her, his head jerked up, as if he'd spotted something on the hill behind her. A second later, a beam of light swept the hillside from above, barely missing her as it stopped and moved back across the slope. In a panic, she stepped out of the creek onto solid ground and ran.

Only when she reached Reinhardt and the shelter of the trees did she look up at the hill again. At the top, two figures were using flashlights to explore the grassy slope. Several dogs were nosing about the bushes.

He hurried her through the trees and over a thick outcropping of rocks. At the water's edge, he stopped. "We're going to wade in the loch. It's quite chilly but shallow along the shoreline. Take care—the bottom is covered with sharp stones."

A moment later, she followed him into the icy water. Although it only came to mid calf, the chill reached all the way to her scalp. Reinhardt turned and began to wade along the shore. Teeth chattering, she forced herself to follow. The rubber boots offered little protection; with each step, the sharp-edged stones jabbed her feet.

It wasn't long before he turned and waded back to her. "I think I'd better carry you," he said. "It's not far, but we have to be out of sight before they get here. When I turn round, climb up and hold on." Reinhardt turned and bent over, and Nicole did as he said, settling behind the backpack. As he straightened up, she wrapped her arms around his neck, her legs around his waist.

They made their way around the end of the cliff and entered the next cove. From her perch, Nicole looked around and felt a wave of despair.

The cove offered no place to hide, nor did there appear to be a route out other than the way they'd just entered. The only cover, unlikely at best, was an occasional cluster of bushes, which had defied gravity by taking root on the face of the rock.

Reinhardt headed determinedly toward a clump of foliage growing near the waterline. "There's a ledge of dry ground here," he said. "I'm going to set you down." He turned around and stood with his back to the ledge so she could climb down. When she was standing on the ledge, he said, "Hold on while I pull myself up."

She grabbed a nearby branch to steady herself, but it came off in her hand, and she found herself teetering on the narrow ledge. Reinhardt dropped back into the water and reached up to hold her. "Sorry," he said. "I meant to warn you not to touch that. Use the rock for support."

Nicole rested her back against the cliff and studied the spot where they'd entered the cove. She could no longer see the lights of their pursuers, just a general glow from that direction. It was impossible to measure its progress. She looked at the tranquil lake, which held the full moon's reflection. Then she turned to stare up at the solid wall of rock behind her, lifting her head to take in its dizzying height.

At that moment, her faith in Reinhardt evaporated. Now, as she looked up at the cliff, she could imagine him attempting to scale it. He'd pull her along by the hand, insisting, "It won't be long now," and "Hang on, it's not far."

Nicole shivered. In minutes, they would be target practice for the men who were after them. She wondered what had possessed her to follow Reinhardt on this long, futile trek when she could have stayed in the basement and died in relative comfort.

She watched Reinhardt as he pulled himself up onto the ledge. Just then she noticed a dark pool accumulating under her left foot. He spotted it, too. "What's that?" he said.

When Nicole lifted her foot, she saw that the sole of her boot had been ripped away and, although she felt no pain, her foot was bleeding profusely.

She crouched down to take a closer look when Reinhardt grabbed her arm and pulled her through a narrow opening in the wall of branches.

On the other side was a damp-smelling space, hidden away behind a lean-to covered with dead branches.

Inside, they were enveloped in darkness. "I don't dare light the torch," he said. "But I think we're safe for the moment. Now, let's find my medical kit and see what we can do about that foot."

Twenty-Seven

In the darkness, Nicole could hear Reinhardt rustling around in his backpack, pulling things out. "Hold out your foot," he said at last. "I'm going to clean the wound with an antiseptic pad. It might smart a bit."

Smart it did, but this was nothing compared to the fiery bite of the iodine he drizzled over the cut. While she clenched her fists and sucked in quick gasps of air, Reinhardt suggested she stay off the injured foot until he had a chance to bandage it properly.

Afterward, they huddled together in silence, and Nicole once again revised her opinion of Reinhardt. Her rescue had been nothing short of miraculous, a tribute to the advance work he'd done when he first arrived on the island, before he was captured: scouting out their escape route and setting up this hiding place.

Not that they were out of danger. At any moment, she expected a spotlight to find the entrance to the cave. A voice on a bullhorn would demand their surrender, followed by a barrage of gunfire. Oddly enough, she wasn't frightened. Perhaps she'd reached her threshold of sustainable terror. A certain numbness had set in, giving everything a sense of unreality. It was almost as if she were a bystander, watching the scene from a distance.

Minutes passed and still they waited. Finally, Reinhardt went to the entrance and peered out. "No sign of them," he whispered, "We'd best get out of these wet things, but we'll have to do it quietly, in case someone is out there."

Using a penlight shielded with his hand, he located some plastic bags at the rear of the cave and rifled through them. Finally, he turned off the light and whispered, "I have some dry clothes. Strip off your wet things and I'll hand them to you."

Nicole removed her remaining boot and peeled off the soggy jumpsuit. Despite the impenetrable darkness, she was acutely aware of Reinhardt standing nearby and of her heart thumping in her chest. When her clothes were off, she stood there shivering until she realized he was waiting, too. "Ready," she said.

He thrust a bundle of soft, dry fabric in her direction. "This is a jumper. Put it on first."

Her fingers recognized the soft, fuzzy texture of a sweatshirt. She felt around until she figured out which way was up, then slipped it over her head. Next came a pair of sweatpants, which she quickly pulled on.

"I'm afraid I don't have anything for you to wear on your feet," he said.

"Really?" She was shivering so much that her voice quavered. "I thought these pants had feet in them."

"I beg your pardon?"

"The legs are too long," she explained. Then, to his continued silence, "It was a joke. Not a very good one."

"Oh," he said, producing a sound that was probably meant to be a chuckle. "Sorry about that."

Nicole grimaced, suddenly weary of Reinhardt's unflagging good manners, the burden of having to make polite conversation when she felt like throwing herself on the ground for a good cry.

A light, dry object brushed her face, and she realized that he was passing her something else. "It's a blanket," he whispered. Then, after a pause, he handed her another packet, identical to the first. "You'd better lie down and cover up," he went on. "That was a nasty cut. You may be in shock."

The "blankets" resembled sheets of packing material composed of papery layers fused to padded plastic. Although she doubted she was in shock, Nicole did as he said. The ground beneath her was hard and cold. Even with dry clothes and the two blankets, she couldn't seem to stop shivering.

On the other side of the cave, she could hear Reinhardt rooting through the supplies again. Then he began to shift about in a way that told her he was changing out of his own wet things. Despite the cold, she was half asleep when she felt him spread another blanket over her.

When she jerked awake, it took a moment before she realized that this was the interior of the cave, now dimly illuminated by the low flame of a gas lantern. The place was smaller than she'd imagined, with craggy walls of dark, stratified rock. Against the rear stood three green plastic trash bags, which she assumed were the source of Reinhardt's supplies. Set on the ground nearby was a camp stove with a pot on its single burner.

A lightweight rowboat covered the entryway. It had been upended and tipped slightly to lean against the exterior wall of the cliff. The bottom of the boat, facing out toward the loch, was covered with a net to which branches had been attached. This was what hid the cave from outside.

"I draped a sheet of black plastic over the entrance, so our light can't be seen from outside," Reinhardt said. "Now, if you don't mind, I'd like to do a proper job of dressing your foot."

Nicole sat up and pulled off the blankets, clutching them around her shoulders while he placed a gauze pad over the wound and secured it with a length of tape.

She studied him while he worked, noting the look of quiet concentration in his eyes, the way he kept pushing his dark hair back from his forehead. At one point, he caught her gazing at him and grinned. That was when she first noticed his smile, how nice it was.

When he was done, he produced a flask of brandy and poured some into a disposable cup. "Drink up," he said. "It's just the tonic for you."

The first swallow of brandy made her cough, but it was warming, and she drank the rest in a couple of gulps. Only when the cup was empty did it occur to Nicole that alcohol might not be a good idea on an empty stomach. Already she could feel its effect.

She lay down again, expecting to drift back to sleep, but when she shut her eyes, the scene in the basement flooded back, etched in crisp detail. She could feel the weight of the sledgehammer as she brought it down on Kevin's head, hear the sound of the weapon as it landed. His skull had given way like the shell of a soft-boiled egg with a smack of the spoon.

Aside from the horror of that memory, she couldn't bear the idea of having killed another human being. It was contrary to everything she believed in, unthinkable in the humane and orderly world she'd always inhabited.

Nicole shifted about, trying to think of anything but the mess she'd made of Kevin's head. Finally, she propped herself on her elbows and looked at Reinhardt. He was leaning against the wall of the cave, staring into space while he took an occasional sip from his cup. He wore a grim expression, as if he, too, were thinking about the man he'd killed.

He must have felt her gaze, for he looked up. When their eyes met, she felt her own fill with tears. "Do you really think he's dead?" she said.

Reinhardt stared at her. "Who?"

"Kevin, the man I ..." She stopped, unable to say the word.

"Killing a grown man is not as easy as you think," he said. "You gave him a good knock on the head, no doubt about that. But he's probably recovered enough to be out with the others, trying to track us down."

Reinhardt spoke soothingly, as if reassuring a child who'd just awakened from a nightmare. Yet something in his voice told her that he, too, thought Kevin was dead. She covered her face with her hands and began to cry.

Reinhardt came over, squatted beside her, and reached out to pat her shoulder. "You were brave back there," he whispered. "You saved my life. I want to thank you."

She could see that her tears made him uncomfortable. Yet she couldn't seem to stop crying. Instead, she leaned against him and began to sob in earnest.

At last she grew quiet, and he started to pull away. Without speaking, she reached out and caught his sleeve.

He hesitated and, with a sigh she couldn't interpret, sat down beside her and put his arms around her. His body was tense, as if poised for a quick getaway. She ignored this, snuggling into his warmth and resting her face into the curve of his neck. Against her forehead, the stubble of his beard was somehow reassuring.

For the first time since they waded into the loch, Nicole stopped trembling. Breathing in his scent—a faint remnant of aftershave mixed with the salty smell of the loch—she felt a slow stirring of desire. It's the brandy, she thought. It's made me drunk. Then, all at once, she was overcome by an irresistible wave of drowsiness. Resting against him, she dozed. She started awake as he lowered her to the ground. "That's all right," he said, pulling the blankets over her. "Get some rest."

Drowsily, she watched Reinhardt take what appeared to be a small black box out of his backpack and walk over to the cave's entrance. He looked over at her. "This is a GPS device," he said. "I need to let my teammates know where we are." He pushed a button on it for a good long moment then returned it to his backpack.

Nicole sat up and hugged her knees, no longer quite as sleepy. “What happens now?” she asked. “Are they coming to pick us up? Or do we row this thing to the mainland?” She gestured toward the rowboat.

He took out the flask and poured some brandy into a fresh cup. “The dinghy?” he said. “We will be taking it to return to Hayes' compound. But we can't leave the island just yet, I'm afraid,” he said, walking over to hand her the cup. “Hayes' people are bringing in a drug shipment late tonight,” he went on. “The loch is actually an inlet from the coast; it's deep enough for a good-sized ship to dock. We're all set to raid Hayes' operation.”

She stared at the brandy, considering it before venturing a tiny sip. “Who is we?” she said.

“Oh, sorry. I'm with a special drugs intelligence unit assigned to gather evidence on our friend Hayes and put an end to his operation,” he said. “We scheduled the raid for last Thursday, the evening you arrived. But Lowry's disappearance put a spanner in the works. Several months ago he turned Queen's witness. He learned we had evidence against him and offered to cooperate in the hope that things might go easy for him. He provided us a wealth of information: the location of this island as the base for Hayes' drugs running, the schedule of the next few shipments. We still lacked some details, but Lowry was to have it...”

Reinhardt broke off and hissed “Shhhh! I hear something!” Then he put out the lamp and made a lunge for her, pulling her flat so both of them were lying on the ground.

Now Nicole heard it, too, the rhythmic splashing of someone rowing a boat. It was growing louder, coming in their direction.

“No sign of 'em,” a man said, his voice echoing off the rocks.

“Here, give me that light,” a second man said. It sounded like Chazz. “He says there's caves out here.”

The splashing stopped. A thin wedge of light poked its way into the cave, darted away, and then was back, slanting in from a different angle. For a long moment, the light hung suspended on the cave wall. Nicole sucked in her breath and held it.

At last the light disappeared, leaving them in darkness. There was an interminable silence before one of the voices outside said, "Nothing. We'd better get back." The rowing sound resumed, faster now and retreating.

When it was quiet, Reinhardt got up and peered through the opening. Returning to his seat next to her, he whispered, "They're gone, but we'd best wait a bit before turning on the light. Let me ask you something. Hayes seems to think you know where Lowry put his money. Is this true?"

Only as Reinhardt said this did Nicole realize that she'd been expecting this question and dreading it. She was silent for a long moment, gathering her thoughts. Then she began the story of how, after being duped into retrieving the money, she'd ended up mailing it to herself in Chiswick. She also told him about finding Muriel's passport and gave him Keaton's account of Alice's death.

"I'd heard that Alice McConnehy had a falling out with Hayes and Lowry," he said. "She was in league with them, you know, recruiting runners. In exchange, they made contributions to some save-the-whales organization she worked for. Apparently, she decided the whales deserved more money and tried to blackmail Hayes and Lowry. I suppose they'd had enough of her. After Lowry disappeared, Muriel must have decided it would be best to hide in plain sight, as Alice." He paused a moment, then he added, "About the parcel you mailed off to Chiswick …"

Now that she'd admitted what she'd done with the money, Nicole felt profoundly uneasy. "I was planning to turn the money to the authorities in London, I really was," she said. "I just wanted to make sure it went directly to the team investigating the car bombing."

"That makes sense," he said. "But you weren't there to receive the parcel when it arrived, were you? What do you suppose your husband has done with it?"

"Well, I don't think he'd open it," she said. "It's not unusual for me to mail packages home when I travel, things I've bought that won't fit in my suitcase. Brad probably left it on the hall table for me to take care of when I get back."

"The hall table," he repeated slowly. "We don't know Muriel's whereabouts, but she does have a key to the house."

"Right," Nicole said in a small voice.

They both grew quiet. Despite what she'd just said about Brad, it now occurred to her that he would eventually open the box if he hadn't heard from her and had started to worry.

But she could also picture Muriel letting herself into the house while Brad was at work. As soon as Muriel saw the label, with Nicole listed as both sender and addressee, she'd know what it was. And she'd have no compunctions about taking it.

"In a bit we'll take the dinghy back to Hayes' compound," Reinhardt was saying. "There's an unused boat house that will make a good hiding place for you. The raid should be fairly routine. We'll outnumber them, and despite what you've heard about the police here, we will be armed. Aside from my group, HM Customs and Excise is sending a cutter with a special team we call the rummage crew. They'll take possession of the yacht Hayes uses for drug smuggling."

"A while ago," Nicole said, "when you sent that GPS signal. How do you know you got through?"

"We've tested the equipment, so we know it works. We have to be careful. Today's drug smugglers are extremely sophisticated with electronics—scanning police frequencies, that sort of thing. It would be child's play for them to listen in on a conversation and track us down. On the other hand, with that shipment coming in tonight, I rather think they have their hands full."

He flashed the penlight on his watch again. "We'll wait to be certain they've given up the search. Meanwhile, I'm going to get out some rations. Once we've had something to eat, I suggest you try to rest."

Later, with Reinhardt rowing the dinghy, the two of them made their way back around the island. From time to time, the water's dark surface reflected the moon peeking out from the clouds.

Nicole was feeling better since the light meal Reinhardt had fixed of freeze-dried tuna-noodle casserole, cheese and crackers, and dried fruit. He'd reconstituted the tuna mixture with bottled water, heated on the camp stove. To Nicole, the dish tasted mainly of salt. Reinhardt ate quite a lot of it while she concentrated on the cheese, crackers, and dried fruit.

After eating, he had mumbled something about the toilet arrangement. In Nicole's case, this seemed to involve carrying a bucket to the outside ledge of the cave, squatting over it and then emptying it into the loch. He was vague on the details, and she felt it indelicate to ask. Nor was it in her to point out the difficulties, in view of female anatomy and the narrow width of the ledge. Instead, she bit her lip and hauled the bucket onto the ledge while Reinhardt waited inside. It had been a humbling experience.

Before they got into the dingy, Reinhardt gave her a plastic bag to put over her bandaged foot. Her rubber boots were no longer waterproof, although he'd managed to mend the ripped sole with some water-resistant tape and a sturdy piece of plastic. He also came up with another sweatshirt, which Nicole put on over the first.

Several times, Reinhardt had warned her that Hayes' men were sure to be on the alert. Now she was almost afraid to breathe.

Nicole stared at Reinhardt's silhouette against the moonlit clouds. With their knees almost touching, she couldn't help wondering about his personal life. He didn't wear a wedding ring. But it was impossible to imagine a man as attractive as Reinhardt going home every night to an empty—What did they call it?—bedsit. She pictured the two of them in a tiny, one room apartment with a bed that pulled down from the wall.

She drew a curtain on the daydream and pushed it away, although she understood where it had come from. It wasn't just physical attraction, but the growing bond between them: He'd saved her life, and in a way she'd saved his. But Reinhardt's interest in her well being, she reminded herself, was purely professional. This was his job. She could see that uninvited crushes would be an occupational hazard for policemen, firemen, and (she supposed) doctors who, in the course of their duties, occasionally saved people. She wondered how often, in the normal routine of his job, Reinhardt encountered more gratitude than he bargained for.

At that moment, the boat gave a lurch, and the bottom scraped something. "We've reached the shallows near the boathouse," he whispered.

Overhead branches brushed against Nicole's face, but it was too dark to make out much of anything.

The dinghy gave another lurch as Reinhardt got out. He steadied it with his hands and, with Nicole still inside, began to half pull, half drag the boat ashore. When it was firmly wedged between two rocks, he got out a rope and secured the boat to a tree.

"All set," he said. "Here, put your arms around my neck, and I'll lift you out."

"That's okay," she said. "A little water won't hurt me." She made an attempt to stand, but the movement set the boat rocking, and she was forced to sit down again.

"I can't allow that," he said. "With an open cut on your foot, there's too much danger of infection." With a soft grunt, Reinhardt lifted her out of the boat.

When they reached dry ground, he put her down. Walking beside him, she wondered about his unfailing politeness. Surely there were moments when he put good manners aside and the real Reinhardt made an appearance.

He moved closer, putting his left arm around her and cupping her left elbow while, at the same time, linking his right arm through hers. It was the same way a Boy Scout might guide an old lady across the street, one more reminder that his solicitousness was simply a matter of duty. He was responsible for delivering her safely to the mainland, and he was doing his job.

By now they'd reached a huge dark shape Nicole recognized as the boathouse. Reinhardt opened the door and ushered her inside to an interior so devoid of light that it seemed a great, empty void.

Twenty-Eight

As Nicole and Reinhardt entered, they were assailed by a cascade of sound, like the roar of an angry mob. Then Reinhardt closed the door, and the wind died away, leaving just the faint, rhythmic sound of lapping water.

He snapped on the flashlight and moved the beam around, revealing the interior of the boathouse with its high rafters. The walls were of narrow wood slats in a style favored by carpenters a century ago. Suspended from the rafters was a large hook and pulley, used to haul boats out of the water for storage or repair. Above them, three skylights revealed black squares of night sky.

The lapping sound came from a dark gap to the right of the wooden platform where they were standing. On their left was a row of empty racks that would have made perfect storage for surfboards and water skis. Considering the age of the boathouse, however, the builder had probably intended them for punts and small canoes. Ahead, at the end of the structure that overhung the water, two enormous garage-type doors could be slid open to admit a boat.

Nicole touched Reinhardt's hand and pointed to a corner where garden furniture was stacked under plastic drop cloths. "Didn't you tell me this place was deserted?" she said.

He aimed the flashlight beam at the furniture then let it drop to the floor. "Lowry told us that Hayes built a large, modern dock near the house to accommodate his yacht. He outfitted this place for fishing and picnics for his houseguests, but it's rarely used."

He moved to the edge of the platform and directed the flashlight beam into the darkness below. "Hello," he said. "What's this?"

She went over to look. Docked beneath them was a black boat of a sort she'd never seen before. It was small, no more than ten or twelve feet long, constructed of plastic inflatable tubes, like a life raft, but more streamlined. It was an attractive, sporty design with a small engine perched at the back.

"This wasn't here when I came through before," Reinhardt said. "This kind of boat is known as an R.I.B.—all the rage for water hobbyists these days. I wonder if you'd mind stepping to the rear of the boathouse while I go down and take a look." He pointed the light at the area where the furniture was stacked.

Goosebumps rose on the back of Nicole's neck. "Why can't I wait here?"

"You've been hurt. I want to be sure you're safe."

"I'll be safe here."

Reinhardt studied her a moment and said, "Sorry, but I must insist you wait at the other end. I don't want to turn round and find you following me down the ladder."

Nicole opened her mouth to argue, then shut it again. Why make things more difficult? "All right," she said, taking his arm and allowing herself to be led along the platform. The floorboards creaked beneath their feet while the moving flashlight threw eerie, dancing shadows.

"Listen," she said, "since we don't know who the boat belongs to, I don't think this is a good place for me to wait."

"Agreed. I'll just take a quick look at the boat. Then we'll find another spot."

As Reinhardt disappeared down the ladder, Nicole began to wonder if he'd insisted she get out of the way because he thought the boat might be booby-trapped. She remembered how benign the Lowrys' car had looked parked in front of the house that day. Even after Mr. McGiever got the engine started, everything had seemed perfectly normal until the blast knocked her off her feet.

Several loud clicks pierced the darkness. A well-tuned engine purred to life and immediately cut off. Nicole leaned forward to peer into the slot where the boat was docked, but all she could see was the reflected glow of Reinhardt's flashlight. There was a silence of perhaps fifteen seconds—an eternity—before he began up the ladder again. Already she was hurrying back along the platform to meet him.

Reaching the top, he held up a key. "This was left in the ignition," he said. "Either someone's been careless, or they're covering their bases for a quick escape. Let's get out of here."

Nicole felt an enormous sense of relief as they emerged into the night. He took her arm and guided her uphill, through the shrubs that covered the slope behind the boathouse. It wasn't long before their destination came into view—a somewhat ramshackle, low-slung structure just below the crest of the hill.

"It's an old stable," he explained. "And I am certain it's abandoned."

She trailed him along the row of stalls, shivering, unable to throw off the damp chill. They stopped at each stall, while Reinhardt flashed his light around. The floors were clean except for a thin layer of hay, which lent a sweetness to the air.

The last stall, which overlooked the water, was slightly larger than the others. Here, Reinhardt stopped and went inside. Nicole stood in the doorway a moment, gazing at the moon suspended over the loch, the gently-sloped hills covered with fir trees. If drug runners or a shipload of narcs were on the way, there was no sign of them.

In the reflected moonlight, she watched Reinhardt sling off his backpack, get out a cutting tool, and snip the wire on a bale of hay that was sitting in a corner of the stall. "Hang on while I find something for you to sit on," he said. From the backpack, he retrieved the light-weight blankets salvaged from the cave. He also produced the flask of brandy and handed it to Nicole.

While he spread a blanket over the hay, she uncapped the flask and took a sip. The brandy was just as raw as before and made her choke in the same way. While she was coughing, Reinhardt came over and patted her back. She sat down on the covered mound of hay and watched while he got out the second blanket and wrapped it around her shoulders.

"Do you have to go?" she asked.

"Not yet," he said. "I'll wait until Hayes' yacht arrives. I suspect that won't be for several hours."

"Look," she said, "if this is such a routine arrest, why can't I come with you?"

He shook his head. "It's against policy. Don't worry. You'll be safe here." His tone of voice, which had turned cool again, made her think of their very first conversation, when he'd turned up on the Lowrys' front porch.

A realization clicked into place. "You know, something still bothers me about the day I arrived, when you turned up at the house," she said. "You must have known the Lowrys' disappearance left us in a potentially dangerous situation. Why didn't you warn us?"

"At that point, there was no reason to think you were in danger," he said. "We weren't expecting Lowry to bolt, and we were unaware he'd bilked Hayes out of a large sum of money. Looking back, we now know he'd been planning this for some time. Arranging the home exchange so his house would be occupied."

"Then, when the car bomb went off," she said, "I told Keaton that Chazz and Kevin were responsible, but she insisted it was terrorists. I can't understand why Keaton didn't tell us what was going on."

"Detective Keaton didn't have the full story," he said. "We never involve outsiders in an undercover investigation, not even our fellow officers. No one is privy to this information except the investigation team itself. That's our policy.

"You have to understand," he went on. "If we let the whole division in on it, there's danger of a leak that could risk officers' lives. Despite what you see on television, we never allow a private citizen to get involved in an undercover investigation—especially a foreign tourist like yourself. It would put you in too much danger."

"Too much danger!" she repeated. She was too angry to listen to him anymore. Getting up, she stalked out of the stable and walked a short distance down the hill.

Reinhardt was right behind her. "We did do our best to protect you," he said. "But you kept evading us. You're rather good at that, you know. But I do owe you an apology. We completely underestimated the ability of those men to plan a crime and carry it off." He reached out and put a hand on her shoulder, gently pulling her around to face him. "Nicole, you must believe me when I say I'm truly sorry. We were wrong. We should have warned you, even if it meant jeopardizing the investigation."

She looked into his eyes, and her anger evaporated. He was genuinely sorry; she could see that. She also understood the pressure he was under. As a cop, he was obliged to follow the rules, and the operative rule was that he couldn't tell anyone about his investigation. But he had risked his life to save her from Hayes, and look how she was treating him. My God—what a wreck she was.

As they made their way back into the stable, she said, "I'm sorry I blew up like that. After all you've done." She held up the flask, which was still in her hand, and offered it to him. "Here," she said, "You must be cold, too."

He waved it away. "Sorry. I'm on duty."

"But you said Hayes' yacht might not arrive for hours."

"Ah, but there's our unexplained discovery in the boathouse." Then, after a moment's thought, he added, "Besides, here I am on a moonlit loch with a beautiful woman. If I don't keep my wits about me, there's no telling what might happen."

Smiling to herself, Nicole resumed her seat on the mound of hay and wrapped herself in the blankets. Once she was settled, Reinhardt came over and sat beside her.

For a moment, the two of them gazed at the shimmering water. Nicole was acutely aware of his thigh touching hers, the fact that their relationship had gone through some kind of subtle change.

It was Reinhardt who broke the silence. "I imagine you won't be sorry to see the last of this place," he said.

This didn't seem to require an answer. Nicole, who was feeling calmer, inched herself backwards and leaned against the wall.

"If things go smoothly," he went on, "we could have you on a boat heading out of here by daybreak. You'd be in Glasgow before noon."

"Hmm," she said. "What about you? Will you be glad to leave?"

She felt him turn and look at her. "It's always good to finish an assignment," he said.

"Do you have someone waiting at home?" she asked.

"I'm divorced," he replied. "Men in my line of work don't make very good husbands, I'm afraid. The hours are bad, and you can never predict what time you'll be home. There are missed dinners, birthdays, anniversaries. Everything we do is teamwork, and your assignments often call you out at the odd hour—the middle of the night, or just as you're setting off on holiday. The women don't like it."

She turned to look at him. "You haven't answered my question."

He was lying back, propped against his elbows. When he answered, he sounded drowsy. "I'm afraid I've forgotten what it was."

"If there was anyone waiting at home."

"Not at the present moment. You are inquisitive, aren't you?"

"Born that way, I'm afraid," she said. "Insatiably curious. Want to know everything about the people I meet. I'm not usually this aggressive, though. It must be the brandy."

"Have some more," he laughed.

"If you do."

"Sorry," he said.

"You must be freezing."

"It is a bit chilly," he agreed.

"Look, why don't we share the blankets?" Nicole said. "I mean, if we bundle together, we'll be warmer." Without waiting for his answer, she unwrapped the blankets from her shoulder and stretched them around him.

Already she felt warmer, but as she tried to nestle against him, she could feel how tense he was. "Here, relax," she said, ducking her head under his arm and wrapping it around her shoulder. She pulled the blanket more snugly around them. "There," she said.

Reinhardt took a breath, as if he were about to say something, then stopped. After another long pause, he cleared his throat. "I'll bet you'll be happy to get back to your husband."

"That's one bet you'd lose," she said. "I've left him."

Nicole could sense Reinhardt turning to stare at her, feel his breath on her cheek. Through an act of will, she continued gazing out at the night sky and its rippling reflection. "As soon as I get back to London," she went on, "I'm going to pack my bags, fly back to L.A., and file for divorce."

"I say, I don't mean to pry, but isn't this a bit sudden?"

"Not really." Nicole was quiet, trying to think of a way to explain. She was still too angry with Brad to discuss their problems calmly, especially with someone she barely knew.

"The thing is," she began carefully, "we've been growing apart for some time. Brad is the sort of person who compartmentalizes things. He has other areas of interest—perhaps the most important parts of his life—he isn't willing to share with me. It wasn't much of a marriage."

He took in a breath. "Well, the man's a fool."

"It's all right. Really! I'm fine with it." And as she said this, she realized it was true. She picked up the flask, uncapped it, and took another sip. This time, when she handed it to Reinhardt, he took a substantial gulp.

Emboldened, she reached out and touched his cheek. With that touch, he turned to look at her, and it was as if a door had opened; a decision had been made.

"I wish you didn't have to leave," she said.

Without answering, Reinhardt leaned over and brushed his lips against hers. His touch was so gentle it almost wasn't a kiss. Then he pulled her against him and kissed her again, much more earnestly. Just as she moved her hands to the back of his neck and let herself melt against him, he drew back.

"I can't do this," he whispered, burying his face in her hair. "I'm on duty."

Reinhardt released her and pulled away to sit beside her, both of them looking out at the loch. Nicole inched close enough to rest her head against his shoulder. He put his arm around her.

She was sure she hadn't dozed, but when she opened her eyes, she was lying on the straw, and the blankets were tucked around her. She breathed his name.

"I'm over here," he said.

When she sat up, she could see Reinhardt standing just outside the doorway. He came over and crouched down beside her. "The ship has entered the loch," he said. "I have to go."

Then she heard it, too. It was more a vibration than a sound, like a fly buzzing in the distance.

"I need to give you a few things," he said. "There isn't much time."

When Nicole saw the gun, she said, "Take that with you. I have no idea how to use a gun."

"Don't worry. I have my own," he said. Despite her protest, he quickly explained how to release the safety catch and aim the weapon. "I'm also leaving a flare gun, so you can signal if you get into trouble. I don't expect you'll need it. But you never know."

Reinhardt handed her the key to the boat. "This will start the boat's engine," he said. "It has an ignition switch, much like a car. To steer, you move the rubber-coated handle on the motor to the right or left. The boat responds to a light touch, so it's only necessary to move the handle a few degrees to turn the bow. In a pinch, I think you could manage. Remember—the plan is for you to wait here until I come back. Promise me you won't leave."

"What if they set the place on fire?"

He smiled. "I'll count on you to use your own good sense." The final item out of his backpack was a large Cadbury bar. "In case you get hungry," he said as he handed it to her. "You take care of yourself.

"The whole thing will be boringly routine. I promise," he added. "You're not to worry." Reinhardt bent down to get his backpack and slip it on. He kissed Nicole quickly on the top of her head and then disappeared through the shrubbery alongside the stable.

Twenty-Nine

After Reinhardt was gone, Nicole settled down on the pile of hay, not knowing quite what to do with herself. She felt weary and, at the same time, too restless and prickly to sit still. Sleep was out of the question. Her hands and feet were like ice, and the blankets were little use against the cold. She thought of the brandy but lacked the energy to get up and see if there was any left.

She couldn't stop thinking about Reinhardt, the long hours ahead, and all the dangers they posed for him. Other thoughts raced through her mind. What if he were killed before she had a chance to know him? And even if the raid went according to plan? Then what? They didn't even live in the same country. The whole thing was impossible.

She got up and went to the doorway. Everything was still, as if the whole island were waiting, holding its breath.

Despite her promise, she couldn't possibly wait up here, cut off from any news of the raid. She had to find out what was going on. And, really, what difference did it make where she spent the next few hours, as long as she kept out of the way?

Nicole picked up one of the blankets and struggled to tear it in half. It was surprisingly sturdy, and she had to use her teeth to make the first rip. In one triangular half, she rolled up the things Reinhardt had left for her: the key to the motorboat, the flashlight, the candy bar, the other blanket, and the remaining piece of the torn one. As she tied the bundle into a makeshift knapsack, she eyed the two items remaining on the floor. The gun appeared small and deadly in contrast to the bulkier shape of the flare gun next to it. On an impulse, she selected the flare gun and tucked it into the top of her knapsack.

She headed downhill along the same route Reinhardt had taken. It was a relief to be going somewhere, to have a sense of purpose. Once she made her way through the first stand of trees, the pier came into view, and she stopped to stare.

A large white yacht was docked there, and several men had begun unloading it. The craft was about eighty to ninety feet in length and appeared to be built for both power and speed. Its hull, dotted with portholes, was broad and deep enough to hold a sizable cargo. Yet the ship, with its flying banners and fringed awnings, looked more like a rich man's toy than a working transport for smuggling narcotics. That was probably why Hayes had chosen it.

Nicole edged farther downhill to a point about a hundred feet above the access road that ran along the shore. This, she decided, was as close as she dared. She headed for a large fir tree with branches that came within a few feet of the ground. Crawling under them, she settled herself on a nest of pine needles. Then she placed her knapsack against the trunk of the tree and rested her back against it.

Through the lower branches, she had a good view of the house and pier, as well as the road connecting them. Six men were using dollies to haul heavy-looking wooden crates from the hold of the yacht, down the pier, and into the back of a truck. Two other vehicles were parked behind it, almost identical to the first; they were all unmarked and of the same indeterminate make. In the still night air, she caught the sound, if not the sense, of occasional snatches of conversation.

Despite the residual tumult of her stomach, she found the scene reassuring. The men were immersed in their work, and their concentration suggested they suspected nothing of the raid. As for Reinhardt and the others, they must be safely holed up somewhere, waiting for the cutter. Maybe the whole thing really would go according to plan, just as Reinhardt had said.

Her thoughts shifted to the time spent together, the feelings he'd awakened in her. She knew almost nothing about him in particular, nor about policemen in general, at least on a personal level. She'd always wondered what inspired people to go into law enforcement, half suspecting it was a symptom of an authoritarian personality, the need to order others around and hold power over them. Yet she saw no sign of this in Reinhardt. Whatever had taken him into police work, he seemed to genuinely care about people.

With the same clarity, she also saw that any relationship they might have would be doomed. There were too many obstacles, not the least of which was geography. If that could be overcome, there were the demands and dangers of his work. Even now, when she thought about the raid and the risks he faced, she felt almost sick with worry.

Yet there was no denying the chemistry between them. How often did that come along? Maybe they could work something out. Even a long distance romance or an occasional holiday together would be better than nothing. But there was the question of whether this possibility would occur to him or if his interest would last beyond the scope of this assignment, when he was no longer responsible for her.

At that moment, Nicole caught movement against the hull of the yacht. A spider-like figure in black was silently leaving the ship, using a rope to climb down from the deck. Meanwhile, the men continued working, apparently oblivious to the activity behind them. She held her breath as the man dropped to the pier and disappeared, still unnoticed, into the shadows.

It occurred to her that this stranger might be with the police. Was the raid underway? Had they decided to go ahead without waiting for the cutter?

For a minute, perhaps two, nothing happened. The men continued carrying the crates into the vans. Then a man hurried off the ship and shouted an order she couldn't quite make out. The men loading the trucks immediately stopped what they were doing. Two of them began running toward the house, while the others scrambled onto the yacht, leaving the pier deserted. The lights on the ship went out; a moment later, the pier went dark.

Nicole got up, felt around for her things, and scrambled out from under the branches. Her instinct told her to run for the stable, where she'd be safe, but she paused for a last look. The white yacht was standing at the dock, silent and seemingly deserted. The three trucks remained parked nearby with rear doors open, the wooden crates stacked on the ground.

Someone must have tipped off Hayes' men. She thought of the stranger she'd seen climbing off the yacht. But if he'd come to warn them, why would he sneak away?

She was starting up the hill when she heard the hum of a motor and turned to see a white van speeding toward her on the road from the house. She recognized it as the same vehicle she'd seen parked near the house earlier.

As the car swung along a curve in the road, she was caught in the glare of headlights. She stood frozen, half blinded by the beams, until they released her. Seconds later, as the vehicle screeched to a stop, she turned and started running up the slope.

Behind her, a car door opened, and she heard someone scrambling after her. She tried to move faster, but the hillside was steep, and she felt herself losing ground. Abandoning the climb, she headed across the face of the hill toward the boathouse. As soon as she reached the shrubs surrounding it, she pushed her way into the foliage and lay flat, holding her breath. Seconds later, her pursuer came crashing through the bushes and began to circle her. It wasn't until she heard it panting that she realized it was a dog, an enormous one. Whoever was after her had sent the animal to track her down.

In slow, careful movements, Nicole got to her feet, loosened the knot on her knapsack, and pulled out the chocolate bar. By now the dog had taken a position nearby and was growling, poised to jump. She recognized it as one of the huge, shaggy hounds she'd seen in Hayes' library. She snapped the bar in half and held out a piece. The growling stopped. She threw the candy as hard as she could, but the dog leapt up and caught it midair. After devouring it, wrapper and all, he moved closer, staring at her with a rapt attention that was almost as menacing as his growl. She broke the remains of the candy bar into two pieces and raised her arm to throw one, concentrating on the need to hurl it farther.

At that moment, someone grabbed her from behind. "Look what we 'ave 'ere," he said. From the rank breath and fractured diction, she knew immediately who it was. He was pulling her against his huge stomach, tightening his arm around her neck when the dog jumped up and braced its enormous paws against her. The thrust knocked both her and Chazz off balance. All three of them tumbled to the ground.

The dog grabbed the remaining chocolate and darted away, crunching it in his teeth. Nicole scrambled to her feet. Before Chazz could grab her again, she reached into her knapsack, still dangling from her arm, and pulled out the flare gun. She swung the weapon at him, striking him squarely across the nose. He screamed in pain and stumbled backward a few steps. She stumbled with him, trying to get away, but he had a firm hold on her shirt. She hit him again. He let out another howl but didn't let go.

In desperation, she shoved the muzzle of the flare gun against his face and pulled the trigger. For a second, nothing happened. Then there was a queer whistling sound followed by a small explosion and a burst of light.

In that moment, Chazz's face was illuminated, and she saw a deep, bloody gash next to his nose, where he'd taken the impact of the flare. The rest of his face was covered with a thick coat of grayish powder that ignited into tiny flames. They quickly spread and, with a sudden swoosh, the entire surface of his face was alight. As the skin blackened, he began to beat at it, emitting a horrible keening sound.

He couldn't have been standing there for more than ten or fifteen seconds before he staggered backward and slipped, disappearing down the slope as if he'd been sucked away by a powerful force. Only then did the smell of burning flesh register in Nicole's brain. She turned and ran, her stomach heaving with disgust and horror.

By the time she reached the entrance to the boathouse, she was sweating and gasping for breath. She had no idea what had happened to the dog but suspected he was still out there in the bushes, nosing around for more chocolate.

She took a deep breath, fighting back a wave of nausea and reached for the doorknob; at that moment, someone grabbed her and shoved her against the wall. A cold piece of metal was pressed to her temple. "Don't make a sound," a voice hissed, "or I'll kill you."

Thirty

Nicole was forced into the boathouse at the point of a gun. "Lie down on the floor," the stranger said, "and see that you're quick about it.

Only now did Nicole recognize the voice. It sounded different without the Irish accent, more British than American. Under the circumstances, she decided not to let on that she knew it was Muriel, at least not yet. "Alice," she said. "It's me, Nicole."

After the slightest hesitation, the hand on the back of Nicole's neck relaxed and the gun was withdrawn. A moment later, she was blinded by the beam of a high-powered flashlight.

"Nicole! It is you," Muriel said. The Irish accent was back, her tone softer. "But you're so pale, and what's that blood on your face? Are you hurt?"

Nicole reached up to touch a tender spot on her cheek. "I'm all right. It's just a scratch."

"We'll see about that." Muriel guided her to a corner of the boathouse where a tap and drain provided a crude wash-up area. Here, Muriel turned on the faucet. "Splash the water on your face, and you'll feel better," she said. "That's the way. Put your face under the tap."

The water was cold and bracing. After Nicole washed, she opened her mouth and took a long drink. She had nothing to dry her hands and face—her sweats were filthy—so she shook off as much water as she could and, still dripping, turned back to Muriel.

"It is just a scratch," the woman said after checking Nicole's face again. "That's all right, then."

In the reflected glow of the flashlight, Nicole noticed Muriel's clothes. She was dressed all in black from her pants, sneakers, and pullover to the knit cap covering her hair.

"Alice," Nicole said slowly. "That was you I saw climbing off the yacht, wasn't it? What were you doing there?"

"The less you know about it, the better," Muriel said. "I will say this: I heard Hayes was receiving another shipment of drugs, and I wanted to make sure it was his last."

"Are you trying to tell me you're with the police?"

"Don't be daft," Muriel said. "I've already explained. I have a score to settle with these people."

"Your brother," Nicole repeated. It was hard to keep the sarcasm out of her voice.

"I told you all about that, Nicole. Remember?" Muriel said. "Now, listen. We're in serious danger here. I have a boat waiting to take us away."

"I can't go," Nicole said. "I promised I'd wait."

"Not in here, Nicole. It's too dangerous."

"Right," Nicole agreed. "In the stable on top of the hill."

"That's up to you then," Muriel said, starting toward the edge of the platform. "But I'm warning you: Get a move on. The whole thing is about to go up."

"Neither of us is going anywhere until you explain a few things," Nicole said.

"Suit yourself." Already Muriel was starting down the ladder that would take her to the boat.

"The key to the boat isn't where you left it," Nicole called out, "and I won't tell you where it is until you answer my questions. I know who you are, Muriel."

Muriel stopped and turned, pointing the flashlight at Nicole. "Give me the key, Nicole," she said, abandoning the Irish accent. "We both have to get out of here before all hell breaks loose."

Nicole held up a hand to shade her eyes from the light. "Just answer one question," she said. "Why did you tell me all those lies?

"Oh, all right," Muriel hissed. "If I tell you that much, will you give me the key?"

Nicole murmured her assent, and Muriel began, her words tumbling out in a rush: "I couldn't let you know who I was. You were supposed to think Freddy and me were on our way to Los Angeles. But the plan was for me to wait at the house in Chiswick until I heard from him. Then I'd ship the money and join him in Ecuador. While I was waiting, I had to stay out of sight so the neighbors wouldn't see me. So I dyed my hair and made some changes to my appearance. When you arrived, I was still waiting for Freddy to contact me. I was beginning to think he'd left me in the lurch, and I was pretty angry and upset. To get my mind off my worries, I thought I'd make myself busy, showing you around, and making sure you enjoyed London."

"Making sure I enjoyed London!" Nicole said. "From that first day, you were using us. We were decoys to make your house look occupied." She continued, "I guess I understand why you said you were Alice, but what about the rest of it, all that stuff you told me about your dead brother and getting revenge on Lowry?"

"Nicole, please! I'm truly sorry you got swept up in this," Muriel said. "And I will tell you everything. But right now we haven't time; we've got to get out of here! I can't use the motor because the noise will give me away. I'm going to row to the other side of the island. Why don't you give me a hand? While we're rowing, we'll talk. Then I'll let you off at a spot on the other side. It's an easy climb up to the stable."

After a moment's hesitation, Nicole got up and followed Muriel to the edge of the platform. The doors leading to the loch were open, revealing the quiet water beyond. Muriel descended the ladder first. Then she waited, shining the flashlight on the rungs so Nicole could see the way.

The boat, which was made of inflatable plastic, didn't have much heft. It bucked and swayed as they climbed aboard. When they were finally seated side by side, Muriel said, "Let's have the key, Nicole. We'll start out rowing, but I want to be sure I'll be able to start the engine." Nicole quickly located the key in her knapsack and handed it over. Muriel slipped the key into the ignition and turned it until it started, then turned the engine off again.

The oars were fastened lengthwise, along the inflatable tubes that made up the boat's exterior. Muriel released the oar on her side and let the paddle end drop into the water. Nicole did the same with hers.

"All right, now," Muriel said. "It'll take a minute to coordinate our movements."

Nicole had never rowed before. She was surprised at what hard work it was, despite the boat's light weight. At first, they only managed to make the boat turn in circles. Before long, however, they got the hang of it. The craft began moving in the right direction. They slipped silently out of the boathouse before making a ninety-degree turn to parallel the shore. They were heading toward the southern tip of the island.

"Remember, Nicole," Muriel whispered as the boat slid silently along. "We have to keep our voices low. You have no idea how easily sound carries on water. Now, what do you want to know?"

"When you took Alice's identity, did you already know she was dead?"

"I had a suspicion," Muriel said in a low voice. "Alice and I were friends, good friends. She had a deal with Freddy, providing couriers for him. She had connections with people, mostly unemployed young men in the neighborhoods where she did her nursing. Every cent went to some wildlife group. Alice seemed to think it was her job to save the planet. When she figured out Freddy's plan to disappear, she realized it meant an end to the arrangement, and she was furious. She called Hayes and proposed a deal between them; he must have decided she was a threat because he had her killed. That call of hers also blew the whistle on Freddy."

Already, Nicole was winded from the exertion of rowing. In contrast, Alice didn't seem to feel it at all. She wielded the oar easily, while Nicole had to use both hands and every ounce of strength into pulling hers through the water. Raw spots were developing on her palms. But the effort seemed to be paying off. The boat was picking up speed. Before long, they'd almost reached the southern tip of the island.

For a few minutes, they were both quiet, concentrating on keeping the boat off the rocks while they maneuvered around the point. When the turn was complete, Nicole said, "What about getting revenge for your brother's murder?" she said. "Was there any truth to that?"

"Sorry about that." Muriel said, "I guess I got carried away. After the first few days, when I still didn't hear from Freddy, I didn't know what to do. I couldn't risk running into anyone who might know me, and I had the feeling you'd noticed the way I was sneaking around. I needed to come up with some kind of explanation.

"I borrowed the story about the dead brother from something I saw on TV," she went on. "You have to understand—I was crazy with worry by that time. Then, a few days ago, Hayes had me dragged up to this God-forsaken island. He said he'd have me killed the way he'd done Freddy. Hayes told me they caught him on his way to the airport."

Nicole thought about the grave above the tropical garden but decided it would be best not to mention it.

"Wait, stop!" Muriel said.

They both stopped rowing. In the silence, Nicole inspected her palms with her fingertips. The skin was raw, and she could feel blisters rising. Meanwhile Muriel was feeling around in her pockets. Only when she blew her nose, snuffling a bit, did Nicole realize her friend was crying.

"You probably think Freddy was a bad man," Muriel said as they started rowing again. "But he wasn't. He just got caught in a bad situation. In the old days, when Freddy started out, even Hayes wasn't that bad. He dealt only in marijuana, a bit of hashish. I begged Freddy to get out of the life, but you could make good money selling weed in those days. Then high-grade heroin, crack, and designer drugs came on the market, and Hayes decided he'd have to branch out or go out of business.

"At that point, Freddy did try to quit, but Hayes threatened to have him killed. Then, a few months ago, the police closed in on Freddy. He didn't know what to do. If he ratted on Hayes, Hayes' people would kill him. If he didn't, the cops would put him away for years, and Hayes would probably make sure he never got out alive. So Freddy pretended to cooperate with the police to buy some time so he could plan our escape. Just as we were getting ready to leave, Hayes got stuck with a shipment of cocaine. There had been a big police crackdown, and his regular contacts couldn't get rid of it. So he gave Freddy a load on consignment. Freddy decided to take the profits and run. He saw it as his retirement fund, a chance to start over."

"Earlier," Nicole said, "you were Hayes' prisoner at the house. When was that?"

"Four days ago."

"That was just before they brought me here," Nicole said. "How did you escape?"

"I paid someone off."

"Paid someone off?" Nicole repeated. "With what?"

"Let's say I had a little windfall."

"The money I shipped to the house," Nicole said, "You took it, didn't you? Muriel, that money is important evidence against Hayes; you have to turn it in to the police."

"I'm sorry, Nicole," Muriel said. "The police have plenty of evidence. Besides, Hayes will never serve a day in jail, and I have a right to that money. Hayes was telling the truth when he said he killed Freddy, or I would have heard from him by now. My only regret is that I had to hand a good bit of money over to that no-good Ben."

"Ben is dead, Muriel."

Muriel continued as if she hadn't heard. "Do you know what's happening back there? The police are about to arrive, and Hayes and his men are hiding aboard that ship, ready to make their escape. They'll lose the drugs they already unloaded, but there's still plenty onboard. All kinds of drugs, you understand, not just the weed Hayes is always going on about. Once his boat is on the open sea, he's a free man. After everything he did, all the people he had killed—Freddy, Alice, Mr. McGiever.

"Poor Mr. McGiever," Muriel continued, "he was the dearest man. We were in the Chiswick Thespians together; he was quite an actor. You'd be surprised."

"The Chiswick Thespians," Nicole repeated. "That explains a lot—your Irish accent, your flair for the dramatic."

"I trained as an actress," Muriel said. "I'll bet you didn't know that. I never had much talent, though. The instructors were always telling me I was over-the-top. But I did have a knack for dialect …" Her voice trailed off.

"One more thing," Nicole said. "Why are you so sure Hayes is going to escape? The police will be here any minute now; he'll be in jail by morning."

"Well, where are they?" Muriel said. "Do you really believe they'll pull it off?" Then she added, almost to herself, "Never, never."

They rowed silently for a few more minutes. Then Muriel said, "Over to our left. See those flat rocks jutting out just above the water? That's where I'll let you off."

After they made their way close to the shore, they turned the boat to bring it parallel to the rocks. Muriel jumped out first and pulled the boat alongside the rocky formation.

It wasn't until this moment, when she was no longer rowing, that Nicole realized how sore her arms were. She rubbed them a bit, then stood up and began to get out of the boat while Muriel held it. The rocks were slick, and as Nicole climbed up, Muriel reached up to steady her.

As soon as Nicole was safely on shore, Muriel looked up at her. "I'm sorry, Nicole," she said. "Sorry I got you involved in this terrible mess. When we set up the house exchange, you were just a stranger who was going to stand in for us for a few days—no harm done. I had no idea you'd end up in such danger, or that I'd grow so fond of you ..."

She went silent, then added, "I hate to be the bearer of bad news, but I thought you'd want to know. The police took your husband away day before yesterday. I saw them from Mr. McGiever's house."

Somehow, this didn't come as a surprise. Nicole drew in a deep breath. "I'm sorry to hear it," she said, "but I've left him."

"I'd figured as much," Muriel said. "You two were married for a good while, weren't you? You share a past. No matter how angry you are or how much you think you hate him, you wouldn't wish this kind of trouble on him."

"I guess you're right," Nicole said. "But it's out of my hands; I can't save him from himself."

"Amen," Muriel said. "No one knows that better than I do. Well, take care of yourself, Nicole. Just head straight up the hill to the stable. No more wandering around. I want you to promise."

"I promise," Nicole said. "You take care, too. By the way, what happens when you start the engine? Aren't you afraid they'll hear it?"

"It isn't a half mile to the mainland," Muriel said, "and I have a car waiting. By the time they get their forces mobilized, I'll be gone. Are you sure I can't persuade you to come along? I'll drop you anywhere you want. Glasgow? Chiswick? Heathrow? We could take the Chunnel to Paris. Have you ever been to Paris?"

"I can't," Nicole said, "I gave my word."

"Goodbye then." Muriel turned the key to start the motor and, with a wave, began moving the boat away from the rocks. Then she made a tight U-turn, reversing direction. Only then did Nicole remember seeing Muriel's black-clad figure climbing down from the yacht. "Wait!" she called out, "You never told me! What you were doing on Hayes' yacht?"

Her question went unanswered. The boat was already speeding away.

Nicole began the climb uphill. When she reached the crest, and the other side of the island came into view, she stopped to take in the quiet scene below. The yacht was still there, docked at the pier. Everything was quiet and dark, just as before.

Just then, she heard the yacht's engine start up, and she realized what Muriel had been doing on that ship; she wasn't talking about the raid when she said all hell was going to break loose.

Nicole hesitated only a few seconds before dashing the short distance to the stable. She reached it just as the explosion struck. As a deafening roar shook the earth, she rolled herself into a ball. She sensed, rather than saw, the white-hot blast. Next came several lesser explosions and a loud swoosh!. Ringing filled her head, eliciting a sense of déjà vu that turned her insides to jelly. Hot wind rushed in, lifting the hay from the floor, whipping it around the stall, and hurling it down on her.

When the fury subsided, Nicole got up; finding herself uninjured, she went to the doorway. The smoke made her eyes water, turning the scene into an impressionistic painting of flames dancing on water, the night sky lit up, the air billowing with smoke. For a while she stood leaning against the doorway, staring, her mind empty of thought. Then, still in a state of shock, she remembered Reinhardt. He was out there somewhere. Heart pounding, she began to hurry down the hill.

The branches on some of the trees were smoldering. Only when she reached the point on the hill where the trees began to thin was she able to get a good look at the burning yacht. Whatever explosives had been used, the charge must have been enormous. Portions of the ship's hull had been blown away, and the wooden skeleton supporting it had collapsed. The fire was furiously consuming the remains.

Nicole remembered what Reinhardt had told her. His team planned to wait until the cutter from customs arrived before boarding the yacht. The cutter was nowhere in sight. She hoped this meant that he and his cohorts were still hiding.

Clearly, Muriel had been right. Customs wouldn't have arrived in time to prevent Hayes' escape. This seemed to confirm Nicole's own view of the police, the haphazardness of their results, the random way some criminals were caught while others walked away, free to do the same thing all over again.

If Muriel hadn't taken the law into her own hands, Hayes would be heading onto the Sea of Hebrides and, from there, to the Atlantic. As Nicole thought about Muriel's violent act, she could see a certain justice in it. Clearly, sabotaging the yacht wasn't right, but it wasn't right for Hayes and his goons to go free either.

Nicole's thoughts shifted to the small motorboat that had carried Muriel away. She pictured it reaching the shore, its occupant getting into a sleek, dark sedan and speeding away. She closed her eyes and sent up a prayer for Muriel's safe passage.

Someone touched Nicole's shoulder, and she looked around to see Reinhardt standing beside her. "You all right, then?" he said. He put his arms around her and pulled her close, briefly resting his head against hers.

"I'm fine. How about you?"

Reinhardt gave her another squeeze and turned to stare at the burning ship. Although he didn't speak, the anguish on his face showed what he was feeling. Even though Hayes and the drug ring had been destroyed, the explosion was anything but a victory for Reinhardt and his fellow officers. They were left without a case, all those months of work wasted. As Nicole considered her own complicity in Muriel's escape, she wondered why she didn't feel any regret. Perhaps it would make an appearance at some future date. For the moment, however, her conscience was clear and unclouded by doubt.

Watching the fire, she began to wonder about the advance work required to blow up a yacht. How, for example, had Muriel managed to carry enough explosives on board to destroy it so completely? Then she remembered an item she'd read in *The Times* a few days before, about an incident off the coast of Japan. Radical environmentalists, enraged at the snaring of dolphins in tuna nets, had used a boat's own fuel system to blow it up.

So perhaps it wasn't necessary for Muriel to carry a ton of explosives onboard. All she'd needed was the latest recipe for blowing up a large boat, no doubt easily available on the Internet.

It was Reinhardt who broke the silence. "My God, what a waste," he said. "That's our evidence going up in flames, our whole case, and there must have been five or six men on board." After a moment's silence, he added, "Not that any of them were choir boys. But, bloody hell, the system had a right to try them and decide what price they should pay."

"What do you think happened to the ship?"

He paused and shook his head. "These people don't bother with licensed crew. You can bet the men they hire think nothing of using drugs. All it takes is a moment of carelessness. You know the kind of thing. Someone lights a cigarette too near the fuel tank…"

"The boat from Customs," she said. "Where is it?"

"We had a message that it was delayed an hour or so, lending a hand in a rescue operation a bit south of here," he said. "We thought we had time while Hayes' people were busy unloading the ship."

"Don't you think—" Nicole stopped, then began again, "I mean, I'm pretty sure I heard the engines on Hayes' yacht start up."

"Yes, we heard it, too. It appears they were getting ready to make a run for it. They hadn't finished unloading, so perhaps they'd gotten wind of something. But we were prepared. We have equipment that can shoot a tracking device into a ship's hull. We had one of these in place and were poised to track them to their next port. Then we would have notified local drug authorities. Believe me, they would have been caught—if they hadn't all been blown to kingdom come…"

His voice trailed off as several men emerged from the shadows, all dressed in dark jump suits. Nicole could tell they were Reinhardt's colleagues, for he hurried over to join them.

The men gathered for a talk, heads together like a football team discussing their next play. In this case, they were no doubt rehashing their failed raid. If Muriel hadn't blown up the boat, Nicole wondered, would their tracking device have done its job, allowing them to find Hayes and arrest him? Considering the bad luck that had dogged the case so far, she had her doubts.

As Nicole watched Reinhardt confer with his teammates, she was overcome with despair. She had the feeling that, once they left the island, she would never have another moment alone with him, perhaps she'd never even see him again. And it seemed to her that of all the things she'd had to endure since her plane set down at Heathrow, this was the cruelest.

Thirty-One

Nicole was filled with apprehension as the police cutter carried her away from the Isle of Benbarra and from Reinhardt who, with several members of his team, remained behind to finish the investigation.

The day was gray with a thick mist that reflected her mood. As soon as they arrived on the mainland, she was handed a phone so she could let her family know she was all right.

Knowing that Brad had been picked up by the police, Nicole didn't bother to call his cell or the house in Chiswick. Instead, she called her sister in Los Angeles. "My God, Nicole," Stephanie had said when she heard about her sister's ordeal. "I'm going to drop everything and catch the next flight over. You shouldn't be alone right now."

"Please don't do that," Nicole said. "I'm fine. Besides, I'll be coming home in a couple of days." The truth was, she needed some time to herself so she could digest what had happened and try to make sense of it.

Around 10:30 a.m., when she was delivered to the house, she was astonished to find Brad pacing anxiously in front. Only as she stepped out of the police car, did she realize she was no longer angry; she no longer felt much of anything at all for him.

As soon as the police were gone and Nicole and Brad were alone, he confessed that the new business he'd said had belonged to his employer was, in fact, his own. He wasn't entirely truthful, however, in that he made it sound more like an investment management firm than a money laundering service. "I got greedy and made some stupid mistakes," he admitted. "And now I'm in trouble with the police. I might even lose my job."

Under Nicole's questioning, he explained what had happened when the police picked him up. "They had a bunch of questions about this outside business I started. The truth of the matter is that some of the stuff we did was, well, pretty questionable, and they started making noises about money laundering charges. But then I volunteered to turn over my records and some other…" he paused and seemed to consider this, "assets and help them sort out information about my clients. So they released me. I'm on leave from work now, helping the police on several high-profile cases."

Brad continued, "Everything was going pretty well until this morning. I wake up and they're out there banging on the front door. They show me a search warrant and say they're looking for some package they claim you shipped to the house. I swear to God, Nick—I never saw it. Then, as they're leaving, one of them says to me…"

At this point he screwed up his face and affected an exaggerated British accent: "'By the way, old chap, did you hear? Your wife has been released by those kidnappers who were holding her up in Scotland.' I almost croaked. I didn't even know you were missing. I mean, you never said when you were coming back, and I figured you were too mad at me to answer when I tried reaching you on your cell."

Nicole nodded, waiting for Brad to finish speaking so she could retreat upstairs. He hadn't mentioned Hayes, and she was too weary to pursue the point. Nor did she question him about the missing package. She knew he was telling the truth about this. Muriel had found it and disappeared with the money long before Brad arrived home from work. Or was that the day the police picked him up? Somehow these questions didn't seem worth pursuing.

"But you haven't told me anything about what happened," he said, as she started up the stairs. "Are you all right? Don't you want to talk about it?"

"Not really," Nicole said. All she wanted to do was wash up, change into a clean nightgown, and climb into bed. Brad had the good sense not to follow her.

She had a shock when she reached into the bureau and found a hefty bundle of £50 notes nestled among her bras and panties. Tucked in with the bills was an unsigned note that said, "Buy something lovely for yourself, Nicole."

She recognized the handwriting, just as she knew the money, £5,000 in all, was a payoff for retrieving the drug loot from the storage locker. Her first reaction was indignation, a resolve to march it right down to the police.

She was looking around for a bag to pack the money in when she began to have second thoughts. She could see that returning the £5,000 might focus unwanted attention on the infinitely larger sum she'd taken from Lowry's storage locker. True, she'd admitted this to Reinhardt. Apparently he'd handed the information on to the London police, who'd come banging on Brad's door that morning. But she had a hunch that Reinhardt had minimized her role as Muriel's messenger. With a closer look, the London police might take a dim view of this behavior.

She also questioned the use British authorities were likely to make of the recovered money. No doubt it would be tossed into the general fund where most government revenues end up.

Ultimately, it would be used for something really stupid, like the next coronation. The amount was too small to accomplish much.

Nicole had a sudden urge to see the money used to undo some of the harm Hayes had done. For the rest of the day, she remained upstairs, napping and gazing out the bedroom window, deep in her own thoughts. She saw Brad leave and, much later, heard him come back. Around 7:00 p.m., when she went downstairs to fix something to eat, he was sitting at the kitchen table, reading the newspaper.

"Take a look at the afternoon paper," he said, holding up the front page. A huge headline across the top read, "Drug Yacht Blown to Kingdom Come".

Below that, in smaller letters, it said, "Search on for Missing Drug Lord". Taking the paper from him, Nicole sat down at the table and quickly devoured the stories about Hayes, his operation, the failed drug raid, and the yacht's explosion. As a sidebar, the paper even ran a body count.

LIST OF DEAD AND MISSING IN HAYES DRUGS CASE

The following includes those dead or unaccounted for in connection with missing international drug lord Alexander Hayes. According to sources in West Scotland, the loch surrounding Hayes' Isle of Benbarra compound is too deep to be dragged for bodies.

Dead: Edgar McGiever, 67, retired manager of the maintenance department of the Greater London Council's Board of Public Works; victim of the Chiswick car bombing, now believed to have been the work of Hayes' operatives.

Dead: Alice McConnehy, 30, the Lowrys' tenant, whose body was found in the Thames. Police believe she was murdered by Hayes' operatives.

> Dead: Frederick Lowry, 52, of gunshot wounds. Body discovered in a shallow grave in the Hayes compound on the Isle of Benbarra.
>
> Dead: Kevin Smithson, 28, of head injuries, also on Isle of Benbarra.
>
> Dead: Benjamin (Ben) Manning, 45, Hayes' top enforcer, of injuries suffered during a struggle with police on Isle of Benbarra.
>
> Dead: Andrew Crump, 23, Greg Lawson, 25, and Colin Durfield, 28, crew members of Alexander Hayes' yacht, the Summer Wind. They were killed when the vessel exploded as the result of an unexplained engine fire.
>
> Missing: Alexander Hayes, 55, believed to have been in the vicinity of his yacht, the Summer Wind, at the time of the explosion; body never recovered.
>
> Missing: Charles (Chazz) Reilly, 26, employee of Alexander Hayes, also in the vicinity of the yacht's explosion. Body never recovered.
>
> Missing: Muriel Lowry, age unknown, wife of Frederick Lowry (see above). Police believe this woman may have fled the U.K.

When she was done reading, she tore out the story, put it in the pocket of her robe and began to assemble ingredients for an omelet. Every once in a while, she'd pause, pull out the clipping, and consult it again, as if it could explain why so many whose lives had touched hers were now dead or missing. Perhaps the real issue was how she had managed to survive, a question that continued to mystify her. For here she was, unharmed (at least in any visible way), and perfectly able to function at normal daily tasks, like cooking.

"Look, Nick," Brad said while she looked through the cupboards for an eggbeater. "I want to tell you what happened, but I'm afraid—Well, why not just come out with it?" He gestured toward the newspaper. "This guy Hayes, the one who kidnapped you? Well, I was doing some, uh, business with him. That's how I heard about Lowry and ended up getting us this house. What I mean to say is that I'm to blame for the whole thing, all that horrible stuff you went through. But I had no idea. I mean, if you only knew how bad I feel about it, you'd forgive me."

Nicole listened without comment while she finished the omelet, sprinkling it with cheese, and placing it under the broiler. Almost without thinking about it, she'd made enough for both of them.

It wasn't until they'd finished the meal that Brad had talked himself out. At that point, Nicole told him their marriage was over. She was heading back to L.A. to file for divorce. "But there's no reason you can't stay here at the house in Chiswick," she added. "The agreement we signed with the Lowrys gives us the house until mid-September."

Brad refused to accept her decision about the divorce as final. He did seem to understand, however, that he'd been evicted from the bedroom. Even so, Nicole took the precaution of locking the door.

The next day, she arranged for the two of them to consult with the solicitor who was handling Brad's case. She had no intention of getting involved in his defense. But with community property, her finances were entangled with his, and she thought it was important for her to have a clear picture of his legal problems.

The solicitor explained that money laundering carried a fairly heavy maximum penalty in the U.K.—fourteen years. Although Brad was giving the police his full cooperation, the British courts had no formal system of plea bargaining. So there were no guarantees. "At the end of the day," he added, "I think it's very likely that Mr. Graves will be facing some prison time."

After they left the office, Brad shrugged off the solicitor's assessment. "Talk about worst-case scenario," he said. "What a total load of crap!"

"I checked out his references, Brad," Nicole said. "This guy knows what he's talking about."

"He's just trying to cover his ass," Brad scoffed. "They'll never send me to jail."

What surprised Nicole was the way Brad refused to accept the idea that he might have to pay some kind of penalty. He didn't believe charges would be brought or, if brought, that they would stick. Nor did he seriously think he'd lose his job. In fact, he seemed to regard his predicament as a minor scrape that could, if he played his cards right, open some great opportunities. He mentioned the possibility of a book contract, or starting a brand new business to shepherd small investment companies through the thicket of laws governing international currency exchanges. He was so doggedly upbeat and optimistic that she realized this was no act. He was truly delusional.

From the solicitor's office, Brad took the tube to the police station, where he was spending long days helping investigators with cases related to his money laundering scheme. Nicole caught a cab back to the house. On her way inside, she stopped to chat with Mr. McGiever's son and teenage grandson, who were working on the blackened shambles of his front yard. They'd already begun hacking up the charred skeleton of the hedge that had formerly stood between the two houses. Young McGiever explained that he was fixing up the house so he could sell it. He was terribly nice—thin and wispy like his father—and kept apologizing to Nicole about her ordeal, as if it had somehow been the old man's fault.

As he was talking, Nicole remembered her recent windfall and realized that Mr. McGiever's garden was exactly the kind of project she had in mind. She'd spend the money helping them repair the damage, replant the garden, and replace the burnt hedge. It felt right: direct reparation, however small, of the harm Hayes and his men had done. After making some inquiries at a local nursery, she postponed her flight back to L.A.

She bought herself some gardening gloves and hired McGiever's grandson, Edgar III, to assist her. The two of them spent several days planting Mr. McGiever's ravaged flowerbeds with roses and a bank of azaleas. She also followed the nurseryman's suggestion of putting in a small ornamental pear by the front window. This done, Nicole gave the boy a box of scouring pads and put him to work removing the sooty splotches the blast had left on the house's brick facade. Then they repainted the front door while a crew from the local nursery rolled down a carpet of thick green turf. She'd had to bribe the nurseryman to avoid the usual three-to-six-week wait. Since it wasn't her money, she didn't haggle.

Until this moment, the neighbors had been peeking out from behind their curtains, but the sight of workmen laying down a ready-made lawn drew them outside to watch. Instant landscaping was taken for granted in Los Angeles, where a full botanical garden, complete with a grove of palm trees, could appear overnight. Clearly, this wasn't the case in Chiswick.

For Nicole, the most therapeutic part of the project was the moment each afternoon when Reinhardt arrived, and the two of them retreated inside to work on Nicole's "debriefing." For the most part, these sessions took the form of languid hours upstairs in the Lowrys' double bed, getting better acquainted, talking, or not talking, as the mood struck them.

On his first visit, Reinhardt arrived in official capacity, with a list of questions, including the very ones she'd been dreading. What did she know about the disappearance of the inflatable motorboat they'd found in the boathouse? More significantly, what had happened to the key to that boat, which he'd left in her charge?

She gave the answers she'd rehearsed, praying that they sounded convincing. About the boat, she explained, "I have no idea what happened to it." And, in a way, this was true. Of the key, she told him she'd put it in her make-shift knapsack before leaving the stable. "Later," she lied, "I noticed the knapsack was gone. I'm not sure, but I think Chazz might have grabbed it when I was trying to get away from him."

At that, Reinhardt's eyes brightened, as if she'd just imparted an important piece of information. "You know, that does explain a great deal," he said. "It's entirely possible that our missing suspects escaped in that boat."

She knew, of course, they had done no such thing, but she said nothing to Reinhardt.

Between Reinhardt's visits, Nicole continued to work on the McGievers' yard. When that was finished, she had some money left, so she replaced the charred rose bushes in the Lowrys' front yard. If anyone had asked, she couldn't have explained why she was doing this. Whatever the reason, it gave her a sense of closure.

Even then, she still had more than £100 left over. She changed it into £5 notes and took a last ride on the tube, handing it out, two or three bills at a time, to panhandlers and street musicians.

Her destination was the Knightsbridge Station. There, she got off and headed into Harrods for a stroll through the hat department. To her disappointment, the stock had completely changed since her last visit. In place of the wide-brimmed, flowered hats, the display tables were filled with exaggerated stovepipes, squashed flowerpots, and bullet-shaped helmets. All were made of a heavy felt that seemed to suggest summer was over, although July had yet to begin.

When a salesgirl approached and asked if she needed help, Nicole's eyes inexplicably filled with tears. Unable to speak, she dashed out of the store and down into the tube. At the bottom of the long escalator, she blindly dumped the remaining bills into the open cello case of an old man sawing out a weary rendition of Ravel's Bolero.

On her last day in Chiswick, Nicole was able to pack her things in her one remaining bag. Memory of that long-lost bag brought back the moment when she noticed it was gone, that first sharp stab of loss. She still had no idea if its disappearance had been a random mishap or the starting point, the moment when Frederick Lowry's vanishing act took possession of her life.

Since then, of course, she'd lost countless other belongings, as if shedding bits of herself all over Britain. There had been the wonderful rose-trimmed hat, which had disappeared during her scuffle in the National Gallery. Gone, too, was her purse, her cell phone, the butter-soft leather suitcase she'd bought in Glasgow, and the lovely clothes inside. She'd even lost the things she was wearing when Chazz and Kevin snatched her from the hotel room.

There were high-ticket items, as well, such as her marriage. Nicole knew their relationship had been in trouble before she and Brad arrived in London, but these last few weeks had sent it well beyond hope. Perhaps even more than the end of her marriage, she grieved the end of—What was it? Her innocence?—which had vanished when she brought the bludgeon down on Kevin's head.

She gave the house a final check before she brought her suitcase downstairs. The entry hall still reeked of fresh paint. She set the bag down by the hall table, where the Lowrys' mail was stacked in two neat piles. Although it was doubtful anyone would ever claim it, she'd saved everything, even a few soot-smudged envelopes that had survived the car bombing.

At the sound of a key in the lock, Nicole looked up. The door opened, and Brad was standing there.

She stared at him. "Damn it, Brad. We both agreed not to make a big deal about my leaving. No goodbyes, remember?"

He shrugged. "I told them you were going home today. And, well, they gave me the morning off. Look, Nick, I was a fool. I made some pretty terrible mistakes, and you have a right to be angry. But you've got to let me make it up to you." He gave her a pleading look. "I love you."

Without answering, Nicole turned away and picked up her bag. She'd explained at least a dozen times, as clearly as she knew how, that the marriage was dead. As for his professed feelings for her—she knew it wasn't love, but a fondness for the comfort and order she brought to his life.

Brad reached for her suitcase, and they struggled over it until he pulled it out of her hands. "At least you could let me take you to the airport," he said.

"I told you. I have a ride."

Brad refused to be discouraged, following her out the front door, down the stairs, and along the path. From here, Nicole could see the new hedge that now separated the Lowrys' yard from the next. She stopped a moment to admire the red and white blossoms on the bushes in the front garden. Then, leaving Brad by the front gate, she continued along the sidewalk until she had a good view of the McGievers' yard, now brightened by the flowers and the square of perfect, velvety turf.

Somehow this activity had restored her soul. It seemed strange that a task as mundane as gardening could become a holy mission, yet, as she packed dirt around the roots of the new shrubs, it had felt as if she were setting the world back in orbit after finding it seriously off course.

After a long look, she returned to the Lowrys' front gate, where Brad still waited with her suitcase. Nicole glanced at her watch. It was 12:03, and her ride was late. She felt a sudden flutter of anxiety. What if he'd been called away at the last minute? Just then, a black sports car appeared around the corner and rolled up to the curb. Reinhardt got out and walked around to take her suitcase from Brad, who handed it over without a fuss. With a nod in Brad's direction, Reinhardt opened the door for Nicole and put the bag in the trunk. Until they turned the corner, she could see Brad in her rear-view mirror, staring glumly after them.

Reinhardt drove expertly, weaving in and out of the narrow streets along an unfamiliar back route. At first they passed houses much like the Lowrys'. After a few blocks, they turned in another direction, entering a business district where modern crackerboxes alternated with ornate brick Victorians and more austere Regency graystones.

They turned onto a block packed with tantalizing boutiques, as well as several large bookstores. Shoppers strolled up and down, looking in windows, while others queued for lunch at a packed wine bar. "What a wonderful street!" she exclaimed. "Will you bring me here when I come back?"

"Done," Reinhardt said. He looked up from the road and smiled, releasing the gearshift to caress her right knee. She placed her hand on his and gave it a squeeze.

They zipped past a great green park ringed with a black wrought-iron fence featuring a gilded motif of lions and thistles. Next, they made their way through a dizzying labyrinth of roundabouts. Cars sped by, jockeying for position according to a rule of the road that everyone but Nicole seemed to understand. Then they were on the main motorway bound for Heathrow.

They passed the same bleak-looking brick high rises Nicole had seen on the ride in. She recalled the way she'd felt that morning, debilitated from the long flight and feverish with anticipation. That ride, less than three weeks before, seemed a lifetime ago.

Despite all she'd been through, she felt restored. Except for the flashbacks, she was almost herself again, ready to put her life back together. She could barely remember the Nicole who had embarked on this trip, the innocent who'd sat up late at night, composing a list of all the sites she was going to visit: museums, historic monuments, theaters, restaurants, shops. She'd done almost none of it.

But she would be back once the dust settled. This was something she'd promised herself. Oh, yes, she would be back.

About the Author

The Swap is Nancy Boyarsky's debut novel and the first of the *Nicole Graves Mystery* series. Her second novel in the series, *The Bequest*, is scheduled for release Summer 2017.

Nancy has been a writer and editor for her entire working career. She coauthored *Backroom Politics*, a *New York Times* notable book, with her husband Bill Boyarsky. She has written several textbooks on the justice system as well as written articles for publications such as the *Los Angeles Times*, *Forbes*, and *McCall's*. She also contributed to political anthologies, including *In the Running*, about women's political campaigns, and *The Challenge of California* by the late Eugene Lee. In addition to her writing career, she was communications director for political affairs for ARCO.

Nancy is a graduate of U.C. Berkeley with a major in English literature. She lives in Los Angeles. Readers can connect with her online at her website nancyboyarsky.com.

Acknowledgements

I want to thank my family, especially my husband Bill, for their continuing support for this project. I also thank the many friends who helped and encouraged me along the way, most especially my sister Susan Scott, brother-in-law Jeff Boyarsky, Cathy Watkins, Claudia Luther, Joyce Brownfield, Keri Pearson, Chuck Rosenberg, Layne Staral, Sid Spies, Ed Wright, Larry Pryor, Nadine Leveille, Carol Finizza, and Tony Finizza.

Nicole Graves Mysteries

BY NANCY BOYARSKY

The Swap
Book 1

The Bequest
Book 2
(Summer 2017)

...you might also like

The Peter Savage Series

BY DAVE EDLUND

Crossing Savage
Book 1

Relentless Savage
Book 2

Deadly Savage
Book 3

Hunting Savage
Book 4
(Fall 2017)